The Story of
Sir
LAUNCELOT
and his
Companions

The Story of
Sir
LAUNCELOT
and his
Companions

by
HOWARD PYLE.

TEXset Press, Stillwater, 74074
http://www.texset.com

First edition published 2011

ISBN: 978-0-9835194-2-3

The Story of Sir Launcelot and his Companions

Originally published 1907
Typset with Garamond No. 8 using LATEX. Text prepared by Sharon Verougstraete, Suzanne Shell and the Online Distributed Proofreading Team at http://www.pgdp.net.

Foreword.

ITH THIS *begins the third of those books which I have set my-self to write concerning the history of King Arthur of Britain and of those puissant knights who were of his Court and of his Round Table.*

In the Book which was written before this book you may there read the Story of that very noble and worthy knight, Sir Launcelot of the Lake; of how he dwelt within a magic lake which was the enchanted habitation of the Lady Nymue of the Lake; of how he was there trained in all the most excellent arts of chivalry by Sir Pellias, the Gentle Knight— whilom a companion of the Round Table, but afterward the Lord of the Lake; of how he came forth out of the Lake and became after that the chiefest knight of the Round Table of King Arthur. All of this was told in that book and many other things concerning Sir Launcelot and several other worthies who were Companions of the Round Table and who were very noble and excellent knights both in battle and in court.

So here followeth a further history of Sir Launcelot of the Lake and the narrative of several of the notable adventures that he performed at this time of his life.

Wherefore if it will please you to read that which is hereinafter set forth, you will be told of how Sir Launcelot slew the great Worm of Corbin; of the madness that afterward fell upon him, and of how a most noble, gentle, and beautiful lady, hight the Lady Elaine the Fair, lent him aid and succor at a time of utmost affliction to him, and so brought him back to health again. And you may herein further find it told how Sir Launcelot was afterward wedded to that fair and gentle dame, and of how was born of that couple a child of whom it was prophesied by Merlin (in a certain miraculous manner fully set forth in this book) that he should become the most perfect knight that ever lived and he who should bring back the Holy Grail to the Earth.

For that child was Galahad whom the world knoweth to be the flower of all chivalry; a knight altogether without fear or reproach of any kind, yet, withal, the most glorious and puissant knight-champion who ever lived.

So if the perusal of these things may give you pleasure, I pray you to read that which followeth, for in this book all these and several other histories are set forth in full.

Contents

OF ILLUSTRATIONS

he Lady Elaine the Fair.

ir Mellegrans interrupts the
sport of the Queen. *****

Prologue.

IT BEFEL upon a very joyous season in the month of May that Queen Guinevere was of a mind to take gentle sport as folk do at that time of the year; wherefore on a day she ordained it in a court of pleasure that on the next morning certain knights and ladies of the court at Camelot should ride with her a-maying into the woods and fields, there to disport themselves amid the flowers and blossoms that grew in great multitudes beside the river.

Of this May-party it stands recorded several times in the various histories of chivalry that the knights she chose were ten in all and that they were all Knights of the Round Table, to wit, as followeth: there was Sir Kay the Seneschal, and Sir Agravaine, and Sir Brandiles, and Sir Sagramour the Desirous, and Sir Dodinas, and Sir Osanna, and Sir Ladynas of the Forest Sauvage, and Sir Persavant of India, and Sir Ironside and Sir Percydes, who was cousin to Sir Percival of Gales. These were the ten (so sayeth those histories aforesaid) whom the Lady Guinevere called upon for to ride a-maying with her all bright and early upon the morning of the day as aforesaid.

And the Queen further ordained that each of these knights should choose him a lady for the day. And she ordained that each lady should ride behind the knight upon the horse which he rode.

How the Lady Guinevere rode a-maying

3

And she ordained that all those knights and ladies and all such attendants as might be of that party should be clad entirely in green, as was fitting for that pleasant festival.

Such were the commands that the Queen ordained, and when those who were chosen were acquainted with their good fortune they took great joy therein; for all they wist there would be great sport at that maying-party.

So when the next morning was come they all rode forth in the freshness of dewy springtide; what time the birds were singing so joyously, so joyously, from every hedge and coppice; what time the soft wind was blowing great white clouds, slow sailing across the canopy of heaven, each cloud casting a soft and darkling shadow that moved across the hills and uplands as it swam the light blue heaven above; what time all the trees and hedgerows were abloom with fragrant and dewy blossoms, and fields and meadow-lands, all shining bright with dew, were spread over with a wonderful carpet of pretty flowers, gladdening the eye with their charm and making fragrant the breeze that blew across the smooth and grassy plain.

For in those days the world was young and gay (as it is nowadays with little children who are abroad when the sun shines bright and things are a-growing) and the people who dwelt therein had not yet grown aweary of its freshness of delight. Wherefore that fair Queen and her court took great pleasure in all the merry world that lay spread about them, as they rode two by two, each knight with his lady, gathering the blossoms of the May, chattering the while like merry birds and now and then bursting into song because of the pure pleasure of living.

They feast very joyously So they disported themselves among the blossoms for all that morning, and when noontide had come they took their rest at a fair spot in a flowery meadow that lay spread out beside the smooth-flowing river about three miles from the town. For from where they sat they might look down across the glassy stream and behold the distant roofs and spires of Camelot, trembling in the thin warm air, very bright and clear, against the blue and radiant sky beyond. And after they were all thus seated in the grass, sundry attendants came and spread out a fair white table-cloth and laid upon the cloth a goodly feast for their refreshment—cold pasties of venison, roasted fowls, manchets of white bread, and flagons of golden wine and ruby wine. And all they took great pleasure when they gazed upon that feast, for they were anhungered with their sporting. So they ate and drank and made them merry; and whilst they ate certain minstrels sang songs, and certain others recited goodly contes and tales for their entertainment. And meanwhile each fair lady wove wreaths of herbs and flowers and therewith bedecked her knight, until all those noble gentlemen were entirely bedight with blossoms—whereat was much merriment and pleasant jesting.

Thus it was that Queen Guinevere went a-maying, and so have I told you all about it so that you might know how it was.

Now whilst the Queen and her party were thus sporting to- *A knight* gether like to children in the grass, there suddenly came the sound *cometh forth* of a bugle-horn winded in the woodlands that there were not a very *from the* great distance away from where they sat, and whilst they looked with *forest* some surprise to see who blew that horn in the forest, there suddenly appeared at the edge of the woodland an armed knight clad cap-a-pie. And the bright sunlight smote down upon that armed knight so that he shone with wonderful brightness at the edge of the shadows of the trees. And after that knight there presently followed an array of men-at-arms—fourscore and more in all—and these also were clad at all points in armor as though prepared for battle.

This knight and those who were with him stopped for a little while at the edge of the wood and stood regarding that May-party from a distance; then after a little they rode forward across the meadow to where the Queen and her court sat looking at them.

Now at first Queen Guinevere and those that were with her wist not who that knight could be, but when he and his armed men had come nigh enough, they were aware that he was a knight hight Sir Mellegrans, who was the son of King Bagdemagus, and they wist that his visit was not likely to bode any very great good to them.

For Sir Mellegrans was not like his father, who (as hath been already told of both in the Book of King Arthur and in The Story of the Champions of the Round Table) was a good and worthy king, and a friend of King Arthur's. For, contrariwise, Sir Mellegrans was malcontented and held bitter enmity toward King Arthur, and that for this reason:

A part of the estate of Sir Mellegrans marched upon the borders of Wales, and there had at one time arisen great contention between Sir Mellegrans and the King of North Wales concerning a certain strip of forest land, as to the ownership thereof. This contention had been submitted to King Arthur and he had decided against Sir Mellegrans and in favor of the King of North Wales; wherefore from that time Sir Mellegrans had great hatred toward King Arthur and sware that some time he would be revenged upon him if the opportunity should offer. Wherefore it was that when the Lady Guinevere beheld that it was Sir Mellegrans who appeared before her thus armed in full, she was ill at ease, and wist that that visit maybe boded no good to herself and to her gentle May-court.

Sir Mellegrans affronts the May-party

So Sir Mellegrans and his armed party rode up pretty close to where the Queen and her party sat in the grass. And when he had come very near he drew rein to his horse and sat regarding that gay company both bitterly and scornfully (albeit at the moment he knew not the Queen who she was). Then after a little he said: "What party of jesters are ye, and what is this foolish sport ye are at?"

Then Sir Kay the Seneschal spake up very sternly and said: "Sir Knight, it behooves you to be more civil in your address. Do you not perceive that this is the Queen and her court before whom you stand and unto whom you are speaking?"

Then Sir Mellegrans knew the Queen and was filled with great triumph to find her thus, surrounded only with a court of knights altogether unarmed. Wherefore he cried out in a great voice: "Hah! lady, now I do know thee! Is it thus that I find thee and thy court? Now it appears to me that Heaven hath surely delivered you into my hands!"

To this Sir Percydes replied, speaking very fiercely: "What mean you, Sir Knight, by those words? Do you dare to make threats to your Queen?"

Quoth Sir Mellegrans: "I make no threats, but I tell you this, I do not mean to throw aside the good fortune that hath thus been placed in my hands. For here I find you all undefended and in my power, wherefore I forthwith seize upon you for to take you to my castle and hold you there as hostages until such time as King Arthur shall make right the great wrong which he hath done me aforetime and shall return to me those forest lands which he hath taken from me to give unto another. So if you go with me in peace, it shall be well for you, but if you go not in peace it shall be ill for you."

Then all the ladies that were of the Queen's court were seized with great terror, for Sir Mellegrans's tones and the aspect of his face were very fierce and baleful; but Queen Guinevere, albeit her face was like to wax for whiteness, spake with a great deal of courage and much anger, saying: "Wilt thou be a traitor to thy King, Sir Knight? Wilt thou dare to do violence to me and my court within the very sight of the roofs of King Arthur's town?"

"Lady," said Sir Mellegrans, "thou hast said what I will to do."

At this Sir Percydes drew his sword and said: "Sir Knight, this shall not be! Thou shalt not have thy will in this while I have any life in my body!"

Then all those other gentlemen drew their swords also, and one and all spake to the same purpose, saying: "Sir Percydes hath spoken; sooner would we die than suffer that affront to the Queen."

"Well," said Sir Mellegrans, speaking very bitterly, "if ye will it that ye who are naked shall do battle with us who are armed, then let it be even as ye elect. So keep this lady from me if ye are able, for I will herewith seize upon you all, maugre anything that you may do to stay me."

Then those ten unarmed knights of the Queen and their attendants made them ready for battle. And when Sir Mellegrans beheld what was their will, he gave command that his men should make them ready for battle upon their part, and they did so.

Then in a moment all that pleasant May-party was changed to dreadful and bloody uproar; for men lashed fiercely at men with sword and glaive, and the Queen and her ladies shrieked and clung in terror together in the midst of that party of knights who were fighting for them.

And for a long time those ten unarmed worthies fought against *Of the battle* the armed men as one to ten, and for a long time no one could tell *with the party* how that battle would end. For the ten men smote the others down *of Sir* from their horses upon all sides, wherefore, for a while, it looked as *Mellegrans* though the victory should be with them. But they could not shield themselves from the blows of their enemies, being unarmed, wherefore they were soon wounded in many places, and what with loss of blood and what with stress of fighting a few against many without any rest, they presently began to wax weak and faint. Then at last Sir Kay fell down to the earth and then Sir Sagramour and then Sir Agravaine and Sir Dodinas and then Sir Ladynas and Sir Osanna and Sir Persavant, so that all who were left standing upon their feet were Sir Brandiles and Sir Ironside and Sir Percydes.

But still these three set themselves back to back and thus fought on in that woful battle. And still they lashed about them so fiercely with their swords that the terror of this battle filled their enemies with fear, insomuch that those who were near them fell back after a while to escape the dreadful strokes they gave.

So came a pause in the battle and all stood at rest. Meantime all around on the ground were men groaning dolorously, for in that battle those ten unarmed knights of the Round Table had smitten down thirty of their enemies.

So for a while those three stood back to back resting from their battle and panting for breath. As for their gay attire of green, lo! it was all ensanguined with the red that streamed from many sore and grimly wounds. And as for those gay blossoms that had bedecked them, lo! they were all gone, and instead there hung about them the dread and terror of a deadly battle.

Then when Queen Guinevere beheld her knights how they stood bleeding from many wounds and panting for breath, her heart was filled with pity, and she cried out in a great shrill voice: "Sir Mellegrans, have pity! Slay not my noble knights! but spare them and I will go with thee as thou wouldst have me do. Only this covenant I make with thee: suffer these lords and ladies of my court and all of those attendant upon us, to go with me into captivity."

Then Sir Mellegrans said: "Well, lady, it shall be as you wish, for these men of yours fight not like men but like devils, wherefore I am glad to end this battle for the sake of all. So bid your knights put away their swords, and I will do likewise with my men, and so there *The Queen* shall be peace between us."

putteth an Then, in obedience to the request of Sir Mellegrans, the Lady
end to the
battle Guinevere gave command that those three knights should put away

their swords, and though they all three besought her that she should suffer them to fight still a little longer for her, she would not; so they were obliged to sheath their swords as she ordered. After that these three knights went to their fallen companions, and found that they were all alive, though sorely hurt. And they searched their wounds as they lay upon the ground, and they dressed them in such ways as might be. After that they helped lift the wounded knights up to their horses, supporting them there in such wise that they should not fall because of faintness from their wounds. So they all departed, a doleful company, from that place, which was now no longer a meadow of pleasure, but a field of bloody battle and of death.

✠   ✠   ✠

Thus beginneth this history.

And now you shall hear that part of this story which is called in many books of chivalry, "The Story of the Knight of the Cart."

For the further history hath now to do with Sir Launcelot of the Lake, and of how he came to achieve the rescue of Queen Guinevere, brought thither in a cart.

The Chevalier of the Cart

HERE FOLLOWETH *the story of Sir Launcelot of the Lake, how he went forth to rescue Queen Guinevere from that peril in which she lay at the castle of Sir Mellegrans. Likewise it is told how he met with a very untoward adventure, so that he was obliged to ride to his undertaking in a cart as aforesaid.*

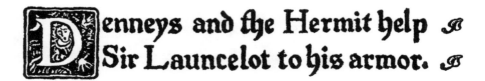

Denneys and the Hermit help Sir Launcelot to his armor.

Chapter First

How Denneys Found Sir Launcelot, and How Sir Launcelot Rode Forth for to Rescue Queen Guinevere from the Castle of Sir Mellegrans, and of What Befell him upon the Assaying of that Adventure.

NOW AFTER that sad and sorrowful company of the Queen had thus been led away captive by Sir Mellegrans as aforetold of, they rode forward upon their way for all that day. And they continued to ride after the night had fallen, and at that time they were passing through a deep dark forest. From this forest, about midnight, they came out into an open stony place whence before them they beheld where was built high up upon a steep hill a grim and forbidding castle, standing very dark against the star-lit sky. And behind the castle there was a town with a number of lights and a bell was tolling for midnight in the town. And this town and castle were the town and the castle of Sir Mellegrans.

Now the Queen had riding near to her throughout that doleful *How Denneys* journey a young page named Denneys, and as they had ridden upon *escaped* their way, she had taken occasion at one place to whisper to him: "Denneys, if thou canst find a chance of escape, do so, and take news of our plight to some one who may rescue us." So it befell that just as they came out thus into that stony place, and in the confusion that arose when they reached the steep road that led up to the castle, Denneys drew rein a little to one side. Then, seeing that he was unobserved, he suddenly set spurs to his horse and rode away with might and main down the stony path and into the forest whence they had all come, and so was gone before anybody had gathered thought to stay him.

Then Sir Mellegrans was very angry, and he rode up to the Queen and he said: "Lady, thou hast sought to betray me! But it matters not, for thy page shall not escape from these parts with his life, for I shall send a party after him with command to slay him with arrows."

So Sir Mellegrans did as he said; he sent several parties of armed men to hunt the forest for the page Denneys; but Denneys escaped them all and got safe away into the cover of the night.

And after that he wandered through the dark and gloomy woodland, not knowing whither he went, for there was no ray of light. Moreover, the gloom was full of strange terrors, for on every side of him he heard the movement of night creatures stirring in the darkness, and he wist not whether they were great or little or whether they were of a sort to harm him or not to harm him.

How Denneys rideth through the forest Yet ever he went onward until, at last, the dawn of the day came shining very faint and dim through the tops of the trees. And then, by and by, and after a little, he began to see the things about him, very faint, as though they were ghosts growing out of the darkness. Then the small fowl awoke, and first one began to chirp and then another, until a multitude of the little feathered creatures fell to singing upon all sides so that the silence of the forest was filled full of their multitudinous chanting. And all the while the light grew stronger and stronger and more clear and sharp until, by and by, the great and splendid sun leaped up into the sky and shot his shafts of gold aslant through the trembling leaves of the trees; and so all the joyous world was awake once more to the fresh and dewy miracle of a new-born day.

So cometh the breaking of the day in the woodlands as I have told you, and all this Denneys saw, albeit he thought but little of what he beheld. For all he cared for at that time was to escape out of the thick mazes of the forest in which he knew himself to be entangled. Moreover, he was faint with weariness and hunger, and wist not where he might break his fast or where he could find a place to tarry and to repose himself for a little.

But God had care of little Denneys and found him food, for by and by he came to an open space in the forest, where there was a neatherd's hut, and that was a very pleasant place. For here a brook as clear as crystal came brawling out of the forest and ran smoothly across an open lawn of bright green grass; and there was a hedgerow and several apple-trees, and both the hedge and the apple-trees were abloom with fragrant blossoms. And the thatched hut of the neatherd stood back under two great oak-trees at the edge of the forest, where the sunlight played in spots of gold all over the face of the dwelling.

So the Queen's page beheld the hut and he rode forward with intent to beg for bread, and at his coming there appeared a comely woman of the forest at the door and asked him what he would have. *How Denneys findeth food*
To her Denneys told how he was lost in the forest and how he was anhungered. And whilst he talked there came a slim brown girl, also of the woodland, and very wild, and she stood behind the woman and listened to what he said. This woman and this girl pitied Denneys, and the woman gave command that the girl should give him a draught of fresh milk, and the maiden did so, bringing it to him in a great wooden bowl. Meanwhile, the woman herself fetched sweet brown bread spread with butter as yellow as gold, and Denneys took it and gave them both thanks beyond measure. So he ate and drank with great appetite, the whiles those two outland folk stood gazing at him, wondering at his fair young face and his yellow hair.

After that, Denneys journeyed on for the entire day, until the light began to wane once more. The sun set; the day faded into the silence of the gloaming and then the gloaming darkened, deeper and more deep, until Denneys was engulfed once more in the blackness of the night-time.

Then lo! God succored him again, for as the darkness fell, he heard the sound of a little bell ringing through the gathering night. Thitherward he turned his horse whence he heard the sound to come, and so in a little he perceived a light shining from afar, and when he had come nigh enough to that light he was aware that he had come to the chapel of a hermit of the forest and that the light that he beheld came from within the hermit's dwelling-place.

As Denneys drew nigh to the chapel and the hut a great horse neighed from a cabin close by, and therewith he was aware that some other wayfarer was there, and that he should have comradeship—and at that his heart was elated with gladness.

Denneys cometh to the chapel of the hermit

So he rode up to the door of the hut and knocked, and in answer to his knocking there came one and opened to him, and that one was a most reverend hermit with a long beard as white as snow and a face very calm and gentle and covered all over with a great multitude of wrinkles.

(And this was the hermit of the forest several times spoken of aforetime in these histories.)

When the hermit beheld before him that young lad, all haggard and worn and faint and sick with weariness and travel and hunger, he took great pity and ran to him and catched him in his arms and lifted him down from his horse and bare him into the hermitage, and sat him down upon a bench that was there.

Denneys said: "Give me to eat and to drink, for I am faint to death." And the hermit said, "You shall have food upon the moment," and he went to fetch it.

Then Denneys gazed about him with heavy eyes, and was aware that there was another in the hut besides himself. And then he heard a voice speak his name with great wonderment, saying: "Denneys, is it then thou who hast come here at this time? What ails thee? Lo! I knew thee not when I first beheld thee enter."

Then Denneys lifted up his eyes, and he beheld that it was Sir Launcelot of the Lake who spoke to him thus in the hut of the hermit.

Denneys findeth Sir Launcelot

At that, and seeing who it was who spake to him, Denneys leaped up and ran to Sir Launcelot and fell down upon his knees before him. And he embraced Sir Launcelot about the knees, weeping beyond measure because of the many troubles through which he had passed.

Sir Launcelot said: "Denneys, what is it ails thee? Where is the Queen, and how came you here at this place and at this hour? Why look you so distraught, and why are you so stained with blood?"

Then Denneys, still weeping, told Sir Launcelot all that had be-fallen, and how that the Lady Guinevere was prisoner in the castle of Sir Mellegrans somewhere in the midst of that forest.

But when Sir Launcelot heard what Denneys said, he arose very hastily and he cried out, "How is this! How is this!" and he cried out again very vehemently: "Help me to mine armor and let me go hence!" (for Sir Launcelot had laid aside his armor whilst he rested in the hut of the hermit). *Sir Launcelot rides forth to save the Queen*

At that moment the hermit came in, bringing food for Denneys to eat, and hearing what Sir Launcelot said, he would have persuaded him to abide there until the morrow and until he could see his way. But Sir Launcelot would listen to nothing that might stay him. So Denneys and the hermit helped him don his armor, and after that Sir Launcelot mounted his war-horse and rode away into the blackness of the night.

So Sir Launcelot rode as best he might through the darkness of the forest, and he rode all night, and shortly after the dawning of the day he heard the sound of rushing water.

So he followed a path that led to this water and by and by he came to an open space very stony and rough. And he saw that here was a great torrent of water that came roaring down from the hills very violent and turbid and covered all over with foam like to cream. And he beheld that there was a bridge of stone that spanned the torrent and that upon the farther side of the bridge was a considerable body of men-at-arms all in full armor. And he beheld that there were at least five-and-twenty of these men, and that chief among them was a man clad in green armor.

Then Sir Launcelot rode out upon the bridge and he called to those armed men: "Can you tell me whether this way leads to the castle of Sir Mellegrans?"

They say to him: "Who are you, Sir Knight?"

"I am one," quoth Sir Launcelot, "who seeks the castle of Sir Mellegrans. For that knight hath violently seized upon the person of the Lady Guinevere and of certain of her court, and he now holds her and them captive and in duress. I am one who hath come to rescue that lady and her court from their distress and anxiety."

Upon this the Green Knight, who was the chief of that party, came a little nearer to Sir Launcelot, and said: "Messire, are you Sir Launcelot of the Lake?" Sir Launcelot said: "Yea, I am he." "Then," said the Green Knight, "you can go no farther upon this pass, for you are to know that we are the people of Sir Mellegrans, and that we are here to stay you or any of your fellows from going forward upon this way."

Then Sir Launcelot laughed, and he said: "Messire, how will you stay me against my will?" The Green Knight said: "We will stay you by force of our numbers." "Well," quoth Sir Launcelot, "for the matter of that, I have made my way against greater odds than those I now see before me. So your peril will be of your own devising, if you seek to stay me."

How Sir Launcelot assailed his enemies Therewith he cast aside his spear and drew his sword, and set spurs to his horse and rode forward against them. And he rode straight in amongst them with great violence, lashing right and left with his sword, so that at every stroke a man fell down from out of his saddle. So fierce and direful were the blows that Sir Launcelot delivered that the terror of his rage fell upon them, wherefore, after a while, they fell away from before him, and left him standing alone in the centre of the way.

Sir Launcelot, his horse is slain Now there were a number of the archers of Sir Mellegrans lying hidden in the rocks at the sides of that pass. These, seeing how that battle was going and that Sir Launcelot had driven back their companions, straightway fitted arrows to their bows and began shooting at the horse of Sir Launcelot. Against these archers Sir Launcelot could in no wise defend his horse, wherefore the steed was presently sorely wounded and began plunging and snorting in pain so that Sir Launcelot could hardly hold him in check. And still the archers shot arrow after arrow until by and by the life began to go out of the horse. Then after a while the good steed fell down upon his knees and rolled over into the dust; for he was so sorely wounded that he could no longer stand.

But Sir Launcelot did not fall, but voided his saddle with great skill and address, so that he kept his feet, wherefore his enemies were not able to take him at such disadvantage as they would have over a fallen knight who lay upon the ground.

So Sir Launcelot stood there in the midst of the way at the end of the bridge, and he waved his sword this way and that way before him so that not one of those, his enemies, dared to come nigh to him. For the terror of him still lay upon them all and they dreaded those buffets he had given them in the battle they had just fought with him.

Wherefore they stood at a considerable distance regarding Sir Launcelot and not daring to come nigh to him; and they stood so for a long time. And although the Green Knight commanded them to fight, they would not fight any more against Sir Launcelot, so the Green Knight had to give orders for them to cease that battle and to depart from that place. This they did, leaving Sir Launcelot standing where he was.

Thus Sir Launcelot with his single arm won a battle against all that multitude of enemies as I have told.

But though Sir Launcelot had thus won that pass with great credit and honor to himself, fighting as a single man against so many, yet he was still in a very sorry plight. For there he stood, a full-armed man with such a great weight of armor upon him that he could hardly hope to walk a league, far less to reach the castle of Sir Mellegrans afoot. Nor knew he what to do in this extremity, for where could he hope to find a horse in that thick forest, where was hardly a man or a beast of any sort? Wherefore, although he had won his battle, he was yet in no ease or satisfaction of spirit.

Thus it was that Sir Launcelot went upon that adventure; and now you shall hear how it sped with him further, if so be you are pleased to read that which followeth.

How Sir Launcelot rode errant in a cart. *Ⅎ Ⅎ Ⅎ Ⅎ*

Chapter Second

How Sir Launcelot rode in a cart to rescue Queen Guinevere and how he came in that way to the castle of Sir Mellegrans.

OW AFTER Sir Launcelot was thus left by his enemies standing alone in the road as aforetold of, he knew not for a while what to do, nor how he should be able to get him away from that place.

As he stood there adoubt as to what to do in this sorry case, he by and by heard upon one side from out of the forest the sound of an axe at a distance away, and thereat he was very glad, for he wist that help was nigh. So he took up his shield on his shoulder and his spear in his hand and thereupon directed his steps toward where he heard that sound of the axe, in hopes that there he might find some one who could aid in his extremity. So after a while, he came forth into a little open glade of the forest where he beheld a fagotmaker chopping fagots. And he beheld the fagotmaker had there a cart and a horse for to fetch his fagots from the forest.

But when the fagotmaker saw an armed knight come thus like a shining vision out of the forest, walking afoot, bearing his shield upon his shoulder, and his spear in his hand, he knew not what to think of such a sight, but stood staring with his mouth agape for wonders.

Sir Launcelot said to him, "Good fellow, is that thy cart?" The fagotmaker said, "Yea, Messire." "I would," quoth Sir Launcelot, "have thee do me a service with that cart," and the fagotmaker asked, "What is the service that thou wouldst have of me, Messire?" Sir Launcelot said: "This is the service I would have: it is that you take me into yonder cart and hale me to somewhere I may get a horse for to ride; for mine own horse hath just now been slain in battle, and I know not how I may go forward upon the adventure I have undertaken unless I get me another horse."

Now you must know that in those days it was not thought worthy of any one of degree to ride in a cart in that wise as Sir Launcelot said, for they would take law-breakers to the gallows in just such carts as that one in which Sir Launcelot made demand to ride. Wherefore it was that that poor fagotmaker knew not what to think when he heard Sir Launcelot give command that he should be taken to ride in that cart. "Messire," quoth he, "this cart is no fit thing for one of your quality to ride in. Now I beseech you let me serve you in some other way than that."

But Sir Launcelot made reply as follows: "Sirrah, I would have thee know that there is no shame in riding in a cart for a worthy purpose, but there is great shame if one rides therein unworthily. And contrariwise, a man doth not gain credit merely for riding on horseback, for his credit appertains to his conduct, and not to what manner he rideth. So as my purpose is worthy, I shall, certes, be unworthy if I go not to fulfil that purpose, even if in so going I travel in thy poor cart. So do as I bid thee and make thy cart ready, and if thou wilt bring me in it to where I may get a fresh horse, I will give thee five pieces of gold money for thy service."

Now when the fagotmaker heard what Sir Launcelot said about the five pieces of gold money, he was very joyful, wherefore he ran to make ready his cart with all speed. And when the cart was made ready, Sir Launcelot entered into it with his shield and his spear.

Sir Launcelot rideth in a cart So it was that Sir Launcelot of the Lake came to ride errant in a cart, wherefore, for a long time after, he was called the Chevalier of the Cart. And many ballads and songs were made concerning that matter, which same were sung in several courts of chivalry by minstrels and jongleurs, and these same stories and ballads have come down from afar to us of this very day.

Meantime Sir Launcelot rode forward at a slow pass and in that way for a great distance. So, at last, still riding in the cart, they came of a sudden out of the forest and into a little fertile valley in the midst of which lay a small town and a fair castle with seven towers that overlooked the town. And this was a very fair pretty valley, for on all sides of the town and of the castle were fields of growing corn, all green and lush, and there were many hedgerows and orchards of fruit-trees all abloom with fragrant blossoms. And the sound of cocks crowing came to Sir Launcelot upon a soft breeze that blew up the valley, and on the same breeze came the fragrance of apple blossoms, wherefore it seemed to Sir Launcelot that this valley was like a fair jewel of heaven set in the rough perlieus of the forest that lay round about.

So the fagotmaker drove Sir Launcelot in the cart down into that valley toward the castle, and as they drew near thereunto Sir Launcelot was aware of a party of lords and ladies who were disporting themselves in a smooth meadow of green grass that lay spread out beneath the castle walls. And some of these lords and ladies tossed a ball from one to another, and others lay in the grass in the shade of a lime-tree and watched those that played at ball. Then Sir Launcelot was glad to see those gentle folk, for he thought that here he might get him a fresh horse to take him upon his way. So he gave command to the fagotmaker to drive to where those people were.

But as Sir Launcelot, riding in the fagotmaker's cart, drew near to those castle-folk, they ceased their play and stood and looked at him with great astonishment, for they had never beheld an armed knight riding in a cart in that wise. Then, in a little, they all fell to laughing beyond measure, and at that Sir Launcelot was greatly abashed with shame.

Then the lord of that castle came forward to meet Sir Launcelot. He was a man of great dignity of demeanor—gray-haired, and clad in velvet trimmed with fur. When he came nigh to where Sir Launcelot was, he said, speaking as with great indignation: "Sir knight, why do you ride in this wise in a cart, like to a law-breaker going to the gallows?"

"Sir," quoth Sir Launcelot, "I ride thus because my horse was slain by treachery. For I have an adventure which I have undertaken to perform, and I have no other way to go forward upon that quest than this."

Then all those who heard what Sir Launcelot said laughed again with great mirth. Only the old lord of the castle did not laugh, but said, still speaking as with indignation: "Sir Knight, it is altogether unworthy of one of your degree to ride thus in a cart to be made a mock of. Wherefore come down, and if you prove yourself worthy I myself will purvey you a horse." *The lord of a castle chideth Sir Launcelot*

But by this time Sir Launcelot had become greatly affronted at the laughter of those who jeered at him, and he was furthermore affronted that the lord of the castle should deem him to be unworthy because he came thither in a cart; wherefore he said: "Sir, without boasting, methinks I may say that I am altogether as worthy as any one hereabouts. Nor do I think that any one of you all has done more worthily in his degree than I have done in my degree. As for any lack of worship that may befall me for riding thus, I may say that the adventure which I have undertaken just now to perform is in itself so worthy that it will make worthy any man who may undertake it, no matter how he may ride to that adventure. Now I had thought to ask of you a fresh horse, but since your people mock at me and since you rebuke me so discourteously, I will ask you for nothing. Wherefore, to show you that knightly worthiness does not depend upon the way a knight may ride, I herewith make my vow that I will not mount upon horseback until my quest is achieved; nor will I ride to that adventure in any other way than in this poor cart wherein I now stand."

So Sir Launcelot rode away in his cart from those castle-folk. And he rode thus down into the valley and through the town that was in the valley in the fagotmaker's cart, and all who beheld him laughed at him and mocked him. For, as he passed along the way, many came and looked down upon him from out of the windows of the houses; and others ran along beside the cart and all laughed and jeered at him to see him thus riding in a cart as though to a hanging. But all this Sir Launcelot bore with great calmness of demeanor, both because of his pride and because of the vow that he had made. Wherefore he continued to ride in that cart although he might easily have got him a fresh horse from the lord of the castle.

Now turn we to the castle of Sir Mellegrans, where Queen Guinevere and her court were held prisoners.

First of all you are to know that that part of the castle wherein she and her court were held overlooked the road which led up to the gate of the castle. Wherefore it came about that one of the damsels of the Queen, looking out of the window of the chamber wherein the

Queen was held prisoner, beheld a knight armed at all points, coming riding thitherward in a cart. Beholding this sight, she fell to laughing, whereat the Queen said, "What is it you laugh at?" That damsel cried out: "Lady, Lady, look, see! What a strange sight! Yonder is a knight riding in a cart as though he were upon his way to a hanging!"

Then Queen Guinevere came to the window and looked out, and *The Queen* several came and looked out also. At first none of them wist who it *beholds Sir Launcelot* was that rode in that cart. But when the cart had come a little nearer *riding in a* to where they were, the Queen knew who he was, for she beheld the *cart* device upon the shield, even from afar, and she knew that the knight was Sir Launcelot. Then the Queen turned to the damsel and said to her: "You laugh without knowing what it is you laugh at. Yonder gentleman is no subject for a jest, for he is without any doubt the worthiest knight of any who ever wore golden spurs."

Now amongst those who stood there looking out of the window *Sir Percydes is* were Sir Percydes and Sir Brandiles and Sir Ironside, and in a little *offended with Sir Launcelot* Sir Percydes also saw the device of Sir Launcelot and therewith knew who it was who rode in the cart. But when Sir Percydes knew that that knight was Sir Launcelot, he was greatly offended that he, who was the chiefest knight of the Round Table, should ride in a cart in that wise. So Sir Percydes said to the Queen: "Lady, I believe yonder knight is none other than Sir Launcelot of the Lake." And Queen Guinevere said, "It is assuredly he." Sir Percydes said: "Then I take it to be a great shame that the chiefest knight of the Round Table should ride so in a cart as though he were a felon law-breaker. For the world will assuredly hear of this and it will be made a jest in every court of chivalry. And all we who are his companions in arms and who are his brethren of the Round Table will be made a jest and a laughing-stock along with him."

Thus spake Sir Percydes, and the other knights who were there and all the ladies who were there agreed with him that it was great shame for Sir Launcelot to come thus to save the Queen, riding in a cart.

But the Queen said: "Messires and ladies, I take no care for the manner in which Sir Launcelot cometh, for I believe he cometh for to rescue us from this captivity, and if so be he is successful in that undertaking, then it will not matter how he cometh to perform so worthy a deed of knighthood as that."

Thus all they were put to silence by the Queen's words; but nevertheless and afterward those knights who were there still held amongst themselves that it was great shame for Sir Launcelot to come thus in a cart to rescue the Queen, instead of first getting for himself a horse whereon to ride as became a knight-errant of worthiness and respect.

✛   ✛   ✛

Now you are to know that the Green Knight, who was the head of that party that tried to stand against Sir Launcelot at the bridge as aforesaid, when he beheld that the horse of Sir Launcelot was shot, rode away from the place of battle with his men, and that he never stopped nor stayed until he had reached the castle of Sir Mellegrans. There coming, he went straightway to where Sir Mellegrans was and told Sir Mellegrans all that had befallen, and how that Sir Launcelot had overcome them all with his single hand at the bridge of the torrent. And he told Sir Mellegrans that haply Sir Launcelot would be coming to that place before a very great while had passed, although he had been delayed because his horse had been slain.

Sir Mellegrans feareth Sir Launcelot At that Sir Mellegrans was put to great anxiety, for he also knew that Sir Launcelot would be likely to be at that place before a very great while, and he wist that there would be great trouble for him when that should come to pass. So he began to cast about very busily in his mind for some scheme whereby he might destroy Sir Launcelot. And at last he hit upon a scheme; and that scheme was unworthy of him both as a knight and as a gentleman.

So when news was brought to Sir Mellegrans that Sir Launcelot was there in front of the castle in a cart, Sir Mellegrans went down to the barbican of the castle and looked out of a window of the barbican and beheld Sir Launcelot where he stood in the cart before the gate of the castle. And Sir Mellegrans said, "Sir Launcelot, is it thou who art there in the cart?"

Sir Launcelot replied: "Yea, thou traitor knight, it is I, and I come to tell thee thou shalt not escape my vengeance either now or at some other time unless thou set free the Queen and all her court and make due reparation to her and to them and to me for all the harm you have wrought upon us."

To this Sir Mellegrans spake in a very soft and humble tone of voice, saying: "Messire, I have taken much thought, and I now much repent me of all that I have done. For though my provocation hath been great, yet I have done extremely ill in all this that hath happened, so I am of a mind to make reparation for what I have done. Yet I know not how to make such reparation without bringing ruin upon myself. If thou wilt intercede with me before the Queen in this matter, I will let thee into this castle and I myself will take thee to her where she is. And after I have been forgiven what I have done, then ye shall all go free, and I will undertake to deliver myself unto the mercy of King Arthur and will render all duty unto him." *Sir Mellegrans speaketh to Sir Launcelot*

At this repentance of Sir Mellegrans Sir Launcelot was very greatly astonished. But yet he was much adoubt as to the true faith of that knight; wherefore he said: "Sir Knight, how may I know that that which thou art telling me is the truth?"

"Well," said Sir Mellegrans, "it is small wonder, I dare say, that thou hast doubt of my word. But I will prove my faith to thee in this: I will come to thee unarmed as I am at this present, and I will admit thee into my castle, and I will lead thee to the Queen. And as thou art armed and I am unarmed, thou mayest easily slay me if so be thou seest that I make any sign of betraying thee."

But still Sir Launcelot was greatly adoubt, and wist not what to think of that which Sir Mellegrans said. But after a while, and after he had considered the matter for a space, he said: "If all this that thou tellest me is true, Sir Knight, then come down and let me into this castle as thou hast promised to do, for I will venture that much upon thy faith. But if I see that thou hast a mind to deal falsely by me, then I will indeed slay thee as thou hast given me leave to do." And Sir Mellegrans said, "I am content."

So Sir Mellegrans went down from where he was and he gave command that the gates of the castle should be opened. And when the gates were opened he went forth to where Sir Launcelot was. And Sir Launcelot descended from the fagotmaker's cart, and Sir Mellegrans kneeled down before him, and he set his palms together and he said, "Sir Launcelot, I crave thy pardon for what I have done." *Sir Mellegrans kneels to Sir Launcelot*

Sir Launcelot said: "Sir Knight, if indeed thou meanest no further treachery, thou hast my pardon and I will also intercede with the Queen to pardon thee as well. So take me straightway to her, for until I behold her with mine own eyes I cannot believe altogether in thy repentance." Then Sir Mellegrans arose and said, "Come, and I will take thee to her."

So Sir Mellegrans led the way into the castle and Sir Launcelot followed after him with his naked sword in his hand. And Sir Mellegrans led the way deep into the castle and along several passage-ways and still Sir Launcelot followed after him with his drawn sword, ready for to slay him if he should show sign of treason.

Sir Launcelot falleth into the pit Now there was in a certain part of that castle and in the midst of a long passageway a trap-door that opened through the floor of the passageway and so into a deep and gloomy pit beneath. And this trap-door was controlled by a cunning latch of which Sir Mellegrans alone knew the secret; for when Sir Mellegrans would touch the latch with his finger, the trap-door would immediately fall open into the pit beneath. So thitherward to that place Sir Mellegrans led the way and Sir Launcelot followed. And Sir Mellegrans passed over that trap-door in safety, but when Sir Launcelot had stepped upon the trap-door, Sir Mellegrans touched the spring that controlled the latch with his finger, and the trap-door immediately opened beneath Sir Launcelot and Sir Launcelot fell down into the pit beneath. And the pit was very deep indeed and the floor thereof was of stone, so that when Sir Launcelot fell he smote the stone floor so violently that he was altogether bereft of his senses and lay there in the pit like to one who was dead.

Then Sir Mellegrans came back to the open space of the trap-door and he looked down into the pit beneath and beheld Sir Launcelot where he lay. Thereupon Sir Mellegrans laughed and he cried out, "Sir Launcelot, what cheer have you now?" But Sir Launcelot answered not.

Then Sir Mellegrans laughed again, and he closed the trap-door and went away, and he said to himself: "Now indeed have I such hostages in my keeping that King Arthur must needs set right this wrong he hath aforetime done me. For I now have in my keeping not only his Queen, but also the foremost knight of his Round Table;

wherefore King Arthur must needs come to me to make such terms with me as I shall determine."

As for Queen Guinevere, she waited with her court for a long time for news of Sir Launcelot, for she wist that now Sir Launcelot was there at that place she must needs have news of him sooner or later. But no news came to her; wherefore, as time passed by, she took great trouble because she had no news, and she said: "Alas, if ill should have befallen that good worthy knight at the hands of the treacherous lord of this castle!"

But she knew not how great at that very time was the ill into which Sir Launcelot had fallen, nor of how he was even then lying like as one dead in the pit beneath the floor of the passageway.

The Damsel Elouise the Fair rescues Sir Launcelot

Chapter Third

*How Sir Launcelot was rescued from the pit and how he over-
came Sir Mellegrans and set free the Queen and her court from
the duress they were in.*

OW WHEN Sir Launcelot awoke from that swoon into which
he was cast by falling so violently into the pit, he found
himself to be in a very sad, miserable case. For he lay there
upon the hard stones of the floor and all about him there was a darkness so great that there was not a single ray of light that penetrated
into it.

So for a while Sir Launcelot knew not where he was; but by and
by he remembered that he was in the castle of Sir Mellegrans, and he
remembered all that had befallen him, and therewith, when he knew
himself to be a prisoner in so miserable a condition, he groaned with
dolor and distress, for he was at that time in great pain both of mind
and body. Then he cried out in a very mournful voice: "Woe is me
that I should have placed any faith in a traitor such as this knight
hath from the very beginning shown himself to be! For here am I
now cast into this dismal prison, and know not how I shall escape
from it to bring succor to those who so greatly need my aid at this
moment."

*Sir Launcelot
lyeth in the
pit*

So Sir Launcelot bemoaned and lamented himself, but no one
heard him, for he was there all alone in that miserable dungeon and
in a darkness into which no ray of light could penetrate.

Then Sir Launcelot bent his mind to think of how he might escape from that place, but though he thought much, yet he could not
devise any way in which he might mend the evil case in which he
found himself; wherefore he was altogether overwhelmed with despair. And by that time it had grown to be about the dead of the
night.

Now as Sir Launcelot lay there in such despair of spirit as aforetold of, he was suddenly aware that there came a gleam of light shining in a certain place, and he was aware the light grew ever brighter

31

and brighter and he beheld that it came through the cracks of a door. And by and by he heard the sound of keys from without and immediately afterward the door opened and there entered into that place a damsel bearing a lighted lamp in her hand.

The Lady Elouise findeth Sir Launcelot At first Sir Launcelot knew not who she was, and then he knew her and lo! that damsel was the Lady Elouise the Fair, the daughter of King Bagdemagus and sister unto Sir Mellegrans; and she was the same who had aforetime rescued him when he had been prisoner to Queen Morgana le Fay, as hath been told you in a former book of this history.

So Elouise the Fair came into that dismal place, bringing with her the lighted lamp, and Sir Launcelot beheld that her eyes were red with weeping. Then Sir Launcelot, beholding that she had been thus weeping, said: "Lady, what is it that ails you? Is there aught that I can do for to comfort you?" To this she said naught, but came to where Sir Launcelot was and looked at him for a long while. By and by she said: "Woe is me to find thee thus, Sir Launcelot! And woe is me that it should have been mine own brother that should have brought thee to this pass!"

Sir Launcelot was much moved to see her so mournful and he said: "Lady, take comfort to thyself, for whatever evil thing Sir Mellegrans may have done to me, naught of reproach or blame can fall thereby upon thee, for I shall never cease to remember how thou didst one time save me from a very grievous captivity."

The Lady Elouise said: "Launcelot, I cannot bear to see so noble a knight as thou art lying thus in duress. So it is that I come hither to aid thee. Now if I set thee free wilt thou upon thy part show mercy unto my brother for my sake?"

"Lady," said Sir Launcelot, "this is a hard case thou puttest to me, for I would do much for thy sake. But I would have thee wist that it is my endeavor to help in my small way to punish evil-doers so that the world may be made better by that punishment. Wherefore because this knight hath dealt so treacherously with my lady the Queen, so it must needs be that I must seek to punish him if ever I can escape from this place. But if it so befalls that I do escape, this much mercy will I show to Sir Mellegrans for thy sake: I will meet him in fair field, as one knight may meet another knight in that wise. And I will show him such courtesy as one knight may show another in time of battle. Such mercy will I show thy brother and meseems that is all that may rightly be asked of me."

Then Elouise the Fair began weeping afresh, and she said: "Alas, Launcelot! I fear me that my brother will perish at thy hands if so be that it cometh to a battle betwixt you twain. And how could I bear it to have my brother perish in that way and at thy hands?"

"Lady," said Sir Launcelot, "the fate of battle lyeth ever in God His hands and not in the hands of men. It may befall any man to die who doeth battle, and such a fate may be mine as well as thy brother's. So do thou take courage, for whilst I may not pledge myself to avoid an ordeal of battle with Sir Mellegrans, yet it may be his good hap that he may live and that I may die."

"Alas, Launcelot," quoth the Fair Elouise, "and dost thou think that it would be any comfort to me to have thee die at the hands of mine own brother? That is but poor comfort to me who am the sister of this miserable man. Yet let it be as it may hap, I cannot find it in my heart to let thee lie here in this place, for thou wilt assuredly die in this dark and miserable dungeon if I do not aid thee. So once more will I set thee free as I did aforetime when thou wast captive to Queen Morgana le Fay, and I will do my duty by thee as the daughter of a king and the daughter of a true knight may do. As to that which shall afterward befall, that will I trust to the mercy of God to see that it shall all happen as He shall deem best."

So saying, the damsel Elouise the Fair bade Sir Launcelot to arise *The Lady* and to follow her, and he did so. And she led him out from that *Elouise* place and up a long flight of steps and so to a fair large chamber that *Launcelot out* was high up in a tower of the castle and under the eaves of the roof. *of a pit* And Sir Launcelot beheld that everything was here prepared for his coming; for there was a table at that place set with bread and meat and with several flagons of wine for his refreshment. And there was in that place a silver ewer full of cold, clear water, and that there was a basin of silver, and that there were several napkins of fine linen such as are prepared for knights to dry their hands upon. All these had been prepared for him against his coming, and at that sight he was greatly uplifted with satisfaction.

So Sir Launcelot bathed his face and his hands in the water and he dried them upon the napkins. And he sat him down at the table and he ate and drank with great appetite and the Lady Elouise the Fair served him. And so Sir Launcelot was greatly comforted in body and in spirit by that refreshment which she had prepared for him.

Then after Sir Launcelot had thus satisfied the needs of his hunger, the Lady Elouise led him to another room and there showed him where was a soft couch spread with flame-colored linen and she said, "Here shalt thou rest at ease to-night, and in the morning I shall bring thy sword and thy shield to thee." Therewith she left Sir Launcelot to his repose and he laid him down upon the couch and slept with great content.

So he slept very soundly all that night and until the next morning, what time, the Lady Elouise came to him as she promised and fetched unto him his sword and his shield. These she gave unto him, saying: "Sir Knight, I know not whether I be doing evil or good in the sight of Heaven in thus purveying thee with thy weapons; ne'ertheless, I cannot find it in my heart to leave thee unprotected in this place without the wherewithal for to defend thyself against thine enemies; for that would be indeed to compass thy death for certain."

Sir Launcelot hath his weapons again Then Sir Launcelot was altogether filled with joy to have his weapons again, and he gave thanks to the Lady Elouise without measure. And after that he hung his sword at his side and set his shield upon his shoulder and thereupon felt fear of no man in all of that world, whomsoever that one might be.

After that, and after he had broken his fast, Sir Launcelot went forth from out of the chamber where he had abided that night, and he went down into the castle and into the courtyard of the castle, and every one was greatly astonished at his coming, for they deemed him to be still a prisoner in that dungeon into which he had fallen.

Sir Launcelot challenges the castle So all these, when they beheld him coming, full armed and with his sword in his hand, fled away from before the face of Sir Launcelot, and no one undertook to stay him in his going. So Sir Launcelot reached the courtyard of the castle, and when he was come there he set his horn to his lips, and blew a blast that sounded terribly loud and shrill throughout the entire place.

Meantime, there was great hurrying hither and thither in the castle and a loud outcry of many voices, and many came to the windows and looked down into the courtyard and there beheld Sir Launcelot standing clad in full armor, glistening very bright in the morning light of the sun.

Meantime several messengers had run to where Sir Mellegrans was and told him that Sir Launcelot had escaped out of that pit wherein he had fallen and that he was there in the courtyard of the castle in full armor.

At that Sir Mellegrans was overwhelmed with amazement, and a great fear seized upon him and gripped at his vitals. And after a while he too went by, to a certain place whence he could look down into the courtyard, and there he also beheld Sir Launcelot where he stood shining in the sunlight.

Now at that moment Sir Launcelot lifted up his eyes and espied Sir Mellegrans where he was at the window of that place, and immediately he knew Sir Mellegrans. Thereupon he cried out in a loud voice: "Sir Mellegrans, thou traitor knight! Come down and do battle, for here I await thee to come and meet me."

But when Sir Mellegrans heard those words he withdrew very hastily from the window where he was, and he went away in great terror to a certain room where he might be alone. For beholding Sir Launcelot thus free of that dungeon from which he had escaped he knew not what to do to flee from his wrath. Wherefore he said to himself: "Fool that I was, to bring this knight into my castle, when I might have kept him outside as long as I chose to do so! What now shall I do to escape from his vengeance?"

So after a while Sir Mellegrans sent for several of his knights *Sir Mellegrans* and he took counsel of them as to what he should do in this pass. *taketh counsel* These say to him: "Messire, you yourself to fulfil your schemes have brought yonder knight into this place, when God knows he could not have come in of his own free will. So now that he is here, it behooves you to go and arm yourself at all points and to go down to the courtyard, there to meet him and to do battle with him. For only by overcoming him can you hope to escape his vengeance."

But Sir Mellegrans feared Sir Launcelot with all his heart, wherefore he said: "Nay, I will not go down to yonder knight. For wit ye he is the greatest knight alive, and if I go to do battle with him, it will be of a surety that I go to my death. Wherefore, I will not go."

Then Sir Mellegrans called a messenger to him and he said: "Go down to yonder knight in the courtyard and tell him that I will not do battle with him."

So the messenger went to Sir Launcelot and delivered that message to him. But when Sir Launcelot heard what it was that the messenger said to him from Sir Mellegrans, he laughed with great scorn. Then he said to the messenger, "Doth the knight of this castle fear to meet me?" The messenger said, "Yea, Messire." Sir Launcelot said: "Then take thou this message to him: that I will lay aside my shield and my helm and that I will unarm all the left side of my body, and thus, half naked, will I fight him if only he will come down and do battle with me."

So saying, the messenger departed as Sir Launcelot bade, and came to Sir Mellegrans and delivered that message to him as Sir Launcelot had said.

Sir Launcelot offers to fight Sir Mellegrans in half-armor Then Sir Mellegrans said to those who were with him: "Now I will go down and do battle with this knight, for never will I have a better chance of overcoming him than this." Therewith he turned to that messenger, and he said: "Go! Hasten back to yonder knight, and tell him that I will do battle with him upon those conditions he offers, to wit: that he shall unarm his left side, and that he shall lay aside his shield and his helm. And tell him that by the time he hath made him ready in that wise, I will be down to give him what satisfaction I am able."

So the messenger departed upon that command, and Sir Mellegrans departed to arm himself for battle.

Then, after the messenger had delivered the message that Sir Mellegrans had given him, Sir Launcelot laid aside his shield and his helm as he had agreed to do, and he removed his armor from his left side so that he was altogether unarmed upon that side.

After a while Sir Mellegrans appeared, clad all in armor from top to toe, and baring himself with great confidence, for he felt well assured of victory in that encounter. Thus he came very proudly nigh to where Sir Launcelot was, and he said: "Here am I, Sir Knight, come to do you service since you will have it so."

Sir Launcelot said: "I am ready to meet thee thus or in any other way, so that I may come at thee at all."

After that each knight dressed himself for combat, and all those who were in the castle gathered at the windows and the galleries above, and looked down upon the two knights.

Then they two came slowly together, and when they were pretty nigh to one another Sir Launcelot offered his left side so as to allow Sir Mellegrans to strike at him. And when Sir Mellegrans perceived this chance, he straightway lashed a great blow at Sir Launcelot's unarmed side with all his might and main, and with full intent to put an end to the battle with that one blow.

But Sir Launcelot was well prepared for that stroke, wherefore he very dexterously and quickly turned himself to one side so that he received the blow upon the side which was armed, and at the same time he put aside a part of the blow with his sword. So that blow came to naught.

But so violent was the stroke that Sir Mellegrans had lashed that he overreached himself, and ere he could recover himself, Sir Launcelot lashed at him a great buffet that struck him fairly upon the helm. *Sir Launcelot slayeth Sir Mellegrans* And then again he lashed at him ere he fell and both this stroke of the sword and the other cut deep through the helm and into the brain pan of Sir Mellegrans, so that he fell down upon the ground and lay there without motion of any sort. Then Sir Launcelot stood over him, and called to those who were near to come and look to their lord, and thereat there came several running. These lifted Sir Mellegrans up and removed his helmet so as to give him air to breathe. And they looked upon his face, and lo! even then the spirit was passing from him, for he never opened his eyes to look upon the splendor of the sun again.

Then when those of the castle saw how it was with Sir Mellegrans and that even then he was dead, they lifted up their voices with great lamentation so that the entire castle rang presently with their outcries and wailings.

But Sir Launcelot cried out: "This knight hath brought this upon himself because of the treason he hath done; wherefore the blame is his own." And then he said: "Where is the porter of this castle? Go, fetch him hither!"

So in a little while the porter came, and Sir Launcelot made demand of him: "Where is it that the Queen and her court are held prisoners? Bring me to them, Sirrah?"

Then the porter of the castle bowed down before Sir Launcelot and he said, "Messire, I will do whatever you command me to do," for he was overwhelmed with the terror of Sir Launcelot's wrath as he had displayed it that day. And the porter said, "Messire, have mercy on us all and I will take you to the Queen."

Sir Launcelot rescueth the Queen So the porter brought Sir Launcelot to where the Queen was, and where were those others with her. Then all these gave great joy and loud acclaim that Sir Launcelot had rescued them out of their captivity. And Queen Guinevere said: "What said I to you awhile since? Did I not say that it mattered not how Sir Launcelot came hither even if it were in a cart? For lo! though he came thus humbly and in lowly wise, yet he hath done marvellous deeds of knightly prowess, and hath liberated us all from our captivity."

After that Sir Launcelot commanded them that they should make ready such horses as might be needed. And he commanded that they should fetch litters for those knights of the Queen's court who had been wounded, and all that was done as he commanded. After that they all departed from that place and turned their way toward Camelot and the court of the King.

But Sir Launcelot did not again see that damsel Elouise the Fair, for she kept herself close shut in her own bower and would see naught of any one because of the grief and the shame of all that had passed. At that Sir Launcelot took much sorrow, for he was greatly grieved that he should have brought any trouble upon one who had been so friendly with him as she had been. Yet he wist not how he could otherwise have done than as he did do, and he could think of naught to comfort her.

So ends this adventure of the Knight of the Cart with only this to say: that after that time there was much offence taken that Sir Launcelot had gone upon that adventure riding in a cart. For many jests were made of it as I have said, and many of the King's court were greatly grieved that so unworthy a thing should have happened.

More especially were the kinsmen of Sir Launcelot offended at *His kinsmen* what he had done. Wherefore Sir Lionel and Sir Ector came to Sir *chide Sir* Launcelot and Sir Ector said to him: "That was a very ill thing you *Launcelot* did to ride to that adventure in a cart. Now prythee tell us why you did such a thing as that when you might easily have got a fresh horse for to ride upon if you had chosen to do so."

To this Sir Launcelot made reply with much heat: "I know not why you should take it upon you to meddle in this affair. For that which I did, I did of mine own free will, and it matters not to any other man. Moreover, I deem that it matters not how I went upon that quest so that I achieved my purpose in a knightly fashion. For I have yet to hear any one say that I behaved in any way such as a true knight should not behave."

"For the matter of that," said Sir Ector, "thy knighthood is suffi-ciently attested, not only in this, but in many other affairs. But that which shames us who are of thy blood, and they who are thy com-panions at arms, is that thou shouldst have achieved thy quest in so unknightly a fashion instead of with that dignity befitting a very wor-thy undertaking. For dost thou not know that thou art now called everywhere 'The Chevalier of the Cart' and that songs are made of this adventure and that jests are made concerning it?"

Then Sir Launcelot was filled with great anger, and he went to *Sir Launcelot* his inn and took his shield and laced a sheet of leather over the *covereth his* face thereof. Thereafter he painted the leather covering of the shield *shield* a pure white so that it might not be known what was the device thereon, nor who was the knight who bare that shield. Then after he had done this he armed himself and took horse and rode forth errant and alone, betaking his way he knew not whither but suffering his horse to wander upon whatsoever path it choose.

Thus Sir Launcelot departed in anger from the court of King Arthur, and after that, excepting one time, he was not seen in the court of the King again for the space of two years, during which time there was much sorrow at the court, because he was no longer there.

The Story of Sir Gareth of Orkney

AND NOW *followeth the history of Sir Gareth of Orkney, who came unknown to the court of his uncle, King Arthur; who was there treated with great indignity by Sir Kay the Seneschal; who was befriended by his brother, Sir Gawaine, and who afterward went errant with a damsel hight Lynette, meeting whilst with her several beladventures which shall hereinafter be duly told of.*

So if you would know how it fared with that young knight, you must cease to consider the further adventures of Sir Launcelot at this place, and must now read of those other adventures of this youth, who was the youngest son of King Lot and Queen Margaise of Orkney. But after they are ended, then shall the further history of the adventures of Sir Launcelot be considered once more.

ir Gareth of Orkney ♂ ♂ ♂

Chapter First

How Sir Gareth of Orkney came to the Castle of Kynkennedon where King Arthur was holding court, and how it fared with him at that place.

THE YOUNGEST son of King Lot of Orkney and of his Queen, *Of Gareth of Orkney* who was the Lady Margaise, sister of King Arthur, was a youth hight Gareth of Orkney. This young, noble, high-born prince was the most beautiful of all his royal race, for not only was he exceedingly tall and stalwart of frame—standing a full head bigger than the biggest of any at his father's court—and not only was he the strongest and the most agile and the most skilful at all knightly sports, and not only was he gentle in speech and exceedingly courteous in demeanor to all with whom he held discourse, but he was so beautiful of countenance that I do not believe that an angel of Paradise could be more fair to look upon than he. For his hair was bright and ruddy, shining like to pure gold, his cheeks were red and they and his chin were covered over with a soft and budding bloom of beard like to a dust of gold upon his face; his eyes were blue and shining and his neck and throat were round and white like to a pillar of alabaster.

Now King Lot and Queen Margaise loved Gareth above any of *How they of the court praise Gareth* their other children, and so it befell that all those who dwelt at the

43

King's court took every occasion to praise young Gareth, both to his face and before the faces of the King and Queen, his father and mother. For these would sometimes say: "Lo! this youth sendeth forth such a glory of royal beauty and grace and dignity from him that even were he clad in fustian instead of cloth of gold yet would all the world know him to be of royal strain as plainly as though he were clothed in royal attire fitting for such a princely youth to wear. For, behold! the splendor of his royalty lieth in his spirit and not in his raiment, and so it is that it shineth forth from his countenance."

Queen Margaise bespeaketh Gareth Now it came to pass that when Gareth was twenty years of age, his mother, Queen Margaise, called him to her in her bower where she was with her maidens, and she bade him to sit down beside her and he did as she commanded, taking his place upon a couch spread with purple cloth embroidered with silver lions whereon the Queen was sitting at that time. Then Queen Margaise gazed long upon her beautiful son, and her heart yearned over him with pride and glory because of his strength and grace. And by and by she said: "My son, now that thou hast reached to the fulness of thy stature and girth and art come to the threshold of thy manhood, it is time for thee to win for thyself the glory of knighthood such as shall become thee, earning it by such deeds as shall be worthy of the royal race from which thou hast sprung. Accordingly, I would now have it that thou shouldst go to the court of my brother, King Arthur, and that thou shouldst there take thy stand with that noble and worthy companionship of the Champions of the Round Table, of whom thy brothers shine forth like bright planets in the midst of a galaxy of stars. So I would have it that thou shouldst go to the court of the great King, my brother, a week from to-day, and to that end I would have it that thou shouldst go in charge of three of the noblest lords of this court and in such a state of pomp and circumstance as may befit one who is, as thou art, the son of a royal father and mother and the nephew of that great King who is the overlord of this entire realm."

Gareth departeth for the court of King Arthur Thus spake Queen Margaise, and in accordance with that saying Gareth set forth a sennight from that time for the court of King Arthur. With him there rode three very noble haughty lords of the court as the Queen had ordained, and with these went esquires and attendants to the number of threescore ten and four. In the midst of that company young Gareth rode upon a cream white horse, and all the harness and furnishings of the horse upon which he rode were of gold, and the saddle upon which he sat was stamped with gold and riveted with rivets of gold, and Gareth himself was clad all in cloth of gold, so, what with all of these and his fair beautiful face in the bright sunlight (the day being wonderfully clear and fair) the royal youth appeared to shine with such a glistering splendor that it was as though a star of remarkable glory had fallen from the heavens and had found lodgment in his person upon the earth.

So it was that the young Gareth rode forth upon his way to the court of his uncle, the King.

That evening, he and his company rested for the night in a glade of the forest and there the attendants set up a pavilion of purple silk for him. Around about this pavilion were other pavilions for those three lords who accompanied him as his companions in the journey and for their esquires and attendants.

Now that night Gareth lodged alone in his pavilion saving only that his dwarf, Axatalese, lay within the tent nigh to the door thereof. And it came to pass that Gareth could not sleep that night but lay awake, looking into the darkness and thinking of many things. And he said to himself: "Why is it that I should go thus in state to the court of the King and in that wise to win his especial favor? Lo! It were better that I should go as any other youth of birth and breeding rather than in this royal estate. For, if I am worthy, as men say of me, then my worth shall be made manifest by my deeds and not because of the state in which I travel."

Thus Gareth communed within himself and he said: "I will go to the court of mine uncle the King as a simple traveller and not as a prince travelling in state."

So somewhat before the dawning of the day, he arose very softly and went to where the dwarf lay, and he touched Axatalese upon the shoulder, and he said, "Axatalese, awake." Thereupon the dwarf awoke and sat up and looked about him in the darkness of the dawning, bewildered by the sleep that still beclouded his brain.

Then Gareth said, still speaking in a whisper: "Listen to what I say, but make no noise lest you arouse those who lay around about us." And Axatalese said, "Lord, I listen, and I will be silent."

Then Gareth said: "Axatalese, arise and fetch me hither some garments of plain green cloth, and aid me to clothe myself in those garments. Then thou and I will go forward alone and without attendants to King Arthur's court. For so I would come before the King in that guise and not travelling in the estate of a prince who may claim his favor because of the chance of birth. For I would have it that whatsoever good fortune I win, that fortune should come to me by mine own endeavor, and not because of the accident of birth."

Then Axatalese was greatly troubled, and he said: "Lord, think well of what you do, for, lo! your mother, the Queen, hath provided this escort for you; wherefore, haply, she will be very angry if you should do as you say, and should depart from those whom she appointed to accompany you."

"No matter," quoth Gareth; "let that be as it may, but do you as I tell you and go you straightway, very quietly, and carry out my commands. And see to it that no one shall be disturbed in your going or coming, for it is my purpose that we two shall go privily away from this place and that no one shall be aware of our going."

Gareth escapeth from his companions So spake Gareth, and Axatalese was aware that his command must be obeyed. So the dwarf went very quietly to do Gareth's bidding, and anon he returned with the clothes of a certain one of the attendants, and the clothes were of plain green cloth, and Gareth clad himself in that simple raiment. Then he and the dwarf went forth from the pavilion and they went to where the horses were, and they chose two of the horses and saddled them and bridled them with saddles and harness and trappings of plain leather, such as the least of the attendants might use—and in all of that time no one of those in attendance upon Gareth was aware of what he had done. Then Gareth and the dwarf rode away from that place and still all the others slept, and they slept for a long while after.

And be it here said that when those three lords who were in charge of Gareth awoke and found that he and Axatalese were gone, they were filled with terror and dismay, for they wist not why he was gone nor whither, and they dreaded the anger of the Queen, Gareth's mother. Then the chief of those lords said: "Lo! here are we betrayed by this young prince and his dwarf. For he hath left us and taken himself away, we know not whither, and so we dare not return to the court of Orkney again. For should we return without him they will assuredly punish us for suffering him to depart, and that punishment may come even to the taking of our lives."

Then another of those lords said: "Messire, those words are very true, so let us not return unto the court of Orkney, but let us escape unto some other part of the realm where the wrath of the King and Queen may not reach us."

So it was as that lord said, for straightway they departed from that place and went to a part of the realm where neither the King and Queen of Orkney nor King Arthur might hear of them, and there they abode for that time and for some time afterward.

Now at this time King Arthur was celebrating the Feast of Pentecost at the Castle of Kynkennedon. With him sat all the great lords of his court and all the Knights-companion of the Round Table who were not upon adventure in some other part of the realm. As they so sat at high feast, filling the hall with a great sound of merriment and good cheer, commingled with the chanting of minstrels and the music of harps and viols, there came one to where the King sat, and he said to him: "Lord, there is a fellow without who demandeth to have speech with you, face to face. Nor know we what to do in this case, for he will not be gainsaid, but ever maketh that demand aforesaid." *How King Arthur sat at feast*

Then King Arthur said: "Hah! say you so? Now what manner of man is he? Is he a king or a duke or a high prince that he maketh such a demand as that?" "Lord," said the messenger, "he is none of these, but only a youth of twenty years, tall and very large of frame and beautiful of face, and very proud and haughty in bearing. And he is clad like to a yeoman in cloth of plain green, wherefore we know not what to think of that demand he maketh to have speech with you." King Arthur said, "What attendants hath he with him?" And the messenger said, "He hath no attendants of any kind, saving only a dwarf who followeth after him."

Quoth the King: "Well, at this Feast of Pentecost far be it from me to deny any man speech with me. So fetch this one hither that we may see what manner of man he is."

Therewith in obedience to the King's command, that attendant went forth and anon he returned, bringing Gareth and the dwarf Axatalese with him. And Gareth walked very proudly and haughtily *Gareth cometh before the King* up the hall and all who looked upon him marvelled at his height and his girth and at the beauty of his countenance. And many said: "Certes, that is a very noble-appearing man to be clad in such plain raiment of green, for, from his manner and his bearing, he would otherwise appear to be some nobleman's son, or some one of other high degree."

So Gareth walked up the length of the hall with all gazing upon him, and so he came and stood before the King and looked the King in the face, regarding him very steadfastly and without any fear or awe—and few there were who could so regard King Arthur.

Now Sir Kay the Seneschal stood behind the King's seat and when he beheld how young Gareth fronted the King, look for look, he was very wroth at the demeanor of that youth who stood thus before that royal majesty. So he spoke aloud before all those who sat there in hall, saying, to Gareth: "Sirrah, who are you who darest thus to stand with such assurance in the presence of the Great King? Wit you it is not for such as you to stand before such majesty, and have speech with it. Rather you should veil your face and hang your head in that awful presence."

Then Gareth looked at Sir Kay very calmly and he said, "Who are you who speak such words to me?" and all were amazed at the haughtiness of his tones and voice.

And King Arthur was also much astonished that a youth, clad thus like a yeoman, should thus speak to a great lord of the court such as Sir Kay. Wherefore the King wist not what to think of such a bearing. Then anon he said: "Fair youth, whence come you and who are you who speaketh thus so boldly to a great lord of our court and before our very face?" And Gareth said: "Lord, I am one who hath come hither from a great distance to crave two boons of you."

Quoth the King: "At this time, and at this Feast of Pentecost I may not refuse any one a boon who asketh it of me. So, if these two boons are fit for one of your condition to have, they shall be granted unto you."

Gareth asketh his boon   Then Gareth said: "Lord, this is the first boon that I would ask of thee. I ask not for knighthood nor for courtly favor. All that I ask is that thou wilt permit me to dwell here at court for a year and that thou wilt provide me with lodging and with clothing and with meat and with drink for that time. Then at the end of a year, if I have proved myself patient to wait, I shall crave a second boon of thee."

Now many who were there heard what it was that strange youth asked as a boon, and that he besought not knighthood or honor at the King's hands, but bread and meat and drink and lodging, wherefore several of them laughed a great deal at the nature of that boon. As for the King, he smiled not, but he inclined his head very calmly and said: "Fair youth if that is all the boon thou hast to ask of us at this time, then thou shalt have thy will with all welcome." And he said: "Kay, see to it that this youth hath his desires in these things, and that he hath lodging and clothing and food and drink for an entire year from this time."

Then Sir Kay looked very scornfully upon Gareth and said: "It shall be as you will. As for thee, fellow, I will see to it that thou art fed until thou art as fat as any porker."

So spake Sir Kay, and when young Gareth heard the words his face flamed red with wrath and the veins stood out upon his forehead like cords. But he controlled his anger to calmness and anon he said: "Messire, you do but hear my words, knowing nothing of the purpose that lyeth within my mind. Wherefore then do you scorn me since you know naught of my purpose?"

Then Sir Kay looked upon the youth with anger and he said: "Sirrah, thou speaketh very saucily to those who are thy betters. Learn to bridle thy tongue or otherwise it may be very ill with thee."

So spake Sir Kay, but Gareth answered him not. Otherwise he turned to the King and bowed low, as though he had not heard the speech that Sir Kay had uttered.

Then he turned and went away from the King's presence with the dwarf Axatalese following close after him.

Now Sir Gawaine sat not far distant from the King and so he had heard all that had passed. And he beheld the indignation of Gareth against Sir Kay, and the heart of Sir Gawaine went out very strongly toward this haughty and beautiful youth—albeit he wist not why it was that he felt love for him, nor that Gareth was his own brother. So it befell that after Gareth had departed from the King's presence in that wise, Sir Gawaine arose and followed after him; and when he had come up with Gareth he touched him upon the arm and said, "Come

Sir Gawaine loveth Gareth

with me, fair youth." And Gareth did so. So after that Sir Gawaine led Gareth to another place, and when they were come thither he said to him: "Fair youth, I prythee tell me who you are and whence you come, and why it is that you asked such a boon as that from the King's Majesty."

Then Gareth looked upon Sir Gawaine and knowing that it was his brother whom he gazed upon he loved him a very great deal. Ne'ertheless he contained his love and said: "Messire, why ask you me that? See you not from the raiment I wear who I am and what is my degree? As for the boon which I asked, wit you that I asked it because I needed a roof to shelter me and meat and drink to sustain my life."

Then Sir Gawaine was astonished at the pride and haughtiness of the youth's reply, wherefore he said: "Fair youth, I know not what to think; yet I well believe it was not for the sake of the food and drink and lodging that thou didst so beseech that boon of the King, for methinks that thou art very different from what thou appearest to be. Now I find that my heart goeth out to thee with a very singular degree of love, wherefore I am of a mind to take thee into my favor and to have thee dwell near me at mine inn." And Gareth said to his brother, "Sir, thou art very good to me."

Sir Gawaine traineth Gareth in knightly skill

So it was that after that time Sir Gawaine took Gareth into his favor and did many acts of kindness unto the youth. And so Gareth dwelt nigh to Sir Gawaine, and Sir Gawaine instructed him in the use of arms. And ever Sir Gawaine was astonished that the youth should learn so quickly and so well the arts of chivalry and of knighthood. For Sir Gawaine wist not that Gareth had been taught many of these things, and that others came easily to him by nature, because of the royal and knightly blood from which he had sprung.

Sir Kay scorneth Gareth

And ever in the same measure that Sir Gawaine bestowed his favor upon Gareth, in that degree Sir Kay scorned him. So it came to pass that when Sir Kay would meet Gareth he would say to whomsoever was present at that time, some such words as these: "Lo! you! this is our kitchen knave who had no spirit to ask of the King's Majesty any higher boon than this, that he be allowed to sup fat broth in the kitchen." So Sir Kay ever called Gareth a kitchen knave, and so calling him he would maybe say, "Sirrah, get thee upon the other side of me, for the wind bloweth toward me and thou smellest vilely of the kitchen." And because Sir Kay perceived that the hands of Gareth were soft and very white he named the youth "Beaumains," saying, "Look you at this kitchen knave, how fat and white are his hands from dwelling in lazy idleness." So Gareth was known as "Beaumains" by all those who were of the King's court.

But when Sir Gawaine heard this talk of Sir Kay he remembered him of how Sir Percival had been one time scorned by Sir Kay in such a manner as this. And Sir Gawaine said: "Messire, let be, and torment not this youth, lest evil befall thee. Remember how thou didst hold Sir Percival in scorn when he was a youth, and how he struck thee such a buffet that he nigh broke thy neck."

Then Sir Kay looked very sourly upon Sir Gawaine, and said, "This Beaumains is not such as Sir Percival was when he was young." And Sir Gawaine laughed and said, "Nevertheless, be thou warned in season."

So it was that Gareth dwelt for a year at the King's court, eating the meat of idleness. And many laughed at him and made sport of him who would have paid him court and honor had they known who he was and what was his estate. Yet ever Gareth contained himself in patience, biding his time until it should have come, and making no complaint of the manner in which he was treated.

And now if you would hear how young Gareth won him honor and knighthood, I pray you read that which followeth, for therein are those things told of at some length.

The Damsel Lynette . . ✦ ✦

Chapter Second

How Gareth set forth upon an adventure with a young damsel hight Lynette; how he fought with Sir Kay, and how Sir Launcelot made him a knight. Also in this it is told of several other happenings that befell Gareth, called Beaumains, at this time.

O PASSED a year as aforetold, and Gareth lodged with the household of King Arthur and had food and drink as much as he desired. And in all that time Gareth ate his food and drank his drink at a side table, for Sir Kay would not permit him to sit at the same table with the lords and knights and ladies of the King's court. For Sir Kay would say, "This kitchen knave shall not eat at table with gentle folk but at a side table by himself," and so Gareth fed at a table by himself. And ever Sir Kay called Gareth "Beaumains" in scornful jest and all the court called him "Beaumains" because Sir Kay did so.

Now at the end of that year when the Feast of Pentecost had King Arthur sitteth again at feast come again, King Arthur was holding his court at Caerleon-upon-Usk, and at the high Feast of Pentecost there sat, as usual at the King's table, the lords and the ladies of the court and all the Knights of the Round Table who were not upon adventure that took them elsewhither.

As they so sat eating and drinking there came into the hall a slen- A damsel appeareth before the King der maiden of not more than sixteen years old. And the maiden was exceedingly beautiful, for her hair was as black as ebony and was like to threads of fine black silk for softness and brightness. And her eyes were as black as jet and very bright and shining, and her face was like ivory for clearness and whiteness and her lips were red like to coral for redness. She was clad all in flame-colored satin, embroidered with threads of gold and she wore a bright shining chaplet of gold about her brows so that what with her raiment of flame-color and with her embroidery and ornaments of shining gold, the maiden came up the hall like to a fiery vision of beauty, insomuch that all turned to behold her in passing, and many stood in their places that they might see her the better.

The damsel asketh for a champion Thus the damsel came up the hall until she had reached to that place where King Arthur sat at the head of the feast, and when she had come there she kneeled down and set her hands together as in prayer, palm to palm. And King Arthur looked upon her and was pleased with her beauty, and he said, "Damsel, what is it thou wouldst have of us?" The damsel said: "Lord, I would have the aid of some good worthy knight of thy court who should act as champion in behalf of my sister." And the King said, "What ails thy sister?"

Quoth the damsel: "Lord, my sister is tormented by a very evil disposed knight who maketh demand of her for wife. But my sister hateth this knight and will have naught to do with him, wherefore he sitteth ever before her castle and challengeth whomsoever cometh thitherward, and will not suffer any one to go in to the castle or come out thence without his permission. Now I come hither upon my sister's behalf to seek a champion who shall liberate her from this duress."

Then said the King, "Who is thy sister and who is this knight who tormenteth her?" To the which the damsel made reply: "I may not tell you my sister's name, for she is very proud and haughty, and is very much ashamed that she should be held in duress by that knight against her will. But as for the knight who tormenteth her, I may tell you that he is hight the Red Knight of the Red Lands."

Then King Arthur said: "I know not any such knight as that. Is there any one of you hereabouts who knoweth him?" And Sir Gawaine said: "Lord, I know him very well, for I met him one time in battle and it was such hard ado for me to hold mine own against him that even to this day I know not rightly whether he was better than I or whether I was better than he." Then King Arthur said: "Fair damsel, that must be a very strong and powerful knight, since Sir Gawaine speaketh of him in this wise. But touching this affair of thy sister, know you not that it is not likely that any knight of renown will be found to champion a lady of whose name or degree he knoweth naught? If thou wilt tell the name of thy sister and wilt declare her degree I doubt not there are many good worthy knights of this court any one of whom would gladly champion her cause."

So spake the King, but the damsel only shook her head and said, "Lord, I may not tell my sister's name, for I am forbidden to do so."

Then the King said: "That is a pity for I fear me thou wilt not easily find thee a champion in that case." And he said, "Damsel, what is thy name?" And she said, "Sir, it is Lynette." The King said, "That is a fair name and thou art very fair of face."

Then the King looked about him and he said: "Is there any knight in this court who will undertake this adventure in behalf of that fair lady, even though she will not declare her name and degree? If such there be, he hath my free will and consent for to do so."

So spake the King, but no one immediately answered, for no one cared to take up such a quarrel against so strong a knight, not knowing for whom it was that that quarrel was to be taken up.

Now he whom all called Beaumains was at that time sitting at his side table a little distance away, and he heard all that passed. Likewise he observed how that no one arose to assume that adventure and at that he was very indignant. For he said to himself: "This damsel is very fair, and the case of her sister is a very hard case, and I wonder that no good and well-approved knight will take that adventure upon him."

But still no one appeared to assume that quarrel of the unknown lady and so, at last, Beaumains himself arose from where he sat, and came forward before them all to where the King was and at that time the damsel was still kneeling before the King.

Then the King beholding Beaumains standing there said, "Beaumains, what is it thou wouldst have?" and Beaumains said: "Lord, I *Gareth asketh his second boon* have now dwelt in this court for a year from the time that I first came hither. That time when I first stood before thee I besought two boons of thee and one of them thou didst grant me and the other thou didst promise to grant me. According to that first boon, I had since that time had lodging beneath thy roof and food and drink from thy table, as much as ever I desired. But now hath come the time when I would fain ask that other boon of thee."

Then King Arthur wondered a very great deal, and he said, "Speak, Beaumains, and ask what thou wilt and the boon is thine."

"Lord," said Beaumains, "this is the boon I would ask. I beseech thee that thou wilt suffer me to assume this adventure upon behalf of that lady who will not tell her name."

Now when they of the court who sat near to the King heard what boon it was that the kitchen knave, Beaumains, besought of the King, a great deal of laughter arose upon all sides, for it seemed to all to be a very good jest that Beaumains should assume such an undertaking as that, which no knight of the court chose to undertake. Only King Arthur did not laugh. Otherwise he spake with great dignity saying: "Beaumains, methinks thou knowest not what boon it is thou hast asked. Ne'ertheless, be the peril thine. For since thou hast asked that boon, and since I have passed my promise, I cannot refrain from granting that which thou hast besought of me."

Then Sir Kay came forward and he spake to the damsel, saying, "Fair damsel, know you who this fellow is who asketh to be appointed champion for to defend your lady sister?" and Lynette said, "Nay, I know not; but I pray you tell me who he is."

"I will do so," quoth Sir Kay. "Wit you that this fellow is a kitchen knave who came hither a year ago and besought as a royal boon from the King that he should have meat and drink and lodging. Since then he hath been well fed every day at a table I have set aside for him. So he hath grown fat and proud and high of spirit and thinketh himself haply to be a champion worthy to undertake such an adventure as that which he hath besought leave to assume."

The damsel Lynette is angry

So said Sir Kay, and when the damsel Lynette heard his words her face flamed all as red as fire and she turned to King Arthur and said: "My Lord King, what shame and indignity is this that you would put upon me and my sister? I came hither beseeching you for a champion to defend my sister against her oppressor and instead of a champion you give me a kitchen knave for that service."

"Lady," quoth King Arthur very calmly, "this Beaumains hath besought a boon of me and I have promised him that favor. Accordingly, I must needs fulfil my promise to him. But this I tell thee, that I believe him to be very different from what he appeareth to be; and I tell thee that if he faileth in this adventure which he hath assumed, then will I give thee another champion that shall haply be more to thy liking than he."

But Lynette was very exceedingly wroth and she would not be appeased by the King's words; yet she dared say no word of her indignation to the King's Majesty. Accordingly she turned and went away from that place very haughtily, looking neither to the one side nor to the other, but gazing straight before her as she went out from that hall.

Then after she was gone Sir Gawaine came and stood before the King and said: "Messire and Lord, I have faith that greater things shall come of this adventure than any one hereabouts supposeth it possible to happen. For Beaumains is no such kitchen knave as Sir Kay proclaimeth him to be, but something very different from that, as Sir Kay himself shall mayhap discover some day. For a year this Beaumains hath dwelt nigh me and I have seen him do much that ye know not of. Now I pray you, Lord, to suffer me to purvey him with armor fit for this undertaking and I believe he will some time bring honor both to you and to me—to you because you granted him this boon, to me because I provided him with armor." Then King Arthur said to Sir Gawaine, "Messire, let it be as you say."

So Sir Gawaine took Beaumains away with him to his own lodging-place and here he provided the youth with armor. And he provided him with a shield and a sword and a good stout spear. And he provided him with a fine horse, such as a knight who was to go errant might well care to ride upon. Then when Beaumains was provided in all this way, Sir Gawaine wished him God-speed and Beaumains took horse and departed after the maiden Lynette. And Axatalese the dwarf rode with Beaumains upon a gray mule, as his esquire. *Sir Gawaine armeth Beaumains*

Now by the time all this had been accomplished—to wit, the arming and horsing of Beaumains—Lynette had gone so far upon her way that Beaumains and Axatalese were compelled to ride for two leagues and more at a very fast pace ere they could overtake her.

And when they did overtake her she was more angry than ever to behold that misshapen dwarf accompanying the kitchen knave who was her appointed champion. Wherefore when Beaumains had come nigh to her, she cried out, "Sirrah, art thou Beaumains, the kitchen knave?" And Gareth said, "Aye, I am he whom they call Beaumains." *Lynette scorneth Beaumains*

Then she cried out upon him, "Return thee whence thou hast come for I will have none of thee!"

To this angry address Beaumains replied, speaking very mildly and with great dignity: "Lady, the King hath appointed me to ride with you upon this adventure, wherefore, with you, I must now do as I have been commanded. For having embarked in this affair, I must needs give my service to you, even if you should order me to do otherwise." "Well," quoth she, "if you will not do as I bid you, then I tell you this; that I will straightway take a path that will lead you into such dangers as you have no thought of, and from which you will be not at all likely to escape with your life."

To this Beaumains replied, speaking still very calmly and with great courtesy: "Lady, that shall be altogether as you ordain. And I venture to say to you that no matter into what dangers you may bring me, still I have great hope that I shall bring you out thence with safety and so be of service to you and your lady sister. Wherefore, whithersoever you lead, thither will I follow you."

Then Lynette was still more angry that Beaumains should be so calm and courteous to her who was so angry and uncourteous to him, wherefore she hardened her heart toward him and said: "Sirrah, since I cannot rid me of you, I bid you ride upon the other side of the way, for methinks you smell very strongly of the kitchen in which you have dwelt."

To these words Beaumains bowed his head with great dignity and said, "Lady, it shall be as you command." And therewith he drew rein to the other side of the highway to that upon which she rode. Then Lynette laughed, and she said: "Ride a little farther behind me, for still methinks I smell the savor of the kitchen." And Beaumains did as she commanded and withdrew him still farther away from her.

✠   ✠   ✠

Sir Kay followeth Beaumains Now some while after Beaumains had ridden after Lynette as aforetold, Sir Kay said to certain of those who were nigh him: "I am of a mind to ride after our kitchen knave and to have a fall of him, for it would be a very good thing to teach him such a lesson as he needs." So according to that saying, Sir Kay went to his inn and donned his armor. And he chose him a good stout spear and he took horse and rode away after Beaumains with intent to do as he had said. So he rode at a good pace and for a long time and by and by he beheld Lynette and Beaumains and the dwarf where they rode along the highway at some distance before him. Then Sir Kay called out in a great voice, saying: "Stay, Beaumains, turn thou thitherward. For I am come to overthrow thee and to take that damsel away from thee."

Then Lynette turned her head and beheld Sir Kay where he came, and with that she pointed and said: "Look, thou kitchen knave, yonder cometh a right knight in pursuit of thee. Now haply thou hadst best flee away ere harm befall thee."

But to this address Beaumains paid no heed, otherwise he turned about his horse and straightway put himself into array for defence. And as Sir Kay drew nigh, Beaumains beheld the device upon his shield and knew who was the knight who came thitherward and that it was Sir Kay who followed after him and called upon him to stay.

Then Beaumains remembered him of all the many affronts that Sir Kay had put upon him for all that year past and with that his anger grew very hot within him. And he said to himself: "This is well met; for now my time hath come. For either this is the day of satisfaction for me or else it is the day in which I shall lay my dead body down beside the highroad."

Meantime Sir Kay had come nigh, and finding that Beaumains had prepared himself, he also made himself straightway ready for battle. Then Lynette drew her palfrey to one side of the way and to a place whence she might behold all that befell.

So when Beaumains and Sir Kay were in all ways prepared, each gave shout and drave forward very violently to the assault. And they met in the midst of that course and in that encounter the spear of Sir Kay held and the spear of Beaumains, because it was not very well directed, was broken into several pieces, so that he would have fallen only for the address of horsemanship that Sir Gawaine had taught him in the year that had passed.

Sir Kay doeth battle with Beaumains

But when Lynette beheld how that the spear of Beaumains was broken in that wise, and how that he was nearly cast out of the saddle in that encounter, she laughed very high and shrill. And she cried out in a loud voice: "Hah! thou kitchen knave, if thou showest not better address than that, thou wilt not be likely to succeed in this adventure that thou hast undertaken."

Now Beaumains heard the high laughter of Lynette and the words that she called out to him and with that he was more angry than ever. So therewith he ground his teeth together, and, casting aside the stump of his spear which he still held in his hand, he drew his sword and made at Sir Kay with all his might and main. And he put aside Sir Kay's defence with great violence, and having done so he rose up in his stirrups and lashed a blow at Sir Kay that fell upon his helm like to a bolt of lightning. For in that one blow Beaumains lashed forth all his rage and the indignation of a whole year of the scorn of Sir Kay. And he launched forth all the anger that he felt against the damsel Lynette who had also scorned him.

Beaumains smiteth down Sir Kay So fierce and terrible was that blow he struck that I misdoubt that any knight in all the world could have stood against it, far less could Sir Kay stand against it. For straightway upon receiving that stroke the senses of Sir Kay scattered all abroad and darkness fell roaring upon his sight and he fell down from off his horse and lay there upon the ground as though he was dead. Then Beaumains stood above him smiling very grimly. And he said, "Well, Sir Kay, how like you that blow from the hands of the kitchen knave?" but Sir Kay answered him not one word as you may suppose.

Therewith, having so spoken, Beaumains dismounted from his horse and he called the dwarf Axatalese to him and he said: "Axatalese, dismount from thy mule and tie it to yonder bush and take thou the horse of this knight and mount upon it instead." And Axatalese did as his master commanded. And Beaumains said to Sir Kay when he still lay in his swoon, "Sir Knight, I will borrow of you your spear, since I now have none of mine own," and therewith he took the spear of Sir Kay into his hand. And he took the shield of Sir Kay and hung it upon the pommel of the saddle of the horse of Sir Kay that he had given to Axatalese, and after that he mounted his own horse and rode away from that place, leaving Sir Kay lying where he was in the middle of the way.

And Lynette also rode away and ever Beaumains followed her in silence. So they rode for a while and then at last and by and by the damsel fell alaughing in great measure. And she turned her to Beaumains, and said, "Sirrah, thou kitchen knave, dost thou take pride to thyself?" and Beaumains said, "Nay, Lady." She said: "See that thou takest no pride, for thou didst but overcome that knight by the force of thy youth and strength, whilst he broke thy spear and wellnigh cast thee out of thy saddle because of his greater skill."

Then Beaumains bowed his head and said, "Lady, that may very well be." At that Lynette laughed again, and she said, "Sirrah, thou art forgetting thyself and thou ridest too near to me. Now I bid thee ride farther away so that I may not smell the savor of the kitchen," and Beaumains said, "As you command, so it shall be," and therewith he drew rein to a little greater distance.

And here it may be told of Sir Kay that some while after Beaumains had gone he bestirred himself and arose and looked about him, and for some while he knew not what had befallen him nor where he was. Then anon he remembered and he wist that he had suffered great shame and humiliation at the hands of Beaumains the kitchen knave. And he saw that in that encounter he had lost his shield and his spear and his horse and that naught was left for him to ride upon saving only that poor gray mule upon which the dwarf of Beaumains had been riding.

Then Sir Kay wist not what to do, but there was naught else left *Sir Kay* for him but to mount that mule and ride back again whence he had *returneth to* come. So he did and when he reached the King's court there was such *court,* laughing and jesting concerning his adventure that he scarce dared to *ashamed* lift his voice in speech or to raise his face in the court for a week from that time. But Sir Gawaine made no speech nor jest of the mishap that Sir Kay had suffered, only he smiled very grimly and said, "Sir, you would have done well to have hearkened to what I said to you," and Sir Kay, though at most times he had bitter speech enough and to spare, had naught whatever to say to Sir Gawaine in reply.

And now we turn again to Beaumains and Lynette as they rode onward upon their way as aforetold. *They behold a*
For after that last speech of Lynette's, they went onward in si- *white knight*

lence, and ever Lynette looked this way and that as though she wist not that any such man as Beaumains was within the space of a league of that place. So travelling they came, toward the sloping of the afternoon, to a place nigh to the edge of a woodland where was a smooth and level space of grass surrounded on all sides but one by the trees of the forest. Here they beheld a knight who was just come out of the forest, and he was clad all in white armor and he rode upon a white horse. And the sun was shining so far aslant at that time that the light thereof was very red, like to pure gold. And the beams of the sun fell upon the skirts of the forest so that all the thick foliage of the woodland was entirely bathed in that golden light. And the same light flashed upon the polished armor of the knight and shone here and there very gloriously as though several stars of singular radiance had fallen from heaven and had catched upon that lonely knight-rider, who drew rein at their approach and so sat watching their coming.

Then Lynette turned to Beaumains and she said: "Sir kitchen knave, look you! yonder is a right knight with whom you may hardly hope to have ado. Now turn you about and get you gone while there is yet time, otherwise you may suffer harm at his hands."

To this Beaumains made no reply; otherwise, he rode forward very calmly and when he had come pretty nigh he bespoke that single knight in a loud clear voice, saying, "Sir Knight, I pray you do me battle."

At this address that knight aforesaid was very much astonished, and he said: "Sir, what offence have I done to you that you should claim battle of me in so curt a fashion? Gladly will I give you your will, but wit you not that all courtesy is due from one knight to another upon such an occasion?"

To this Beaumains made no reply, but turning his horse about he rode to a little distance and there made him ready for the encounter that was about to befall. For at that time his heart was so full of anger at the scorn of Lynette that he could not trust himself with speech, and indeed I verily believe that he knew not very well where he was or what he did.

Meantime the White Knight had also put himself into array for battle and when all was prepared they immediately launched the one against the other with such violence that the ground trembled and shook beneath their charge.

So they met with great crashing and uproar in the midst of the course and in that meeting the spear of Beaumains was broken into a great many pieces and he himself was cast out of his saddle and down to the ground with such violence that he was for a little while altogether stunned by the force of his fall.

Then Lynette laughed so high and so shrill that Beaumains heard her even in the midst of his swoon, and with that his spirit came back to him again and straightway he leaped up to his feet and drew his sword. And he cried out to the White Knight: "Sir Knight, come down from off thy horse and do battle with me afoot, for never will I be satisfied with this mischance that I have suffered."

Then the White Knight said: "Messire, how is this? I have no such cause of battle with you as that." But all the more Beaumains cried out with great vehemence, "Descend, Sir Knight, descend and fight me afoot."

"Well," quoth the White Knight, "since you will have it so, so it shall be."

Thereupon he voided his horse and drew his sword and straight- *Beaumains* way setting his shield before him, he came forward to the assault of *doeth battle* Beaumains. Then immediately they met together, each lashing very *White Knight* fiercely at the other, and so that battle began. And so it continued, each foining and tracing this way and that like two wild bulls at battle, but ever lashing stroke upon stroke at one another. Soon the armor of each was stained in places with red, for each had suffered some wound or hurt at this place or at that. Yet ever Beaumains fought with might and main, for he was so strengthened by his passion of rage that rather would he have died than yield in that battle.

So they fought with astounding fierceness for a considerable while, and then, at last, the White Knight called out, "Sir, I pray you stay this battle for a little," and with that Beaumains ceased his lashing and stood leaning upon his sword, panting for breath.

And the White Champion also leaned upon his sword and panted, and anon he said, "Sir, I pray you tell me your name. For I make my vow to you that never have I met any knight who hath fought a greater battle than you have fought this day—and yet I may tell you that I have fought with a great many of the very best knights of this realm."

"Messire," quoth Beaumains, "I may not declare my name at this present, for there are several good reasons why I will not do so. But though I may not do as you demand of me, nevertheless I beseech you that you will extend that favor unto me and will declare to me your name and your degree."

"Well," said the White Knight, "never yet have I refused that courtesy to any one who hath asked it of me. Wit ye then that I am called Sir Launcelot of the Lake."

Beaumains knoweth Sir Launcelot Now when Beaumains heard this that the White Knight said and when he wist that it was none other than Sir Launcelot against whom he had been fighting for that while, he was filled with great wonder and astonishment and a sort of fear. So straightway he flung aside his sword and he kneeled down before Sir Launcelot and set his palms together. And he said: "Messire, what have I done, to do battle against you? Rather would I have done battle against mine own brother than against you. Know you that you are the man of all others whom I most revere and admire. Now I pray you, Messire, if I have done well in your sight in this battle which I have fought, that you grant me a boon that I have to ask of you and of no other man."

Quoth Sir Launcelot: "What boon is it thou wouldst have? Ask it and if it is meet that I grant it to thee, then assuredly it shall be thine. As for that battle which thou hast done, let me tell thee of a truth that I believe that I have never before met a stronger or a more worthy champion than thou art. So now I prithee ask thy boon that I may have the pleasure of granting it to thee."

Then Beaumains said: "Sir, it is this. Wit you that I am not yet made knight, but am no more than a bachelor at arms. So if you think that I am not unworthy of that honor, I pray you make me a knight at this present and with your own hand."

"Sir," said Sir Launcelot, "that may not be until I know thy name and of what degree and worthiness thou art. For it is not allowed for a knight to make a knight of another man until first he is well assured of that other's degree and estate, no matter what deed of arms that other may have done. But if thou wilt tell me thy name and thy degree, then I doubt not that I shall be rejoiced to make a knight of thee."

Unto this Beaumains said, "Sir, I will tell you my name and degree if so be I may whisper it in your ear." And Sir Launcelot said, "Tell it to me as you list and in such manner as may be pleasing to you." So Beaumains set his lips to Sir Launcelot's ear and he told him his name and his degree. And he told Sir Launcelot many things that had befallen him of late, and Sir Launcelot was astonished beyond measure at all that he heard. Then when Beaumains had told all these several things, Sir Launcelot said: "Messire, I wonder no more that you should have done so great battle as you did against me, seeing what blood you have in your veins and of what royal race you are sprung. Gladly will I make you knight, for I believe in time you will surpass even your own brothers in glory of knighthood, wherefore I shall have great credit in having made you a knight."

Therewith Sir Launcelot took his sword in his hand, and Beau- *Sir Launcelot* mains kneeled. And Sir Launcelot laid the blade thereof upon the *maketh Sir* shoulder of Beaumains and so made him knight by accolade. And *Gareth a* he said, "Rise, Sir Gareth!" and Sir Gareth arose and stood upon his *knight* feet, and his heart was so expanded with joy that it appeared to him that he had the strength of ten men rather than one man in his single body.

Now the damsel Lynette had been observing all this from afar, and from that distance she could hear naught of what one champion said to the other, and she beheld what they did with very great wonderment and perplexity. Anon came Sir Launcelot and Sir Gareth to where she was, and when they were come near she said to Sir Launcelot, "Know you, Messire, who is this with whom you walk?" And Sir Launcelot said, "Yea, damsel, methinks I should know him." Lynette said: "I believe that you do not know him, for I am well assured that he is a kitchen knave of King Arthur's court. He hath followed me hither against my will, clad in armor which I believe he hath no entitlement to wear, and I cannot drive him from me."

Then Sir Launcelot laughed and he said: "Damsel, you know not what you say. Peace! Be still, or else you will bring shame upon yourself."

Then Lynette regarded Sir Launcelot for a while very seriously and anon she said, "Messire, I pray you tell me who you are who take me thus to task." And at that Sir Launcelot laughed again and said: "Damsel, I will not tell you my name, but mayhap if you ask my name of this worthy gentleman who is with you, he will tell you what it is."

Sir Launcelot leaveth Sir Gareth Then Sir Launcelot turned him to Sir Gareth and he said: "Friend, here I must leave you, for I have business that taketh me in another direction. So God save you and fare you well until we shall meet again. And if you will keep upon yonder path and follow it, it will bring you by and by to a fair priory of the forest, and there you and your damsel may have lodging for the night."

Thereupon Sir Launcelot bowed in courtesy both to Sir Gareth and to the damsel Lynette and so took his departure, wending his way whither he was minded to go and so in a little was lost to sight.

Then Lynette and Sir Gareth and the dwarf also went their way, taking that path that led to the priory of which Sir Launcelot had spoken; and there they found lodgment for the night—the damsel at one place, Sir Gareth at another.

✠   ✠   ✠

And now if you would hear more concerning Sir Gareth and Lynette and of what befell them, I pray you read further, for these things shall there be duly set forth for your entertainment.

ir Gareth doeth Battle with the Knight of the River Ford.

Chapter Third

How Sir Gareth and Lynette travelled farther upon their way; how Sir Gareth won the pass of the river against two strong knights, and how he overcame the Black Knight of the Black Lands. Also how he saved a good worthy knight from six thieves who held him in duress.

NOW WHEN the next morning had come, all bright and dewy and very clear like to crystal, Lynette arose and departed from that forest priory where she had lodged over-night, giving no news to Sir Gareth of her going. And at that time the birds were singing everywhere with might and main. Everywhere the May was abloom, the apple orchards were fragrant with blossoms, and field and meadow-land were spread thick with a variegated carpet of pretty wild flowers of divers colors, very fair to see.

So Lynette rode alone, all through the dewy morn, amid these fair meadow-lands and orchards belonging to the priory, making her way toward the dark and shady belt of forest that surrounded those smooth and verdant fields upon all sides. And ever she gazed behind her very slyly, but beheld no one immediately following after her.

For it was some while ere Sir Gareth arose from his couch to find the damsel gone. And when he did arise he was vexed beyond measure that she had departed. So he donned his armor in all haste and as soon as might be he followed hard after her, galloping his horse very violently through those fair and blooming meadows aforesaid, with the dwarf Axatalese following fast after him upon Sir Kay's warhorse.

So Sir Gareth made all speed, and by and by he perceived the *Sir Gareth* damsel where she was, and at that time she was just entering into *followeth* the forest shades. So he drove forward still more rapidly and anon *Lynette again* he came up with her and thereupon he saluted and said, "Save you, Lady!" Upon that salutation Lynette looked about, as though in surprise, and said, "Hah, thou kitchen knave, art thou there?" And Sir

69

Gareth said, "Yea, Lady." And Lynette said: "Methought thou hadst enough of adventure yestereve when that same White Knight rolled thee down into the dust and beat thee in a fair fight afterward." Sir Gareth said, "Lady, thou speakest bitter words to me!" and Lynette laughed, and she said: "Well, Sir Knave, it seems that I cannot speak words that are so bitter as to prevent thee from following after me for I see that I am not to be free from thee in spite of my will to that end." And then she said: "Now I bid thee to ride a little farther away from me, for even yet thou savorest very strongly of the kitchen, and the savor thereof spoileth the fair savor of the morning."

So spake Lynette, and thereupon Sir Gareth drew rein a little farther, and so followed after her some distance away as he had done the day before.

Lynette telleth Sir Gareth of the robber knights
After that they went a considerable ways in silence, and then by and by Lynette turned her head toward Sir Gareth and spake, saying: "Sirrah, knowest thou whither this path upon which we travel will lead us?" And Sir Gareth said, "Nay, Lady, I know not." "Alas for thee," quoth Lynette, "for I am to tell thee that this path leadeth toward a certain ford of a river, which same ford is guarded by two strong and powerful knights who are brothers. Of these two knights I heard yesternight at the priory that they are very savage robbers, and that, of those who would pass the ford of the river, some they slay and others they rob or else make captive for the sake of ransom. Now I am making my way toward that place where are these two knights in the belief that they may rid me of thee. So be thou advised whilst there is yet time; withdraw thee from this adventure and return whither thou hast come, or else, mayhap, a very great deal of harm may befall thee."

"Lady," quoth Sir Gareth, "were there twenty knights instead of two at that ford and were each of those twenty ten times as strong as either of the two are likely to be, yet would I follow after thee to the end of this adventure. Mayhap it may be my good fortune to rid the world of these two evil knights."

Then Lynette lifted up her eyes toward Heaven. "Alas," quoth she, "I see that never will I be rid of this kitchen knave until all the pride is beaten out of his body." And after that they rode their way without saying anything more at that time.

Anon, and when the sun had risen pretty high toward the middle of the morning, they came out of the forest and into a fair open plain of considerable extent. Here Sir Gareth perceived that there was a smooth wide river that flowed down through the midst of the plain. And he perceived that the road ran toward the river and crossed it by a shallow gravelly ford. And he perceived that upon the other side of the river was a tall, grim, and very forbidding castle that stood on high and overlooked the ford, and so he wist that this must be the ford guarded by those two knights of whom Lynette had spoken.

So as they drew nearer to the ford, Sir Gareth beheld a pillar of stone beside the way, and he saw that a great bugle horn of brass was chained fast to this pillar. Then Lynette pointed to the bugle horn and she said: "Sir Kitchen Knave, seest thou yon bugle horn? Thou had best not blow upon that horn for if thou dost thou will arouse those two knights who guard this ford and they will come forth from the castle and it will certes fare very ill with thee."

Then Sir Gareth said, "Say you so, Lady?" Therewith he went *Sir Gareth* straight to where the horn hung by its chain, and he seized it in both *challengeth* hands and blew upon it so violently that it was as though the brazen *knights* horn would be burst with his blowing. For the sound thereof flew far and wide, and came echoing back from the distant walls of the castle as though the trump of doom had been sounded in those parts.

Therewith, and after a little while, the portcullis of the castle was uplifted and the drawbridge let fall and there issued forth two knights very large and stout of frame and very forbidding of appearance. These two knights rode down toward the ford and when they had come nigh to it he who was the bigger of the two drave down to the edge of the water and called across to Sir Gareth, "Who are you who dareth to blow so loudly upon our bugle horn?" And to him Sir Gareth replied: "Sir, I blew upon that horn to let you know that I was here and that I come with intent to rid the world of you, if so be God shall be with me in mine endeavor."

At that the knight upon the other bank was so enraged that he cast aside his spear and drew his sword and drave straightway into the waters of the ford, splashing with a noise like to thunder. And Sir Gareth also cast aside his spear and drew his sword and drave into the ford with great violence.

Sir Gareth overthroweth the knight of the ford So they met in the midst of the river and the knight of the ford lashed at Sir Gareth a most terrible and vehement blow, which stroke Sir Gareth put aside with great skill so that it harmed him not. Then Sir Gareth upon his part lifted himself on high and lashed at the knight so woful and terrible a blow that his horse tottered under the stroke and the knight himself catched at the pommel of his saddle to save himself from falling. Then Sir Gareth lashed at him another stroke and with that the knight swooned away into darkness and fell out of his saddle and into the water. And the river where he fell was very deep so that when he sank beneath the water he did not rise again, although Sir Gareth waited some while for him to do so.

Sir Gareth overthroweth the second knight Then Sir Gareth, perceiving how that he had finished this enemy, drave his horse very violently across the ford, and to the farther bank, and the knight who was there upon that side of the river drave down against Sir Gareth with his spear in rest with intent to thrust him through the body. But Sir Gareth was aware of his coming and so when the knight of the river was immediately upon him, he put aside the point of the spear with his shield with great skill and address. Then he rode up the length of the spear and when he had come nigh enough he rose up in his stirrup and lashed at the knight of the river so dreadful deadly a blow that nor shield nor helm could withstand that stroke. For the sword of Sir Gareth clave through the shield of the knight, and it clave through the helm and deep into his brain-pan. And with that the knight of the river fell headlong from his saddle and lay upon the ground without life or motion wherewith to rise again. Then Sir Gareth leaped very nimbly out of his saddle and ran to him to finish the work that he had begun. And Sir Gareth plucked away the helm of the knight and looked into his face and therewith beheld that his work was very well done, for already that fallen knight was in the act of yielding up the ghost.

Then Sir Gareth wiped his sword and drave it back again into its sheath; and he remounted his horse and rode very quietly back to where the damsel waited for him upon the farther bank. And the damsel looked at Sir Gareth very strangely but Sir Gareth regarded her not at all.

So Sir Gareth brought Lynette safely across the ford and afterward they rode on their way as they had aforetime done—the damsel in the lead and Sir Gareth and Axatalese following after at a distance.

So after they had ridden a long while the damsel turned her about *Lynette* in the saddle and looked at Sir Gareth and she said, "Hah, Beaumains, *mocketh at* dost thou take pride in what thou hast done?" And Sir Gareth said, *Sir Gareth* "Nay, Lady; God forbid that I should take pride in any such thing as that." Quoth Lynette: "I am glad that thou dost not take pride in it; for I beheld thy battle from afar and I saw how fortune favored thee. For the first of those two knights, his horse stumbled in the river and so he fell into the water and was drowned; and thou didst strike the second knight with thy sword ere he was well prepared for his defence and so thou wert able to slay him."

"Lady," quoth Sir Gareth very calmly, "that which thou sayest doth not in anywise change the circumstances of what I did. For now my work is done and so I leave it to God His mercy to judge whether I did that thing well or whether I did it ill." "Hah," said Lynette, "meseemeth you speak very saucily for a kitchen knave." And Sir Gareth said, still speaking very calmly, "Think you so, Lady?" And Lynette said, "Yea," and she said, "I see that thou still ever forgettest my commands, for thou art riding so nigh to me that methinks I smell the kitchen. Now I prythee draw a little farther away." And Sir Gareth said, "Damsel, it shall be as you command." And therewith he drew rein so as to ride at a little greater distance, and Lynette laughed to see him do so.

Now some little while about the prime of the day they came to a certain grassy place of considerable extent, and at that place was a black hawthorn bush, very aged and gnarled and full of thorns that stood alone beside the highroad, and as they drew nigh to it they perceived that there was hung upon the thorn bush a great black shield bearing the device of the red gryphon, and they saw that a great black spear, bearing a black pennon with the device of a red gryphon leaned beside the shield. And they beheld that near by the bush was a noble black horse with trappings and housings all of black, and the horse cropped the grass that grew at that place.

All this they beheld, and as they came still nearer they perceived *They behold* that upon the other side of the hawthorn bush there was a knight *the black* clad all in black armor, and they saw that the knight sat beside a *knight at his* great flat stone and ate his midday meal that lay spread out upon the *meal* stone. And the knight was unaware of their coming but ever ate with great appetite of the food that was spread before him.

Then Lynette drew rein while they were yet at some distance and she laughed and pointed toward the hawthorn bush, behind which sat the knight, and she said: "Sir Kitchen Knave, look you yonder and behold that knight. Seest thou the device upon his shield? I know that device very well and so I may tell thee that that knight is hight Sir Perard and that he is brother of Sir Percevant of Hind, and that he is a very strong, worthy, noble knight and one of great renown in deeds of arms. This is a very different sort of knight from those thou didst overcome at the ford of the river, wherefore be thou advised by me and turn thee about and get thee gone ere yonder knight seest thee, or else harm will certainly befall thee."

Quoth Sir Gareth: "Damsel, having followed you so far and through several dangers it is not very likely that I shall turn back at this, even if there be as much peril in it as you say."

"Very well," said Lynette, "then if ill befall thee thou art to blame thyself therefor and not blame me." Therewith speaking, she tightened the rein of her palfrey and so rode forward toward that hawthorn bush aforesaid.

Now when they had come a little more close to that place, the Black Knight, Sir Perard, was aware of their coming and looked up and beheld them. Then, seeing that it was an armed knight and a damsel that were coming thitherward, Sir Perard arose very slowly and with great dignity and set his helm upon his head, and so he made him ready for whatsoever might befall. Then when he had so prepared himself he came out into the road for to meet them. Then when Sir Gareth and the damsel were come pretty nigh, Sir Perard bespake Sir Gareth, saying: "Sir Knight, I pray you of your courtesy for to tell me who you are and whither you go?"

Quoth Sir Gareth: "I may not tell you who I am, but ask you this damsel and she will tell you."

Then Sir Perard was greatly surprised at that reply and he said, "Is this a jest?" And he said: "Damsel, since I am directed to you, I pray of you tell to me the name and the degree of this knight."

Upon this Lynette fell alaughing in great measure and she said: "Messire, since you ask me that thing, I have to tell you that this fellow is a certain kitchen knave, hight Beaumains, who hath followed me hither from the court of King Arthur, and I have to tell you further that many times I have bid him begone and leave me, but he will not do so, but continually followeth after me."

"Fair damsel," quoth the Black Knight, speaking with great dignity, "you are pleased to jest with me, for this is no kitchen knave I trow but a very good worshipful knight of whom you are pleased to say such things."

Then Sir Gareth spake very sternly, saying, "Messire, I will not have you or any man gainsay what this lady sayeth." And the Black Knight, still speaking with great dignity, said: "How may I do otherwise than gainsay her, seeing that you wear armor that is indented with the marks of battle? For who ever heard of a kitchen knave wearing such armor?" "Ne'ertheless," quoth Sir Gareth, "either you must acknowledge what this lady sayeth of me, or else you must do battle with me so that I may defend what she sayeth."

"Sir," said the Black Knight, "in that case I will do battle with you, for I cannot accept the saying of this lady."

So therewith Sir Perard took down his shield from off the black-thorn bush and he took his spear into his hand and whistled his horse to him. And he mounted his horse and made him in all ways ready for battle. Meanwhile Sir Gareth waited very composedly and with great calmness of bearing until the other was in all wise prepared. Then Sir Perard said, "I am ready, Messire." And therewith each knight drew rein and withdrew to such a distance as was fitting for a course to an assault. Then when this was accomplished, each knight shouted to his steed and each charged forward against the other with a terrible speed and violence. So they met in the midst of the course with a crash that might have been heard for two furlongs. In that meeting the spear of each knight was broken into many pieces, even to the hand that held it, and the horse of each staggered back and would haply have fallen had not the knight rider brought him to foot again with shout and prick of spur and with great address of horsemanship. Then each knight voided his horse and each drew his sword and therewith rushed to an assault at arms. And each smote the other again and again and yet again, lashing such blows that it sounded as though several blacksmiths were smiting amain

Sir Gareth doeth battle with the Black Knight

upon their anvils, and for a while neither knight had any advantage over the other, but each fought for that time a well-matched battle. Then of a sudden Lynette cried out very shrilly: "Sir Perard! Sir Perard! Noble, worthy knight! Wilt thou suffer a kitchen knave to have his will of thee?"

So she cried out very loud and shrill and Sir Gareth heard the words she uttered. Then a great anger came upon him so that he was uplifted by it, as though the strength of several had entered into his body. So straightway he redoubled his battle to twice what it had been before, giving stroke upon stroke, so that the Black Knight was forced to bear back before the fierceness and violence of his assault. Then Sir Gareth perceived that Sir Perard began to weary a very great deal in that fight and to bear his defences full low, and therewith he redoubled his blows and smote Sir Perard upon the helm so fiercely that his brains swam like water and his head hung low upon his breast.

Then, perceiving how that Sir Perard fainted, Sir Gareth ran to him and catched him by the helm and dragged him down upon his knees, and he rushed off the helm of Sir Perard, and catched him by the hair and dragged down his neck so that he might have slain him had he chosen to do so.

Then Sir Perard, perceiving how near death was to him, catched Sir Gareth about the knees, and cried out on high, "Messire, spare my life, for so thou hast it at thy mercy." Quoth Sir Gareth, "Sir Knight, I will not spare thy life unless this lady beseech it of me."

Then Lynette cried out: "Fie upon thee, thou saucy varlet! Who art thou that I should ask a favor of thee?"

Lynette asketh the life of the Black Knight Then Sir Perard cried out, "Fair Lady, I beseech thee that thou beg my life at the hands of this knight," and thereupon Lynette said: "Fie upon it that it must needs be so. But indeed I cannot suffer so worshipful a knight as thou art, Sir Perard, to be slain by the hand of a kitchen knave. So, Sirrah Beaumains, I bid thee stay thy hand and spare this knight his life."

Upon this speech, Sir Gareth released his hold upon Sir Perard and said, "Arise, Sir Knight, for I will spare thy life upon this lady's behest." And therewith Sir Perard arose and stood upon his feet. And Sir Perard said: "Sir, thou hast conquered me in fair battle and for that reason I have yielded me to thee. Now, I prythee tell me, hast thou any commands that thou wouldst lay upon me?" Quoth Sir Gareth: "Yea, Messire, I have a command to lay upon you and this is that command: It is that you straightway go to the court of King Arthur and pay your duty unto him. And you are to say unto King Arthur that Beaumains, the kitchen knave, hath sent you unto him. And I pray you give him news of me and tell him it fareth well with me." And Sir Perard said, "Messire, it shall be done according to your bidding." And Sir Gareth said, "See that it is so."

Now in all these things that Sir Gareth did and said he ever bore himself with such dignity and haughtiness that a knight of ten years' standing would not have acted with more dignity than he. And after he had settled those affairs in that wise, he turned to Lynette and addressed himself to her, saying, "Lady, if so be thou art now ready to depart I am ready to accompany thee," and with that the damsel took her departure and Sir Gareth and Axatalese followed after her. So they left that place of battle and soon after they had gone Sir Perard departed upon his way to the court of King Arthur as he had been commanded to do by Sir Gareth as aforesaid.

Now after Lynette and Sir Gareth had ridden some while in silence, Lynette turned her face and looked upon Sir Gareth. And she said, "Sir Kitchen Knave, I would I knew who thou really art." To the which Sir Gareth answered very calmly, "Thou hast declared several times who I am and that I am a kitchen knave from King Arthur's court." Then Lynette laughed and she said, "True, I had nigh forgot." And she said, "Ride not so near to me for still, I believe, thou savorest of the kitchen." And thereupon Sir Gareth withdrew to that same distance he had assumed before.

Now somewhile toward the approach of eventide, Sir Gareth and Lynette and Axatalese came away from that part of the country and to where the forest began again. And it befell that as they approached the forest they beheld of a sudden one who came spurring out of the woodlands riding upon a white horse, driving very furiously and at full speed. This rider when he was come nigh suddenly drew rein, and flinging himself from the saddle he ran to Sir Gareth and catched him by the stirrup, crying out: "Sir Knight! Sir Knight! I crave you of your worship that you will lend your aid in a case of woful need!"

They behold one fleeing from the forest

Then Sir Gareth beheld that this one who had come to him in this wise was an esquire, clad in green and yellow and that he was one of good appearance and of quality. And Sir Gareth said: "Fair Friend, I prythee tell me what service it is that thou wouldst have of me?"

"Sir," cried that esquire, "my master, who is a knight of these marches, is beset within the forest yonder by several thieves and I fear they will slay him unless help cometh to him in short order." Sir Gareth said, "Where is your master?" And the esquire said, "Follow me and I will bring you to him."

Sir Gareth driveth to rescue the wounded knight So the esquire mounted his horse again and drave away with all speed and Sir Gareth set spurs to his horse and also drave away at speed, and Lynette and the dwarf followed with speed after Sir Gareth. So anon they entered the forest and coursed therethrough for a little ways and then Sir Gareth perceived where at a short distance there was a knight set with his back against a tree defending himself against six great and brawny villains clad in full armor. And Sir Gareth beheld that there were three other villains who lay dead upon the ground, but that the knight was in a sorry case, bleeding from several wounds and very weary with his battle. Thereupon, beholding this, Sir Gareth drew his sword and cried out in a very loud voice: "Have at ye, villains! Have at ye!" and therewith drave into the midst of that contest. And the thieves were astonished at the violence of his coming so that they knew not what to do, for Sir Gareth drave into their midst without let or pause of any sort. And ere they recovered from their astonishment, Sir Gareth struck one of the villains to the earth at a single blow and then he smote down another. And a third would have defended himself, but Sir Gareth rose up in his stirrups and he smote him so full and terrible a buffet that he clave through his morion and through his head to the very teeth of his head.

Sir Gareth slayeth the thieves Then beholding that dreadful terrible blow that Sir Gareth had struck their companion, the other three villains were adread for their lives, and fled shrieking away into the forest. But Sir Gareth would not let them escape but charged after them with great fury. And the three thieves found that they could not escape, and that there was naught else for them to do but to turn and stand at bay and so they did. But Sir Gareth would not be stayed by this, but he drave straightway into their midst and struck upon this side and upon that, so that maugre their defence all three of those villains were presently stretched, all bathed in their blood, upon the ground. Then Sir Gareth rode back again, wiping his sword very calmly ere he put it back into its sheath.

So anon he came to where was that knight whom he had saved and at that time Lynette and Axatalese and the esquire were lending such aid to the wounded man as his case demanded.

But when that knight beheld Sir Gareth returning from his battle, he broke away from the others and came to Sir Gareth and embraced him about the knee and said, "Messire, you have certes saved my life." And he said: "I pray you tell me what great and worshipful knight you are who doeth such wonderful battle as I beheld. Never would I have supposed it possible that any single knight could have overthrown six armed men with such ease as I have beheld you do this day."

Now Lynette was standing by at that time and her eyes were *Lynette* wonderfully bright and shining and she looked very strangely upon *mocketh Sir* Sir Gareth. Then hearing what that knight said whom Sir Gareth *Gareth* had rescued she burst out laughing very shrilly and piercingly and she cried out, "Sir Knight, wit you who this is who hath saved your life?" The knight said, "Nay, damsel, I know not." She said: "Wit you then that this is a kitchen knave of King Arthur's court hight Beaumains, so hight because of the whiteness of his hands. He hath followed me hither against my will, and I cannot drive him from me."

Then that knight was very much astonished and he said: "Fair damsel, certes you jest with me, for indeed this is some very noble and well-approved knight of great worship. For no one but such a knight as that could have done such deeds of arms as I beheld this day."

Now at that time Sir Gareth was very weary with the battles *Sir Gareth* he had fought during the day, and his body was sore with several *rebuketh the* wounds that he had suffered, and his spirit was very greatly vexed *knight* with the scorn with which Lynette had ever treated him for all this while, wherefore he had but little patience to deal to any man. So straightway he turned him toward that knight and he spake very sternly to him, saying: "Messire, do you intend to gainsay that which this lady sayeth to you concerning me? Wit you that I will not suffer her word to be put in question in any wise. Wherefore, if she is pleased to say that I am a scullion lad, so for her sake you must believe it to be."

At this that knight was more astonished than before, and he wist not what to think. So anon he said: "Messire, certes I meant no offence to you, for how should I mean offence to one who hath done me such service as you have rendered to me this day?"

"Well," quoth Sir Gareth, "in this I am greatly offended that you should gainsay that which this lady is pleased to say. Wit you that for this while I am this lady's champion, and so I will suffer no one to gainsay her." So said Sir Gareth, and when he had ended that saying, Lynette laughed and laughed again with all her might and main. And she cried out, "Well said, thou kitchen knave!" unto the which speech Sir Gareth made no reply.

Then that knight said to Sir Gareth and to Lynette: "Messire, and thou, fair damsel, I know not what all this meaneth but haply you know. But I see, Sir Knight, that thou art wounded in several places, and I doubt not that you are both aweary with your travels, wherefore I pray you that you will come with me to my castle which is not a very great distance away from this, and I beseech you there to lodge and to refresh you for this night."

To this Lynette said: "That which thou sayest pleases me very greatly, Messire, for indeed I am aweary and would fain rest me a little. So let us go forward to your castle. But this Beaumains must ride not so close to us for indeed I cannot abide the odor of the kitchen."

So after that they all departed from that place, and ever Sir Gareth rode at a distance as the damsel had commanded him to do.

They come to the castle of the knight Now after they had gone a considerable way they came out of the forest and into a valley wherein stood the castle of that knight. And it was a very fair and noble castle and the valley was exceedingly fertile with many rich fields and meadows and with several plantations of trees, both of fruit trees and otherwise. Through this fruitful valley they came to the castle and they rode into the castle courtyard with a great noise of horses' hoofs upon the cobblestones, and at that coming many of the attendants of the castle came running for to take their horses and to serve them.

Then Lynette gazed about her and she said to the knight of the castle, "Messire, who are these?" He said: "Fair damsel, these are they who would take your horse and the horse of that noble knight your companion, and others are they who would wait upon you and upon him to serve you both." Then Lynette said: "Not so, Sir Knight, my horse they may take and me they may serve, but it is not meet that a kitchen knave such as Beaumains should be waited upon in that wise, wherefore I bid you to suffer him to wait upon himself."

Upon this speech Sir Gareth turned him to the knight of the *Sir Gareth* castle and his face was very calm, albeit his eyes shone like sparks of *serveth* fire and he said, speaking very haughtily: "Messire, whitherward is *himself* the stable? I pray you to tell me so that I may house my good horse and wait upon myself as this lady, whom I have undertaken to serve, hath commanded me to do." Then the knight of the castle was much troubled and knew not what to reply; yet anon he said, "Messire, I know not what to say in this case but an you ask me I must say the stable lieth yonderways."

So spake the knight, and thereupon Sir Gareth turned him without another word and rode away, still very calmly, leaving them alone.

So after that the knight and Lynette entered the castle. But the knight, when he was alone, called to him the steward of the castle and he said to him: "Go you and search out that noble and worthy knight, for assuredly he is some great and famous champion. See you that he is served in all wise that such an one should be served, and spare naught to comfort him and put him at his ease, for this day he hath certes saved my life." So the steward did as he was bidden and that evening Sir Gareth was served in all wise befitting for a knight royal such as he really was.

Now when the next day was come, and when it was time for Lynette and Sir Gareth and Axatalese the dwarf to depart from that place, the knight of the castle came to Sir Gareth where he sat upon his horse. And he laid his hand upon the stirrup of Sir Gareth and he said: "Messire, I pray you tell me, is there any service that I may do you that you would have of me?"

Sir Gareth biddeth the knight to do service Then Sir Gareth looked down upon that knight and he said: "Sir, there is a service you could render me an you chose to do so, and this is that service: it is that you should go to the court of King Arthur with all the estate that is befitting for one of your degree. And when you have come to the court I would fain have you tell King Arthur that Beaumains, the kitchen knave, hath sent you to him for to pay your court unto him. And I would have you tell the King and Sir Gawaine how it hath fared with me so far as you are aware of." Thus said Sir Gareth, and to him the knight of the castle made reply: "Sir, it shall be done as you ordain; for all those things I will do exactly as you commanded me."

So after that they three departed upon their way, the damsel Lynette riding ahead and Sir Gareth and the dwarf riding some distance behind.

And now if you would hear what other adventures befell Sir Gareth and Lynette at this time I pray you to read further, for there these several things are told of in due order.

he Lady Layonnesse. *F F F*

Chapter Fourth

*How Sir Gareth met Sir Percevant of Hind, and how he came to
Castle Dangerous and had speech with the Lady Layonnesse. Also
how the Lady Layonnesse accepted him for her champion.*

SO THE damsel Lynette followed by Sir Gareth and the dwarf
travelled for all that morning and a part of the afternoon
without let or stay of any sort and without meeting with
any adventure whatsoever, and in all that time the damsel said no
word to Sir Gareth whether of good or ill, but ever kept her eyes
fixed straight before her as though very much occupied with thought.

So about two hours or three after the prime of the day they came *They behold a*
to the top of a very long steep hill, and there beneath them in the val- *fair pavilion*
ley that lay below the hill, Sir Gareth perceived that a considerable *in a valley*
company and one that appeared to be of great estate were foregath-
ered. For at that place there were a number of pavilions of divers
colored silk and above each pavilion there flew a silken banner bearing the device of the owner of that pavilion. And in the midst of all
those other pavilions there was one that was manifestly the pavilion
of the knight-champion or of the overlord of all the others. For that
pavilion was of crimson silk embroidered with figures in threads of
silver and black, and above the pavilion there flew a banner of very
great size, which same was also of crimson silk embroidered in silver
and black with the figure of a leopard couchant.

And from where he stood upon the heights, Sir Gareth saw that
all these pavilions were spread in a fair level meadow with grass well
mown, as smooth as a cloth of green velvet, and all bright with gay
and pretty flowers. And this meadow and other meadows beyond it
stretched away to a great distance and at the extremity of the distance
was a fair tall castle and a goodly town of many towers, all shining
very bright in the clear transparent daylight.

All this Sir Gareth beheld very plain, as it were upon the palm of
his hand, and he beheld how above all that level, fruitful valley the

sky arched like to a roof of crystal—warm and perfectly blue, and filled full of a very great many clouds.

Then Lynette said: "Hah, Beaumains, see you yonder pavilions and see you that pavilion which is in their midst?" And Sir Gareth said, "Yea, damsel, I behold them all."

Lynette telleth Sir Gareth of Sir Percevant Quoth Lynette: "Wit you that that central pavilion belongeth to Sir Percevant of Hind, for well do I know the device embroidered upon his banner. And I have to tell you that Sir Percevant is one of the very greatest of the knights champion of this realm and that he hath fought many battles with some of the chiefest Knights of the Round Table and hath come forth with great credit in all those encounters. Now, Beaumains, this is a very different sort of knight from any of those with whom you have hitherto had to do, wherefore be you advised that it is not meet for a kitchen knave to have to do in such an adventure as this. So turn you about and get you gone or else of a surety some great ill will befall you in this affair."

Then Sir Gareth looked very calmly upon Lynette and he said: "Lady, it may well be that a man who assumeth to have credit and honor may fail in an undertaking of this sort, but when have you ever heard that such a man of credit or of honor hath withdrawn him from an adventure because there is great danger in it?"

Then Lynette laughed and she said: "Hah, Beaumains, thou speakest with a very high spirit for one who is but a kitchen knave. Now if harm befalleth thee because of this undertaking, blame thyself therefor." And Sir Gareth said: "So will I do, and rest you well assured, fair damsel, that never shall I blame you for that or for anything else that may befall me." And at that Lynette laughed again.

Then Sir Gareth drew rein and turned downhill to where were those pavilions aforesaid, and so they all three descended from the height into the valley and so came toward that fair meadow wherein the silken tents had been erected.

Now as they drew near to the pavilions, they beheld several esquires who were sitting at a bench playing at dice. These, beholding Sir Gareth coming in that wise with the fair damsel and the dwarf, they all arose, and he that was chief among them said: "Sir, what knight are you, and what is your degree, and why come you hitherward?" Him answered Sir Gareth, saying: "Friend, it matters not who I am saving only that I am of sufficient worth. As for my business, it is to have speech with Sir Percevant of Hind, the lord of this company."

Quoth the esquire: "Sir, you cannot come past this way nor may you have speech with Sir Percevant of Hind without first making known your name and your degree, for otherwise you come upon him at your peril." Then Sir Gareth laughed, and said, "Say you so?" and therewith he drave past all those esquires and Lynette and the dwarf went with him and no one dared to stay him. So they came to the pavilion of Sir Percevant and Sir Percevant was within his pavilion at that time.

Now before the pavilion there was a tall painted post set into the ground, and upon the post there hung a great shield, bearing upon it the device of a leopard couchant in black and white, and so Sir Gareth perceived that this was the shield of Sir Percevant.

Then Sir Gareth drew his sword and he went forward and smote the shield such a blow that it rang like thunder beneath the stroke that he gave it.

Therewith came Sir Percevant of Hind out of his pavilion and his countenance was all aflame with anger and he cried out very fiercely: "Messire, who are you who dare to smite my shield in that wise?"

But Sir Gareth sat his horse very calmly, and he said: "Messire, I struck your shield for to call you forth so that I might have speech with you. As for my name, I will not tell you that nor my degree. But if you would know these things, I bid you for to ask them of this lady who is my companion." *Sir Gareth challengeth Sir Percevant*

Then Sir Percevant turned him to Lynette, and he said, "Damsel, who is this knight?" And Lynette said: "Sir, I know not otherwise than that he is a kitchen knave of King Arthur's court who hath clothed himself in armor. He is called Beaumains, and fain would I have been rid of him several times, but could not; for ever he followeth me, and, maugre my wishes, will ever serve as my champion."

Then Sir Percevant turned unto Sir Gareth with great anger and he said: "Sir, I know not what is this jest that you and your damsel seek to put upon me, but this I do know, that since you have appointed her to speak for you, and since she declareth you to be a kitchen knave, so must I believe you to be. Wherefore, unless you straightway declare your name and your degree to me upon your own account, and unless you prove to me that you are otherwise than this damsel sayeth, I shall straightway have you stripped of your armor and shall have you bound and beaten with cords for this affront that you have put upon my shield."

Then Sir Gareth spake very calmly, saying: "Sir, that would be a pity for you to do, for I have to tell you that, whether I be a kitchen knave or no, nevertheless I have had to do with several good and worthy knights of fair repute. For I have to tell you that one of these knights was Sir Launcelot of the Lake and that he made me knight. And I have to tell you that another one of these was your own brother, Sir Perard, whom I overcame yesterday in battle and whom I would have slain only that this damsel besought his life at my hands. And I have to tell you that Sir Perard is even now upon his way to the court of King Arthur, there to pay his duty to the King upon my demand upon him to that end."

Then Sir Percevant cleared his brow of its anger, and he said: "Sir, I perceive from all that you tell me that you are some knight of very good quality and merit. Wherefore I will withdraw that which I said and will do you battle because you have struck my shield. And it will go hard with me but I shall serve you in such a way as shall well wipe out that affront in your warm red blood. For I promise you that I shall not let or stay in the battle against you."

So spake Sir Percevant and straightway he withdrew him into his tent and several of the knights who were his companions and several esquires who had gathered about in this while of talk, went into his pavilion with him and there aided him to don his armor and to fit himself for battle.

Of the meadow of battle So anon Sir Percevant came forth again in all wise prepared for that battle. And his esquires brought to him a noble horse as white as milk and they assisted him to mount thereon. And Sir Percevant took a great spear into his hand and so turned and led the way toward a fair smooth level lawn of grass whereon two knights might well run atilt against one another. And all they who were of that company followed Sir Percevant and Sir Gareth to that lawn of grass, and the damsel Lynette and the dwarf Axatalese went thither along with the others.

So coming to that place a marshal of the lists was appointed, and thereafter each knight was assigned a certain station by that marshal. Then, everything being duly prepared, the word for the assault was given, and each knight launched forth against the other with all the speed with which he was able to drive. So they met in the midst of the course with a great roar and crashing of wood and metal and in that encounter the spear of each knight was broken into small pieces and the horse of each staggered back from beneath the blow and would have fallen had not the knight rider recovered him with rein and spur and voice.

Then each knight leaped down from his horse and drew his sword and rushed to the assault afoot with all the fierceness of two wild boars engaged in battle. And thereupon they fell to lashing such blows at one another that even they who looked on from a distance were affrighted at the violence and the uproar of that assault. For the two champions fought very fiercely, and the longer they fought the more fiercely they did battle. And in a little while the armor of each was all stained red, and the ground upon which they fought was all besprinkled with red, yet neither knight had any thought of yielding to the other in any whit or degree, but still each fought on with ever-increasing fury against the other. *Sir Gareth doeth battle with Sir Percevant*

Now at this time neither knight had aught of advantage against the other, and no man might have told how that battle would have gone, but at the moment of the greatest doubt, Lynette uplifted her voice aloud, as it were in terror, crying out very shrilly and vehemently: "Good worthy knight Sir Percevant, will you then let a kitchen knave and a scullion stay you thus in your battle?"

Then it befell as it had befallen before when Sir Gareth fought with the Black Knight, Sir Percevant's brother, for Sir Gareth heard the words that Lynette cried out, and straightway it was as though the new strength of several men had entered into his body because of his anger at those words. And that anger consumed all else that was before it, whether that other were of prudence or of temper. For straightway Sir Gareth flung aside his shield and seized his sword in both hands and rushed upon Sir Percevant and struck blow upon blow so fiercely and so violently that nor skill nor strength might withstand his assault. Then Sir Percevant fell back before that as- *Sir Gareth overcometh Sir Percevant* sault and could not do otherwise, and he bore his shield full low; but ever Sir Gareth followed him and smote him more and more violently so that Sir Percevant could no longer hold up his shield against the assault of his enemy. And Sir Gareth perceived that Sir Percevant waxed feeble in his defence and with that he rushed in and smote Sir Percevant upon the helm so woeful a blow that Sir Percevant could no longer stand upon his feet but sank slowly down upon his knees before Sir Gareth. Then Sir Gareth ran to Sir Percevant and catched him by the helm and rushed the helm off from his head and with that Sir Percevant wist that death overshadowed him. Then Sir Percevant catched Sir Gareth about the thighs and, embracing him, cried out: "Messire, spare my life and do not slay me!" And all those knights and esquires who were in attendance upon Sir Percevant pressed about Sir Gareth where he stood, and lifted up their voices, also crying out: "Sir Knight, do not slay that good worthy knight our champion, but spare his life to him."

Then Sir Gareth, all wet with the blood and sweat of battle and panting for breath said in a very hoarse voice: "Ask ye not for this knight's life for I will not spare his life to him except upon one condition, and that condition is that the damsel whose champion I am shall ask his life at my hands."

Now at that time Lynette was weeping amain, though whether with dread of that fierce battle or because of something else, who may tell? Yet ever she wept, and ever she laughed and wept again. And she cried out: "Thou saucy knave, Beaumains, who art thou to make such a demand as that?"

But Sir Gareth said: "If I be saucy, let it pass, yet so it is as I have said, and I will not spare this knight his life unless thou ask it of me," and therewith he catched Sir Percevant by the hair and lifted his sword on high as though to separate the head of Sir Percevant from off his body.

Lynette beseecheth Sir Percevant's life Then all those knights and esquires crowded around Lynette and besought her that she would ask for the life of Sir Percevant. And Lynette said: "Stay thy hand, Beaumains, and slay him not, for it would be a pity for so good and worthy a knight as Sir Percevant of Hind to lose his life at the hands of a kitchen knave such as thou art."

Then Sir Gareth said: "Arise, Sir Knight, and stand up, for the word of this lady hath saved thy life." And therewith Sir Gareth released his hold of Sir Percevant and Sir Percevant arose and stood up.

Then Sir Percevant said: "Sir, thou hast beaten me in a very fair and bitter battle and so I yield myself to thee. Now I pray thee tell me what are thy commands upon me?" And Sir Gareth said: "Sir, thou *Sir Gareth commandeth service of Sir Percevant* sayest well, and these are my commands: that thou, together with all this thy company of knights and esquires, do take your departure from this field and that ye all go to the court of King Arthur. And it is my desire that when thou hast come to the court of the King thou shalt pay thy duty to him and say to him that Beaumains, the kitchen knave, hath sent thee to pay that duty."

Then Sir Percevant bowed his head before Sir Gareth and said: "Sir, it shall be as you command." And after that he said, "Sir, I pray you that you will do me this favor; I pray you that you will come with me to yonder castle at that town which you see afar off. For that is my castle and my town and I am fain that you should rest you ere you go farther upon your way, and that you should refresh yourself at my castle. I perceive that you are wounded in several places, and I would fain that you should have your wounds searched and dressed and that you should have rest and ease ere you go forward, so that your wounds may be healed and that you may be made hale when you undertake your further adventures."

To this Sir Gareth said: "Sir, I thank you well for your courtesy and it will pleasure me greatly to go to your castle with you and there to rest me awhile. For indeed it hath been a sore battle that I have fought with you this day and I suffer a very great deal of pain. Moreover I have fought other battles of late and am aweary and in no fit case to go farther at this present."

So after Sir Gareth and Sir Percevant had rested them a little, they and all of their companies departed thence and betook their way to the castle of Sir Percevant. There Sir Gareth was bathed and his wounds were searched and dressed and he was put in all ease that was possible.

And Sir Percevant gave command that ever a company of knights should stand guard over Sir Gareth where he lay so that no harm *Sir Gareth rests him in the castle of Sir Percevant* should befall him, and it was done according to that command. So Sir Gareth abided at the castle of Sir Percevant for five days and in all that time he saw nothing whatsoever of the damsel Lynette; for he lay in one part of the castle and she dwelt in another part. Then at the end of five days, Sir Gareth was well healed of his wounds and was in all ways hale and strong to carry out his further adventures.

✛ ✛ ✛

Lynette maketh peace with Sir Gareth Now when those five days aforesaid were past, Sir Gareth made him ready to depart, and Lynette also made herself ready to depart, and so they took their leave of the castle of Sir Percevant. And they rode out through the gateway of the castle and into the sunlight that lay beyond, and it was a wonderfully bright cheerful pleasant day with all the little birds singing amain and the blossoms falling like snow whensoever that the wind blew through the branches of the apple-trees. Thus they departed and after that they rode for a long while. So they came two or three leagues upon their way, and in that time neither said anything to the other but both rode in silence. Then at last Lynette turned her about and Sir Gareth perceived that her eyes shone very bright. And Lynette said, "Sir, have you anger against me?" Then Sir Gareth, who was riding some little distance away, as he had aforetime done upon her bidding, came nearer to her and said: "Nay, fair damsel; why think you that I should anger have against you? Have I shown you any anger, that you should say those words to me?" She said: "Nay, Messire, never at any time have you shown anger toward me, but you have ever been to me all that it was possible for any noble and worthy knight to be to a lady who had treated him with all consideration and regard, and this you have done in spite of the scornful way in which I have treated you. And also I have very well perceived the manner in which you have borne yourself in these several contests at arms which you have fought, and I have beheld you to be as brave and haughty toward those knights who were strong and valiant, as you have been gentle and kind to me who am a woman."

Then Sir Gareth smiled and he said: "Lady, you make much of that which is very little. Know you not that it behooves all true knights to be gentle and patient with all such as are not so strong as they? So it is that in being courteous to you I have done naught except that which I have been taught to do in such a case. As for those bitter words you spake to me, I may tell you that any anger which I might have felt therefor I visited upon those knights against whom I fought. For when you gave me those bitter words, then I gave them bitter blows therefor, and the more you scorned me the more strongly and vehemently did I fight."

Then Lynette said: "Sir, you are certes a very high, noble, and worthy knight, and she unto whom you vouchsafe to give your belle regard that lady will be as fortunate as any of whom I ever heard tell. For I believe that it is not possible for any knight ever to have been so tried as I have tried you for all this while that we have journeyed together; wherefore, if you have proved yourself so worthy in this thing, how much more will you prove yourself worthy in those greater things that shall in time come unto you?"

So spake Lynette and thereat Sir Gareth laughed a little and said: "Fair damsel, have I now leave to ride beside you, and is there now peace betwixt us?" And Lynette said, "Yea, Messire." So therewith Sir Gareth rode forward until he was come beside Lynette, and from that time forward there was peace and concord betwixt them; for Lynette was now as kind and humble to him as she had been saucy and uncivil before.

And so as they journeyed together Lynette told Sir Gareth many *They journey* things concerning the adventure which he was entered upon that he *together in* had not known before. For she told him that this lady who was her *concord* sister was hight the Lady Layonnesse and that she was but eighteen years of age. And she told him that the Lady Layonnesse was one of the most beautiful ladies in the world, and she told him that the lady was the countess of a very great and rich town, hight Granderegard, and of a noble castle appertaining to the town, which same was called the Castle Dangerous. And she told him that the marches over which the Lady Layonnesse was countess extended for several leagues upon this side and upon that side of the town and the castle, and she told him that the Knight of the Red Lands, who opposed her sister, was so strong and so doughty a knight that she believed it would be hard to find in any part of the realm so powerful a knight as he. And she said to Sir Gareth: "In good sooth, Messire, I have great fear that you will have sad ado to hold your own against this Red Knight of the Red Lands, for as Sir Perard was greater and bigger than those two knights at the ford whom you overthrew so easily, and as Sir Percevant of Hind was greater and bigger than Sir Perard, so I believe is this Red Knight of the Red Lands greater and bigger than Sir Percevant."

"Well, Lynette," quoth Sir Gareth, "so far it hath been that I have had success in all my battles but one, and in that one I suffered no dishonor. So I believe I may hope to have a fair fortune with this knight also, for wit you that the fortunes of any knight lie in the hands of God and not in man's hands, wherefore if it is His will that I fare well in this undertaking, then shall I assuredly do so."

Thus they talked in great amity of many things, and so they travelled for all that day and the next day and for a part of the day after that. And somewhat early in the morning of the third day they came to the summit of a certain highland whence Sir Gareth beheld a great plain, well tilled and very fertile, spread out beneath that high place where he stood. And he beheld that the plain was very broad and very long and that in the midst thereof there was a hill and that upon the hill there stood a castle and that behind the castle was a town of many fair and well-built houses.

They behold the pavilions of the Red Knight Then Lynette pointed, and she said to Sir Gareth: "See you that castle and that town? That castle is my sister's castle and that town is her town. And, yonder, beneath the walls of the town and of the castle, you may see a number of pavilions spread upon a considerable meadow. Those are the pavilions of the Red Knight of the Red Lands and of the knights and esquires attendant upon him. For there he keepeth continual watch and ward over the castle of my sister, so that no one may either come out thereof or enter thereinto without his leave for to do so." And Sir Gareth said, "Let us go down unto yonder place."

So straightway they descended from the highland into the plain, and so went forward upon their way toward the town and the castle of the Lady Layonnesse.

Now as they drew more nigh to that place where the pavilions of the Red Knight of the Red Lands and of his companions at arms had been spread, they went past a great many pollard willow-trees standing all in a row. And Sir Gareth beheld that upon each tree there hung either one shield or two or three shields and that each shield bore some device of knighthood. At that sight he was greatly astonished, and he said: "Fair damsel, I prythee tell me what is the meaning of this sight and why those shields are hung to yonder pollard willow-trees?" Quoth Lynette: "Sir, each one of those shields is the shield of some knight whom the Red Knight of the Red Lands hath overthrown. And some of these knights have been slain in battle by the Knight of the Red Lands, and some have not been slain, but all those who were not slain have been disgraced in the encounter which they have fought. For from each knight which he hath overthrown the Red Knight of the Red Lands hath taken his shield and his horse and hath sent him away afoot, unarmed and horseless, wherefore it is thought by some that it were better to have been slain in battle than to have suffered such disgrace as that."

Then Sir Gareth said: "Certes, Lynette, that must have been a very doughty champion to have overcome so many knights as these. Now, if it is my fortune to overthrow him in that battle which I am come to fight with him, then do I believe I shall win for myself more honor and credit than ever fell to any young knight of my age since first Sir Percival of Gales assumed his knighthood."

So said Sir Gareth, and after that he and Lynette rode onward a little farther until they had come to that meadow where were the pavilions of the Red Knight of the Red Lands and of his knights companion.

And Sir Gareth and the damsel rode straight through the midst of those pavilions and many knights and esquires came out thence to see who they were who came thitherward. But ever Sir Gareth and Lynette and the dwarf rode onward until they had come to the center pavilion of all and that was the pavilion of the Red Knight aforesaid.

Here at this place were several pages and of one of them Sir Gareth demanded where was that Red Knight. They say, "Sir, he is within his pavilion resting after his midday meal." Sir Gareth said, "Go ye and tell him that there is one come who would have speech with him."

So those esquires departed, and anon there came forth the Red Knight from his pavilion, and he was clad all in a loose robe of scarlet silk trimmed with miniver. And Sir Gareth looked upon him and

Sir Gareth beholdeth the Red Knight

beheld that he was very big of bone and thew and that the hair of his head and his beard was exceedingly red and that his countenance was terribly lowering and forbidding.

Then the Red Knight when he saw Sir Gareth, said, "Who art thou, Sir Knight, and what is thy business here?" And Sir Gareth said: "Messire, I am one come from King Arthur's court to take up the quarrel of the Lady Layonnesse of this place and to serve as her champion therein."

Then the Knight of the Red Lands said: "Who are you? Are you a knight of repute and fame at arms?" and Sir Gareth said: "Nay, Sir, not so; for I have only been made knight fortnight, and I have but little service at arms."

Then the Red Knight laughed very boisterously and said: "How is this, and what sort of a green knight are you, who dares to come against me! Know that I have laid more than twoscore better knights than you very low in the dust."

Quoth Sir Gareth: "That may very well be, Sir Knight. Yet is the fate of every one in the hands of God and so mayhap He will cause me to overthrow you upon this occasion." And Sir Gareth said: "Now, I pray you that you will let me go up to yonder castle and have speech with the lady thereof and if so be she will accept me for her champion, then will I return hitherward immediately to do battle with you." And the Red Knight said, "Go and speak with her."

So Sir Gareth went up toward the Castle Dangerous and Lynette went with him. And when they had come pretty nigh to the castle, the lady thereof appeared at an upper window and called down to Sir Gareth, saying, "Sir, who are you and whence come you?"

Sir Gareth beholdeth the Lady Layonnesse Then Sir Gareth looked up and beheld the lady where she stood at the window, and he beheld her face that it was very exceedingly beautiful. For, though she had dark hair like to Lynette's, and though she had cheeks resembling in their clear whiteness the cheeks of Lynette, and though her lips were red as coral like to Lynette's, yet was she ten times more beautiful than ever was Lynette. So, beholding how beautiful she was, the heart of Sir Gareth leaped straightway up to her, even as a bird flyeth upward, and there it rested within her bosom.

Then Sir Gareth said to her: "Lady, you ask me who I am, and I am to tell you that I am one come from King Arthur's court to serve you as your champion if so be you will accept me as such."

Then the Lady Layonnesse said, "Sir, are you a knight of good fame and service?" And Sir Gareth said, "Nay, Lady, but only a green knight very little used to arms. For I have but been a knight for these few days and though I have fought several battles with good fortune in that time, yet I know not as yet what may be my fate when I meet such a knight as the Red Knight of the Red Lands. Yet this is true, Lady, that though I be but very young and untried at arms, yet is my spirit very great for this undertaking."

Then the Lady Layonnesse said: "Sir, what is your name and what is your degree?" And Sir Gareth said: "I may not tell you that at this present, for I will not declare my name until that my kindred (who yet do not know me) shall have acknowledged me." To this the Lady Layonnesse said: "This is very strange, and I am much affronted that King Arthur should have sent to me from his court a knight without a name and without any credit at arms for to serve as my champion." And Sir Gareth said, "Lady, there was reason for it."

Then the Lady Layonnesse said, "Is not that my sister Lynette whom I behold with thee?" and Sir Gareth said, "Yea, Lady." The Lady said, "Who is this knight, Lynette?" and Lynette replied, "I know not, my sister, saving only that I have good reason to believe that he is the noblest and the haughtiest and the most worthy of all knights whom I have ever beheld." "Well," quoth the Lady Layonnesse, "if thou dost thus vouch for him, then upon thee be the peril of my choosing." And Lynette said, "Let it be so."

Then the Lady Layonnesse said, "Sir Knight, I take thee for my champion." And therewith she let fall from the window where she stood a fair scarf of green samite embroidered with threads of gold. And Sir Gareth catched the scarf with such joy that it was as though his heart would burst for happiness. And he wrapped the scarf about his arm, and immediately it was as though the virtue of his strength had been increased threefold.

The Lady Layonnesse giveth Sir Gareth her scarf

✚   ✚   ✚

Now if so be you would know how Sir Gareth sped in his business with the Red Knight of the Red Lands, I beg of you for to read that which followeth, for therein withal it shall be immediately declared.

The Lady Layonnesse cometh to the Pavilion of Sir Gareth

Chapter Fifth

*How Sir Gareth fought with the Red Knight of the Red Lands
and how it fared with him in that battle. Also how his dwarf was
stolen, and how his name and estate became known and were
made manifest.*

OW AFTER Sir Gareth had received the scarf of the Lady Layonnesse as aforetold, he and Lynette and the dwarf returned
to a certain meadow nigh to the pavilions where it had been
ordained that the battle should be held. There they found that the
Red Knight of the Red Lands had made himself in all ways ready for
that battle. For he was now clad all in armor as red as blood, and in
his hand he bore a great spear that was also altogether red; and on the
tip of the spear was a red banneret that was likewise as red as blood.

At that field that had been prepared for battle, there was a great
concourse of people assembled and there also the damsel Lynette
took her stand at a place that had been assigned unto her; and the
dwarf Axatalese was near by in attendance upon her. And there had
been a marshal of the field appointed to judge of the battle that was to
be fought, and as each knight came to the field, the marshal led him
to where he was to take his stand—which stand was in such a place
as should offer a fair course and so that the sun should not shine into
the eyes of either of the knights contestant.

So when everything was duly prepared for battle and when the
knights had taken each his place and when each knight was in all
ways ready for the course to be run, the marshal cried out the call
to the assault. Thereupon each knight immediately leaped his horse
away from where it stood and hurtled the one against the other like a
whirlwind with a great thunder of galloping hoofs. So they came together in a cloud of dust and with a terrible crashing of splintered
wood. For in that encounter each knight shattered his lance into
pieces, even to the hand that held it, and so violent was the blow
that each gave the other that both horses staggered back as though

they had struck each against a solid rock instead of against an armed rider.

Then each knight voided his tottering horse, and each drew his sword, and immediately they rushed together with such eagerness that it was as though the lust of battle was the greatest joy that the world could have for them. So they fell to fighting with the utmost and most terrible fury, lashing such blows that the sound of the strokes of iron upon iron resembled the continual roaring of thunder.

Of the battle of Sir Gareth with the Red Knight So they fought for so long a while that it was a wonder that any man of flesh and blood could withstand the blows that each gave and received. For ever and anon the sword would find its place and upon such a blow some cantel of armor would maybe be hewn from the body of that knight who received the stroke. And the book that telleth of this battle sayeth that the side of each knight was in a while made naked in places because that the armor had been hewn away from it. And it sayeth the armor of Sir Gareth was wellnigh as red as was the armor of his enemy because of the blood that dyed it that ensanguine color. And the same history says that they were somewhile so bemazed by the blows that they endured that either would at times seize the sword of the other for his own, for it is recorded in that history that they fought in that wise for more than two hours at a stretch without taking any rest from battle.

But although the battle continued for that long time, yet by and by their blows waxed somewhat faint and feeble compared to what they had at first been, and each knight tottered upon his feet at times because of his weakness and loss of blood. So at last the Red Knight of the Red Lands cried out to Sir Gareth: "Sir Knight, stay thy hand and let us rest, for I see that neither of us can fight this battle to its end as we are now fighting." So said the Red Knight, and at that saying Sir Gareth held his hand and said, "So be it, Sir Knight, as you ordain."

So they stinted their fighting for that while and they sat them down to rest, each upon a bank of earth. And a page came to the Red Knight of the Red Lands and unlaced his helm and the dwarf Axatalese did the same for Sir Gareth, and the page and the dwarf took each the helm from off the head of his master, and so they two sat where the wind might blow cold upon their faces.

Then anon Sir Gareth lifted up his eyes and he beheld where that the Lady Layonnesse stood at the high window of the castle aforesaid, and several of the chief folk of the castle stood with her at that time. Then Sir Gareth saluted the Lady Layonnesse and when she beheld him salute her she cried out, in a very shrill and piercing voice: "Alas, Sir Knight! Fail me not! For whom have I to depend upon but thee?" So she cried out in that very shrill voice, and Sir Gareth heard her words even from that distance. Then when he heard those words his heart grew big within him once more and his spirit waxed light and he called out, "Sir Red Knight, let us at our battle again!"

Therewith each knight resumed his helm and when each helm was laced into place, Axatalese and the page of the Red Knight leaped aside, and the two came together once more, greatly refreshed by that rest which they had enjoyed.

So they fought for a great while longer, and then they had pause again for a little. Then Sir Gareth perceived that the Red Knight was panting as though his bosom would burst and therewith he rushed at his enemy with intent for to smite him one last blow and so to end the battle. But the Red Knight was very wary and he was expecting that assault, wherefore he quickly avoided Sir Gareth's stroke, and thereupon he himself launched an overthwart blow that smote Sir Gareth upon the hand, and upon that blow the sword of Sir Gareth fell down out of his hand into the grass of the field.

Then the Red Knight leaped upon Sir Gareth and he struck him *Sir Gareth* again and yet again and he struck him a third time a blow upon the *falleth and is* helm and at that third blow the brains of Sir Gareth melted within *in great* him and he fell down upon his knees and then down to the ground *danger* for he had not power to stand. Then the Red Knight leaped upon Sir Gareth and fell upon him with intent to hold him down so that he might finish with him and Sir Gareth could not put him away.

But when the damsel Lynette beheld how that Sir Gareth was beneath his enemy and was in danger of being slain, she shrieked out aloud in a very shrill penetrating voice, crying, "Alas, Beaumains! Do *Sir Gareth* you fail your lady, and are you but a kitchen knave after all?" *overcometh*

Now Sir Gareth heard those words, even through the swooning *the Red* *Knight* of his senses, and therewith it was with him as it had been twice before; for as he heard the words there came new strength into his body, and with that he heaved himself up and cast the Red Knight from him. And he leaped to his feet and rushed to where his sword lay in the grass. And he catched up his sword and sprang upon the Red Knight and smote him a very terrible blow. And Sir Gareth so smote him again and yet again. And he smote him a fourth time so woeful a blow upon the helm that the Red Knight fell down to the earth and could not rise again. Then Sir Gareth fell upon the Red Knight and held him where he was upon the ground. And he drew his miseracordia and cut the thongs of the helm of the Red Knight and plucked the helm from off the Red Knight's head. And he set his miseracordia to the throat of the Red Knight and with that the Red Knight beheld Death, as it were, looking him in the face.

Then all they who were thereabouts came running to where the two knights lay, and they cried out aloud to Sir Gareth, saying, "Sir Knight! Sir Knight! Spare the knight our champion and slay him not!" And the Red Knight said in a voice very faint and weak, "Sir Knight, spare me my life!"

Then Sir Gareth cried out, "I will not spare this knight unless he yield him altogether to my will." And the knight said, "I yield me." And Sir Gareth said, "Still I will not spare this knight his life unless yonder damsel crave his life at my hands."

Lynette asketh for the life of the Red Knight Then Lynette came forward to where Sir Gareth still held his enemy to earth and she was weeping a very great deal. And she said: "Brave Sir Beaumains, be ye merciful as well as powerful and spare this good worshipful knight his life." And Sir Gareth said, "So will I do at thy demand."

Sir Gareth layeth his commands upon the Red Knight Therewith Sir Gareth got him up upon his feet and the Red Knight arose also, and so sore had been their battle that both knights had to be held upon their feet by those who stood near by. Then the Red Knight said, speaking in a very weak and fainting voice, "Fair Sir Knight, what are thy commands upon me?" and Sir Gareth said: "These are my commands: that so soon as you shall be sufficiently healed of your hurts you and all these your people shall depart hence and take your way to the court of King Arthur. And my command is that you shall tell King Arthur that Beaumains, the kitchen knave, hath sent you thither for to pay your homage unto him. And because you have dishonored other knights as you have done by taking away their shields and horses, it is my will that you shall also be dishonored; for I ordain that your shield shall be taken away from you and that it shall be hung upon one of these willow-trees where you have hung the shields of those knights whom you have overcome in battle as I have overcome you. And I ordain that your horse shall be taken away from you and that your armor shall be taken away from you and that you shall travel to the court of King Arthur afoot; for so you have made other knights walk afoot whom you have beaten in battle as I have beaten you."

Then the Red Knight bowed his head full low for shame and he said: "This is a very hard case, but as I have measured to others so it is meted unto me, wherefore, Messire, it shall be done in all ways as you command."

Then Lynette came to Sir Gareth and took him by the hand and set his hand to her lips and she was still weeping at that time. Then Sir Gareth smiled upon her and said, "Hah! Lynette, have I done well?" and Lynette still wept, and she said, with all her weeping, "Yea, Messire." And anon she said: "I pray you, Messire, that you will go with me up to the castle of my sister so that you may there be cherished and that your wounds may be looked to and searched and dressed."

But to this Sir Gareth said: "Not so, Lynette; for behold I am sorely wounded and I am all foul with the blood and dust and sweat of battle and so I will be refreshed and made clean ere I appear before that most fair lady your sister. So this night I will lie in the pavilion of this Red Knight, there to be cleansed of my hurts and to be refreshed. Then to-morrow I will come up unto my lady your sister."

And so it was done as Sir Gareth would have it, for that night *Sir Gareth* he lay in the pavilion of the Red Knight and he was bathed and re- *abideth in the* freshed, and a skillful leech came and dressed his hurts. And the Red *pavilion of the Red* Knight of the Red Lands had a guard of several knights set around *Knight* about the pavilion so that the repose of Sir Gareth should not be disturbed.

✛　　✛　　✛

Now after that battle aforetold the damsel Lynette betook her way to the castle of her sister, and she entered into the castle and there was great rejoicing at her return. Then they who first met her said to her: "Thy sister awaiteth thee and she is in that room in a turret where she keeps her bower." And Lynette said, "I will go thither."

So she went to that place and there she found the Lady Layonnesse, and her brother (who was Sir Gringamore) was with her. And Lynette ran to her sister and embraced her and kissed her. And she said: "Save you, my sister and give you joy that the champion whom I brought hither hath freed you from your enemy."

The Lady Layonnesse said: "Where is that knight and why hast thou not brought him hither with thee so that I may render to him my thanks?"

To this Lynette made reply: "Sister, he hath been sore wounded in his fight and he is moreover so befouled with the blood and dust of battle that he would not come hither at this present but lyeth in the pavilion of the Red Knight until the morrow."

Lynette telleth her sister of Sir Gareth Then the Lady Layonnesse said: "I pray you tell us who is this champion who hath thus set me free from my oppressor?" and Lynette said: "That I know not, only this I may tell you: that at the court of King Arthur there would no knight undertake the adventure because I would not declare your name and your degree before the King's court there assembled. Then there arose a youth of whom Sir Kay made great scorn and said that he was a kitchen knave hight Beaumains and the youth did not deny that saying. And King Arthur gave him leave to go with me and undertake this quest, and the youth did so. So we travelled together. And I was very angry because I thought that King Arthur had given me a kitchen knave for my champion instead of a good worthy knight, and so I treated Beaumains with great scorn, but ever he repaid all my scorn with very patient and courteous speeches. So he followed me hither and now he is that champion who hath just now overthrown thine enemy."

Then the Lady Layonnesse cried out, "What matters it if this young knight is a kitchen knave? Lo! he is my champion and hath risked his life for my sake. So because he hath fought that battle for me I will even raise him up to sit beside me, so that whatsoever honors are mine, they shall be his honors also. For if so be he is now lowly, then by me shall he be exalted above the heads of all you that are hereabouts."

So said the Lady Layonnesse, and thereat Lynette laughed with great heartiness. And when she had ended her laughter, she said, "My sister, I believe that it shall not be necessary for you to lift up this young knight. For if we should come to know who he really is, it might well be that we should discover that it is he who would exalt you rather than you would exalt him. For this champion can be no such kitchen knave as he pretends to be, but rather is he some one of great worth and of high degree. For several days I have so tried the patience of this knight that I do not believe that any one was ever so tried before. But although I so tried him very sorely he was always passing patient and gentle with me. Think you that any kitchen knave would be so patient as that? Moreover, I have beheld this knight in this short while fight six battles, and always he bore himself with such haughtiness and courage that were he an old and well-seasoned Knight of the Round Table of the King he could not have proved himself to be more noble or more worthy. You yourself have beheld to-day how he did battle against the Red Knight who is certes one of the greatest knights in the world, seeing that he hath never before been overcome; you have beheld how he hath suffered wounds and the danger of death; think you then that any kitchen knave could have fought such a battle as you beheld him fight? Nay, my sister, rather this young knight is someone of a very great and high estate."

Lynette defendeth Beaumains

Then Sir Gringamore spake, saying: "Lynette speaketh very truly, my sister, and in good sooth I believe that this is no kitchen knave, but one who is sprung from the blood of right champions. Now tell me, Lynette, I pray thee, is there no one who knoweth this knight who he really is?" and Lynette replied: "Yea, there is one who knoweth and that is the dwarf Axatalese. He could tell us who this knight really is, for he hath followed him for a long time every where he hath gone."

Then Sir Gringamore bethought him for a little while, and anon he said: "Meseemeth it is needful that we have this dwarf for so only shall we come to know who that knight is. Now thou and I and

Lynette will go down to the place of those pavilions. And thou shalt go to the pavilion of the knight and bring the dwarf out thence, for I doubt not he will come at thy bidding. Meantime, whilst thou are finding that dwarf I shall be hidden in some secret place, and when thou hast brought him near enough to me I will leap out upon him and will catch him. Then we will fetch him hither, and it will go hard but we learn who this knight is."

So it was done as Sir Gringamore said; for he and the damsel Lynette went to a place nigh to the place of pavilions where there was a hedge. And Sir Gringamore hid him behind the hedge and so after he was hidden Lynette went alone to the pavilion of the Red Knight where Sir Gareth lay. Now at that time they all slept, even to the guard that surrounded the tent. And so Lynette passed through their midst and none heard her. And Lynette came to the pavilion where Sir Gareth lay and she lifted the curtain of the door of the tent and looked within and beheld Sir Gareth where he lay sleeping upon a couch with a night-light burning very faintly near by him. And she beheld where the dwarf Axatalese lay sleeping near to the door of the tent.

Then Lynette entered the pavilion very softly and she reached out and touched Axatalese upon the shoulder and therewith he immediately awoke. And Axatalese was astonished at beholding the damsel at that place, but Lynette laid her finger upon her lips and whispered very low to him, "Say naught, Axatalese, but follow me." And Axatalese did so.

So the maiden brought Axatalese out of the pavilion and he followed her in silence. And she brought him through the other pavilions and still ever he followed her in silence and no one stayed them in their going. So Axatalese followed Lynette and she led him by a path that brought them out of the field where the pavilions were and to that place near by where Sir Gringamore lay hidden behind the hawthorn hedge. Then when Axatalese was come very close to that place Sir Gringamore leaped out of a sudden from the thicket and catched him. And Axatalese lifted up his voice and fell to yelling very loud and shrill, but anon Sir Gringamore clapped his hand upon the mouth of the creature and silenced him. And Sir Gringamore drew his miseracordia and set it at the throat of Axatalese and said to him,

"Sirrah, be silent, if you would live." And at that Axatalese ceased to struggle and was perfectly silent. Then Sir Gringamore released his hand from the mouth of Axatalese and Axatalese was afraid to utter any further outcry.

So after that Sir Gringamore and Lynette brought Axatalese to the castle and into the castle. And they brought him to that place where the Lady Layonnesse awaited their coming. Then, when they were safely come to that place, Sir Gringamore said to Axatalese, "Sirrah Dwarf, tell us who is that knight, thy master, and what is his degree?" And Axatalese cried out, "Alas, Messire, harm me not." Quoth Sir Gringamore, "No harm shall befall thee, only speak as I bid thee and tell us who thy master is." *They bring Axatalese to the castle*

Then Axatalese trembling with fear, said: "Fair Messire, the knight my master is hight Sir Gareth and he is the son of King Lot of Orkney and the Queen Margaise, the sister of King Arthur, and so it is that he is right brother of those noble worthy champions, Sir Gawaine and Sir Gaheris, and he is the brother of Sir Mordred of Orkney." *Axatalese telleth of Sir Gareth*

Now when Lynette heard the words that Axatalese spoke she smote her hands very violently together and she cried out in a loud and piercing voice: "Said I not so? Well did I know that this was no kitchen knave, but otherwise that he was some very noble and worthy knight. So he is, for there is none better in all the world than he. Rejoice, my sister, for here indeed is a great honor that hath befallen thee. For this is a very worthy champion to have saved thee from thy distresses."

And the Lady Layonnesse said: "Sister, I do indeed rejoice and that beyond all measure." And she turned her to Sir Gringamore and said: "My brother, let us straightway hasten and go to this worthy knight so that we may give him such thanks as is fitting for one of his degree to receive."

"Nay," quoth Sir Gringamore, "not so. Rather let us wait until to-morrow and until he has altogether rested himself from this day of battle. Meantime, I will take this dwarf back whence we brought him and to-morrow we will pay Sir Gareth all due honor."

So it was as Sir Gringamore ordained. For first he took Axatalese back to the place of the pavilions, and after that they waited until *Sir Gringamore payeth court to Sir Gareth* the morn. And when the morn was come Sir Gringamore and the Lady Layonnesse and Lynette went down to that place of the pavilions and to the pavilion of Sir Gareth, and the Lady Layonnesse and the damsel Lynette waited outside of the tent and Sir Gringamore entered thereinto. And Sir Gringamore came to where Sir Gareth lay and he saluted Sir Gareth saying, "Save you, Sir Gareth of Orkney."

Then Sir Gareth was greatly astonished and he said: "How know you my name and my degree, Messire?" And Sir Gringamore said: "Sir, my sister the damsel Lynette, and I, catched thy dwarf last night and took him away to my sister's castle. There we compelled him to tell us who you were, and so we had knowledge of your name and your condition." And Sir Gringamore said: "Sir Gareth, we are rejoiced beyond measure that you have so greatly honored us as to come hither and to serve as the champion of my sister, the Lady Layonnesse. Now if you will suffer her to have speech with you, she standeth without the door of the pavilion." And Sir Gareth said, "Let her come in for I would fain see her near at hand."

The Lady Layonnesse cometh to Sir Gareth So Sir Gringamore went out of the pavilion and immediately he returned, bringing the Lady Layonnesse and Lynette with him. And the Lady Layonnesse came and kneeled down beside the couch whereon Sir Gareth lay. And Sir Gareth saw her face near by and he saw that it was ten times more beautiful than he had supposed it to be when he saw it from a distance at the upper window of the Castle Dangerous as aforetold of. And Sir Gareth loved her from that moment with all his heart and from that time forth his love never wavered from her.

That day they brought Sir Gareth to the castle in a litter and Sir Gareth abided at the castle for a fortnight and in that time he was altogether healed of his hurts that he had got in his battle with the Red Knight.

And ever Sir Gareth loved the Lady Layonnesse more and more and ever she loved him in like manner. So they were continually together and it was said of all that heaven had never sent to the earth two more beautiful young creatures than they.

Then at the end of that fortnight aforesaid, Sir Gareth said: "Now it behooves me to return to the court of the King to proclaim myself to my brothers. For since I have succeeded in overthrowing the Red

Knight of the Red Lands and so of achieving this adventure, I believe I am not unworthy to proclaim myself even unto my brothers."

So spake Sir Gareth, and to this the Lady Layonnesse replied: "Sir, it is indeed well that you return to the court of the King. But when you go I beseech you that you will permit my brother, Sir Gringamore, and my sister Lynette, and I myself for to go with you. For so you who departed alone will return with a company of those who love and honor you." Thus said the Lady Layonnesse for it had come to pass by this time that she could not bear to be parted from Sir Gareth even for so short a while as a few days.

Accordingly, it was done as she said and straightway preparation was made for their departure. So the next day they took leave of the Castle Dangerous for a while, betaking their way with a considerable court of knights, esquires, and attendants to the King's court at Carleon where the King was at that time still abiding. *They all depart for the court of the King*

Now return we to the court of King Arthur ere those others shall come thither, so that we may see how it befell at that place after the departure of the kitchen knave Beaumains.

Now it hath been told how that Sir Kay departed to follow after Beaumains for to have a fall of him; and it hath been told how that Sir Kay returned to court upon a gray mule; and it hath been told how that Sir Kay was made the mock and laughing-stock, all because of the misadventure that had befallen him.

After that there passed five days, and at the end of that time there came Sir Perard to the court with the word that Sir Gareth had bidden him for to carry thither; to wit, that the kitchen knave, Beaumains, hath beaten him in battle and had sent him thither for to pay his duty unto the King.

Then King Arthur said: "Fore Heaven! What sort of a kitchen knave is this to overcome so brave and well-seasoned a knight as Sir Perard? This can be no kitchen knave, but rather is he some youth of very heroic race who hath been dwelling for all this while unknown in our midst, in the guise of a kitchen knave." So said the King. And Sir Gawaine said, "Lord, I may well believe that what you say is indeed the case." *How the several knights do homage*

Then two days after Sir Perard had come to Carleon in that wise, there came thither that knight whom Sir Gareth had saved from the six thieves. And he brought a very considerable court of esquires and attendants with him; and he also told of the further doings of Sir Gareth. And when they at Carleon heard those things, both the King and the court made loud marvel and acclaim that Beaumains should have become so wonderful a champion as to do those things that were told of him.

After that there passed a week and at the end of that time there came Sir Percevant of Hind with a great court of knights and esquires accompanying him; and he also brought the same word that Sir Perard had done; to wit, that Beaumains, the kitchen knave, had overcome him in battle and had sent him to the King's court for to pay his duty to the King. And at that King Arthur and all of his court knew not what to think of a kitchen knave who should do such wonderful works.

So passed a fortnight and at the end of that time there came the Red Knight of the Red Lands, walking afoot and without shield or armor but surrounded by even a greater court of knights and esquires than Sir Percevant had brought with him. And he also brought the same word to the King—that the kitchen knave, Beaumains, had overcome him and had sent him thither to pay his duty to the King. And besides this he told the King many things concerning this same Beaumains that the others had not told; to wit, how Beaumains had carried his adventure of the Castle Dangerous through to a worthy ending and how that he was even then lodging at the castle of the Lady Layonnesse of Granderegard.

So when King Arthur and his court heard all these things, he and they wist not what to think, but marvelled as to who this extraordinary young champion was.

Queen Margaise cometh to court Now the day after the Red Knight of the Red Lands had come to Carleon as aforetold, it befell that there came to the court of the King an herald; and the herald brought news that Queen Margaise of Orkney was even then upon her way for to visit the King.

Then King Arthur was very glad that his sister was coming thither for he loved her above all others of his kin. So it came to pass that when the day after the next day had come, Queen Margaise reached the court of the King as she had promised to do, and the King and the court gave her royal greeting.

Then Queen Margaise looked all about and by and by she said, "Where is my son Gareth whom I sent thitherward a year ago?"

At that King Arthur was very much astonished, and for a little he wist not what to think; then he said, "I know of no such one as Gareth."

Upon this Queen Margaise was filled with anxiety, for she wist not what to believe had happened to her son. So her color changed several times and several times she tried to speak and could not. Then at last she did speak, saying: "Woe is me if harm should have befallen him, for certes he is the very flower of all my children." *Queen Margaise grieveth for Sir Gareth*

Then King Arthur took suddenly thought of Beaumains and he said: "Sister, take heart and look up, for I believe that no harm but rather great honor hath befallen thy son. Now tell me, did he come hither about the time of the feast of Pentecost a year ago?" And the Queen said, "Yea." Then King Arthur said: "Tell me, was thy son fair of face and had he ruddy hair and was he tall and broad of girth and had he a dwarf named Axatalese with him?" And the Queen said, "Yea, that was he!" Then King Arthur said: "He hath been here, but we knew him not." And the Queen said, "What hath befallen him?"

Then King Arthur told the Queen his sister all that had befallen. For he told her how that Gareth had come thither and in what guise; and he told her how Gareth had dwelt all that year unknown at the court under the name of Beaumains because of the whiteness of his hands; and he told her how that Beaumains had gone forth upon that adventure to the Castle Dangerous; and he told her how he had succeeded in that adventure; and he told her of the several other things that are herein told, and ever Queen Margaise listened to him.

But when King Arthur had finished his telling the Queen was very angry and she said: "Methinks, my brother, that you should have known my son for one of high and noble degree, even though he were clad in green as you tell me and even though he did beseech no greater boon of you than food and drink and lodging. For certes there was ever that in his bearing that bespake better things than these."

King Arthur placates Queen Margaise
Then King Arthur, speaking very mildly, said: "My sister, how may one know another, his name and his degree, only by looking in his face? Yet wit you that had I not thought there was somewhat high and noble about this youth I had not given him leave to undertake this adventure in which he hath succeeded so very gloriously."

So spake King Arthur, but Queen Margaise was hardly yet appeased, nor was she pacified for a long time afterward. Then, at last, she was pacified.

Now a day or two after this time the King called Sir Gawaine and Sir Gaheris to him and he said to these two: "Take you a noble court of knights and gentlemen and go you forth and find your brother and bring him hither to our court in all such royal estate as is befitting for such a knight to enjoy. For of a surety it will be a great honor for to have such a knight amongst us."

Then Sir Gawaine and Sir Gaheris were much pleased that the King should so favor their brother, wherefore they fulfilled that command to the full, for they chose them such a court as was as noble as possible, and they set forth upon that journey as the King had commanded.

Sir Gawaine and Sir Gaheris depart to find Sir Gareth
So they travelled for one whole day and for a part of another day, and toward the afternoon of that second day they beheld a great company of knights and lords and ladies ahorseback coming toward them. And many esquires and attendants accompanied that fair company, and they so shone with cloth of gold and with many jewels and with bright shining armor that it bedazzled the eyes to look upon them. And Sir Gawaine and Sir Gaheris wondered what lordly company that could be. And when that company had come nearer, they two perceived that at the head thereof there rode two knights in armor and two ladies upon ambling palfreys and they saw that the two ladies were very beautiful. And when that company had come still nearer Sir Gawaine and Sir Gaheris perceived that one of those knights who rode with the ladies was none other than him whom they had aforetime called "Beaumains"; and that one of the damsels was the damsel Lynette who had come to court a short time before.

They meet Sir Gareth upon the way
Then when Sir Gawaine and Sir Gaheris perceived their brother at the head of that company they immediately set spurs to horse and raced forward to meet him with all speed they could command.

And when they had come to where Sir Gareth was, they leaped down from off their horses and ran to him, crying aloud, "Brother, Brother!" and Sir Gareth leaped down from his horse and ran to them and so they kissed and embraced each other upon the highroad, weeping for joy.

Thus it was that Sir Gareth was acknowledged by those two noble and worthy knights-champion, his brothers, and so his kindred met him and gave him welcome.

And now it remains but few things to say; for there remaineth only to be said that Sir Gareth was received at the court with such rejoicings as you may well suppose. And it remaineth to be said that at that same time there suddenly appeared upon one of the seats of the Round Table near to the seat of Sir Launcelot of the Lake a name in letters of gold, and the name was this:

Sir Gareth becometh a Knight of the Round Table

Gareth of Orkney

For from that time Sir Gareth became a Knight of the Round Table, being elected thereto in that miraculous way that was usual in the case of those who were chosen for that high and worshipful companionship.

And it remaineth to be told that in a little while Sir Gareth was wedded to the Lady Layonnesse with great pomp and ceremony and that thereafter he returned with her to the Castle Dangerous of which he was now the lord.

And in after times Sir Gareth became one of the most famous of all the knights of the Table Round, so that much is told of him in divers books of chivalry. Yet there shall be no more told of his adventures at this place, albeit there may be more said concerning him in another book which shall follow this book. Yet it is to be said that these are the most famous adventures that befel him, and that the history of Gareth and Lynette is the one which is most often told of in stories and sung in ballads and poems.

So endeth the Story of Gareth of Orkney, which same was told at this place in part because it is a good worthy history to tell at any place, and in part because that time in which he did battle with and was knighted by Sir Launcelot, as aforetold, was the only time that Sir Launcelot was seen by any of the court of King Arthur until after he had accomplished the Adventure of the Worm of Corbin.

For that which followeth dealeth of the adventure of the Worm of Corbin and with how that Sir Launcelot overcame that dragon and became acquainted with the Lady Elaine the Fair, who was the mother of Sir Galahad, who was the flower of all chivalry. Wherefore, if you would know that part of the history of Sir Launcelot that relates to those things, you must needs read that which is written hereinafter.

The Story of Sir Launcelot and Elaine the Fair

HERE FOLLOWETH *the history of Sir Launcelot's wanderings and of how he came to the town of Corbin, and of how he slew the great Worm of Corbin that for somewhiles brought sorrow and death to the folk of Corbin. Here you shall also read the history of Elaine the Fair, the King's daughter of Corbin, and of how for her sake Sir Launcelot fought in the tournament at Astolat.*

All these and several other things are herein duly set forth, so that, should you please to read that which is hereafter written, I believe you shall find a great deal of pleasure and entertainment in that history.

How Sir Launcelot held discourse with ẙ merry Minstrels.

Chapter First

How Sir Launcelot rode errant and how he assumed to undertake the Adventure of the Worm of Corbin.

ND NOW you shall be told how it befell Sir Launcelot after that he had fought with Sir Gareth and had made him knight as told in the history of Sir Gareth.

You are to know that after Sir Launcelot left Sir Gareth he went his way very cheerfully, and many times he bethought him of how the damsel Lynette had taken Sir Gareth to be a kitchen knave, and at that thought he would laugh with great joy of so excellent a jest.

So with great cheerfulness of spirit he rode ever onward upon his way, whilst the daylight slanted farther and farther toward sunset. And, after awhile, the sun sunk in the West, and the silence of the twilight fell like to a soft mantle of silence upon the entire earth. The darkness fell, the earth melted here and there into shadow and every sound came very clear and loud as though the bright and luminous sky that arched overhead was a great hollow bell of crystal that echoed back every sudden noise with extraordinary clearness. Then Sir Launcelot was both hungry and athirst and he wist not where he might find refreshment to satisfy the needs of his body.

Sir Launcelot rideth errant

Sir Launcelot meeteth the strolling minstrels

So, thinking of food and drink, he was presently aware of the light of a fire shining in the gray of the falling twilight and thitherward he directed his way, and in a little pass, he came to where there was a merry party of strolling minstrels gathered around about that bright and cheerful fire. Some of these fellows were clad in blue and some in yellow and some in red and some in green and some in raiment pied of many colors. And all they were eating with great appetite a savory stew of mutton and lentils seasoned with onions and washed down with lusty draughts of ale and wine which they poured forth, ever and anon, from big round-bellied skins into horns and cups that were held to catch it.

These jolly fellows, beholding Sir Launcelot coming to them through the dusk, gave him welcome with loud voices of acclaim and besought him to descend from horseback and to eat with them, and Sir Launcelot was right glad to do so.

So he dismounted from his horse and eased it of its saddle and turned it loose to browse as it listed upon the grass of the wayside. And he laid aside his shield and his spear and his sword and his helmet and he sat him down with those minstrels and fell to eating and drinking with might and main. And the minstrels bade him to take good cheer and to eat and drink all that he desired and Sir Launcelot did so.

The minstrels Then, after Sir Launcelot and the minstrels had supped their fill, *chaunt* those lusty fellows brought forth other skins of wine and filling again the several cups and flagons they all fell to drinking and making merry. And several of the minstrels brought forth lutes and others brought forth viols, and anon he who was the chief minstrel called upon one to stand forth and sing, and that fellow did so, chaunting a rondel in praise of his sweetheart's eyes. After that, another sang of battle and still another sang in praise of pleasant living; meantime the others accompanied, with lute and viol, those who sang, and Sir Launcelot listened to their music with great pleasure of heart.

All about them lay the deep silence of the moonlit night with only that one red spot of fire and of cheerful mirth in the midst of it, and the fire shone very bright upon the armor of the knight and lit up all those quaint fellows in red and green and yellow and blue

and pied so that they stood forth against the blackness behind them
as though they had been carved out from it with a sharp knife.

Then he who was chief among the minstrels said to Sir Launcelot,
"Messire, will ye not also sing?" At this Sir Launcelot laughed, and
quoth he: "Nay, good fellows, I cannot sing as ye do, but I will tell
ye a story an ye list to hear me."

At that they all cried out to tell them that story and thereupon he *Sir Launcelot*
did so, telling them a certain goodly conte of two knights who loved *telleth a conte*
a lady, but she loved neither of them, having set her heart upon an
esquire of low degree. So of these two knights the one became an
hermit and the other by force of his knighthood brought it to pass
that the esquire was exalted from his squirehood to become a king.
But when the esquire became a king the lady would have none of
him, but turned her love to the knight who had exalted him to his
high estate. So the lady left the esquire who was king and married the
noble knight who had made him king, and so, having made choice of
the greatest and the noblest of all the three, she dwelt happily with
him to the end of her life.

To this the minstrels listed in silence and when Sir Launcelot had
finished they gave him great applause without measure.

After that the minstrels sang again and Sir Launcelot told them
another tale of chivalry; and so with good cheer the night passed
pleasantly away until the great round moon, bright and full like to
a bubble of shining silver, floated high in the sky above their heads,
very bright and as glorious as day and bathing all the world in a flood
of still white light, most wonderful to behold.

Then perceiving it to be midnight, Sir Launcelot bestirred him- *Sir Launcelot*
self, and he said: "Good fellows, I thank ye with all my heart for the *would leave*
the minstrels
entertainment ye have given me, but now I am refreshed I must go
again upon my way."

To this he who was chief among the minstrels said: "Sir Knight,
we would fain that you would remain with us to-night and would
travel with us upon our way to-morrow, for indeed you are the pleas-
antest and cheerfulest knight that ever we met in all of our lives."

At this Sir Launcelot laughed with great good will, and he said: *He asketh of*
"Good fellows, I give you gramercy for your fair regard. Ye are indeed *some*
adventure
a merry company and were I not a knight methinks I would rather

be one of your party than one of any other company that ever I fell in with. But it may not be, for, lo! I am a knight and I must e'en go about my business as becometh one who weareth spurs of gold. So here and now we part. Ne'ertheless you may haply do me one service, and that is to tell me whether anywhere hereabout is to be found an adventure such as may beseem a knight of good credit to undertake."

Upon this one of those minstrels spake saying: "Messire, I know where there is an adventure, which, if you achieve it, will bring you such great credit that I believe Sir Launcelot of the Lake himself would not have greater credit than you."

At this Sir Launcelot laughed with great good will. "Well," quoth he, "I would not be overbold, yet this I may say, that anything Sir Launcelot of the Lake might not fear to undertake, that also I shall not fear to assume, and whatever he might find strength to do that also I may hope to accomplish. For indeed I may tell ye that I hold myself to be altogether as good and worthy a knight as ever is Sir Launcelot of the Lake."

"Ha!" quoth the chief minstrel, "I perceive, Sir Knight, that thou hast a very good opinion of thyself. Now, were Sir Launcelot here, haply thou wouldst not venture to reckon thyself so high as thou now dost."

At that all those minstrels laughed in great measure, and Sir Launcelot laughed with them as loud as any. "Good fellows," said he, "I believe I reckon myself to be no better than another man born of woman, yet this I have to say: Oftentimes have I beheld Sir Launcelot and sometimes have I contended against his will, but never at any time have I found him to be stronger or worthier than am I myself. But let us not debate so small a matter as this. Let us instead learn what is that adventure concerning which yonder good fellow hath to advise us."

"Messire," quoth the minstrel, "have ye ever heard tell of the Worm of Corbin?"

"Nay," said Sir Launcelot, "but tell thou me of it."

The minstrel telleth of the Worm of Corbin "Sir," said the minstrel, "I will do so. You are to know that some ways to a considerable distance to the eastward of this place there is a very large fair noble town hight Corbin; and the King of that country is King Pelles. Now one time it chanced that Queen Morgana le Fay and the Queen of North Wales were upon a visit to Corbin, and whilst they were there there was given in that place a great jousting and feast in their honor.

"Whilst King Pelles sat at table with the two queens (all of his *Of the damsel* court and his daughter Elaine the Fair being with him) there came *who came to* into the pavilion where the feast was held a wonderfully fair damsel, *King* tall and straight and clad from top to toe in flame-colored satin. In her hand she bare a paten of silver and upon the paten was a napkin, and on the napkin there was a wonderful ring of gold set with a clear blue stone. And the damsel spoke in a voice both high and clear, saying: 'Lords and Ladies, here have I a ring that may only be worn by the fairest and worthiest lady in this room.'

"At these words, as you may suppose, there was a great deal of wonder and much expectation, and a great deal of talk. For some said that one lady should by rights have that ring and some said that another lady should have it.

"Now the first to essay that ring was Queen Morgana le Fay, for *Of how* she supposed that this was a masque devised by King Pelles in honor *Queen* of her. So she took the ring in her hand and essayed to pass it upon *Morgana* her finger, but lo! it would not pass the first joint thereof. *ring*

"At that Queen Morgana was filled with wrath, but still she dissembled her anger and sat, waiting to see what would next befall.

"So after Queen Morgana le Fay had thus failed to wear that ring, *Of how the* the Queen of North Wales said unto herself, 'Haply King Pelles may *Queen of* intend this ring for me.' So she also took the ring and would have *North Wales* placed it upon her finger, but lo! it grew so large that it would not *ring* stay where it was placed, but fell off upon the table before the whole court of the King.

"At this many who were there laughed aloud, and thereat the Queen of North Wales was filled with anger and mortification as much as Queen Morgana le Fay had been. But she also dissembled her anger before the court and sat to watch what would befall.

"So after these two queens had so essayed, several others of the ladies who were there each tried to put the ring upon her finger, but no one could do so, for either it was too large, or else it was too small. Then last of all the Lady Elaine the Fair, the King's daughter, essayed the adventure of the ring, and lo! it fitted her as exactly as though it had been made for her.

"At this both of those two queens aforesaid were more angered than ever, for each said to herself, 'Certes, this King hath done this to put affront upon us.' So that night they communed together what they should do to punish King Pelles of Corbin and the Town of Corbin for that affront which they deemed themselves to have suffered.

Of how Queen Morgana layeth a curse upon the town "Now the next morning those two queens quitted the court, and as they and their attendants passed by the market-place of the town they perceived where there lay a great flat stone that marked the centre of the town. Then Queen Morgana le Fay cried out: 'See ye yonder stone! Beneath that slab there shall breed a great Worm and that Worm shall bring sorrow and dole to this place ten thousand times more than the shame which I suffered here yesterday. For that stone shall be enchanted so that no man may lift it. And beneath that stone the Worm shall live; and ever and anon it shall come forth and seize some fair young virgin of this town and shall bear her away to its hiding-place and shall there devour her for its food.'

"So it was as the Queen said, and now that Worm dwelleth at Corbin beneath the stone, and ever bringeth sorrow and death to that place. And it cometh out only at night, so that the terror of the Worm of Corbin is greater than it would otherwise be, for no eye hath ever beheld it in its comings and its goings. So if any champion shall achieve the death of that Worm, he shall be held to have done a deed worthy of Sir Launcelot of the Lake himself."

"Friend," said Sir Launcelot, "thou sayest true and that were indeed a most worthy quest for any knight to undertake. As for me, I am so eager to enter upon that quest that I can hardly stay my patience."

With this saying, Sir Launcelot rose from where he sat; and he whistled his horse to him and when his horse had come to where he was he put the saddle upon its back. And he took his shield and spear in his hand and mounted upon his charger and made him ready to leave that place.

But ere he departed, the chief minstrel and several others came to him, and the chief minstrel laid his hand upon the horse's neck and he said: "I pray you, Messire, tell us who you are who have seen Sir Launcelot of the Lake so often and who declare yourself to be as good a knight as he."

Then Sir Launcelot laughed and he said: "Good friend, I am riding errant as you behold. In these my travels I would fain withhold my name from the knowledge of men. Nevertheless, since we have eaten and drunk together, and since we have cohabited in good fellowship together, I will tell you that I myself am that very Sir Launcelot whom ye appear to hold in such high regard. Wherefore it is that I am, certes, as good as he could possibly be, let that be saying much or saying little." *Sir Launcelot revealeth himself to the minstrels*

So saying, Sir Launcelot set spurs to his horse and rode away and left them astonished at his words. And long after he had left those merry fellows he could hear their voices in the distance babbling together very loud with wonder that Sir Launcelot of the Lake had been amongst them for all that time without any one of them suspecting him who he was. For by this time all the world knew Sir Launcelot of the Lake to be the greatest champion that ever the world had seen from the very beginning unto that time.

After that, Sir Launcelot rode forward upon his way toward the eastward through the moonlit night, and by and by he entered a great space of forest land. And somewhile after he had entered that woodland the summer day began to dawn and all the birds began at first to chirp and then to sing very blithely and with a great multitude of happy voices from out of every leafy thicket. Then up leapt the jolly sun and touched all the upper leafage of the trees and turned them into gold.

And anon the sun rose high and higher and when it was very high in the heavens Sir Launcelot came out of the forest into an open country of level meadows and of pasture-lands. And in the midst of that place, a great way off, he beheld where there was a fair walled town set upon a hill with a smooth shining river at its foot, and he *Sir Launcelot beholdeth Corbin* wist that this must be the Town of Corbin of which the strolling minstrels had told him the night before.

So Sir Launcelot rode forward and drew near the town. And as he drew closer to it he thought that this was one of the fairest towns that ever he had beheld in all of his life. For the castle of the town and the houses of the town were all built else of stone or else of brick, and a thousand windows sparkled in the brightness of the day, shining like to stars in heaven. And the river that flowed beside the town wound down between fair green meadows which lay upon either side, and betwixt banks of reeds and rushes and pollard willows, and it was like to a great serpent of pure silver lying in the grass. The walls of the castle and the walls of the town came down to the river, and stood with their feet, as it were, in the clear and crystal-bright water, and there were trees that overhung the water upon this side and upon that, and there was a bridge with three arches that crossed over the river and led to the town. All these things Sir Launcelot beheld and so it was that the town appeared exceedingly pleasant to his eyes.

Sir Launcelot bespeaks the town's folk Now when Sir Launcelot had come pretty close to the town he met a party of town-folk with several pack-mules hung with bells and laden with parcels of goods. These Sir Launcelot bespoke, saying, "I pray ye, fair folk, tell me, is this the Town of Corbin?" Thereunto they replied, "Yea, Sir Knight, this is that town." Sir Launcelot said, "Why are ye so sad and downcast?" Whereunto the chief of that party—a right reverend man with a long white beard—made reply: "Sir Knight, wherefore do you ask us why we are sad? Whence come you that you have not heard how we are cursed in this town by a Worm that torments us very grievously; and how is it that you have not heard tell how that Worm devoureth every now and then a tender virgin from our midst?"

"Sir," quoth Sir Launcelot, "I have indeed heard of this Worm that bringeth you so much woe and dole. Know ye that it is because of this very Worm that I have come hither. For I purpose, if God's grace be with me, to destroy that vile thing and so to set ye all free from the curse that lies upon you!"

"Alas, Sir Knight," quoth the old man, speaking very sorrowfully, "I do not doubt that you are possessed of all the courage necessary for this undertaking, yet for all that you may not hope to succeed in your quest. For even if you were able to slay the Worm, yet you could not come at it. For you are to know that it lyeth beneath a great stone and that the stone is sealed by magic which Queen Morgana le Fay set upon it so that no man may raise it from where it lyeth."

Then Sir Launcelot spoke words of good cheer to that old man *Sir Launcelot* and to his companions, saying: "Let that be as it may, yet for all *speaketh words of cheer* that ye need not despair of succor. Know ye not that naught can be achieved until it first be essayed? As for that enchantment that lyeth upon the stone, I tell ye this: Behold this ring which I wear upon my finger! It is sovereign against all magic whatsoever, wherefore I know that the spells which bind this stone into its place cannot prevail against the counter magic of this ring. So ye shall be well assured that I shall lift that stone, and after that, when it shall be lifted and when it shall come to battle betwixt me and that Worm, then shall the issue lie altogether with God, His Grace and Mercy."

Now when those who were there heard what Sir Launcelot said, *How Sir* their hearts were filled with hope and joy, for it seemed to them that *Launcelot entered* here indeed might be a champion who should deliver them out of *Corbin* their distresses. Wherefore when they heard his words they presently lifted up their voices in loud acclaim, some crying, "God be with you!" and some crying, "God save you from destruction!" some crying this, and some crying that.

Then Sir Launcelot smiled upon them and said, "Save you good people," and therewith set spurs to flank and rode away.

But many of those who were there went with him, running beside his horse, seeking to touch him and even to touch the horse which he rode. And all the time they gave him loud acclaim without measure and without stint.

For the virtue of Sir Launcelot went forth from him like a shining light wherefore it seemed to them that here was one who should certainly free them from the curse that lay upon them.

And thus it was that Sir Launcelot of the Lake rode across that three-spanned bridge and into the Town of Corbin and so to his adventure with the Worm of Corbin.

ir Launcelot slayeth the Worm of
Corbin:

Chapter Second

How Sir Launcelot slew the Worm of Corbin, and how he was carried thereafter to the Castle of Corbin and to King Pelles and to the Lady Elaine the Fair.

O THUS it was that Sir Launcelot entered the town of Corbin to slay the Dragon that lay beneath the stone. And with his coming a great multitude gathered very quickly, hurrying from all sides, crying out and blessing him as he rode forward upon his way. And ever a great roar of voices sounded all about him like to the noise of many waters. *The folk of the town welcome Sir Launcelot*

So, upborn by that multitude, Sir Launcelot went forward very steadfastly toward the market-place of the town, in the midst of which lay that great stone, aforetold of, with the Worm beneath it. And when he had reached the place, he bade the multitude abide where they were. *Sir Launcelot cometh to the place of the Dragon*

So, upon that command, the people stood afar off, and Sir Launcelot went forward alone to where was the slab of stone. And he looked down upon the slab and beheld that it was very flat and wide and so big that three men might hardly hope to lift it. Besides this, he beheld that it had been sealed by magic as had been reported to him, for many strange letters and figures had been engraved into the face of the stone.

Now you are to remember that it was aforetold of in the "Book of the Champions of the Round Table" that Sir Launcelot wore upon his finger a ring which the Lady of the Lake had given him when he quitted the Lake; and you all remember that that ring was of such a sort that he who wore it might dissolve all evil magic or enchantment against which he should direct his efforts. Wherefore it was that Sir Launcelot was aware, as he had already told the people outside of the walls of the town, that he might lift that stone even if another, because of the magic that was upon it, should not be able to stir it where it lay.

So Sir Launcelot put aside his sword and his shield and he went forward to the slab and he seized the slab in both of his hands. And he bent his back and lifted, and lo! the bands of enchantment that lay upon the stone were snapped and the slab moved and stirred in the bed wherein it lay.

Sir Launcelot lifteth the stone

Then when the multitude of the people who gazed upon him beheld the slab how it moved and stirred in its bed, a great shout went up from several thousand lips like to one mighty voice of outcry. Therewith Sir Launcelot bent again to the stone and heaved with all his might. And lo! he lifted the stone and he raised it and he rolled it over upon the earth.

Then he looked down into the hole that was beneath the stone and he was aware that there lay something in the hole that moved. And anon he beheld two green and glassy eyes that opened upon him and looked up at him from out of the hole; and he beheld that those eyes were covered over as with a thin film to shelter them from the dazzling light of the daytime. And as Sir Launcelot gazed he beheld that that thing which lay within the hole began to crawl out of the hole, and Sir Launcelot beheld that it was a huge worm, covered all over with livid scales as hard as flint. And the Worm lifted the fore part of its body to the height of a tall man and gaped very dreadfully with a great mouth an ell wide, and all glistening with three rows of white and shining teeth. And Sir Launcelot beheld that the Worm had as many as a thousand feet, and that each foot was armed with a great claw like the claw of a lion, as hard as flint, and very venomous with poison. And the Worm hissed at Sir Launcelot. And its breath was like the odor of Death.

The Worm of Corbin cometh forth

Such was that dreadful terrible Worm that lay beneath the stone at Corbin. And when the people of the town saw it thus appear before them in the broad light of day, they shrieked aloud with the terror of that which they beheld. For it was like to something that had come to life out of a dreadful dream, and it did not seem possible that such a thing should ever have been beheld by the living eyes of man.

But Sir Launcelot beholding the Worm in all its terror leaped to where was his sword and he seized his sword in both hands and he ran at the Worm and lashed at it a blow so mighty that it might easily have split an oak tree. But the scales of the Worm were like adamant for hardness wherefore the stroke of the sword pierced them not but glanced aside without harming the creature.

Then when the Worm felt itself thus smitten, it hissed again in a manner very terrible and loud, and it reached out toward Sir Launcelot and strove to catch him into the embrace of a hundred of its sharp claws. But Sir Launcelot sprang aside from the embraces of the Worm and he smote it again and again, yet could not in any wise cut through the scales that covered its body. And at every blow the Worm hissed more terribly and sought to catch Sir Launcelot into its embraces.

Thus for a long time Sir Launcelot avoided the Worm, but, by and by it came to pass that he began to wax faint and weary with leaping from side to side, weighed down as he was with his armor. *Sir Launcelot doeth battle with the Worm* So, at last, it befell that the Worm catched Sir Launcelot in the hook of one of its claws, and thereupon they who looked on at that battle beheld how in a moment it had embraced Sir Launcelot in several hundred of its claws so that his body was wellnigh hidden in that embrace. And the Worm, when it so held Sir Launcelot in its embrace, tore at him with its claws and strove to bite him with its shining teeth. And anon it catched its claws in the armor of Sir Launcelot and it tore away the epaulier upon the left side of Sir Launcelot's shoulder, and it tore away the iron boot that covered his left thigh, and it cut with its claws through the flesh of the left shoulder of Sir Launcelot and through the flesh of his thigh to the very bone, so that the blood gushed out in a crimson stream and ran down over his armor and over the claws of the Worm.

Then Sir Launcelot, finding himself as it were thus in the very embrace of Death, put forth all his strength and tore away free from the clutches of the Worm ere it was able to do him further harm. And seeing how that the case was now so ill with him, he catched the haft of his sword in both of his hands, and he rushed at the creature and he stabbed with his sword into the gaping mouth of the creature and down into its gullet so that the cross-piece of the sword smote against the teeth of the creature's mouth.

Then when the Worm felt that dreadful terrible stroke driven thus into its very vitals, it roared like a bull in its torments, and it straightway rolled over upon the ground writhing and lashing the entire length of its body, bellowing so that those who heard it felt the marrow in their bones melt for terror.

Sir Launcelot slayeth the Worm But Sir Launcelot, looking down upon the lashings of the Worm, beheld where there appeared to be a soft place nigh to the belly and beneath the scales of the back and sides, and therewith he rushed at the Worm and plunged his sword twice and thrice into that soft spot, whereupon, lo! thick blood, as black as ink, gushed forth after those strokes. Then again Sir Launcelot pierced the Worm twice and thrice in such another place and thereafter it presently ceased to bellow in that wise and lay shuddering and writhing in death, rustling its dry scales upon the earth in its last throes of life.

Then Sir Launcelot beheld that his work was done and he stood leaning upon his sword, panting and covered all over with the blood and slime of that dreadful battle. And the people beholding how that the Worm was now slain, fell to shouting aloud beyond measure. And they came running from all sides to that place like to a flood so that they filled the entire market-place. And they crowded around and gazed upon the Worm with horror, and they gazed upon Sir Launcelot in wonder that Heaven should have sent so wonderful a Champion to save them out of their distresses. And ever Sir Launcelot stood there leaning upon his sword panting and with the blood flowing down from his shoulder and his thigh so that all that side of his body was ensanguined with shining red.

The knights of Corbin do honor to Sir Launcelot So as he stood there, there came a party of knights riding into that place. These thrust their way through the multitude to where Sir Launcelot was in the midst of the crowd as aforesaid. When they had come to Sir Launcelot the chief of those knights said, "Sir, art thou he who hath slain the Worm?" Sir Launcelot said, "Thou seest that I am he." Then he who spoke to Sir Launcelot said, "Messire, I fear me you are sorely hurt in this battle." Quoth Sir Launcelot: "I am hurt indeed, but not more hurt than I have been several times before and yet live as you behold me."

Then those knights went and looked upon the Worm where it lay and they gazed upon it with wonder and with loathing. And they gave great praise beyond measure to the knight who had slain it.

After that they sent for a litter and they laid Sir Launcelot upon the litter and bare him away into the Castle of Corbin where King Pelles of Corbin was then holding his court in royal pomp of circumstance. And they brought Sir Launcelot to a fair chamber of the castle where a number of attendants came to him and eased him of his armor and led him to a bath of tepid water steeped with healing herbs. And there came a skilful leech and searched the wounds of Sir Launcelot and spread soothing unguents upon them and bound them up with swathings of linen. And after that they bare Sir Launcelot to a fair soft couch spread with snow-white linen and laid him thereon, and he was greatly at ease and much comforted in body.

Then after all this was done in that wise, there came King Pelles of Corbin to that place for to visit Sir Launcelot, and with him came his son, Sir Lavaine, and his daughter, the Lady Elaine the Fair. And Sir Launcelot beheld that King Pelles was a very noble haughty lord, for his beard and his hair were long and amplelike to the mane of a lion, and resembled threads of gold sprinkled with threads of silver. And he was clad all in a robe of purple studded over with shining jewels and he wore a fillet of gold about his head set with several gems of great price. Upon the right hand of King Pelles there came his son, Sir Lavaine—a very noble young knight, newly created by the bath—and upon his left hand there came his daughter, the Lady Elaine the Fair. *King Pelles of Corbin doeth honor to Sir Launcelot*

Then Sir Launcelot looked upon the Lady Elaine the Fair and it seemed to him that she was the most beautiful maiden that ever he had beheld in all of his life. For he saw that her hair was soft and yellow and shining like to the finest silk; that her eyebrows were curved and very fine, as though they had been marked with a sharp and delicate pencil; that her eyes were very large and perfectly blue and very lustrous, and as bright as precious jewels; that her forehead was like cream for whiteness; that her cheeks were like roses for softness of blush; that her lips were like coral for redness, and that betwixt her lips her teeth were white, like to pearls for whiteness. *Of the Lady Elaine the Fair*

Such was the Lady Elaine, as Sir Launcelot beheld her, and he was amazed at her surpassing beauty, and at the tender grace of her virgin youth.

Then King Pelles and Sir Lavaine and the Fair Elaine came close to where Sir Launcelot lay upon his couch, and there they kneeled them down upon the ground. And King Pelles spake, saying: "Messire, what thanks shall we find fit to give to you who have freed this entire land from the dreadful curse that lay upon it?" "Lord," said Sir Launcelot, "thank not me but give your thanks to God whose tool and instrument I was in this undertaking." "Messire," quoth King Pelles, "I have not forgot to give thanks to God. Nevertheless seeing the instrument which He hath fitted to His hand is so perfect an instrument, one may praise that also. So we do praise you and give thanks from our heart to you for the deliverance which you have brought to us. Now I pray you tell me who you are who have brought this great succor to our state, for methinks you must be some famous hero, and I would fain thank you in your own name for what you have done to benefit us."

"Lord," said Sir Launcelot, "this you must forgive me if I tell you not my name. For there is supposed to be shame upon my name, wherefore I am now known as le Chevalier Malfait, because in the eyes of those to whom I am accountable I have done amiss."

"Well," quoth King Pelles, "I dare be sworn you have not at any time done greatly amiss in that which you have done. Nevertheless an you will have it so, so it shall be as you will, and with us all of this place you shall be known as le Chevalier Malfait until such time as it pleases you to assume your proper name and title."

Sir Launcelot lyeth sick in Corbin Thus I have told you all the circumstances of that famous adventure of the Worm of Corbin and there remaineth now only this to say: That Sir Launcelot did not recover from his hurt as soon as he had supposed he would. For the venom of the Dragon had got into his blood, wherefore even after a twelvemonth had gone by, he still remained in the castle of King Pelles at Corbin, albeit he was by that time quite healed in his body.

And also there is this to tell—that at the end of the twelvemonth aforesaid, King Pelles came to Sir Launcelot and said to him: "Messire, I would that you would henceforth dwell with us at this court.

For not only would you be a great credit to any court in which you live, but here we all love you as one loveth the apple of his eye."

"Lord," said Sir Launcelot, "ye cannot love me more than I love ye all who have been so good to me in the days of my sickness and disease. So I will be exceedingly rejoiced to remain with ye yet a while longer; for this is indeed a pleasant haven in which to rest in the long and toilsome journey of life, and I have nowhere else to go." *Sir Launcelot remaineth at Corbin*

Then King Pelles took Sir Launcelot into his arms and kissed him upon the brow and so they became plighted in friendship unto one another.

So Sir Launcelot remained at Corbin and went not any farther errant at that time.

But meantime, and for all that while, there was great wonder at the court of King Arthur whither Sir Launcelot had gone and what had become of him that no one in all of the world heard tell aught of him.

ir Launcelot confideth his Shield to Elaine the Fair :•

Chapter Third

*How King Arthur proclaimed a tournament at Astolat, and how
King Pelles of Corbin went with his court thither to that place.
Also how Sir Launcelot and Sir Lavaine had encounter with two
knights in the highway thitherward.*

NOW IT FELL upon a time that King Arthur proclaimed a King Arthur proclaimeth a tournament
great tournament to be held at Astolat, upon Lady's Day
Assumption. And the King sent word of this tournament
throughout all the land, both east and west and north and south. So
it came about that word of the tournament was brought one day by
herald to King Pelles at Corbin, and when this news came to him
he ordained that his court should make them ready to go to Astolat
to that passage of arms, in pursuance of the word that the herald of
King Arthur had brought to Corbin.

Then Sir Launcelot was much troubled in his mind for he said to Sir Launcelot is troubled
himself, "I fear me that if I go unto Astolat with this court there may
be some one there who will know me." For Sir Launcelot was still
very bitterly affronted at his kinsmen because that they had chid him
so greatly for the manner in which he had ridden in a cart upon that
adventure to rescue Queen Guinevere as aforetold of. For the pride of
Sir Launcelot was stiff and stubborn and he could not bring himself
to bend it or to break it. Neither could he bring himself to overlook
such an affront as that which he had suffered from the words that Sir
Lionel and Sir Ector de Marishad said to him. Wherefore, until full
justification had been rendered unto him, he was unwilling that any
of his former companions should behold him or know him who he
was.

Yet did he not see how he could refuse to obey the behest of
King Pelles, for as he was now become a knight of the court of the
King of Corbin he was bound to obey whatsoever that King should
command him to do. Wherefore he wist not what to do in this case, King Pelles talketh with Sir Launcelot
and so was much troubled in mind.

Now King Pelles was aware how it was with le Chevalier Malfait and that he was unwilling to go to the tournament at Astolat. So one day the King took Sir Launcelot aside and he said to him: "Messire, will you not also go with our court to this tournament that King Arthur hath proclaimed?"

To this Sir Launcelot said, "Lord, I would rather that I did not go."

King Pelles said: "Sir Knight, far be it from me to urge you to go if it be greatly against your wishes; yet you are to know that it will be a very sad thing for all of us if you do not go with us. For it is the truth that you are, beyond all others, the foremost of our court, and its most bright and shining light; wherefore it will be sad for us if we go thither without you."

Then Sir Launcelot looked very steadfastly at King Pelles and his heart went out toward the King and he said, "Do you then desire my company so very greatly?" King Pelles said, "Yea." "Well," said Sir Launcelot, "let it be so and I will go with you." And at that saying King Pelles was glad beyond measure.

So when the time came Sir Launcelot made him ready to go with the others to Astolat, and when the day of departure arrived he went with them.

King Pelles and his court journey to Astolat Thereafter they travelled by easy stages toward Astolat, and upon the third day after their departure from Corbin they came to the castle of a certain Earl, which castle stood about three leagues or a little more from the town. This Earl was a kinsman of King Pelles and in great amity with him, wherefore he was glad to have the King and his court to lodge with him at that time. And they of Corbin were also glad, for this was a very noble excellent place in which to lodge and all the other castles and inns nigh to Astolat were at that time very full of folk.

So it came about that King Pelles and his court remained several days at that place, and in all that time Sir Launcelot kept himself ever in retreat, lest some one with whom he was acquainted should chance to see him and know him who he was. To this end, and that he might *The Lady Elaine and Sir Launcelot talk together* conceal himself, Sir Launcelot was most often with the court of the Lady Elaine the Fair and not often with the court of the King.

Now the Lady Elaine was not very well pleased with this, for she held Sir Launcelot in great admiration above all other men, and she would fain have had him stand forth with the other knights who were there, so that his nobility might be manifested amongst them. So one day whilst they two sat together in the garden of the castle of that Earl (the court of the Lady Elaine and several lords of the King's court being near by playing at ball) the Lady Elaine spake her mind to Sir Launcelot upon this point saying: "Fair Sir, will you not take part in this noble and knightly tournament the day after to-morrow?"

To this Sir Launcelot replied, "Nay, Lady."

She said to him: "Why will you not so, Messire? Methinks with your prowess you might win yourself very great credit thereat."

Then for a little Sir Launcelot was silent, and after a little he said to her: "Lady, do you disremember that I call myself le Chevalier Malfait? That name I have assumed because my friends and my kinsmen deem that I have done amiss in a certain thing. Now, since they are of that opinion I am very greatly displeased with them, and would fain avoid them until I am justified in their sight. At this tournament there will be many of those who knew me aforetime and I would fain avoid them if I am able to do so. Wherefore it is that I am disinclined to take part in the battle which the King hath ordained."

After this they were silent for a little, and then by and by the Lady Elaine said: "Sir Knight Malfait, I would I knew who you really are and who are your fellows of whom you speak." At that Sir Launcelot smiled and said: "Lady, I may not tell you at this present who I am nor who they are, but only that they are very good worthy knights and gentlemen." "Aye," quoth the Lady Elaine, "that I may very well believe."

So at that time no more was said concerning this matter but ever the mind of the Lady Elaine rested upon that thing—to wit, that Sir Launcelot should take part in that tournament aforesaid. So at another time when they were alone together, she said: "Sir Knight Malfait, I would that thou wouldst do me a great favor." Sir Launcelot said: "Lady, ask whatsoever thou wilt, and if it is in my power to do that thing, and if it is according to the honor of my knighthood, then I shall assuredly do whatsoever thou dost ask of me."

"Sir," quoth the Lady Elaine, "this is what I would fain ask of thee if I might have it. It is that thou wouldst suffer me to purvey thee a suit of strange armor so that thy friends might not know thee therein, and that thou wouldst go to the tournament disguised in that wise. And I would that thou wouldst wear my favor at that tournament so that I might have glory in that battle because of thee."

Sir Launcelot will take part in the tournament Then Sir Launcelot sighed very deeply, and he looked steadfastly at the Lady Elaine, and he said: "Lady, you know not how great a thing it is you ask of my pride, for I would fain remain unknown as I am at this present. And you know not what it is you ask of my knighthood, for wit ye it must be against my one-time friends and companions-in-arms that you would have me contend. So it is that if I should have success in such an affair as this, whatsoever credit I should win therein shall bring discredit unto them. Moreover, I must tell you that never in all of my life have I worn the favor of any lady, having vowed my knighthood to one who is a queen and the wife of a king. Natheless, though all this is so, yet far be it from me to refuse a boon when it is you who ask it of me. For I speak the truth, Lady, when I say that I would freely lay down my life at your bidding. So in this case, maugre all that I have said, I will even do as you ask me, wherefore, if you will purvey me that armor of which you speak, I will do your will in all ways that I am able."

So spake Sir Launcelot, and thereat the Lady Elaine smiled upon him in such wise and with such great loving-kindness that it was as though both her joy and her great love stood revealed in the midst of that smile. Quoth she: "Assuredly I shall gain great honor and glory at thy hands. For I believe that thou art indeed one of the very greatest and foremost knights in all of the world, as well as the perfect peer of all noble gentlemen."

Now the Earl, the lord of that castle, had a son hight Sir Tyre, who was then lying abed, ill of a flux, and the armor of Sir Tyre was at that place. So the Lady Elaine went to the Earl and she besought him to lend her that armor for the use of Sir Launcelot, and the Earl listened to her and gave it to her.

So she had the armor of Sir Tyre brought to Sir Launcelot and thus the Lady Elaine purveyed him in all wise for that tournament so that no one might know him who he was.

Then, after all this had been accomplished, the Lady Elaine came *The Lady*
to the chamber where Sir Launcelot was, and her brother Sir Lavaine *Elaine giveth*
was with her. And the Lady bore in her hand a sleeve of flame- *her sleeve to*
colored satin very richly bedight with many pearls of great price. *Sir Launcelot*
And she said to Sir Launcelot: "I beseech you to take this sleeve, Sir
Knight, and I beseech you that you wear it as a favor for my sake."

Then Sir Launcelot smiled very kindly upon the Lady Elaine and
he said, "Will this give you pleasure?" and she said, "Yea." Then Sir
Launcelot smiled again and he said, "It shall be in all things as you
will have it." So he took the sleeve, and he wound it about the crest of
the helmet he was to wear at the tournament, and the sleeve formed
a wreath of satin about the helmet like to a wreath of fire. And the
pearls upon the wreath were like to drops of dew as you behold them
of an early morning. Wherefore because of the brightness of that
wreath and because of the pearls upon it, the favor of the Lady Elaine
was of such a sort that all the world could not but see it what it was.
And so Sir Launcelot accepted the favor of the Lady Elaine the Fair.

Then after Sir Launcelot had thus accepted that favor, Sir Lavaine
spake and said: "Sir Knight Malfait, I beseech you that you will take
me with you unto this tournament as your knight-companion. For I
believe that in your company I shall assuredly gain me great honor
and much glory and renown, wherefore I ask of you that you will
grant me this great courtesy."

Then Sir Launcelot looked upon Sir Lavaine and smiled upon *Sir Launcelot*
him and loved him exceedingly, and he said to Sir Lavaine: "Friend, *accepteth Sir*
I will gladly accept thee as my companion-in-arms, and I believe in *Lavaine as his*
very sooth that it would be hard for me to find any one whom I *companion*
would be better pleased to have with me at such a time." And so it
was that Sir Lavaine also had his will with Sir Launcelot.

Then Sir Launcelot turned him to the Lady Elaine and said,
"Lady, see you this shield and this armor of mine?" And she said,
"Yea, I see them."

Sir Launcelot said: "Lady, this shield is a very precious thing to
me, for it and all mine armor was given to me by a very wonderful
lady who is not of this world in which we mortals dwell. Since that
time she gave mine armor to me I have sought ever and in all wise
to use those defences as became a gentleman so that whatever mark

of battle there should be upon them there should be no mark of dishonor to mar their brightness. Now I beseech you for to take this shield and that armor to your maiden bower and to hold them there in trust for me and that as sacredly as though they were your very life." Therewith Sir Launcelot gave the Lady Elaine his shield and he said: "I charge you, Lady, for to let no one touch this shield or to meddle with it until I return hither to reclaim it and mine armor of you." And the Lady Elaine said: "It shall be as you say, and I shall hold this shield and this armor as sacred as my life."

Sir Launcelot and Sir Lavaine depart for Astolat So these matters were all brought to settlement and the next day Sir Launcelot in the armor of Sir Tyre, and Sir Lavaine in his own armor, rode out from the castle of that Earl and away from that place and so betook their way toward Astolat.

Now it chanced that same day that two very worthy knights of King Arthur's court were upon that road on which Sir Launcelot and Sir Lavaine travelled to Astolat, and these two knights were Sir Gawaine and Sir Mador de la Porte. With these were several lords who paid homage and respect to them, and all that party stood beneath the shade of several trees nigh to a water-mill where it was very cool and pleasant. And some of those who were there sat upon their horses, and some had dismounted therefrom and were lying in the cool and pleasant grass beneath the shade.

Then Sir Gawaine perceived where Sir Launcelot and Sir Lavaine came riding and he said to those who were with him: "Behold yonder two knights coming hitherward. Now I am of a mind that Sir Mador de la Porte and I shall try a fall with them, so stand ye by and see what happeneth."

Sir Gawaine and Sir Mador bespeak Sir Launcelot and Sir Lavaine So Sir Gawaine and Sir Mador took horse and rode a little forward and met the two and saluted them very courteously, and Sir Launcelot and Sir Lavaine saluted those others in like manner. Then Sir Gawaine said: "Messires, I pray ye tell me who ye are and whither ye go upon this pass."

Now Sir Launcelot knew very well who those two knights were because of the devices upon their shields. Wherefore he changed his voice a little when he answered Sir Gawaine so that Sir Gawaine should not know him. And he said: "Messire, I know not by what right ye demand such knowledge of us, nevertheless I may tell you that I am called le Chevalier Malfait, and this, my comrade, is hight Sir Lavaine of Corbin. As for our journey and its purpose, I may furthermore tell you that we intend, God willing, to enter the tournament at Astolat to-morrow, in which friendly battle you also, doubtless, intend to take a part."

Then Sir Gawaine said: "Tell me, Sir Knight Malfait, will you and your companion try a fall with me and my companions-in-arms?"

Now Sir Launcelot had no very great relish for such an encounter as that for he feared by some hap he should betray himself who he was. Yet he wist that he must accept the challenge of Sir Gawaine, wherefore after a little while of silence he said: "Sir Knight, we two would fain go our way in peace, but an it cannot be otherwise we must needs accept your challenge. But will you not let be and suffer us to pass onward?"

"Well," said Sir Gawaine, "this is a strange thing that you should pretend to aspire to that tournament of to-morrow and yet have no heart to meet in friendly tilt two knights whom you encounter upon the way."

"Sir," quoth Sir Launcelot, "we fear you not in any wise, wherefore, make yourselves ready in God's name, and we upon our side will do our endeavor."

So Sir Gawaine and Sir Mador de la Porte made themselves ready *The four* as Sir Launcelot had advised, and when they were in all ways pre- *knights run a* pared they withdrew to a little distance so as to have a good course *tilt* to run. Then when all were ready for that encounter, each knight *Sir Gawaine* shouted and set spurs to his horse, and all four thundered together *is overthrown* with such violence that the ground trembled beneath them. So they met in the middle of the course and so furious was the meeting of those four good knights that you might have heard the roar of that encounter for half a mile away or more. In that encounter both Sir Lavaine and Sir Mador broke each his spear upon his enemy and neither of them suffered a fall. But Sir Gawaine had no such fortune for his spear broke into splinters unto the very truncheon thereof, and the spear of Sir Launcelot held, so that Sir Gawaine was lifted out from his saddle and flung upon the ground with such violence that he rolled thrice or four times over and over before he ceased to fall.

Now those who looked upon that encounter were well assured that Sir Gawaine would easily overthrow his opponent into the dust, for Sir Gawaine was held to be one of the very greatest knights in all of the world. Wherefore it was that when they beheld how violently he had been flung to earth by that unknown knight against whom he had tilted, they were astonished beyond all bounds of wonderment.

But Sir Mador de la Porte, when he beheld how Sir Gawaine lay there in the dust as though dead, voided his horse and ran to the fallen knight where he lay. And he raised the umbril of Sir Gawaine's helmet, and lo! the face of Sir Gawaine was like to the face of one who was dead. And at first Sir Mador thought that he was dead, but after a while Sir Gawaine sighed and then sighed again, and thereupon Sir Mador knew that he was not dead, but in a swoon from the violence of the fall. And Sir Mador rejoiced very greatly that no more ill had come of that encounter.

Then Sir Mador turned to Sir Launcelot, and cried out: "Sir Knight Malfait, go thy way in the fiend's name. For indeed thou art well named Malfait, seeing what an evil thing it is that thou hast done to this worshipful knight. For wit you that this is none other than Sir Gawaine, the nephew of King Arthur himself, whom you have overthrown; and had you slain him, as at first I believed you had, it would have been a very ill thing for you. Moreover, you are to know that this knight was to have been the leader of all those upon King Arthur's side in the battle to-morrow-day, but now God knows if he will be able to wear armor again for many days to come. Wherefore go thy way and trouble us no more."

Quoth Sir Launcelot: "Well, Sir Knight, this quarrel was altogether of your own seeking, and not of ours. Wherefore, if ill hath befallen this worshipful knight, it is of his own devising and not of mine."

But Sir Mador only cried out the more vehemently: "Go your way! Go your way, and leave us in peace!" And thereupon Sir Launcelot and Sir Lavaine drew their bridle reins and set heel to horse and rode away from that place, leaving Sir Mador and those others who were there to cherish Sir Gawaine and to revive him from his swoon as best they might.

Sir Bernard of Astolat followeth Sir Launcelot and Sir Lavaine

Now there was among those knights who were with Sir Gawaine

and Sir Mador a certain old and very worthy knight of Astolat, hight Sir Bernard, surnamed of Astolat. Seeing Sir Launcelot and Sir Lavaine departing in that wise, Sir Bernard hied him after them and when he had come up with them he saluted them, and said, "Messires, I pray ye tell me where it is ye lodge this night."

Sir Launcelot said: "Fair Sir, we know not where we lodge for we go to seek such lodging as we may find in Astolat."

Sir Bernard said: "You will find no lodging in Astolat this night, for all places are full. Now I pray ye that you will lodge with me, for I have a very good and comely house and I shall be greatly honored for to have you lodge with me. For I make my vow, Sir Knight Malfait, that never saw I such a buffet as that which you gave to Sir Gawaine anon. Nor do I believe that ever Sir Launcelot of the Lake himself could have done more doughtily than you did in that encounter. Wherefore, I think that you will win you great glory tomorrow-day, and that I shall have due worship if so be that ye two shall have lodged with me over this night."

Then Sir Launcelot laughed, and he said to Sir Bernard: "Well, Sir Knight, I give you gramercy for your courtesy, and so we will gladly take up our inn with you until the time of the tournament. Only this I demand, that we shall be privily lodged apart from any one else, for we wish it that we shall not be known until to-morrow and after this tournament shall have transpired."

"Messire," quoth Sir Bernard, "it shall all be as you desire."

So those three rode on their way together until they had come to Astolat and to the habitation of Sir Bernard of Astolat.

Now the habitation of Sir Bernard was a very fair house over *Sir Launcelot* against the castle of Astolat where King Arthur and his court had *lodgeth with* taken up their inn. And there was a high terraced garden belonging *Sir Bernard* to the castle of Astolat, and the garden overlooked the garden of *King Arthur* the house of Sir Bernard. That day it chanced that King Arthur was *knoweth Sir* walking back and forth in that terraced garden where the air blew *Launcelot* cool over the plats of flowers and grass. As the King so walked he chanced to look down over the edge of the terrace into the garden of Sir Bernard's house, and at that time Sir Launcelot was walking privily in the garden for to refresh himself, and no one was with him. At that time Sir Launcelot had laid aside his armor for the sake of coolness and was walking in light raiment and bareheaded to the air, wherefore it befell that King Arthur immediately knew him who he was.

Then the King was much astonished to see Sir Launcelot in that place, and he said to himself, "What does Sir Launcelot here?" And at first the King was of a mind to send word to Sir Launcelot, bidding him to come to where he was. But afterward he bethought him that mayhap Sir Launcelot would be displeased at being thus summoned to declare himself. For the King perceived that Sir Launcelot did not choose to be known to any one at that time. So King Arthur said to himself: "Well, let be! To-morrow, I dare say, Sir Launcelot will declare himself in such a wise as shall astonish a great many knights who shall do battle against him upon yonder meadow-of-battle. Wherefore, let him e'en declare himself in his own fashion."

Thus it was that King Arthur communed within himself. Wherefore he did not betray the presence of Sir Launcelot to anybody at that time, but kept that matter shut in his own bosom.

Nevertheless, when he had come again to where was his court, he said to the knights there assembled: "Messires, I have this day beheld a certain knight who hath come hither who will I believe play his play with the best of you all at the jousts to-morrow." The knights who were there said to the King: "We pray you, Lord, tell us who that knight is, so that we may pay him such regard as he is worthy of." "Nay," quoth King Arthur, "I will not tell you at this time who is that knight, but haply you will know to-morrow who he is."

Then one of the knights who was there said: "Mayhap that was the knight who overthrew Sir Gawaine this day in the highroad over against the town a little distance away. He calleth himself le Chevalier Malfait, and hath for his companion a youthful knight hight Sir Lavaine, the King's son of Corbin."

Then King Arthur laughed, and said, "Like enough that was he." And so the King departed into his lodging, leaving all those knights much wondering who that knight could be of whom the King spoke to them.

✢   ✢   ✢

Thus it was that Sir Launcelot and Sir Lavaine came to Astolat, and now followeth the history of that famous bout at arms so far as it affected Sir Launcelot of the Lake and his companion-at-arms, Sir Lavaine of Corbin. For in that affair at arms, as you shall presently hear tell, Sir Lavaine gained him such great glory and renown that thereafter he was regarded as one of the great heroes of chivalry, and by and by received that crowning honor of becoming a knight-companion of the Round Table.

ir Launcelot and Sir Lavaine overlook the Field of Astolat:

Chapter Fourth

How Sir Launcelot and Sir Lavaine fought in the tournament at Astolat. How Sir Launcelot was wounded in that affair, and how Sir Lavaine brought him unto a place of safety.

O IT IS true that in these days one may not hope ever to be- *Of the lists at* hold a sight like to the field-of-battle at Astolat upon Lady's *Astolat* Day Assumption, when that tournament proclaimed by King Arthur was about to be fought before the eyes of the King. For upon that morning—which was wonderfully bright and clear and warm—the entire green meadow was altogether covered over with a moving throng of people of all degrees—lords and ladies, knights and dames, esquires, burghers, yeomen and tradesfolk—all moving, each toward some stand from whence he might view the battle that was about to take place. And here were gay attires and bright colors and the fluttering of silk and the flash and sparkle of shining baubles, and because of the sheen and sparkle of all these the whole world appeared to be quick with life and motion.

Yet ever by little and little this confusion of many people pushing themselves hither and thither resolved itself to order as one by one that multitude took seat and brought itself to quietness. And so it came to pass at last that the field prepared for battle was cleared of all save a few who lingered and whom the guardians of the lists pushed back into their places.

Then, all being thus brought to order, the Marshal of the Tour- *The knights-* ney blew his trumpet, and straightway there entered upon this side *contestant enter the* of that wide meadow and upon that side thereof the two companies *field-of-battle* of knights who were to contend the one against the other.

Then, lo! how the sunlight flashed upon shining armor! How it catched the pens and bannerets so that they twinkled at tips of lances like to sparks of fire! How war-horses neighed for love of battle! How armor clashed and shield plates rang as those goodly companies of knights brought themselves by degrees into array for battle!

Upon the one end of the meadow there gathered the knights-champion who were of the party of King Arthur, and the chiefs of that party were the King of Scots and the King of Ireland, and with them were many knights of the Round Table, much renowned both in song and battle. And the number of knights of that company were two hundred and ten in all.

Of the two parties-contestant Upon the other end of the meadow of battle there assembled the party of those who were to withstand the party of King Arthur; and the chiefs of that company were the King of North Wales and the King of an Hundred Knights, and the King of Northumberland and Galahaut the High Prince. And though there were no knights of the Round Table in that company, yet there were many champions of very great renown and high credit in courts of chivalry. And the number of that party were two hundred thirty and two.

Sir Launcelot and Sir Lavaine overlook the field of Astolat Now near to a certain part of the field-of-battle the trees of the forest came down close to the meadow, and made, as it were, a green wall of foliage circumjacent to that part of the field. Here, beneath the shade of the green trees of the forest where it was cool and shady and very still, Sir Launcelot and Sir Lavaine had taken stand at a certain place whence they could look out upon those two parties of knights there gathered in battle array. And, that while, the eyes of Sir Lavaine shone like sparks of light and his cheeks were flaming red, like as though they were on fire, and his breath was thick and stifled when he breathed it. For this was the first great battle in which he had ever taken a part and he wist not what was to befall him in that affair at arms.

But that same while Sir Launcelot neither moved nor spake but sat his horse like to a statue made of iron; calm and steadfast and gazing very steadily out upon that plain before him.

Then Sir Lavaine spake in a voice wonderfully high and clear. "Messire," said he, "upon what side do you will that we take part in this battle?"

Quoth Sir Launcelot: "To neither party do I yet will that we shall join us. Rather let us wait a while and observe the issue of this battle, and when we behold that one side is about to lose in the battle then will we join with that side. For if so be we aid to bring victory out of defeat for that party, then shall our credit and our glory be magnified in that same degree." And Sir Lavaine said, "Sir, thou speakest with great wisdom."

Then, as those two watched in that wise, they beheld that three knights-champion came forth from one side and that three champions came forth from the other side and they wist that these six champions were to engage man to man and so to test the strength of this side and of that ere the two arrays should join in battle-royal. And Sir Launcelot knew these six champions very well and he declared to Sir Lavaine who they were. To wit, he declared that the champions upon King Arthur's side were the King of Scots and the King of Ireland and Sir Palamydes, and that the knights of the other party were the King of Northumberland, and the King of an Hundred Knights, and Galahaut the High Prince.

Then, even as Sir Launcelot was telling Sir Lavaine who were *How the* these six champions who thus stood forth to undertake battle against *battle openeth* one another, the herald blew his trumpet very loud and shrill. And therewith, in an instant of time, each knight had set spurs to his horse, and each horse leaped forward from his station and rushed forward, and so they came, three knights against three, like to thunderbolts launched against one another. So they met together in the midst of the course with a crash of splintering wood and a roar of armor that might easily have been heard a mile away. In that meeting Sir Palamydes and Sir Galahaut the High Prince smote down one another into the dust. And the King of an Hundred Knights smote down King Angus of Ireland with such terrible violence that he lay like dead upon the ground and had to be borne away out of the field by his esquires and could not again do battle that day. As to the King of Northumberland and the King of Scots, they broke each his lance upon the other without suffering a fall. So that first encounter was somewhat to the advantage of the party against King Arthur.

Then all who beheld that noble encounter of knight against *Of the grand* knight shouted aloud in acclaim, and the shout of that vast acclaim *assault at* was like the multitudinous roaring of a strong wind in the forest. *arms* Thereupon in the midst of all that roaring the herald blew his trump again and therewith the two parties contestant rushed the one upon the other, the earth shaking and trembling beneath that charge like to an earthquake. So in another moment they met together in such an uproar of iron and cracking of splintered wood that the ears of those who heard that meeting were stunned with the crash thereof. Then all the air was full of dust and splinters of wood and scraps and shreds of silk and of plumes. Anon, out of a thick red cloud of dust there arose the roar of a mighty battle; the shouts of men, the neighing of horses, the crash of blows and the groans of those who fell. At times, some knight would come forth out of the press reeling in the saddle and all red from some wound he had got. At other times, a party of esquires would run into that cloud, presently to come forth again bearing with them a wounded knight whom they had rescued. At other parts of the field there were knights armed with spears who ran tilt against one another, and ever and anon a knight would be flung from the saddle or else horse and knight would roll together upon the earth all in a smother of dust.

So for a while the battle was toward and yet no one could see how it went. For what with all that dust and the contending of single champions, no one could tell whether it inclined to this side or to that.

But after a while the dust lifted a little, and those who contended became fewer upon one side than upon the other and so stinted the fierceness of their battle.

Then it was that those who looked down upon that battle beheld that the party of King Arthur was pushing their opponents back, little by little, toward the barriers upon their side of the field (and if so be they were pushed altogether against that barrier then was their battle lost for good).

Then Sir Launcelot said to Sir Lavaine: "Behold yonder company of noble knights, how that they hold together and stand against their enemies in spite of that defeat which must certainly fall upon them in the end."

"I see it," said Sir Lavaine, "and have great pity for them."

"Hast thou so?" said Sir Launcelot. "Then let us take side with that side which is so sore bestead, for I believe that if you will help me a little we may well aid them and maybe stay the ill-fortune that seems like to overwhelm them."

"Sir," quoth Sir Lavaine, "spare not, and I upon my side will do the best that I am able for to help you."

So with that Sir Launcelot and Sir Lavaine rode out from the forest wherein they had sheltered themselves, and they set their spears in rest and they drove forward to where those knights were doing combat. And they drove faster and faster forward until they drove full tilt into the thickest of the press.Sir Launcelot and Sir Lavaine take part in the battle

The history of these things saith that in this charge and in other charges that he made in that onset, Sir Launcelot smote down Sir Brandiles, and Sir Sagramore, and Sir Dodinas, and Sir Kay, and Sir Griflet, and the history saith that he smote down all those good knights of the Round Table with one spear ere that spear burst asunder. And the same history saith that Sir Lavaine smote down Sir Lucian the botteler and Sir Bedivere with one spear in that charge and that then that spear also was burst into pieces. And the history saith that Sir Launcelot got him another spear and that Sir Lavaine did likewise and that thereafter they two charged again as they had done before. And it saith that in this second assault Sir Launcelot smote down Sir Agravaine, and Sir Gaheris and Sir Modred and Sir Melyot of Logres, and that Sir Lavaine smote down Sir Hozanna le Cure Hardy, and that after that those second spears were burst in assault as the first had been.

Then Sir Lavaine withdrew a little to get another spear, but by that time the madness of battle was upon Sir Launcelot so that he drew his sword and he ran into the thickest of the press and smote upon the right hand and the left hand with all his might and main so that in a wonderfully short pass he had smitten down Sir Safir and Sir Epynogris and Sir Galleron. And so terrible were the buffets he gave that all who were nigh to him drew away from him from fear of the terrible blows which he bestowed upon whomsoever came within his reach.

By now all who looked upon that field were aware of how terrible a battle it was that the knight of the red sleeve fought against his enemies, wherefore they shouted aloud with a great voice of outcry and loud acclaim. And the Lady Elaine the Fair beheld how her champion did battle, and seeing him she could not contain the passion of her joy, but laughed and wept and trembled for that joy. And she catched King Pelles ever by the arm and cried out to him, "Lord! Lord! see what our champion doeth and what my brother doeth!"The Lady Elaine taketh joy in the battle and King Pelles said, "I see! I see!" and held tight hold of the rail of the dais before him.

Then King Arthur where he sat said to those about him: "Behold yonder champion, what battle it is he doeth. Saw ye ever a better battle than that?" And they say, "Nay, never so great a battle!"

But when Sir Gawaine beheld the flame-colored sleeve that the champion wore about his helmet, he said to King Arthur, "Yonder knight is he who cast me down yesterday into the dust of the highway over against the town," and Sir Gawaine said, "because of that and because of the battle he now doeth, I would deem yonder knight to be none other than Sir Launcelot of the Lake. And yet it cannot be Sir Launcelot, for this knight weareth the sleeve of some lady as a favor upon his helmet, and all the world knoweth that Sir Launcelot would never wear the favor of any lady in such a wise as that."

Of the pause in battle Meantime the battle was stayed for a little while, for at that time it seemed as though neither horse nor man could do any more for that while. Yet though the battle was stayed, nevertheless each knight braced himself for a greater battle than that which had gone before. For all knew that now indeed the time had come when either one party or the other must win that battle. So in that pause of battle Sir Launcelot and Sir Lavaine each chose him a good strong new spear of ash wood, and each drank a cup of lusty spiced wine for to refresh his strength.

And, ere they began to battle afresh, Sir Bors de Ganis and Sir Ector de Maris and Sir Lionel upon the other side called together such kindred of their blood as were upon that field: to wit, Sir Blamor de Ganis, Sir Bleoberis and Sir Aliduke, Sir Galihadan, and Sir Bellanger—all these knights being of Sir Launcelot's kin. These say to one another: "If we do not overthrow yonder single knight who fights so wonderfully against us we shall certes lose this battle. For never knight fought so unless it was Sir Launcelot. For lo! he himself is the single bulwark against us in this battle."

His kinsmen take battle against Sir Launcelot So it was that these kinsmen of Sir Launcelot ordained it that they should join themselves together for to overthrow that knight by main strength if need be.

Sir Launcelot is wounded Then anon the battle was called again and anon each side hurled itself against the other side, well knowing that at this time it must be else to conquer or else to lose. And in that charge the kinsmen of Sir Launcelot hurled themselves against that knight of the red sleeve and against those who were by him. And Sir Bors and Sir Ector and Sir Lionel drave three at once at Sir Launcelot and he drave against them—one against three. But so heavy was the might of the assault of those three, that they overthrew the horse of Sir Launcelot by the weight of their three horses so that the horse of Sir Launcelot and Sir Launcelot himself were cast down upon the earth beneath the feet of the horses of those who charged against him. And in that charge the spear of Sir Bors smote Sir Launcelot in the side, and the point of the spear burst through the armor of Sir Launcelot and pierced deep into his side. Therewith the head of the spear brake from the truncheon and remained thrust deep into the side of Sir Launcelot, and Sir Launcelot groaned aloud, deeming that he had got his death wound.

So Sir Launcelot lay upon the ground and could not rise and he would maybe have been beaten to death beneath the feet of the horses. But Sir Lavaine beheld how it was with him, whereat he shouted aloud with a great voice and he and all that party rushed to the aid of Sir Launcelot. And Sir Lavaine smote down the King of Scots at one blow from out of his saddle. And he turned the horse of the King of Scots to where Sir Launcelot lay. And he stood above Sir Launcelot and defended him against the assault of all those others who were around about, and so, maugre their vehement assaults, he brought Sir Launcelot to horse again.

Then Sir Launcelot was clean wode because of the passion of agony he suffered from that grievous wound he had got. Wherefore he drew his sword and he stood up in his stirrups and he smote right and left like a madman. And he smote down one after the other Sir Lionel and Sir Bors de Ganis, and he smote Sir Bleoberis such a buffet that he fell down to the earth in a swoon as if he had been dead. And in that time Sir Lavaine smote down Sir Bellanger, and two other knights of worship and renown. Then Sir Launcelot turned him about and smote Sir Blamor down from off his horse and with that Sir Ector made at him. But Sir Launcelot was blind with his passion of battle and of pain, and he wist not who that was who came against him. Wherefore he turned upon Sir Ector and he smote him so dreadful terrible a buffet, that the head of Sir Ector hung down low upon the neck of his horse. Then Sir Launcelot catched Sir Ector and rushed off the helm from the head of Sir Ector with intent to slay him, for at that time he was so mad that he wist not where he was or what he did.

Sir Launcelot spareth Sir Ector Then he beheld the face of his brother Sir Ector, and he beheld that face all white and wan from the blow he himself had struck, and he beheld his brother's cheeks all white and streaked with blood, and therewith his senses returned to him, and in that instant he wist where he was and what he did. Thereupon he cried out in a great and terrible voice: "Woe! Woe! Woe is me! what is it that I do!" And therewith he rushed away from that place where Sir Ector was, and he rushed into the thickest of the press, striking right and left like a madman in fury.

And it stands recorded that all in all in that battle Sir Launcelot struck down thirty knights with his own hand, and that sixteen of those thirty were knights of the Round Table. And it is recorded that Sir Lavaine struck down fourteen knights and that six of those knights were knights of the Round Table. And it was because of Sir Launcelot and Sir Lavaine that their party prevailed in that battle. For, because beholding how they fought, their party took great heart and added strength to strength and so drave their enemies back across the meadow-of-battle until they were pushed back against the barriers of their side of the meadow and so the battle was won.

And thus that was achieved that else had been lost had not Sir Launcelot and Sir Lavaine lent their aid to that party with whom they joined in battle against the party of King Arthur.

But Sir Launcelot sat wounded nigh to death. Yea, he deemed that the sickness and the sweat of death was even then upon him, for an exceeding faintness overclouded his spirit. To him where he sat came the King of North Wales and the King of Northumberland and the King of an Hundred Knights and these say to him: "Sir, may God bless you, for without your aid, and that of your companion this day had certes been lost to us." And then they said: "Now we pray you that you will come with us to King Arthur so that you may receive at his hands the prize you have so worshipfully deserved." Thus they spake very cheerfully, for not one of those worthies knew that Sir Launcelot had been so sorely wounded in the battle he had fought.

Then Sir Launcelot spake in a very weak voice, so that it sounded like to one speaking from a very great distance away. And he said: *Sir Launcelot would fain depart* "Fair lords, if I have won credit in this I have paid a fair price for it, for I am sore hurt and wist not what to do. Now this I pray of you that you will suffer me to depart from this place, for I am in great pain and would fain go away from here to somewhere I may have aid and comforts."

Then those three kings would have had him go to a fair pavilion for to have his wound searched and dressed, but ever he besought them to suffer him to depart. So they suffered him, and he rode very slowly away from that place, and Sir Lavaine rode with him.

So it was that Sir Launcelot and Sir Lavaine did battle at that famous tournament at Astolat as I have told you.

And now if you would know how it fared with Sir Launcelot after he rode away from that place, wounded as aforesaid, you shall immediately hear of it in that which followeth.

ir Gawaine knoweth the shield of Sir Launcelot

Chapter Fifth

How Sir Launcelot escaped wounded into the forest, and how Sir Gawaine discovered to the court of King Pelles who was le Chevalier Malfait.

O SIR LAUNCELOT and Sir Lavaine rode away from that field of battle. And they rode together into the forest, and all that while Sir Launcelot contained his suffering to himself so that Sir Lavaine wist not how grievous was his wound nor how great was the passion of agony that he then endured because of that hurt. But after they had ridden a mile or two or three into the woodland, Sir Launcelot could no longer thus contain himself, wherefore he let droop his head very low and he groaned with great dolor. Then Sir Lavaine was aware that some grievous hurt must have befallen Sir Launcelot. Wherefore he cried out: "Messire, I fear me ye are sore hurt. Now tell me, I beseech you, how is it with you?"

Then Sir Launcelot groaned again and he said: "Woe is me! I suffer much pain." And therewith he made to dismount from his horse and would have fallen had not Sir Lavaine catched him and upheld him. After that Sir Lavaine aided Sir Launcelot down from his horse, and Sir Launcelot leaned against a tree of the forest, groaning as from the bottom of his soul, and Sir Lavaine wist not what to do to help him. Then Sir Launcelot turned his eyes, all faint and dim, upon Sir Lavaine, and he said: "Oh, gentle knight, Sir Lavaine, for the mercy of God I beseech you to pluck forth the blade of a spear that has pierced into my side, for I suffer a great pang of torment."

Sir Launcelot declareth his wound

Then Sir Lavaine was aware of what sort was that wound and he made haste to strip off the body armor from Sir Launcelot. So, when that body armor was thus removed, Sir Lavaine beheld a grievous wound where the blade of the spear had pierced deep into the side of Sir Launcelot a little above the midriff. And Sir Lavaine perceived that the blade of the spear was yet in the wound and that the hurt was very deep. So beholding that wound Sir Lavaine wept, and cried

159

out: "Dear my Lord! Woe is me! I dare not pull out that blade; for an I do so, I dread me sore that you will die here in the forest ere aid can be brought to you and so it shall be I who killed you."

"No matter," said Sir Launcelot, speaking very faint and with failing breath. "Do as I bid you, for the point of that blade lieth near to my heart and I suffer a great deal of pain from it."

Sir Lavaine draweth for the steel Then Sir Lavaine laid hold of the shaft of the spear, and he strove to draw forth the blade from out Sir Launcelot's side, yet he could not do so. And thereupon Sir Launcelot cried aloud in a very piercing voice, "Spare not! Spare not! but pull forth that steel!" So with that Sir Lavaine plucked again with all his might and he drew the steel forth from out of the wound. And as the blade came forth from out of the flesh, Sir Launcelot cried out again in a voice very loud and shrill, saying, "God! God! that this should be!" And with that a great issue of blood gushed out of the wound like a crimson fountain and Sir Launcelot sank down upon the ground in a swoon that was like the swoon of death.

Then Sir Lavaine believed that he had assuredly slain Sir Launcelot, wherefore he wept aloud with a great passion of grief, smiting his hands together and crying, "Woe is me! For I have slain my dear lord!" Thereupon he kneeled down beside Sir Launcelot and fell to feeling his heart. And he perceived that the heart still beat but very faintly, and so he wist that Sir Launcelot was not dead but only in a deadly swoon.

So Sir Lavaine turned Sir Launcelot where that the wind blew upon him and after a while Sir Launcelot opened his eyes again. Then with his sight all swimming he beheld Sir Lavaine kneeling beside him weeping, and he said, speaking in a voice very weak and faint, "Lavaine, am I yet alive?" And Sir Lavaine said, "Yea, Lord." Sir Launcelot said, "Then bear me away from this place." And Sir Lavaine said, "Whither shall I take you?" Sir Launcelot said: "Listen, Friend, bear me away into the forest to the westward of here. For after a while to the westward of this place you shall find a forest path that runs across your way. And you shall take that path toward the right hand and so you will come after another while to the hut of an hermit of the forest. Bring me to that holy man; for if any one can cure me of this hurt he alone can do so." Sir Lavaine said: "Lord, how shall I take you such a journey as that, so that you shall not die?" Sir Launcelot replied: "I know not how you shall take me, but this I know: that if you take me not to that place I shall certes die here before your eyes in this forest."

So Sir Lavaine, weeping, made a litter of straight young trees and he laid his cloak upon the litter and he bound the litter to the horses. *Sir Lavaine beareth Sir Launcelot thence* Then he lifted Sir Launcelot and laid him upon the litter as though it were a little child whom he laid there. Thereafter he took the foremost horse by the bridle, and so, led away into the forest whither Sir Launcelot had bidden him to go.

So in that wise they travelled in the forest for a great while and by and by night descended and the full moon arose all white and shining into the sky. And it rose ever higher and higher and it shone down upon the forest woodlands so that here it was all bright and there it was all agloom with shadow; and anon Sir Lavaine, as he led the horses in that wise, would walk in that silver silent light and anon he would be lost in those shadows. And all that while Sir Launcelot lay so still that several times Sir Lavaine thought haply he was dead. Then he would say, "Sir, art thou dead?" And ever Sir Launcelot would answer, "Not yet."

Thus they travelled for a great while in that still forest (all so silent and wonderful) and beneath the clear pale moonlight that caused everything to appear like to an enchantment of stillness. So, somewhat after the middle watch of the night, Sir Lavaine beheld before him a little chapel built up against the rocks of a cliff of stone and beneath the black and umbrageous foliage of a large oak tree. And the moonlight shone down past the oak tree and bathed all the front of that little chapel with pure white silvery light, so still and silent that the chapel appeared as in a strange and singular picture as it were seen in a dream.

Thither Sir Lavaine led the horses bearing between them the *They come to the forest chapel* wounded knight, whose face, as white as the moon above, was turned upward against the sky. And when Sir Lavaine had come to the door of the chapel he smote upon it with the butt of his lance; and he smote again, and therewith the door was opened and there appeared in the doorway the figure of an aged man with a long white beard like to snow for whiteness. And that man was the hermit of the forest afore spoken of several times in these histories.

Then when that reverend hermit beheld where Sir Launcelot lay in the litter, so sorely wounded, he came to him and felt of his heart. So, perceiving him to be alive, he aided Sir Lavaine to lift the wounded man from the litter and to bear him into the hut and to lay him upon a soft and fragrant couch of leaves and moss.

At that time Sir Launcelot was in a deep swoon like as though he were dead; yet he was not dead, for after the hermit had bathed his face with strong wine, and after he had set pungent herbs to his nostrils, by and by Sir Launcelot revived so as to sigh very deep and to open his eyes. And Sir Launcelot said, "Where am I? Am I still alive?" The hermit said, "Yea, Messire." Sir Launcelot said, "I wist that maybe I was dead."

Then the hermit searched Sir Launcelot's wound and bathed it and put unguents upon it and bound it about with bandages of linen and so Sir Launcelot was put at ease. And after that Sir Launcelot fell into a deep sleep so still and profound that it was like to the slumber of a little child.

✛   ✛   ✛

Now whilst Sir Launcelot thus slept, Sir Lavaine and the hermit walked in the moonlight upon a little lawn of grass before the door of the hermitage. By and by the hermit said to Sir Lavaine: "Sir Knight, know you who yonder knight is whom you brought hither to-night?" and Sir Lavaine said, "Nay, I know not, save that he calleth himself le Chevalier Malfait."

The hermit declareth Sir Launcelot's name "Well," quoth the hermit, "God knows that all we who live upon His earth may easily do ill in His sight; yet I dare to say that that yonder knight hath done as little ill as any of us. Sir, you must know that he is none other than Sir Launcelot of the Lake."

At this Sir Lavaine cried out aloud in great wonder, saying: "What is it that you tell me! Lo! This knight hath dwelt at the court of my father, King Pelles of Corbin, for more than a year yet no one there wist that it was Sir Launcelot of the Lake whom we entertained in our midst."

"And yet," quoth the hermit, "that wounded man is none other than he."

✠　　✠　　✠

Now that same night whilst Sir Launcelot lay thus wounded in the *King Arthur* hermit's cell in the forest, a great feast was held at Astolat in the *sits at feast* presence of King Arthur. There were set fourteen tables in the great hall of the castle of Astolat, and at those tables there sat down seven hundred in all of the lords and knights and ladies of that land—kings, earls, dukes, barons, knights, and esquires with their dames—fifty at each table.

Then King Arthur looked all about but he beheld no sign of Sir Launcelot, wherefore he said to the King of North Wales who sat nigh to him: "Where is that worthy knight who was with you to-day—he who wore about his helmet a flame-colored sleeve embroidered with fair pearls of price?" To this the King of North Wales replied: "Lord, we know not where that worshipful champion now is. For although we besought him to come hither with us, and although we besought him to come to you so that you might award unto him the prize of battle, yet he would not. For he proclaimed himself to be wounded and craved our leave to withdraw himself—wherefore we gave him that leave and he hied him away and we know not whither he hath gone."

"Now I am right sorry for that," quoth King Arthur, "for I would rather have that knight to feast with us than any one of all those who wear spurs in this hall. And I am still more sorry to hear that so worshipful a champion as that should have met with mishap in this battle of to-day. Yet do I hope that wound which he suffered is not so sore but that he will soon be well again."

"Lord," quoth the King of North Wales, "mefeareth that that noble knight, whomsoever he may be, hath been very grievously hurt; for when he spake to us his voice was passing weak and he appeared to suffer a great deal of pain."

Then King Arthur was much grieved at what he heard and he said: "That is sad news for me, for rather would I lose half of my kingdom than that death should befall that noble champion." So said King Arthur, yet he would not say who was that champion of the red sleeve, for he perceived that Sir Launcelot would fain conceal his name, wherefore neither would he betray it.

Now King Pelles sat not far from King Arthur's high seat at the table, and the Lady Elaine the Fair sat with him and several lords of their court were there also. These heard what was said between King Arthur and the King of North Wales, and when the Lady Elaine the Fair heard how that her champion was so sorely wounded that he was like to die, it was as though a sword of terror had been thrust into her bosom; for hearing those words she turned all as white as ashes and sank back into her chair as though she would swoon.

Seeing her thus, all white and stricken, King Pelles said, "Daughter, what ails thee?" and she said: "My father, did you not hear how that the Chevalier Malfait hath been sorely wounded and mayhap may be even now lying nigh to death?" "Yea, I did hear that," said King Pelles, "but such is the chance of battle that every good knight is called upon to face." Then the Lady Elaine cried out: "Father! Father! I am sorely afraid that great ill hath befallen that noble knight. Now I pray thee, let us go hence." King Pelles said, "Whither shall we go?" She said: "Haply, my brother, Sir Lavaine, will bring him to the castle of the earl our kinsman, wherefore I pray you, sir, let us make haste thither and see if that be so." And King Pelles said, "It shall be as you will have it."

So King Pelles besought leave of King Arthur to quit that feast, and King Arthur gave him leave and King Pelles withdrew with the Lady Elaine and all of his court from that company.

Yet when they returned to the castle of the earl, Sir Launcelot was not there, for, as hath been told, he lay at that time in the hermit's cell in the forest with his soul hanging in the scales betwixt life and death.

But King Arthur ever bore in mind how it was Sir Launcelot had been wounded, wherefore, when that feast was over, he took Sir Gawaine aside, and he said to him: "Sir, I would that you would seek out that knight of the red sleeve where he is and bring him aid and succor." Sir Gawaine said: "Lord, I pray you tell me; know you who is that knight? Methinks he should be Sir Launcelot of the Lake, for I know of no other than he who could do so nobly in battle as that champion did to-day. And yet, he cannot be Sir Launcelot, for you wist very well that Sir Launcelot would not wear the favor of any lady in such a wise as he wore the sleeve about his helm to-day. So I know not who that knight can be."

"Well," said King Arthur, "when you have succored him then you will know who he is."

So Sir Gawaine withdrew from the court to seek that wounded champion. And he remembered him that the knight had called himself le Chevalier Malfait and that his companion-in-arms was Sir Lavaine, the son of King Pelles of Corbin. So Sir Gawaine went to where were a number of knights who knew of King Pelles, and he asked of these and of several others: "Know ye, Messires, where I shall find King Pelles of Corbin?" They say to him, "King Pelles is lodging at such and such a place." So Sir Gawaine took horse and rode forth to the castle of the earl with whom King Pelles had taken up his lodging, and King Pelles and his court were still at that place. Then Sir Gawaine made demand to have speech with King Pelles and therewith he was brought before the King where he was. And the Lady Elaine the Fair was with King Pelles at that time, and Sir Gawaine, when he beheld her, was amazed at her beauty.

Sir Gawaine departs in search of Sir Launcelot

Then Sir Gawaine said to King Pelles: "Fair Lord, can you tell me where I shall find that wounded knight who called himself le Chevalier Malfait?" King Pelles said, "Alas! I know not where he is." Sir Gawaine said, "Lord, I pray you tell me who he is and what is his name." To this King Pelles made reply: "Messire, I know not who that knight is saving only that he came to us somewhat more than a year ago and that he slew the great Dragon of Corbin; and that he was sorely wounded in his encounter with the Dragon. Since that he hath abided at our court but never have we known him by any other name than le Chevalier Malfait."

Then Sir Gawaine said: "Now I pray you tell me who was the lady who gave her sleeve as a favor unto that knight, for no doubt she may know who he is."

Then the Lady Elaine said: "Messire, it was I who gave my sleeve to him, yet neither do I know who he is nor whence he came."

Sir Gawaine said: "Have you naught that you may know him by?" Whereunto the Lady Elaine made reply: "Sir, by leave of our cousin, the earl of this castle, I purveyed armor in which le Chavalier

Malfait might do battle in this tournament. Now when he quitted us he confided his armor and his shield to me that I might hold them in safe keeping for him until his return hither. Perhaps you can tell from his shield who is that worshipful knight."

Sir Gawaine said: "I prithee, fair lady, tell me what device was painted upon the shield?" And the Lady Elaine said: "I know not what was that device for the shield was all encased in leather laced upon it and painted white so that no one might see the device which it beareth."

Then Sir Gawaine said, "Let me see that shield." And thereupon the Lady Elaine sent her attendants to fetch the shield and they brought it to her where they were. Then Sir Gawaine unlaced the leather from the shield and drew the shield forth from its case, and lo! the shield shone all dazzling bright, like to the sun in his glory. And Sir Gawaine beheld the device upon the shield that it was a knight kneeling to a lady upon a field of silver, and by that he knew (and several others who were there knew) that it was the shield of Sir Launcelot. Thereupon Sir Gawaine turned him to the Lady Elaine the Fair and he said: "Lady, it is no wonder that this knight who hath worn thy favor should have done so well in battle yesterday. For wit ye that this is the shield of Sir Launcelot of the Lake and wit ye that it is to none other than he to whom you gave your sleeve. So I wish you much joy of that great honor that hath come to you through him; for you are to know that never hath it ever been heard tell of before this that Sir Launcelot hath worn the favor of any lady when he hath gone to battle."

But as for the Lady Elaine, when she knew that it was Sir Launcelot of the Lake to whom she had given her sleeve, she was filled full of a great joy and also with a sort of terror. For she had much joy that she should have been so wonderfully honored by that noble knight Sir Launcelot of the Lake, and yet when she bethought herself how she had set her regard upon him who regarded no lady in the light of love she was filled with a sort of terror because she forecast that nothing but sorrow could come to her who had placed her heart and all her happiness in the keeping of this knight, who had no heart or happiness to bestow upon any lady in return.

But King Pelles was unaware of what thoughts lay within the heart of his daughter. His spirit was greatly uplifted with the thought that Sir Launcelot should have been a knight of his court for so long a while and he said: "Messire, this is a very wonderful thing that you tell us, for who would have thought that he was Sir Launcelot who has been with us all this time? Now I know not any glory that could come to us that should be greater than that; to wit, to have had that noble, worthy, and glorious champion for to serve as a knight of our court. For now, because of him, this court hath become famous for all time, that otherwise would not have been known very far or for a very long while."

"Lord," said Sir Gawaine, "I do indeed give you great joy of this honor that you have had through him; for I must tell you that yours is the only court in all the world in which Sir Launcelot has ever served as champion, saving only in the Court of King Arthur. Wherefore this is a very singular honor that hath been visited upon you."

So spake King Pelles and so spake Sir Gawaine; but all that while the Lady Elaine the Fair sat in silence saying naught to any one for her soul was so deeply disturbed with joy and pride that Sir Launcelot should have been her champion, and with fear and anxiety upon behalf of her knight—that she wist not very well what was being done or said by any of those who sat around about her.

That night Sir Gawaine abided at the Court of Corbin, and there was a great feast prepared for his entertainment and all honor and regard was paid to him that was possible to pay any man, even were that man a king. And at that feast Sir Gawaine sat at the right hand of King Pelles and the Lady Elaine sat upon the left hand of the King. And Sir Gawaine and the King talked a very great deal together, yet ever the Lady Elaine sat wrapped in silence, very distraught, passing by her food without tasting of it. For always her thoughts dwelt upon Sir Launcelot as aforesaid, and ever her heart was filled with anxiety as to what had befallen him and where he was, and how it fared with him and who was cherishing him in his sickness and his pain. Yea, even, she wondered whether he was living or whether he was dead. Wherefore it was she knew not what passed about her, but sat silent with her spirit remote and afar off from all those who made merry and laughed and talked and jested so nigh to her.

For the soul in such times of trouble and anxiety is oftentimes very solitary and silent; ever wrapped in its own broody thoughts like to a spirit wrapped in a cloud of darkness that shutteth out from its sight all the bright world of gayety and rejoicing that lieth around about it. And so it was with the Lady Elaine at this season.

✠   ✠   ✠

Now, when the morning had come, Sir Gawaine departed from that place to return to the King's court which was still at Astolat, there to bring them news that it was Sir Launcelot who had fought in that battle and that it was he who had been wounded.

Queen Guinevere is angered
But when that news came to Queen Guinevere she was filled full of a great passion of anger and of indignation against Sir Launcelot and against the Lady Elaine. For it is to be remembered that Sir Launcelot had vowed his vows of service unto Queen Guinevere, and she upon her part had accepted those vows and acknowledged him as her knight-champion. Wherefore it was that finding he had worn the favor of another lady in that wise, she was filled with a most consuming passion of anger. At first she would not believe that it was true that Sir Launcelot had worn the sleeve, and when she was convinced that it was true she withdrew herself from the sight of all, and went and locked herself into her chamber—and how it was with her in that place no one could tell.

Queen Guinevere bespeaketh Sir Bors
Then, after a while, she sent for Sir Bors de Ganis, who was the nighest of kin to Sir Launcelot of all those then at court. And the Queen said to Sir Bors: "What is this your kinsman hath done, Messire? He hath forsworn himself and is shamed of his knighthood in my sight and in the sight of all. For who ever heard of any knight of worship who would swear his faith to one lady and yet wear the favor of another? So I say this knight is forsworn and is no true knight."

Quoth Sir Bors: "Lady, there is no man in all the world who would dare to say to me that Sir Launcelot is shamed of his knighthood, but you may say that because you are a lady. Now I pray you tell me why should not Sir Launcelot wear the favor of so kind and so beautiful a lady as that of the Lady Elaine, the King's daughter of

Corbin? Such service cannot injure you, who have always to your service so high and noble a knight as King Arthur himself!"

So spake Sir Bors very sternly, and therewith Queen Guinevere's cheeks flamed like fire and she stamped her foot upon the ground in wrath and cried out in a very loud voice: "Do you dare to speak thus to me who am your Queen? I say this unworthy knight is forsworn in that he swear his faith to me, and that he came not to me to relieve him of that vow ere he accepted the favor of another lady. Now I bid you go, find Sir Launcelot and bring him straightway hither that he may answer me to my face and that he may clear himself if he is able of that unknightly faithlessness."

Then Sir Bors was filled with indignation against the Queen and at the same time he was filled with great pity for her. For many things came into his mind at that time, wherefore he did not choose to look into the Queen's face, but only bowed low before her and said: "Lady, it shall be as you command. I shall straightway go seek my kinsman and will bring your commands to him that he shall come and present himself before you."

So forthwith Sir Bors departed from the court to seek Sir Launcelot. But after he had left her the Queen went into her privy closet and fast locked herself in. And she wept amain; and as she wept she communed in solitude with her soul, saying: "My soul! My soul! Is it anger thou feelest or is it aught else than anger?" *Sir Bors departeth in search of Sir Launcelot*

Sir Launcelot leapeth from the window:

Chapter Sixth

How the Lady Elaine went to seek Sir Launcelot and how Sir Launcelot afterwards returned to the court of King Arthur.

OW EVER the Lady Elaine the Fair, as aforesaid, took great grief beyond all measure concerning the fate of Sir Launcelot. For he lay wounded she knew not where and she knew not whether he were healing or dying. So upon a day she came to her father, King Pelles, where he was, and she had been weeping a great deal—yea, even whilst she spoke to her father she began weeping afresh. So, still weeping, she said: "Sire, I pray thee let me go and seek for this noble champion, Sir Launcelot of the Lake, where he lieth wounded, for mefeareth he hath been so grievously hurt that he may even now be upon the edge of death."

Then King Pelles said: "My daughter, what is this thou wouldst do? Wouldst thou, a young damsel, go thyself errant in search of this wounded knight?" and the Lady Elaine said, "Yea." The King, her father said, "This may not be." Then the Lady Elaine wept all the more and with such passion that it was as though her heart would break. And therewith she kneeled down before her father and cried most vehemently: "Sire, let me go! Else I believe I shall become distracted with my fears lest he be dying of his wounds."

Then King Pelles was very sorry for the Lady Elaine and he lifted her up and embraced her in his arms and kissed her upon the face. And King Pelles sought to comfort her, wiping away the tears from her face. And he said, "My daughter, weep not so." She said, "Lord, I cannot help it." Then he said: "My daughter, weep no more, for it shall be as thou wouldst have it. Go now in God's name upon this quest, if so be it will ease thy heart to do so, and I will send safe escort with thee."

So it was that the Lady Elaine the Fair went upon that quest in search of Sir Launcelot, and her father purveyed for her such an *The Lady Elaine departeth in search of Sir Launcelot* escort as he had said. For he sent with her a company of seven worthy and noble knights with their esquires and attendants; and seven damsels of her court also went with her. These betook their way to Astolat, for it seemed to the Lady Elaine that there they might best hope to have news of the wounded knight. And when they had come to Astolat she took up her inn at that place, and sent forth several to make diligent inquiry if any news might be heard of the wounded knight.

So those whom she sent made inquiry upon all sides, and upon a certain day, they found a woodchopper who had come out of the forest with a cart load of wooden fagots. This woodman brought news of Sir Launcelot and of Sir Lavaine; for he declared that he had seen them when they had entered the forest after the tournament. So her agents brought the woodchopper to where the Lady Elaine was, and she said to him, "What knowest thou, good fellow?"

The woodman telleth of Sir Launcelot To this the woodman made reply: "Lady, I will tell you all. One day whiles I was in the forest I heard the sound of voices talking together, and greatly wondering what those voices were, I made my way privily to that place where I heard them speaking. There I beheld a half-armed knight who lay upon the ground all bathed in his own blood, and another knight, armed at all points, stood beside this knight, and the hands of the second knight were all red with blood. So methought that the armed knight had haply slain his fellow there in the woodlands in foul wise, for so it appeared to be. So whilst I stood there I heard that knight who lay on the ground complaining very grievously that he was hurt nigh to death, and I heard him entreat that knight who was armed that he should bear him to the westward and so by a forest path to the cabin of a certain hermit that dwelleth in those parts. Therewith I went away from that place as privily as I had come thither, for methought that maybe some ill deed had been done at that place and that so I should be punished if I meddled in it; wherefore I went away and left those two knights in that wise."

Then the Lady Elaine the Fair asked that woodman if one of those horses was white and the other piebald and he said: "Yea, as white as milk and piebald with white and black." And the Lady said, "Then that must be they."

So that same day she and her company made them ready and *The Lady* they rode away from Astolat and so came into the forest toward the *Elaine cometh* westward. And after a while they came to a path that went across *to the forest* the way and they took that path to the right hand. So they travelled *chapel* that path for a great while, and by and by they beheld before them the hut of the hermit where it was all built up against a great rock of the forest and overshadowed by the thick foliage of the aged oak tree that grew above it. Then as they drew near they heard the neighing of horses and they wist that they must be the horses of Sir Launcelot and of Sir Lavaine.

Then, as the horses neighed in that wise, and as the horses of the Lady Elaine's party answered their neighing, there came one and opened the door of the hut and stood gazing at the Lady Elaine and her party as they drew near, shading his eyes from the slanting sun. And the Lady Elaine beheld who it was who stood there and she knew that it was Sir Lavaine, wherefore she cried out in a loud and piercing voice, "My brother! My brother!" Then Sir Lavaine, when he heard her, cried out upon his part as in great amazement, "My sister, is it thou?" and therewith he ran to her and he took her hand and she stooped from her horse and kissed his lips.

Then she said to Sir Lavaine, "How is it with him, doth he live?" Whereunto Sir Lavaine said, "Yea, he liveth and will live, albeit he is weak like to a little child." She said, "Where is he?" And Sir Lavaine said, "Come and you shall see."

So he lifted the Lady Elaine down from her horse and he took *The Lady* her by the hand and led her into the hut of the hermit and there *Elaine* she beheld Sir Launcelot where he lay upon a pallet and lo! his face *beholdeth Sir* was white like to white wax and his eyes were closed as though in *Launcelot* slumber and it seemed to the Lady Elaine that he rather resembled a white and sleeping spirit than a living man.

So the Lady Elaine went silently forward to where Sir Launcelot lay and she kneeled down beside the pallet and the tears ran down her face like to sparks of fire. Therewith Sir Launcelot opened his eyes and he beheld her who she was and he smiled upon her. And Sir Launcelot said, "Is it thou?" She said: "Yea, Messire." He said, "Whence cometh thou?" She said, "I come from my father's house." He said, "And have you come hitherward from thence only for to find me?" whereunto she said, "Yea." Sir Launcelot said, "Why have you taken so great trouble as that upon my account?" And at that she bowed her head low and said, "Certes, thou knowest why." And this she spake not above a whisper, and so that I believe they two alone heard her words.

Then Sir Launcelot said no more but lay gazing upon her albeit he could see naught but her head, for her face was hidden from him. So after a while he sighed very deep and said: "Lady, God knows I am no happy man. For even though I may see happiness within my reach yet I cannot reach out my hand to take it. For my faith lieth pledged in the keeping of one with whom I have placed it and that one can never be aught to me but what she now is. And it is my unhappy lot that whether it be wrong or whether it be right I would not have it otherwise, and so my faith remaineth pledged as aforesaid."

Sir Launcelot and the Lady Elaine commune together Now the Lady Elaine wist what Sir Launcelot meant and that he spoke of the Lady Queen Guinevere unto whom he had vowed his faith of knighthood. And Elaine wept and she said, "Alas, Launcelot, I have great pity both for thee and for me." And at that Sir Launcelot sighed again as from the bottom of his heart and said, "Yea, it is great pity."

Then after a while the Lady Elaine came out from where Sir Launcelot lay, and she gave command that they should abide at that place until the wounded knight was healed of his hurt. So the Lady Elaine established her court there in the forest nigh to where Sir Launcelot lay. And they set up pavilions around about that place so that all that erstwhile lonely and silent woodland was presently gay with bright colors and cheerful with the sound of many voices.

And methinks that these days, whilst the Lady Elaine dwelt there in the forest nigh to the chapel of the good old hermit of the forest, and whilst she abided ever close to Sir Launcelot in that time of his grievous sickness, were the happiest days of all her life unto that time. For it was as though Sir Launcelot were all her own and as though there was none in the world but they two. For ever she was nigh to him and cherished him in all ways, the whiles the voices of those others who were there sounded remote and afar off as though they were of a different world than hers.

So ever the Lady Elaine drank deep draughts of love and joy, and thought not of the morrow, but only of the day and of the joys that the day set to the lips of her soul, as it were, in a bright, shining chalice of pure gold.

For so it is, oftentimes, that the soul drinketh deep from that chalice and reckoneth not that at the bottom of the cup there lyeth the dregs of sorrow or of despair that must by and by likewise be quaffed, and which, when drunk, must turn all the life thereafter to bitterness, as though those dregs were compounded of the gall and of the wormwood of death.

Thus the Lady Elaine the Fair abided with her court there in the *They return* forest for nigh a month and by the end of that time Sir Launcelot *to Corbin* was healed of his infirmities, though like to a little child for weakness. And after he was healed she then had a fair litter prepared with several soft cushions of down. And she had that litter hung with hangings of flame-colored satin; and she had them lay Sir Launcelot therein and so they bore him thence. Thus they bore him in that litter by easy stages until they had brought him to Corbin and there he was received with great rejoicing and high honor.

✤　✤　✤

Now it hath been told how that Queen Guinevere bade Sir Bors for to go seek Sir Launcelot and to bear him a command for to return to the court of the King. So Sir Bors did as the Queen bade him, but he did not find Sir Launcelot until after he had been brought back to Corbin as aforetold of.

Thereafter it happened that one day Sir Bors had news that Sir *Sir Bors* Launcelot was lying at the court of King Pelles. So he went thither *cometh to* and there he beheld Sir Launcelot who was then wellnigh entirely *Corbin* recovered from his wound.

But when Sir Launcelot beheld Sir Bors, such joy seized upon him that it was as though his heart would break, wherefore he ran to Sir Bors and he catched him in his arms, and embraced him with great passion and kissed him many times upon the face.

And they of the court of King Pelles were very glad that so famous a knight had come thither, wherefore they paid him great honor.

Only the Lady Elaine was troubled in spirit, for she wist that now Sir Bors was come Sir Launcelot would not stay with them for long, but that he would in a little while desire to return again to the court of King Arthur.

Sir Bors speaketh to Sir Launcelot
And so she had reason for her fears, for the next day after he had arrived at Corbin, Sir Bors took Sir Launcelot aside and he said to him, "Sir Knight, I am a messenger." Sir Launcelot said, "What message have you, and from whom?" Sir Bors said: "I bear a message from Queen Guinevere and it is that you return immediately to the court of King Arthur and that you present yourself to her and pay your duty to her as of old."

Then after Sir Bors had thus spoken, Sir Launcelot turned him away and stood at a window with his back to Sir Bors. And then after a considerable while he said, "Sir, do you not know that my duty lieth here?" Sir Bors said: "That I believe full well. Nor can I find fault with you if you remain here in spite of the message I bring you. That which I am here for is not to command you to come to Camelot, but only to give you the commands of another."

Then Sir Launcelot said: "Would you return to Camelot if you were me and I were you?" Sir Bors said, "That I cannot tell." Then after another while Sir Launcelot cried out: "Nay, I will not go; for though my heart lieth there and not here, yet I hold the happiness of another in my hand and I cannot cast it away."

"Then," quoth Sir Bors, "I will return and tell them at the court of the King that your honor binds you here." And Sir Launcelot said, "Do so." And then he said, "There is but one favor I beseech of you, Messire." Sir Bors said, "What is that?" Sir Launcelot said: "It is this: I pray you of your courtesy that you will depart immediately from this place, for the sight of you bringeth to me such great desire to behold my kinsmen and my friends once more that I believe that I shall not be able to contain myself because of that desire if you remain here any longer." And Sir Bors said, "I will go within the hour."

So that very hour Sir Bors betook himself away from Corbin and returned to the court of King Arthur, and when he had come there he delivered his message to the Queen and thereat she was like one whose heart had been broken. For when she received that news from

Sir Launcelot she withdrew into her bower and no one saw her for a long time thereafter.

Now after Sir Bors had departed from Corbin in that wise, Sir Launcelot was very heavy and sad, and though several days went by, yet was he not less sad at the end of that time, but still walked like one in a dream with his thoughts a great way off.

And all this the Lady Elaine observed and her spirit was troubled *The Lady* because of the sadness of Sir Launcelot. So one day she sent for Sir *Elaine* *biddeth Sir* Launcelot to come to her bower and when Sir Launcelot had come *Launcelot to* thither she said to him, "Launcelot, I know what is in thy heart." Sir *return* Launcelot said, "What is there in my heart?" She said, "It is in thy heart that thou wouldst fain return to the court of King Arthur." "Lady," said Sir Launcelot, "it matters not what may be my inclination at this present, for above all those inclinations it is my will that I remain at this place."

Then Elaine looked very steadfastly at him and she smiled, but there was as it were despair in her face even though she smiled. And after a little she said: "Not so, Messire, for I cannot bear to see you dwell with us thus in sadness. Wherefore, this command I lay upon you that you leave this court and that you return to the court of King Arthur, which same is the place where you do rightly belong."

Then Sir Launcelot turned away from her, for he wist that there was joy in his face at the thought of returning to his kinsmen and his friends once more, and he would not have her see that joy. Then after a while, and with his back turned, he said, speaking as with a smothered voice: "Lady, if that be your command I must needs obey, but if I do obey you it shall be only to go for a little while and then to return after that while." So for a little no more was said, but the Lady Elaine ever gazed upon Sir Launcelot where he stood with his back to her, and after a while she said, "Ah, Launcelot! Launcelot!" Upon that Sir Launcelot turned him about and cried out, "Elaine, bid me stay and I will stay!" But she said, "Nay, I bid thee not, I bid thee go."

Then Sir Launcelot went from that place with his head bowed down upon his bosom, and after he had gone she wept in great measure, for it was as though she had cut off her hope of happiness with her own hand, as though it had been a part of her body.

Sir Launcelot returneth to court

So the next day Sir Launcelot took horse and departed from Corbin, betaking his way toward Camelot, where was the court of King Arthur, and though he thought a very great deal of the Lady Elaine, yet he could not but look forward with joy in coming back again to the court of the King and of beholding the Queen and his knights companions once more.

�֍   ✤   ✤

Sir Launcelot cometh to the Queen

Now when Sir Launcelot reached Camelot the news of his coming spread like fire throughout the entire place and everywhere was heard the noise of loud rejoicing and acclaim. But Sir Launcelot spake to nobody but came straight to where Queen Guinevere was and he stood before the Queen and his face was very gloomy and he said to her, "Lady, here am I."

Then Queen Guinevere gazed at him with great coldness and she said to him, "Sir Knight, what brings thee hither?" Sir Launcelot said: "Lady, it is thy command that brings me. For alas! I find it to be thus with me that thy word hath power to bring me to thee whether it be from glory or from happiness or from peace or from prosperity. Yea; all these things would I sacrifice at thy behest."

Then Queen Guinevere gazed upon Sir Launcelot for a long while and her soul was tossed and troubled with a great ferment of passion, and yet she wist not whether that passion was of indignation or of grief or of anger or of something else that was not like any of these. And first her face had been very white when he stood before her, and anon it flamed red like to fire, and she said: "Sir Knight, one time I sent my word to thee by a messenger and thou heeded him not. Now it matters not that thou comest, for thy coming and thy going are henceforth of no moment to me."

Then Sir Launcelot's heart was filled to bursting with bitterness and despair, and he cried out aloud: "Lady, thou beholdest me a miserable man. For I have left all my duty and all my service and all my hope of peace and happiness and have come to thee. Hast thou not then some word of kindness for me?"

But the Queen only hardened her heart and would not answer.

Then Sir Launcelot cried out in great despair: "Alas! what is there then left for me? Lo! I have cast away from me all my hope of peace and now even thy friendship is withdrawn from me. Nothing then is left to me and my life is dead."

Then Queen Guinevere's eyes flashed like fire, and she cried out: *The Queen is* "Sir Knight, you speak I know not what. Now I bid you tell me *angry* this—is it true that you wore as a favor the sleeve of the Lady Elaine the Fair at the tournament of Astolat?"

Sir Launcelot said, "Yes, it is true."

Then the Lady Queen Guinevere laughed with flaming cheeks and she said: "Well, Sir Knight I see that you are not very well learned in knighthood not to know that it is both unknightly and dishonorable for a knight to sware faith to one lady and to wear the favor of another. Yet what else than that may be expected of one who knoweth so little of the duties and of the obligations of knighthood that he will ride errant in a hangman's cart?"

So spake Queen Guinevere in haste not knowing what she said, her words being driven onwards by her passion as feathers are blown by a tempest over which they have no control. But when she had spoken those words she was terrified at what she had said and would have recalled them. But she could not do that, for who can recall the spoken word after it is uttered? Wherefore, after she had spoken those words she could do nothing but gaze into Sir Launcelot's face in a sort of terror. And as she thus gazed she beheld that his face became red and redder until it became all empurpled as though the veins of his head would burst. And she beheld that his eyes started as though from his head and that they became shot with blood. And she beheld that he clutched at his throat as though he were choking. And he strove to speak but at first he could not and then he cried out in a harsh and choking voice, "Say you so!" and then again in the same voice he cried, "Say you so!"

Therewith he turned, staggering like a drunken man. And there *Sir Launcelot* was a tall window open behind him, and straightway he leaped out *leapeth from* of that window into the courtyard beneath, where he fell with a loud *the window* and dreadful crash.

But yet it was as though he had not fallen for he immediately leaped up to his feet and ran away all bruised and bloody from that place like one gone wode.

Then Queen Guinevere shrieked aloud with a great passion of terror and remorse. And she cried out she knew not what and smote her hands very violently together. Thereat several came running to her and to them she cried out in a voice of vehement passion: "Go you, run with might and main and fetch Sir Launcelot hither to me again!"

So those ran with all despatch but they could not find Sir Launcelot. For immediately after leaving the Queen as aforesaid, he had leaped upon his horse and had thundered away with all speed, and no one knew whither he had betaken himself.

Sir Bors is   Now the word of all this was talked about the court of the King
indignant   almost as soon as it had happened, for all the court was loud with the noise of it. Thereat, when the kinsmen of Sir Launcelot had heard what had passed, they were filled with great indignation at the manner in which he had been treated; and most of all Sir Bors was indignant, for he said to himself: "Lo! this Lady first sends me to seek my kinsman and to bring him to her and when he cometh at her bidding then she treats him with contumely altogether unworthy for a knight to endure. What then must Sir Launcelot think of me who was her foolish messenger to fetch him hither?"

Queen   But Queen Guinevere, not knowing of the indignation of the
Guinevere   kinsmen of Sir Launcelot, sent for three of them to come to her,
bespeaketh the and these three were Sir Ector and Sir Lionel and Sir Bors de Ganis.
kinsmen of When these three had come to her they found her weeping and when
Sir Launcelot they stood before her she said, "Messires, I have done amiss." To this they said nothing lest from anger they should say too much. Yet the Queen beheld their anger, wherefore she dried her tears and spake with pride, saying: "Messires, I ask you not to forgive me who am your Queen, but I would fain ask Sir Launcelot to forgive me and I know that out of his gentleness he will do so. Now as your Queen and sovereign I lay this command upon you, that you straightway go in quest of Sir Launcelot and that you find him and that you bring him hither to me so that I may beseech his forgiveness for all that I have said amiss to him."

So spake Queen Guinevere, and those knights who were there, though they were very angry with her yet they could not but obey the command which she laid upon them.

So began the Quest of Sir Launcelot concerning which a very *Of the Quest* great deal hath been both written and said. For upon that quest *of Sir* *Launcelot* there went forth those three knights as aforesaid, to wit; Sir Ector, Sir Lionel, and Sir Bors de Ganis, and after that there went forth Sir Gawaine and Sir Ewaine and Sir Sagramore the Desirous and Sir Agravaine and Sir Percival of Gales.

All these undertook the Quest of Sir Launcelot and in that quest several adventures happened to them. Yet of all those adventures little of anything shall here be said saving only that which shall concern those adventures that befell Sir Ewaine and Sir Percival and Sir Gawaine; of which more anon.

And now there followeth the story of the Madness of Sir Launcelot, and of how he returned in a very strange manner to the Lady Elaine the Fair—and of how she was made happy by that return.

The Madness of Sir Launcelot

ERE FOLLOWS *the story of how Sir Launcelot went mad from grief and of how he roamed the woods as a wild man of the woods. Also many other adventures that befell him are herein told, wherefore I hope that you may have pleasure in reading that which is here written for your entertainment.*

The Madman of the Forest who was Sir Launcelot:

Chapter First

How Sir Launcelot became a madman of the forest and how he was brought to the castle of Sir Blyant.

NOW WHEN Sir Launcelot had quitted the presence of Queen Guinevere as aforetold, and having leaped to horse as aforetold, he rode very furiously away, he wist not whither and cared not. And he raced like a whirlwind, striving, as it were, to escape from himself and his own despair. Thus he drove onward until he reached the shades of the forest, and he rode through the forest, rending the branches with his body, until his horse was all a lather of sweat. So he pursued his way till night descended upon him, and still he drove ever forward, he knew not whitherward. And he travelled in that wise all that night until about the dawning of the day, what time he came to that part of the woodland where was the hut of the hermit of the forest, and there he beheld the chapel and the cell of the hermit. Here Sir Launcelot leaped down from his horse, and he burst very violently into the dwelling-place of that good man so that the hermit was amazed at his coming. And Sir Launcelot cried out in a loud and violent voice, "God save you!" and therewith he fell forward and lay with his face upon the floor.

Then the hermit ran to him and he lifted up his head and looked in his face and he beheld that Sir Launcelot was in a fit.

So the hermit eased Sir Launcelot of his armor and he loosed the jerkin and the shirt at his throat so that his throat was bare. And he lifted Sir Launcelot and brought him to his own cot and he laid him down thereon and there Sir Launcelot lay for the entire day.

But toward the sloping of the afternoon the sick man opened his eyes and he aroused and sat up and gazed about him, and he said, "Where am I?" The hermit said, "Thou art with me," and he further said, "What aileth thee, Sir Launcelot?"

But to this Sir Launcelot answered naught but ever looked about him as though not knowing who he was or where he was; for he was like to one who is bedazed by a heavy blow he hath received. Then by and by Sir Launcelot said, "I know not what it is that hath happened." Thus he spake because his brains were bewildered by the passion through which he had passed, for even at that time the madness which afterward gat hold of him had begun to ferment in his brains so that he wist not very well what he said or did.

Then the hermit knew that some great trouble had befallen Sir Launcelot, and he thought that maybe if Sir Launcelot would eat he would perhaps be refreshed and might maybe recover his mind once more. So the good man said, "Messire, will you not eat?" and Sir Launcelot said, "Yea, give me to eat."

The hermit cherisheth Sir Launcelot

So the hermit brought bread and milk and honey and fruit and he set those things before Sir Launcelot. And Sir Launcelot fell upon those things and ate of them very fiercely and voraciously, devouring them more like a savage than a worshipful and worthy knight.

Then after Sir Launcelot had thus eaten he said, "I am aweary," and therewith he arose and ungirded his armor, and laid it aside, piece by piece, even to the very last piece thereof. Then when he was thus eased of his armor, he flung himself down in his jerkin and hose upon the hermit's pallet and therewith in a moment had fallen into a slumber so deep that it was like the sleep of death. And as he slept thus the hermit sat beside the pallet whereon Sir Launcelot lay. And he gazed very steadfastly upon Sir Launcelot, and was greatly grieved to see him in that condition.

Now it happened that about the middle of the night the hermit fell asleep where he sat and shortly after that Sir Launcelot awoke and was aware how the old man slept. And Sir Launcelot took of a sudden a great fear of the hermit he wist not wherefore, so that the only thought in his mind was to escape from the hermit. Wherefore he arose and went very softly and in his bare feet out from that place, doing this so silently that he did not awaken the hermit from his sleep.

Thus Sir Launcelot came outside the hermit's hut, and after he had thus escaped therefrom, he took of a sudden great fear lest the hermit should awake and pursue him for to bring him back to the hut again. So straightway he turned him and sped away into the forest with great speed, like as though he were a wild animal pursued by the hunter. And he fled away for all the rest of that night. And when the dawn had come he ceased to fly and he crouched down and hid himself in the thickets of the forest. For in his madness he was ever pursued by the fear that the hermit would follow him and that he was even then hunting for him for to bring him back to the hut again. *Sir Launcelot escapeth from the hermitage*

Thus it was that Sir Launcelot escaped from the hut of the hermit, and after that he abided in the forest for a long while. What time he gathered the wild fruit of the forest for his food. And he drank of the forest fountains and that was all the food and drink that he had. And after a while the clothes of Sir Launcelot were all torn into shreds by the thorns and briars, and his hair grew down into his eyes and his beard grew down upon his breast so that he became in all appearance a wild man of the forest, all naked, and shaggy, and gaunt like to a hungry wolf.

And now and again it chanced that some one who travelled in the forest would see him as he ran through the thickets of the woodland like to a wild creature, and hence it was that much talk of that wild man of the forest went about the countryside, and folk were afraid of all that part of the woodlands because of him. *Sir Launcelot becometh the forest madman*

Now one pleasant morning in the autumn season when the early frosts were come, and when all the trees had taken on their clothing of crimson and russet and gold, Sir Launcelot, in his mad wanderings, came to the edge of the woodland and there before him he beheld a little open plain all yellow and bright in the broad beams of the shining sunlight. And Sir Launcelot beheld that in the midst of that small plain was a fair pavilion of blue silk. And he beheld that near by the pavilion there were three horses tethered browsing upon the autumn grass. And he beheld that a bright shield hung to a tree that grew near the pavilion, and that a fair sword hung nigh the shield, and that a spear leaned against the tree beside the shield and sword.

Then Sir Launcelot was pleased with the bright color of the pavilion and something of knighthood awoke within him at the sight of the shield and the sword and the spear, wherefore he desired to handle the sword and the spear and to touch the shield.

Sir Launcelot beateth upon the shield of Sir Blyant So Sir Launcelot went forward into that plain and he came to the tree where were the sword and the shield and the spear. And he took the pommel of the sword into his hand. Thereupon a great desire for battle came upon him, and he straightway catched the pommel of the sword in both his hands and he drew the blade forth from the sheath. And he whirled the sword about his head and he smote the shield; and he smote it again and again, striking great dents into it with the blade of the sword; and the sound of those blows made such a din and uproar that it was as though ten men were fighting in that place.

Therewith, at all that sudden din and uproar, there came running out of that pavilion a misshapen dwarf very broad of shoulder and strong of limb. And when that dwarf beheld a madman smiting the shield in that wise, he ran at him with intent to take the sword away from him.

But Sir Launcelot beheld the dwarf coming in that wise, and straightway he dropped the sword which he held, and he catched the dwarf by the shoulders and he flung him so violently down upon the earth that the neck of the dwarf was wellnigh broken by that fall.

Then the dwarf was overwhelmed with the terror of Sir Launcelot, wherefore he did not dare to arise from the ground whereon he had fallen, but lay there calling out for help in a loud voice of outcry.

Thereupon, there immediately came forth from out of the pavilion a noble knight clad all in scarlet and wrapped in a scarlet cloak trimmed with miniver. And that knight was Sir Blyant whose castle stood not more than four or five leagues from that place. For at such pleasant season of the year, Sir Blyant was wont to ride forth with his lady, and ever when he chose he would have a pavilion set up in some such pleasant place as this little glade. And sometimes Sir Blyant and his lady would lodge in that pavilion over-night, as was the case at this time.

So Sir Blyant came forth out of the pavilion as aforesaid, and *Sir Blyant* he beheld the dwarf lying upon the ground. And he beheld that Sir *pitieth the* Launcelot had catched up the sword again, and that he stood above *madman* the dwarf, making play with his sword as though there were many enemies thereabouts; and Sir Blyant wist that he whom he beheld must be the Madman of the Forest of whom folk talked so much. Then Sir Blyant pitied that madman a very great deal, and he spake very mildly to him, saying: "Good man, put down that sword, for meseems thou art in greater need of food and of warm clothes and of nourishing and comforting than of playing with a sharp sword in that wise."

But ever Sir Launcelot waved the sword this way and that, crying out in a great loud voice, "Keep thou away or I will slay thee."

Then Sir Blyant perceived that there was great danger in having to do unarmed with that madman, wherefore he called upon his dwarf to arise and come to him, and therewith he withdrew into the pavilion with intent to arm himself and so to take away that sword from Sir Launcelot by force.

So the dwarf, who by that time had arisen from where he lay, *Sir Blyant* went into the pavilion to where Sir Blyant was, and he aided Sir *armeth* Blyant to don his armor, and so Sir Blyant armed himself from head *himself* to foot. When he was thus armed he took sword in hand and went forth from out of the pavilion prepared to deal with the madman in such wise as was necessary to take that dangerous sword from him. For even if it must be that he had to slay that madman, Sir Blyant wist that he must not leave him thus with a sharp sword in his hand. So Sir Blyant came out of the pavilion armed at all points.

But when Sir Launcelot beheld him coming forth thus armed as for battle, the love of battle awoke to full life in his heart, wherefore he shouted aloud. And he rushed at Sir Blyant and he struck Sir Blyant upon the helm so fierce and terrible a buffet that nor guard nor armor could withstand that stroke. And had the sword not turned a little in the hands of Sir Launcelot that had been Sir *The madman* Blyant's last day upon earth. *overthroweth*

Natheless, the sword, though turned, fell with full force upon the *Sir Blyant* crest of Sir Blyant, and at that dreadful, terrible stroke the brains of Sir Blyant flashed fire into his eyeballs. Then blackness came roaring upon him and therewith he fell down in a deathly swoon, the blood running out from his nose and ears from the force of that woeful stroke he had suffered.

So when Sir Launcelot beheld Sir Blyant fall thus beneath the blow, he shouted aloud for joy. And straightway with the naked sword in his hand he ran into the pavilion with intent to find what other enemies there might be in that place.

Now the lady of Sir Blyant was alone in that pavilion, so when she beheld that half-naked madman rush therein with the shining sword in his hand, and a terrible fierce look of madness upon his face, she shrieked with terror and straightway ran forth from the tent upon the other side thereof.

So Sir Launcelot stood and gazed all about him, waving his sword from side to side, but could behold no enemies such as he might assault. And then he saw where there was a fine soft couch spread with a covering of flame-colored linen in that place, and therewith he ran to that bed and leaped into it and straightway covered himself all over with the coverlet.

The Lady is adread When the lady of Sir Blyant ran in that wise out of the pavilion as aforesaid, she beheld where her lord, Sir Blyant, lay stretched out upon the ground, and she beheld the dwarf bending over him, removing the helm from his head. And beholding that sight she shrieked more than ever and ran frantically to where that stricken knight lay. Therewith, beholding his face all white as milk and streaked with blood, she thought that he had certes been killed by that madman, whereupon she flung herself down upon his body, crying aloud in a most piercing voice, "My lord! My lord! Assuredly thou art dead!"

"Not so, lady," said the dwarf, "he is not dead, but aswoon." And even as the dwarf spoke, Sir Blyant sighed very deeply and opened his eyes. And he said: "Where is that madman who struck me anon? Never in all my life felt I such a buffet as that which he gave me." The dwarf said, "Lord, that madman ran but now into the pavilion and drove your lady out thence." "Go, Sirrah," said Sir Blyant, "and see what he is at in the pavilion."

So the dwarf went very fearfully to the door of the pavilion and peeped within, and he beheld where Sir Launcelot lay sleeping upon the couch. Thereupon the dwarf returned to Sir Blyant and he said: "Sir, that madman hath taken to your bed, and he lyeth there now very soundly asleep as he were in a swoon." And then the dwarf said: "Give me leave to take this sword and go thither and I will slay him where he lieth. For only so may we hope to save ourselves from the madness of his phrenzy when he shall awake."

But Sir Blyant pitied the madman and he said: "Let be and harm him not, for I misdoubt this madman is not what he seemeth to be." And he said, "Help me to arise, for my head swimmeth." So the lady and the dwarf helped Sir Blyant to his feet and in a little while he was able to stand and to walk. And anon Sir Blyant went into the pavilion, and he went to where Sir Launcelot lay and he stood and looked down upon him. And he beheld that Sir Launcelot wore a rich ring upon his finger (and that was the ring of magic which the Lady of the Lake had given him) and he beheld that Sir Launcelot's body was covered with many scars of wounds such as a knight might receive in battle. So seeing these things, Sir Blyant said: "This is no common madman, but some great champion who has fallen into misfortune, for I behold that he weareth a ring such as only a knight of great credit might wear, and I behold that he beareth many honorable scars of battle." *Sir Blyant looketh upon the madman*

And Sir Blyant said to the dwarf: "Take thou thy horse and ride with all speed to my castle. When thou art come there, bid my brother Sir Selivant to make haste hither with several men. And bid him to fetch a horse litter with him so that we may be able to bring this mad knight to where he may have succor and where he may haply be cured of his infirmities."

So the dwarf did as Sir Blyant commanded him; he took horse and rode with all speed to the castle of Sir Blyant, and there he gave Sir Blyant's word to Sir Selivant. And straightway Sir Selivant came to that place with those men and a horse litter for to bring Sir Launcelot away; and he reached that place within three hours after the messenger had been sent to him.

So Sir Selivant and Sir Blyant and those men lifted Sir Launcelot as he lay in his bed, and they laid him on the litter and Sir Launcelot *They bear the madman thence* did not awake. And they took him away from that place and still he did not awake; for all that while he lay in a deep slumber that was like to a swoon. Thus they brought him to the castle of Sir Blyant without his ever arousing from that swoonlike sleep.

After that they fetched the barber of the castle and the barber trimmed the hair and the beard of Sir Launcelot and they put fresh decent clothes upon him, and all that time Sir Launcelot did not awake but lay ever in that swoonlike sleep.

Now when they of that castle beheld Sir Launcelot as he lay after he had been thus clothed and clipped; and when they beheld how noble and comely was his appearance, they said, "Certes, this is indeed some noble and haughty champion of high estate, though who he may be we know not."

So they all took great pity for Sir Launcelot, but yet they feared his phrenzy when he should awake. So they sent for the smith of the castle, and the smith fastened light strong chains of steel to the wrists of Sir Launcelot and to his ankles; so that he might do no harm to any one.

The madman is made prisoner So when Sir Launcelot awoke he was a prisoner in chains in the castle of Sir Blyant. And Sir Launcelot remained dwelling in the castle of Sir Blyant for a year and a half, and ever he remained bound with those light strong chains of steel. For still his wits flitted and he wist not where he was or who he was, wherefore they feared he might at any moment break forth into a phrenzy.

But ever the folk of the castle treated Sir Launcelot with great kindness and gentleness. And especially Sir Blyant was kind to him, wherefore Sir Launcelot loved Sir Blyant as some dumb creature loveth its master, and he would follow Sir Blyant about whithersoever he went.

Thus it was that Sir Launcelot went mad and thus he came to be chained in the castle of Sir Blyant.

And now remaineth other adventures to be told that befell at this time.

The Forest Madman saveth ye Life of King Arthur:

Chapter Second

How Sir Launcelot saved the life of Sir Blyant. How he escaped from the castle of Sir Blyant, and how he slew the great wild boar of Lystenesse and saved the life of King Arthur, his liege lord.

OW IT HAPPENED upon a day that Sir Blyant rode in a little *Sir Blyant* wood nigh to his castle, and whilst he was thus alone he *rideth in the* beheld two knights riding side by side all in the clear bright *woodland* springtime. As these drew nigh to him Sir Blyant was aware from the devices upon their shields that one of them was Sir Breuce sans Pitie and that the other was Sir Bertolet his brother, which same, you are to know, were Sir Blyant's bitter enemies. For in the tournament at Astolat Sir Blyant had very grievously hurt a young knight who was their brother, and afterward that knight (whose name was Sir Gelotius) had died of those hurts.

Yet though Sir Blyant wist that this meeting boded ill for him yet would he not withdraw therefrom but went forward. So it came about that when he was pretty close to those two knights, the foremost of them (who was Sir Breuce sans Pitie) rode forth and bespoke him, saying, "Sir Knight, who are you and whither go you?" Sir Blyant said: "Messires, I am a knight of these marches, riding errant in search of adventure." Sir Breuce said, "Art thou not Sir Blyant of the White Castle?" Sir Blyant said, "Thou sayest it and I am he."

Then Sir Breuce sans Pitie spoke very savagely, saying: "Sir Knight, this is well that we meet you here who are the slayer of our brother Sir Gelotius at the tournament of Astolat." To this Sir Blyant said: "Messires, what do you have against me for that? Certes, it is that I overthrew Sir Gelotius and that he died thereafter, yet it was by chance of battle that this happened and with no evil intent of mine. Moreover, your brother, Sir Gelotius, took his chances of battle as did all those who entered that tournament."

"Say no more!" said Sir Breuce. "Say no more! but prepare you straight for battle with us who have every day sought you from that time till now, and so have found you here to our hand."

"Messires," cried Sir Blyant, "would you fall upon me thus, two against one?" They say, "Aye," and thereupon they drew sword and prepared themselves for battle.

Sir Blyant is assailed in the woodland Then Sir Blyant perceiving how it was, and that there was no other way for him to do than to fight this battle against odds, straightway drew his sword and put himself into posture of defence. Then in a moment they three came to battle together in the woods, two of them against the one.

Yet, for a while, although he stood one to two, Sir Blyant defended himself with great courage and address, striking now upon this side and now upon that, anon wheeling his horse away from a stroke, anon lashing a stroke at his enemies. And so great was the defence he made that it was a long time ere that those two knights had their will of him.

But one knight could not hope to fight thus a continued battle against two who were his equals, wherefore it befell that in a little while Sir Blyant was wounded here and there, and in another place; and then, in a little while longer it came about that, what with weariness and what from the loss of blood, he was aware that he must die in that battle alone in the woodlands unless he saved himself from his enemies.

Sir Blyant fleeth Therewith a great despair fell upon him and with that he put his horse straight at Sir Breuce as though to strike him a buffet. Then as Sir Breuce drew aside to avoid that stroke, Sir Blyant drave his horse very fiercely against Sir Breuce's horse, so that Sir Breuce's horse wellnigh fell to the ground with his rider upon his back. Therewith Sir Blyant thrust past his enemy and quickly fled away toward his castle with all the speed that he could drive his horse to make.

Now at first those two knights were astonished at the sudden escape of their enemy. But immediately they awoke to his going and so set spurs to horse upon their part and chased after Sir Blyant; and if he sped fast, they sped as fast after him. And ever and anon they lashed furiously at him, yet because of his speed they could do him no great harm.

So Sir Blyant raced for his castle and he rushed forward beneath the walls of the castle with those two knights thundering after him amain. And because they were so close upon him, Sir Blyant could not draw rein to turn his steed into the drawbridge of the castle, but must needs rush past the drawbridge, calling for aid to those who were within the walls.

Now at that time Sir Launcelot lay (chained as was aforetold) in a certain window of the castle where the sun shone down strong and warm upon him, and Sir Launcelot slumbered there in the sunlight. And as Sir Launcelot so slumbered he was aroused by the sound of galloping horses and a loud noise of shouting and the din of lashing of blows. So, looking forth from that window, he beheld the three knights as they came thundering past the walls of the castle. And Sir Launcelot beheld that the one knight who was pursued by the two knights was his master, Sir Blyant; and he beheld that Sir Blyant was much put to it to save his life; for he was all covered over with blood and, whilst anon he would wheel his horse and strike right and left, yet anon he would wheel again and flee for his life; and Sir Launcelot beheld that Sir Blyant reeled in his saddle under every blow that his enemies lashed at him. Meanwhile, in the castle was a great shouting and calling to arms, wherefore it came to Sir Launcelot to know that Sir Blyant was being slain. *The madman beholdeth Sir Blyant's danger*

Then a great rage of battle awoke in Sir Launcelot's heart against those who pressed his beloved master, Sir Blyant, in that wise, wherefore he would have hastened to the aid of Sir Blyant, but could not because of the chains that bound him. Then, in his madness, and being driven furious at being thus bound, Sir Launcelot catched those strong steel chains in his hands and wrestled with them. And the chains bit deep into his flesh in his wrestlings so that he was sore wounded by the iron. But in spite of that Sir Launcelot put forth his entire strength, and even though the blood flowed from his arms and hands yet he snapped the chains that bound his arms. After that he catched up a great stone in his hands and he beat upon the chains that bound his legs and brake those also, and so he was free again. *The madman breaketh his bonds*

Then Sir Launcelot leaped upon the window-ledge, and he leaped out of the window of the castle and into the moat below and he swam the moat and so came out upon the other side thereof.

Right there came Sir Blyant striving to defend himself against those who followed him, and at that time he was very nigh falling from his horse at every blow he received. This Sir Launcelot beheld and when he saw how those two knights ever smote Sir Blyant and how that Sir Blyant reeled in his saddle beneath those blows, he roared aloud in pity and in rage.

The madman doeth battle for Sir Blyant Therewith, thus roaring, he straightway rushed upon Sir Bertolet, who was nighest to him, and he leaped up and catched that knight about the body and dragged him down upon the pommel of his saddle with great force of strength, and Sir Launcelot catched the sword of Sir Bertolet and he wrestled with Sir Bertolet and so plucked the sword out of Sir Bertolet's hand.

Then Sir Bertolet cried out to Sir Breuce: "Help! Help! my brother! For this madman slayeth me."

Therewith Sir Breuce turned from Sir Blyant for to succor his brother, and upon that Sir Launcelot quitted Sir Bertolet and rushed at Sir Breuce. And Sir Launcelot gave Sir Breuce such a buffet upon the helm with the sword of Sir Bertolet that he smote Sir Breuce with that one blow clean over the crupper of his horse.

Then Sir Bertolet took his spear in hand and therewith rushed his horse upon Sir Launcelot with intent to pierce him through the body. But from that assault Sir Launcelot leaped nimbly aside. Thereupon he rushed in and catched the spear of Sir Bertolet in his hand; and he ran up the length of the spear, and reached forward, and smote Sir Bertolet such a blow that he cut through the epaulier of the shoulder and deep into the shoulder to the very bone thereof, so that the arm of Sir Bertolet was half cut away from the body at that blow. Then Sir Launcelot would have struck again only that Sir Bertolet let go his spear from his hand, shrieking aloud, and wheeled his horse to escape.

Now by that time Sir Breuce sans Pitie had got him to horse again wherefore, beholding that terrible blow and beholding how his brother Sir Bertolet fled away from that madman, he also drove spurs to flank and fled away with might and main.

So it was that Sir Launcelot, unarmed, save for the sword in his naked hand, defeated two strong and doughty knights and so saved his master's life.

Sir Blyant cherisheth the madman But by now the castle folk had come running to where were Sir Blyant and him whom they called the mad fool of the castle, and they beheld them both panting and bleeding. And Sir Blyant looked upon Sir Launcelot and beheld how his arms and hands were torn and bleeding from breaking those chains, and he said, "Poor fool! and hast thou suffered all that for my sake?" And at that Sir Launcelot laughed and nodded. Then Sir Blyant said to the folk of the castle: "Never let those chains be put upon his body again, for he is gentle and kind, and meaneth harm to no one."

So they did not chain Sir Launcelot again, but suffered him to go free, and after that he wandered whithersoever he willed to go, and no one stayed him in his going or his coming. And ever he was kind and gentle to all so that no one in all that place had any fear of him but all were pleased and merry with him.

Yet ever there lay within the heart of Sir Launcelot some remembrance that told him that he was too worthy to content himself with being a mad fool in a lord's castle, wherefore it was always in his will to escape from the castle of Sir Blyant if he was able to do so.

So now, being unchained, it happened one night when none observed him, that he dropped privily from the wall of the castle into the moat thereof, and swam the moat to the other side. And after *The madman escapeth from the castle of Sir Blyant* he had thus escaped into the night he ran on without stopping until he had reached the forest, and there he roamed once more altogether wild as he had been aforetime. For the remnant of his knighthood said to him that it would be better for him to die alone there in the woodlands than to dwell in shame in a lord's castle.

Now at that time there was a great wild boar in those parts that was the terror of all men, and this boar was called the boar of Lystenesse—taking its name from that part of the forest which was called the Forest of Lystenesse.

So word of this great wild boar, and news of its ravages came to the ears of King Arthur, whereupon the King ordained that a day *King Arthur hunts the boar of Lystenesse* should be set apart for a hunt in which the beast should be slain and the countryside set free from the ravages thereof.

Thus it befell that upon a time Sir Launcelot, where he lived in *The madman chases the boar* his madness alone in the forest, was aware of the baying of hounds and the shouting of voices sounding ever nearer and nearer to where he was. Anon the baying of the hounds approached him very near indeed, and presently there came a great cracking and rending of the bushes and the small trees. Thereupon as he gazed, there burst out of the forest that great savage wild boar of Lystenesse. And lo! the jowl of that boar was all white with the foam that was churned by his tusks, and the huge tusks of the boar gleamed white in the midst of the foam. And the bristles of that great beast were like sharp wires of steel, and they too were all flecked with the foam that had fallen from the jowl of the beast. And the eyes of the wild boar gleamed like to two coals of fire, and it roared like to a devil as it fled, rending, through the forest. And ever the hounds pursued the boar, hanging upon its flanks but not daring to grapple with it in its flight, because of the terror that surrounded it.

Then when Sir Launcelot beheld that sight the love of the chase flamed up within his heart and thereupon he shouted aloud and fell to running beside the dogs after the boar, tearing his way through the briars and thorns and thickets, even as the boar and the hounds burst through them. And so Sir Launcelot and the dogs chased the boar for a great while, until at last the beast came to bay, with his back set against a great crag of stone, and there the dogs surrounded it, yelling and baying. And ever Sir Launcelot shouted them on to the assault, yet not one of the hounds dared to grapple with the wild beast because of the terror of its appearance.

So as Sir Launcelot and the dogs joined in assault about the boar, there came the sound of a horseman riding with speed and winding his horn. Then in a moment there came King Arthur himself, bursting out of the forest alone; for he had outridden all his court and was the first of all upon the field.

Then King Arthur, beholding the boar where he stood at bay, set his lance in rest with intent to charge the beast and to pierce him through the body. But the boar, all fierce and mad with the chase it had suffered, did not wait that charge of the King but himself charged the horseman. And at that charge King Arthur's horse was affrighted, with the terror of the beast and flung suddenly aside so that the lance of King Arthur failed of its aim.

The boar overthroweth King Arthur Therewith the boar ran up under the point of the lance and he catched the horse of the King with his tusks and ripped the horse so that both horse and rider fell to the ground; King Arthur beneath the wounded animal, so that he could not free his leg to rise from his fall.

Then it would have been ill indeed with King Arthur but for that forest madman. For beholding the fall of the King, Sir Launcelot ran straightway to him. And he seized the sword of the King and plucked it forth from its sheath. Therewith he leaped at the boar and lashed at it a mighty buffet, and as he did so his foot slipped in the blood of the horse which there lay upon the ground, and he fell flat with the force of that blow which he purposed should destroy the boar.

Thereupon the boar, finding himself thus attacked by another, turned upon that other and ere Sir Launcelot could arise from his fall it was upon him. And the boar ripped Sir Launcelot with its tusks through the flesh of the thigh, even to the hip bone.

Now, when Sir Launcelot felt the pang of that dreadful wound *The madman* which the boar gave him he yelled aloud. At the same time his soul *slayeth the* was filled with a great passion of rage and madness so that, ere the *boar* boar could charge him again, he leaped to his feet and rushed upon the boar. And Sir Launcelot smote the boar such a terrible dreadful stroke that he cut through the bristles of the neck and through the spine of the neck and half-way through the neck itself, so that the head of the boar was wellnigh cut away from its body.

Therewith the boar fell down dead and Sir Launcelot staggered and stood leaning upon the sword, groaning amain with the bitter pangs of pain that racked him.

Right so, as Sir Launcelot stood thus, the other huntsmen of the King's party came bursting out of the forest with the sound of horses and of shouting voices.

Then when Sir Launcelot beheld them he thought, because of his madness and the raging of his torments, that these were they who had hurt him. So therewith he roared like to a wild beast and he ran at those newcomers, whirling the sword of King Arthur like lightning around his head.

Then several of those set their lances in rest with intent to run the madman through the body ere he could do a harm to any one, but King Arthur cried out: "Beware what you do! Do him no harm, for he hath saved my life." So those who would else have charged Sir Launcelot held their hands and drew away in retreat before him.

But already Sir Launcelot's strength was failing him, for his brains were even then swimming with faintness. So in a little he sank down in a swoon and lay all of a heap upon the ground.

Then the King, and the others who were there came to where he lay bleeding and swooning, and all looked down upon him, and because he was all naked and unkempt they knew him not. But nevertheless, they beheld that he was of great girth and that he was covered over with a great many scars of battle, and they all felt deep pity for him as he lay there. Then King Arthur said: "This is the framework of a mighty champion. Pity indeed that he should have come to this as we behold him." And he said: "Lift him up tenderly and bear him hence to where he may have comfort and nourishment."

So they lifted Sir Launcelot with great gentleness, and they bare him away from that place, and they brought him to the hut of that hermit where he had been healed aforetime when he had received that grievous wound in the tournament at Astolat.

So the hermit received Sir Launcelot and wist not who he was. For though he beheld that here was a man of mighty girth and stature, yet was the great champion so changed by his madness and by his continued fasting in the forest that even his nearest friends might not know him. Nevertheless, though the hermit knew him not, yet he had them lay that forest madman upon a cot in his cell, and he searched that wound in the madman's thigh and bathed it with tepid water, and anointed it with balm and bound it up with bands of smooth white linen, so that that wound was in all ways well searched and dressed.

The madman lyeth in the hermit's cell And the hermit looked upon Sir Launcelot and beheld that he was all gaunt and hollow with hunger and he said: "If this poor mad creature is not fed, he will die in a little while." So when Sir Launcelot had revived him from that swoon, the good old man fetched milk and white bread and offered them to the sick man. But he would not touch that food. For, though he was dying of hunger, yet he loathed that food because of his madness.

So Sir Launcelot lay there wounded and famishing and the hermit wist not what to do to make him eat. And he lay in that wise for three days and ever the hermit watched him and tried to make him partake of food, and ever the madman would fling away from the food that was offered him.

Now upon the fourth day, the hermit being at his orisons in the chapel, Sir Launcelot made assay to rise, and in spite of his weakness, he did arise. And having thus arisen, he found strength in some wise for to crawl out of the hut of the hermit, and the hermit at his prayers wist not that the wounded man was gone. And after that Sir Launcelot crept away into the forest and so hid himself, very cunningly, like to a wild creature, so that, though the hermit searched for him ever so closely, yet he was not able to find him. And the hermit said: "Alas for this! For certes this poor madman will die of his wound and of starvation all alone here in the forest, and no one can bring him succor." *The madman escapeth from the cell of the hermit*

So it was that Sir Launcelot escaped from the cell of the hermit a second time. And now it remaineth to be told how he returned to Corbin and to the Lady Elaine the Fair, and how the Lady Elaine cherished him and brought him back to health and strength and comeliness again. So I pray you to read that which followeth if you would fain learn concerning those things.

The Lady Elaine the Fair knoweth Sir Launcelot:

Chapter Third

How Sir Launcelot returned to Corbin again and how the Lady Elaine the Fair cherished him and brought him back to health. Also how Sir Launcelot with the Lady Elaine withdrew to Joyous Isle.

O SIR LAUNCELOT escaped from the cell of the hermit as aforetold. And he lay hidden in the thickets all that day till the night had come. And when the night had come he arose and turned his face toward the eastward and thitherward he made his way.

For death was very close to Sir Launcelot and there was but one thought in his mind and that thought was to return to Corbin. For even through his clouds of madness, Sir Launcelot wist that there at Corbin a great love awaited him and that if he might reach that place he might there have rest and peace; wherefore in this time of weakness and of pain, he willed to return to that place once more. *How Sir Launcelot returneth to Corbin*

So Sir Launcelot made his way toward Corbin, and he travelled thitherward several days and God alone knows how he did so. And one morning at the breaking of the day he came to the town of Corbin, and he entered the town by a postern gate he knew of old. And after he had entered the town he made his way slowly and with great pain up through the streets of the town and the town was still asleep. So he came unseen to the market-place of Corbin where he had aforetime slain the Worm of Corbin as aforetold, and there sat him down upon that slab of stone beneath which the Worm had made its habitation. And why he came there who shall say except that maybe there lay very dimly within his mind some remembrance that here he had one time had great honor and glory of knighthood.

So there he sat, and when the people of the town awoke they beheld sitting there in the midst of that market-place one all naked and famished who gazed about him with wild and terrified looks like to a starving wolf who had come out of the forest driven by hunger. *The people behold the madman*

And many gathered and stared at Sir Launcelot from a distance, and these laughed and jeered at him as he sat there in his nakedness, and not one of those wist that this was he who had aforetime slain the Worm of Corbin and so saved them in a time of their direst need. So they laughed and mocked him and anon some of those who were there began to cast stones at him with intent to drive him away from that place. So, at last, one of those stones struck Sir Launcelot where he sat, and at that his rage flamed up and took possession of him, whereupon he leaped up and ran at those who were tormenting him. And he catched a young man of the town and heaved him up and cast him down so violently upon the earth that he broke the bone of his thigh.

The people assail the madman Upon that all those who were there shouted and screamed and fled away. And anon they returned and began stoning Sir Launcelot where he stood glaring and gnashing his teeth with the man whom he had hurt lying upon the ground at his feet. And many stones struck Sir Launcelot, some wounding him upon the head and some upon the body. And now and then Sir Launcelot would charge the mob in his rage, and the mob would scatter before him like chaff before a gust of wind; but ever they would return and begin stoning him again.

So stoning Sir Launcelot and so Sir Launcelot charging the mob, the people drove him out of the market-place. And they drave him through the town and Sir Launcelot retreated before them toward the castle; for he wist even in his madness that there were friends there who should help him. So he ever retreated until he had come to a postern gate of the castle, and there he took stand with his back set against a wall. So at that place he maintained his stand, facing the mob and glaring upon them, until at last a stone smote him upon the head and he fell to the earth.

They of the castle save Sir Launcelot Then it would have fared very hard with Sir Launcelot, even to his death, had not they within the castle, hearing the uproar of the multitude, flung open the postern gate of a sudden and so come charging out upon the mob. Thereupon the multitude, being thus charged by the armed folk of the castle, scattered upon all sides and ran away, leaving Sir Launcelot lying where he was.

Then they of the castle came and gazed upon Sir Launcelot where he lay, and they beheld what a great and noble frame of man it was that lay there, and thereupon they took great pity that such a man should be in that condition. So the captain of the guard said: "Alas, that such a man as this has been should come to such a pass. Now let us lift him up and bear him away into the castle where he may have care and nourishment."

So they did as that captain said, and they brought Sir Launcelot into the castle of Corbin and to safety.

Now it chanced that the Lady Elaine the Fair happened to be at her window, and looking down therefrom and into the courtyard she beheld where several men at arms bore a wounded man into the castle from that postern gate. As they passed beneath where she was, the Lady Elaine looked down upon the countenance of the wounded man. Then she beheld his face with the sun shining bright upon it, and at that a thought struck through her like to the stroke of a keen, sharp knife, whereat the Lady Elaine clasped her hands and cried out aloud: "My soul! My soul! What is this? Can it be he?" *The Lady Elaine knoweth Sir Launcelot*

Now there was in attendance upon the Lady Elaine at that time a certain very old and sedate lady of the court who had been her nurse and caretaker ever since her mother had died, leaving her a little helpless babe cast adrift upon the world. And the name of that lady was Dame Brysen. So Elaine ran to where Dame Brysen was and she cast herself upon her knees before Dame Brysen and buried her face in Dame Brysen's lap even as though it were her mother who sat there. And she cried out from where she lay with her face in that lady's lap, "Alas! Alas! Alas! Methinks I have beheld a most terrible sight!" Dame Brysen, speaking as in affright, said, "What hast thou seen, my child?" The Lady Elaine said: "Methinks I have beheld Sir Launcelot all starved with famine, and bruised and bleeding, and lying so nigh to death that I know not whether he is dead or not."

Dame Brysen said: "What is this thou sayst, my child? Where sawst thou such a sight as that? Hast thou been dreaming?" The Lady Elaine said: "Nay, I have not been dreaming, for, certes, as I stood at the window a little while ago I saw Sir Launcelot, and several men bore him into the castle courtyard through the postern gate, and he was all naked and starved and wounded and bruised."

The Dame Brysen said: "Nay, child, calm thyself; what ails thee to think so strange a thing as that? That man whom thou didst see was not Sir Launcelot, but was a poor madman whom the townsfolk were stoning at the postern gate."

But the Lady Elaine cried out all the more vehemently: "I fear! I fear! Certes that was Sir Launcelot! Now take me to him so that I may be assured whether it was he or not, for otherwise meseems I shall go mad!"

Then Dame Brysen perceived how it was with the Lady Elaine and that she was like one gone distracted, and she wist that there was naught to do but to let her have her will of this matter. Wherefore she said, "It shall be as thou wilt have it."

The Lady Elaine cometh to Sir Launcelot So Dame Brysen arose and she took the Lady Elaine by the hand and she led her to that place where the madman lay, and they beheld that he lay in a little cell of stone, very gloomy and dark. For the only light that came into that place was through a small window, barred with iron, and the window was not more than two hands' breadth in width. Yet by the dim light of this small window they beheld the wounded man where he lay upon a hard pallet of straw. And they beheld that he was in a sleep as though it were a swoon of death and they beheld that his face was like death for whiteness.

Then in that gloomy light the Lady Elaine came and kneeled down beside the couch whereon he lay and looked down into Sir Launcelot's face and she studied his face as though it were a book written very fine and small; and ever her breath came more and more quickly as it would suffocate her, for she felt assured that this was indeed Sir Launcelot. And anon she took Sir Launcelot's hand, all thin with famine and as cold as ice, and she looked at it and she beheld a ring upon the finger and the ring was set with a clear blue stone, and thereupon the Lady Elaine knew that this was the ring which the Lady of the Lake had given Sir Launcelot aforetime.

The Lady Elaine weepeth Thereupon she knew that this was indeed Sir Launcelot and she cried out in a very loud and piercing voice, "It is he! It is he!" and so crying she fell to weeping with great passion. And she kissed Sir Launcelot's hand and pressed it to her throat and kissed it again and yet again.

Then Dame Brysen leaned over the Lady Elaine and catched her beneath the arm and said: "Lady, Lady! restrain your passion! remember yourself, and that people are here who will see you." Therewith Dame Brysen lifted the Lady Elaine up from where she kneeled, and she brought her out of that gloomy place, still weeping with a great passion of love and pity. But yet the Lady Elaine had so much thought for herself that she drew her veil across her face so that none might behold her passion, and she said to Dame Brysen, "Take me to my father," and so, Dame Brysen, embracing her with one arm, led her to where King Pelles was.

Then, when the Lady Elaine beheld her father standing before her, she flung herself upon her knees and embraced him about the thighs, crying: "Father! Father! I have seen him and he is in this castle!" At this passion of sorrow King Pelles was much amazed and he said, "Whom hast thou seen, my daughter?" She said: "I have seen Sir Launcelot, and it was he whom they fetched into the castle but now to save him from the townsfolk who were stoning him to death at the postern gate." Then King Pelles was amazed beyond measure and he said: "Can such a thing be true? How knowest thou it was he?" She said: "I know him by many signs, for I knew him by my love for him and I knew him by his face, and I knew him by the ring set with a blue stone which he weareth upon his finger." *The Lady Elaine telleth her father of Sir Launcelot*

Then King Pelles lifted up the Lady Elaine where she kneeled at his feet and he said: "Daughter, stay thy weeping and I will go and examine into this."

So he did as he said and he went to the cell and he looked long upon Sir Launcelot as he lay there. And he looked at the ring which the wounded man wore upon his finger. So after a while King Pelles knew that that was indeed Sir Launcelot who lay there, albeit he would not have known him, had not the Lady Elaine first declared that it was he.

So immediately King Pelles bade those who were in attendance to lift Sir Launcelot up and to bear him very tenderly away from that place and to bring him to a fair large room. So they did as King Pelles commanded and they laid Sir Launcelot upon a couch of down spread with a coverlet of wadded satin. And King Pelles sent for a skilful leech to come and to search Sir Launcelot's hurts and he bade the physician for to take all heed to save his life. And all that while Sir Launcelot lay in that deep swoon like to death and awoke not.

And Sir Launcelot slept in that wise for three full days and when he awoke the Lady Elaine and her father and Dame Brysen and the leech alone were present. And lo! when Sir Launcelot awoke his brain was clear of madness and he was himself again, though weak, like to a little child who hath been ill abed.

How Sir Launcelot awoke from his madness That time the Lady Elaine was kneeling beside Sir Launcelot's couch and hers was the face he first beheld. Then Sir Launcelot said, speaking very faint and weak, "Where am I?" and the Lady Elaine wept and said, "Lord, you are safe with those who hold you very dear." Sir Launcelot said, "What has befallen me?" She said: "Lord, thou hast been bedazed in thy mind and hast been sorely hurt with grievous wounds, wherefore thou hast been upon the very edge of death. But now thou art safe with those who love thee."

He said, "Have I then been mad?" And to that they who were there said naught. Then Sir Launcelot said again, "Have I been mad?" and thereupon King Pelles said, "Yea, Messire."

Then Sir Launcelot groaned as from his soul, and he covered his face with one hand (for the Lady Elaine held the other hand in hers) and he said, "What shame! What shame!" And therewith he groaned again.

How Sir Launcelot was cherished Then, ever weeping, the Lady Elaine said, "No shame, Lord, but only very great pity!" and she kissed his hand and washed it with her tears. And Sir Launcelot wept also because of his great weakness, and by and by he said, "Elaine, meseems I have no hope or honor save in thee," and she said, "Take peace, Sir, for in my heart there is indeed both honor for you and hope for your great happiness." And so Sir Launcelot did take peace.

Then after a while Sir Launcelot said, "Who here knoweth of my madness?" and King Pelles said, "Only a very few in this castle, Messire."

Then Sir Launcelot said: "I pray you that this be all as secret as possible, and that no word concerning me goes beyond these walls." And King Pelles said, "It shall be as you would have it, Messire."

So it was that the news of Sir Launcelot's madness and of his recovery was not carried beyond those walls.

Now after a fortnight had passed, Sir Launcelot was fast becoming cured in body and mind. And one day he and the Lady Elaine were alone in that room where he lay and he said, "Lady, meseems you have had great cause to hate me." At this she looked upon him and smiled, and she said, "How could I hate thee, Launcelot?" Sir Launcelot said, "Elaine, I have done thee great and grievous wrong in times gone by." She said, "Say naught of that." "Yea," he said, "I must say much of that, for I have this to say of it, that I would that I could undo that wrong which I did thee by my neglect. But what have I aught to offer thee in compensation? Naught but mine own broken and beggared life. Yet that poor life and all that it holds dearest I would fain offer thee if only it might be a compensation to thee." *Sir Launcelot and Elaine commune together*

Then the Lady Elaine looked very long and intently at Sir Launcelot and she said: "Sir Launcelot, thy lips speak of duty, but that which boots is that thy heart should speak of duty. For if so be that thou hast ever done me wrong, thou canst not hope to remove that wrong by the words of thy mouth. But if from thy heart thou sayst, 'I have wronged this one and I would fain make amends,' then indeed may that wrong be very quickly amended."

Then Sir Launcelot smiled and he said: "And so I have looked well into my heart ere I spake to thee, and so it is my heart that speaks and not my lips. For in my heart meseems I find great love for thee and certes I find all honor and reverence for thee lying therein, and moving me to everything that I now hope to do or to perform. Now tell me, Lady, what can any heart hold more than that?" And Elaine said, "Meseems it can hold no more."

Then Sir Launcelot took her by the hand and drew her to him and she went to him, and he kissed her upon the lips and she forbade him not. So they two were reconciled in peace and happiness.

So when Sir Launcelot was altogether healed of his sickness, they two were married. And after they were married, King Pelles gave to them a very noble castle for to be their dwelling-place and that castle was called the Castle of Blayne. *Sir Launcelot and the Lady Elaine are wedded*

That castle stood upon a very beautiful island in the midst of a lake of pure water as clear as crystal. And the island was covered over with many plantations and orchards of beautiful trees of various foliages. And there were gardens and meadows upon that island and there was a town about the castle so fair that when one stood upon the margin of that lake and gazed across the lake to the town and the castle he beheld such a place as one may see in a shining dream.

So Sir Launcelot, because of the great peace of that island and because of the peace which he hoped to find there, called it the Joyous Isle, and so it was known of all men from that time forth.

✛   ✛   ✛

So endeth this part of the history of Sir Launcelot with only this to say. That he dwelt there in Joyous Isle in seeming peace and contentment.

How Sir Launcelot dwelt in Joyous Isle Yet was it indeed peace and contentment that he felt? Alas, that it should be so, but so it was that ever and anon he would remember him of other days of doughty deeds of glory and renown, and ever and anon he would bethink him of that beautiful queen to whom he had one time uplifted his eyes, and of whom he had now no right to think of in that wise. Then his soul would up in arms and would cry out aloud: "Let us go hence and seek that glory and that other's love once more! Are not all thy comrades waiting for thee to return, and doth not she also look for thee?" Then Sir Launcelot would ever say to his soul, "Down, proud spirit, and think not of these things, but of duty." But ever and anon that spirit would arise again within him and would struggle with the bonds of honor that held it in check. And ever Sir Launcelot would say, "That which remaineth for me is my duty and my peace of soul."

For indeed it is so that the will of a man is but a poor weak defence against the thoughts that arise within a stubborn heart. For, though a man may will to do that which is right, yet may his thoughts ever turn to that which is wrong; and though he may refrain from doing wrong, yet it is in spite of his desirings that he thus refraineth. Yea; there is no help for a man to contain himself within the bounds of duty, save only that he hath the love of God within his heart. For only when his feet are planted upon that rock may he hope to withstand the powerful thoughts that urge him to do that which is wrong.

So it was with Sir Launcelot at that time; for though he ever willed to do that which was right, yet his desires ever called to him to depart from the paths of honor and truth in which he walked, and so he was oftentimes much troubled in his spirit.

The Story of Sir Ewaine and the Lady of the Fountain

*H*ERE BEGINNETH *the story of Sir Ewaine; of how he went forth to search for Sir Launcelot in company with Sir Percival of Gales; of how they two met Sir Sagramore in a condition of great disrepute; and of how Sir Ewaine undertook a very strange adventure, in which he succeeded, after great danger to his life, in winning the most fair Lady of the Fountain for his wife.*

Sir Gawaine, Knight of the Fountain:

Chapter First

How Sir Ewaine and Sir Percival departed together in quest of Sir Launcelot, and how they met Sir Sagramore, who had failed in a certain adventure. Also how Sir Sagramore told his story concerning that adventure.

T HATH already been told in this book how certain knights of King Arthur's court—to wit, Sir Ector de Maris, Sir Lionel, Sir Bors de Ganis, Sir Gawaine, Sir Ewaine, Sir Percival, Sir Sagramore the Desirous and Sir Agravaine went forth upon Queen Guinevere's command to search for Sir Launcelot and to bring him back to the court of the King.

Upon that quest, Sir Percival and Sir Ewaine rode together for the sake of companionship. And they made agreement to travel together in that wise until the fortunes of adventure should separate them. *Sir Percival and Sir Ewaine ride forth together*

So they rode side by side in very pleasant companionship, taking the way that chance led them, yet everywhere seeking for news of Sir Launcelot, of whom they could find no word of any sort.

In those days the world was very fresh and young, so that it was great pleasure to journey in that wise, for anon they two rode beneath blue skies and anon through gentle showers, anon up hill and anon down dale, anon through countryside, anon through town, anon through forest and anon through wold. Yea; in those days,

when the world was young, all things of life were so gay and joyous that it was little wonder that good knights like those twain took
delight in being abroad in that wise, for so they might breathe more
freely, out in the wider expanses of God's world, and so the spirit
within them might expand to a greater joy of life than would be possible in court or in lady's bower.

So those two worthy gentlemen travelled as aforesaid in good-
fellowship together, journeying hither or yon for a fortnight, neither
hearing aught of Sir Launcelot, or meeting with any adventure whatsoever, and lodging them at night at what place chance might happen
to bring them.

They perceive a castle in a valley   At the end of that time—to wit, a fortnight—they came to a certain high hill and from the summit thereof they beheld a valley that
lay stretched out beneath them. And they beheld a fair tall castle that
stood in the midst of that valley, and the castle was surrounded by
a little town and the town was surrounded by many fair fields and
plantations and orchards of fruit-trees. And at that time evening was
coming on apace, and all the golden sky was fading into a pale silver,
wonderfully clear and fine, with a single star, like a jewel, shining in
the midst of the bright yet fading firmament.

Then Sir Ewaine said: "Sir, let us go down to yonder place and
seek lodging at that fair castle, for meseems that must be a very pleasant place to abide for the coming night." To the which Sir Percival
replied, "Let it be so, brother," and therewith they rode down into
that valley and to that castle. And when they had reached the castle,
Sir Percival blew his bugle horn very loud and clear, and straightway
there came several of the attendants of the castle who bade them welcome and led them within the gateway thereof. There, when they
had arrived, came the major of the castle, and requested them that
they would tell what was their name and their degree, and when the
two knights had announced these there was great rejoicing that two
such famous champions had come thitherward. So several ran and
took their horses in charge and others came and assisted them to dismount and others again led them into the castle and thence brought
them each to a fair chamber, well bedight and with a very cheerful
outlook. Then came other attendants and assisted each knight to dis-
arm and to disrobe, and after that they brought each to a bath of tepid

water. Thereafter, when they had bathed and dried themselves with fair linen towels, very soft and fragrant with lavender, these same attendants brought them rich robes of silk and garments of silk, and they dressed them and were at great ease and comfort.

For thus it was that good knights of old were received in such castles and halls wheresoever they chose to abide in that adventurous wise.

Now after Sir Ewaine and Sir Percival had refreshed themselves and bathed themselves and had clad themselves as aforetold, there came to them a certain dignitary of the castle, who brought them word that the lord of the castle desired to have speech with them. So they two went down with that attendant, and he brought them to the great hall of the castle where was the lord thereof, standing to give them welcome. He was a haughty and noble worthy with a long gray beard and he was clad in a dark purple robe embroidered with silver. When he beheld Sir Ewaine and Sir Percival coming into that place, he hastened to meet them and give them greeting and welcome beyond stint. And he said: "Welcome, welcome, fair lords! Thrice welcome to this castle! For certes it is a great glory to us all to have you with us. Moreover, I may tell you that already there is one of your fellows here at this place, and I believe you will be very glad to see him." *Sir Percival and Sir Ewaine refresh themselves at the castle*

Quoth Sir Ewaine, "Sir, who is it that is here?"

"It is Sir Sagramore who hath come hither," said the lord of the castle, and at that Sir Ewaine and Sir Percival cried out with amazement. And Sir Ewaine said, "How came Sir Sagramore hither, fair lord?" *They hear news of Sir Sagramore*

"I will tell you," said the lord of the castle. "A little before you came hitherward, there arrived at this place a knight riding without a shield and seated upon a white mule. This knight requested rest and refreshment for the night, and upon our asking him his name and degree, he at first refused to tell, for shame of his condition; yet afterward he declared that he was Sir Sagramore of King Arthur's court, and a knight of the Round Table. He also declared that he had met with a sad mischance and had lost his shield and his war-horse, wherefore he was travelling in that wise as I have told you."

"Sir," quoth Sir Ewaine, "this is a very strange thing I hear, that Sir Sagramore should be travelling in that unknightly wise. Wit you that as Sir Sagramore is a knight of the Round Table, this matter concerns both Sir Percival and myself very closely. Now I pray you for to let me have speech with him, so that I may know why it is that he hath travelled in that wise and without his knightly shield."

"It shall be as you command, Messire," said the lord of the castle, "and so I will straightway send a messenger to Sir Sagramore with word that you would have speech with him."

Sir Sagramore appeareth
So the lord of the castle sent the messenger as he said, and anon there came Sir Sagramore to where they were. But when Sir Sagramore stood before Sir Ewaine and Sir Percival, he hung his head full low, as though not wishing to look those knights in the face because of shame that they should find him there in such a condition. Then Sir Ewaine said to him: "Sir, I pray you tell me how you came by such a mischance as this, so that you ride without your shield and upon a white mule like to a strolling demoiselle?"

"Messire," said Sir Sagramore, "I will tell you the whole story, for I would have you know that it was through no disgrace but by mishap of battle that I am come to this pass."

Quoth Sir Ewaine, "I may well believe that."

Then the lord of the castle said: "Messires, ere you talk of these things I pray you to come to table and eat and drink and refresh yourselves. After that we may listen with a better spirit to what this knight has to tell us."

They all sit at feast together
So that which the lord of the castle said seemed very good to those knights, wherefore they straightway went in to table in the hall and sat down thereat. And the table was spread with all manner of meats, and there was wine of divers sorts, both red and white, and they ate and drank with much appetite and great good-will. Then when they were satisfied as to their hunger, Sir Ewaine said to Sir Sagramore: "Now, Messire, I pray you to tell us concerning that adventure which hath befallen you."

Sir Sagramore telleth of his adventures

How Sir Sagramore came to a wonderful valley of enchantment
Sir Sagramore said, "I will do so." Then he said:

"You must know that when I travelled forth errant in search of Sir Launcelot, as several of my fellows did, I went forward upon my way, making diligent inquiries concerning him, but still could get no news of him. So I travelled onward in that wise, ever making inquiries as aforesaid, until two days ago, what time in the evening I came to a certain place a considerable distance to the east of this. There I found myself in a valley that I verily believe must be the fairest valley in the world. For in that valley I beheld a very pleasant expanse of meadow-lands all abloom with flowers, and I beheld many glades of trees of an even size, some abloom with blossoms and some full of fruit. And there was a river of very clear water that flowed down through the centre of the valley, and everywhere there were birds of curious plumage that sang very bewitchingly, so from these things I wist that this valley was very likely a place of enchantment. In the midst of that valley I beheld a very noble castle that was of as wonderful an appearance as the valley itself, so I rode forward into the valley and approached the castle.

"As I drew near thereunto I beheld two youths clad in flame-colored satin who shot at a mark with bows and arrows. And the hair of the youths was yellow and curling, and each bore a frontlet of gold upon his head, and they wore upon their feet shoes of embossed leather with latchets of gold upon the insteps.

"These two youths, as I drew near, gave me very courteous greeting, and besought me that I would declare to them my name and degree, and I did so. Then they besought me that I would come with them to the castle, and I went with them with great content of spirit; for it seemed to me that this was likely to be a very fair and cheerful place to lodge over-night. So I entered with those two youths into the castle, and there came attendants and took my horse and there came others who unarmed me and led me to a bath of tepid water. After that I descended to the hall of that castle, and there I beheld that it was all hung with tapestries and fabrics of divers sorts and of very rich and beautiful designs.

"In that hall there were twelve ladies who sat embroidering cloth of satin at a window, and I think I have hardly ever seen any ladies who were so beautiful as they. Immediately I entered that room these twelve ladies arose, and she who was the fairest amongst them came forward and gave me greeting. And immediately I knew that lady that she was the Lady Vivien who beguiled the Enchanter Merlin to his undoing and his ruin. Yet in this time, I do assure you, she has

Sir Sagramore meets the Lady Vivien

grown more beautiful than ever she was before; for her hair, which was ruddy, is now like to pure gold for brightness, and it was enmeshed in a golden net, and yet one could not tell whether the net or the hair shone the more brightly. And her eyes, which are perfectly black are as bright as jewels, and her lips are like red corals and very fragrant, and her teeth are like to rich pearls. Moreover, she was clad in garments of flame-colored satin, and her neck and arms were adorned with ornaments of gold set with jewels of a great many kinds and colors. And well ye wist, Messires, that it was very difficult not to be altogether enchanted by her beauty of face and appearance.

Sir Sagramore
feasteth with
the Lady
Vivien "Yet well knowing how this lady loved mischief, I was for a time very ill at ease, not knowing whether or not she might be minded to cast some evil spell upon me. Yet she made no sign of such intent, but spake me very fair and gave me courteous greeting. And she took my hand and led me into an adjoining apartment where there was a feast set with all sorts of meats and wines, and we two took our places at the board side by side. And as we feasted so together, there came some who sang and others who made sweet music and I felt such great pleasure as I have hardly ever felt in all of my life before. Meanwhile, as we sat at the table, the Lady Vivien conversed with me upon such matters as she deemed would be of entertainment to me. And she inquired of many lords and ladies at the court of the King and spake well of them all. Then after a considerable while she inquired of me whether it would be pleasant to me to tell her upon what errand I was bound, and so I told her I was errant in search of Sir Launcelot.

"'Ha!' quoth she, 'if thou wert in search of adventure, I could bring you to one that would be well worth undertaking.'

"I said to her: 'Lady, though I am errant upon a certain business, yet I am very ready to stay my affairs for a while if so be I may meet with an adventure that may bring me any credit.'

The Lady
Vivien telleth
Sir Sagramore
of an
adventure "At that the Lady Vivien laughed, and she said: 'Sir Sagramore, I know not what credit you may obtain in this adventure, but I will tell you what you are to do to enter into it. To-morrow I will ordain that one of the youths who brought you hither shall conduct you to a certain path that leads through the forest that lies beyond this valley. If you will follow that path, you will by and by come to a mound

of earth, and on that mound you will very likely behold a man of gigantic stature who is herdsman to a herd of cattle thereabouts. Ask him where is the enchanted fountain, and he will direct you still farther upon the way.'

"I said to her: 'Lady, I am very much beholden to you for the information you give me, and I will very gladly take up with this adventure.' Upon this she laughed a very great deal and said: 'Sir Knight, it may be that after you have passed through this adventure, you will not be so pleased either with me or with yourself. Now I have this to ask of you in return for my entertainment of to-night. My request is that you will return hitherward to me after you have finished this adventure so that I may see how it hath happened with you.' I said to the lady, 'It shall be as you ask.'

"So when the next morning had come I arose very early and donned mine armor. And there came to me one of those youths *Sir Sagramore departs upon the adventure* aforetold of, and he aided me to my horse and afterward guided me through that valley. So he brought me to the borders of a woodland that lay beyond the valley and there he showed me a path and bade me take that path and it would bring me to that adventure I sought.

"Thereafter I followed that path, and after I had gone upon the way a considerable distance I came, some time before midday, to that mound whereof the lady had spoken.

"On the top of the mound there sat a man of gigantic size and so hideously ugly that I never beheld his like in all of my life before that time. This being called to me in a voice exceedingly loud and rough, demanding of me whither I went and upon what business. Thereupon I told him that I sought a certain magic fountain and that I would be much beholden to him if he would direct me upon my way. Upon this he laughed very boisterously, and after a while he said: 'Take that path yonder through the glade. Follow that path until you come to a hill. From the hilltop you will find before you a valley, and you will see in the valley a fountain of water that flows into a small lake with many lilies about the margin. At the fountain is a tall tree with wide-spreading branches, and beneath the tree is a marble slab, and upon the slab is a silver bowl attached to it by a chain of silver. Take some of the water of that fountain into the silver bowl and fling it upon the marble slab, and I believe you will find an adventure that will satisfy your desires for a very long time to come.'

Sir Sagramore cometh to the valley of the fountain

"So spake that gigantic oaf. I took the path to which he directed me, and I followed the path until I came to the hill, and I climbed the hill and there I beheld the valley of which he spake. And I beheld the lake of lilies of which he spake and I beheld the fountain that flowed

Sir Sagramore poureth water upon the slab

into the lake and I beheld the tree that overshadowed the fountain, so I straightway rode down into the valley thereunto. And when I had come to the tree I beheld the slab of stone and the bowl of silver just as that gigantic herdsman had said that I would find them. Then I dipped the silver bowl into the water as he had told me to do and I flung the water of the fountain upon the marble slab.

"Then immediately a very singular thing happened, for lo! the earth began to tremble and to shake, and the skies began, as it were, to thunder, and all over the sky there spread a cloud of very great blackness and density so that whilst it was still midday, it began to grow dark like night-time. Then there came a great wind of such strength that I thought it would blow me away, and after that there fell a rain in such quantities and with such deluge that methought I would be drowned by that rain. And the rain roared down in torrents everywhere through that valley as it were a deluge. And, as the rain fell and the thunder burst forth from the sky and the lightning flamed like living fire, I heard, as from a very great distance, the sound of many voices raised in lamentation.

"Then, by and by, the storm passed and the clouds disappeared and the sun came forth with extraordinary brightness. Then lo! there happened another singular thing, for presently there came a great multitude of birds flying through the air, and they lodged in that tree above the fountain, and they sang with such exquisite melody that methought that my heart would break with the joy of their singing.

"Now whilst I sat there listening to those birds, I beheld where, a great way off, there came a horseman riding with extraordinary rapidity across the plain, and as he drew nigh I beheld that he was a knight seated upon a black horse and clad all in black armor. This knight came riding very violently toward where I was, and he called out in a very fierce loud voice: 'Sir Knight, wherefore did you meddle with my fountain. Know that you have brought a great deluge upon this land, and for that I am come hither to punish you. Now defend yourself from my anger, for it is very great.'

"Therewith he made ready to assail me, and I upon my part immediately put myself into a posture of defence, and dressed my shield and my spear, and took post upon the meadow close to the fountain. After that I ran a tilt against that knight and he ran against me, and he cast me out of my saddle with such violence that methinks I have never before felt a buffet like to that which I then received. *Sir Sagramore is overthrown by the Knight of the Fountain*

"Having thus cast me down, he paid no more heed to me than if I had been a billet of wood, but he took from me my shield and he laid it upon the saddle of my horse and he took my horse by the rein and rode away from that place, leaving me still lying upon the ground. And in departing he said not one single word to me. And indeed I do think, Messires, that I was never so abashed in all my life before.

"Then I remembered how that I had pledged myself to return to the Lady Vivien, and at that I was more ashamed than ever. So, in obedience to that promise, I had to make my way back whence I came on foot. When I passed by where was that mound, the gigantic creature who sat thereon made great mock of me. And when I reached the castle, the Lady Vivien looked at me out of a window and laughed at me beyond measure. And when I requested admission to the castle, she denied me entrance thereunto, and when I besought her for to lend me a horse to ride upon my way, she gave me instead a white mule for to bear me thence. So I returned hitherward upon a white mule without any shield, and thus I have confessed everything to you to the last word." *The Lady Vivien mocketh Sir Sagramore*

Such was the story of Sir Sagramore, and thereunto all those who were there listened with great attention and with much amazement. Then Sir Ewaine spake, saying: "That was a very great shame that was put upon you, Messire; and I take it so greatly to heart that had I suffered it in my own person methinks I could not feel much greater shame than I do. For that which hath befallen you is, as it were, a despite put upon all of us who are knights of the Round Table. Wherefore, being a fellow of that company, your despite is my despite also. As for that mischievous Lady Vivien, methinks that she is at the bottom of all this coil, and I am much misled if this hath not all been devised by her to bring shame upon you who are a knight of King Arthur's court and of the Round Table."

Quoth Sir Percival, "That may very well be so, Messire."

Then Sir Ewaine said: "Well, Messires, as for me, I am of no mind to sit down quietly under this affront."

"Sir," said Sir Sagramore, "what would you do?"

"I would do this," said Sir Ewaine. "I would go upon that same quest in which you have failed, and if I succeed therein, then will the shame of your mischance be wiped away from us all."

Thus spake Sir Ewaine with great feeling; for you are to know that those noble knights of the Round Table were so closely knit into brotherly fellowship that whatsoever ill thing befell to the injury of one was in that same measure an injury to all, and that whatsoever quarrel was taken up by one of that company, was a quarrel appertaining to all. Wherefore it was the injury that had been done to Sir Sagramore was also an injury done to Sir Ewaine, and so it was that Sir Ewaine felt himself called upon to undertake that adventure in which Sir Sagramore had failed as aforesaid.

Then Sir Ewaine said: "Now I prithee tell me where that path is that may bring me to this adventure and to-morrow I will part from you and will myself enter upon it. Meantime, do you both resume your quest of Sir Launcelot, and if I should not prosper in this undertaking, I will return hither and leave report of my happenings. Wherefore at this place you may, at any time, easily hear what hath befallen me if you will come hither."

Sir Ewaine departeth upon the Adventure of the Fountain So Sir Sagramore gave Sir Ewaine such directions for that adventure as were necessary and after that they all went to bed to rest them after their travails of the day. And when the next morning had come and while the dew still lay upon the grass, shining like to a thin veil of fine, bright silver spread over the level meadow-lands, Sir Ewaine arose all in the freshness of the early daytime and busked him whilst the rest of the castle still lay fast asleep. And he donned his armor and went down and aroused the sleeping groom and gave command that his horse should be brought to him; and after the groom had apparelled his horse he mounted and rode forth upon that way which Sir Sagramore had advised him would lead him toward the castle of the Lady Vivien.

And now if you would know how Sir Ewaine prospered in that undertaking which he had assumed, I pray you to read further in this history and you shall hear how it befell with him.

ir Ewaine poureth water on
the slab:

Chapter Second

How Sir Ewaine undertook that adventure in which Sir Sagramore had failed, and how it sped with him thereafter.

THUS IT was that Sir Ewaine departed upon that adventure whilst Sir Percival and Sir Sagramore were still asleep, and no one wist of his going saving only the groom. After he wended his way from that place until he had come to the woodlands, and he entered the woodlands and travelled therein for a long while, breaking his fast with the charcoal burners whom he found there at a curious place. About the middle of the morning he came to a high hill, and when he had climbed this hill he beheld before him a very strangely beautiful valley, and he beheld that in the midst of the valley there stood a wonderful castle, and he wist that this must be the castle of the Lady Vivien of which Sir Sagramore had aforetold of.

And Sir Ewaine was astonished at the wonderful appearance of that castle and the valley in which it stood. For this castle was bright and shining as though of polished stone, and the roofs thereof were of bright red tile variegated with dark green tiles and black tiles, laid in sundry figures and patterns very strange to behold. And the valley in which the castle stood was spread out with fair lawns and gardens and meadow-lands and plantations of comely trees. And everywhere there were flowers abloom in incredible quantities, and there were thousands of birds of bright plumage that sang in the trees throughout the valley, so that the multitudinous sounds of their singing came even to Sir Ewaine where he sat so far distant. And ever those birds flitted like bright sparks of color hither and thither through the foliage of the trees, and Sir Ewaine had never beheld their like before in all of his life. So because of the wonderfulness of all that he beheld, Sir Ewaine wist that this must be a land of faery and enchantment with which the Lady Vivien had surrounded her castle and herself and her court. So for a while Sir Ewaine sat there observing all these

Sir Ewaine cometh to the castle of the Lady Vivien

things, and after a while he set spurs to horse and rode down into that valley and toward the castle.

Now when Sir Ewaine had come pretty near to the castle, he beheld two youths with golden hair, clad in garments of flame-colored satin, and he knew that these must be the two fair youths of whom Sir Sagramore had spoken. And he saw that those two youths were playing at ball under the walls of the castle just as Sir Sagramore had beheld them when he had visited that place.

These, when Sir Ewaine drew nigh, ceased their play, and he who was the chief of the twain came forward and greeted that noble knight with great courtesy, saying: "Sir Knight, you are very welcome to these parts where not many ever come. For she who is the lady of this castle ever takes pleasure in giving welcome to such as you who come thitherward. Now I pray you of your courtesy to tell me who you are and upon what quest you are bound and what is your degree, for I would fain announce you with all dignity to the lady of the castle."

Quoth Sir Ewaine: "Fair youth, you are to know that I am a knight of King Arthur's court, and that I am a fellow of the Round Table. My name is Sir Ewaine, and I am King Uriens' son of Gore, my mother being Queen Morgana le Fay. As for your lady, I know very well who she is, and that she is none other than the Enchantress Vivien. Moreover, I know that she is not at all above devising mischief against me because I am a knight of King Arthur and of his Round Table. Yet I will that you bring me before this lady, for I would fain have speech with her."

Upon this, so boldly said by Sir Ewaine, those two fair youths were adoubt, wherefore they withdrew a little to one side and held consultation together. Then he who had before spoken to Sir Ewaine spake again, saying: "Messire, I trust you have it not in your mind to do any ill to the lady of this castle, for unless we are well assured upon that point we will not bring you to her."

"Rest ye easy," quoth Sir Ewaine; "I am a true knight, and mean no ill to any lady, be she evil or good. Only I would have speech with her as presently as may be."

Then the youth who was the speaker for the two said, "Sir, I will take you to her."

So forthwith that youth led the way into the enchanted castle *Sir Ewaine* and Sir Ewaine followed closely after him. And after they had come *cometh to the Lady Vivien* unto the castle and after Sir Ewaine had dismounted from his horse and after they had traversed various spaces, the youth brought Sir Ewaine to where the Lady Vivien was. And she was in her own fair bower with her eleven damsels gathered about her.

Now the news of the coming of Sir Ewaine had gone before him, *The Lady* so that when he came to the Lady Vivien she arose from her seat *Vivien giveth welcome to* and went forward to meet him and received him with her face all *Sir Ewaine* wreathed with smiles. And she said: "Welcome! Welcome! Thrice welcome, Sir Ewaine! Now I pray you to let my attendants conduct you to a fair room where you may bathe and refresh yourself, for we would fain have you stay with us at this place for a day or two or three if so be you will favor us so greatly."

But Sir Ewaine neither smiled nor made acknowledgment of any sort; otherwise he spake with great sternness, saying: "Fair Lady, I know you well, and I know that you have no very good will toward us who are of King Arthur's court. I know that you continually devise mischief and enchantments against all who come near you, and I well believe that could you do so without danger to yourself, you would this moment practise mischiefs against me. Nevertheless, I am not come hither to chide you because of your shortcomings, for though all those things are well known to me and to others, yet I leave it to God to judge you in His own wisdom and am not come hither to be myself your judge. What I have come for is this: not long since you sent my fellow, Sir Sagramore, upon an adventure that brought great shame upon him. Now I pray you that you will direct me to that same adventure so that I may undertake it, for, if so be I have that good fortune, I would fain punish that discourteous knight who so shamed my companion at arms."

Then the Lady Vivien laughed very high and shrill. "Sir," quoth she, "you are very brave for to undertake that adventure wherein so good a knight as Sir Sagramore failed so signally. Gladly will I direct you upon your way, and all that I ask in return is that when you have sped in that adventure, you will also return hither as did Sir Sagramore, so that I may bestow a white mule upon you as I bestowed one to him."

To this Sir Ewaine bowed his head very gravely and said: "Be it so. Show me the way to that adventure, and if I fail therein, then I will submit myself to you so that you may humiliate me as you humiliated Sir Sagramore."

Sir Ewaine entereth into the Adventure of the Fountain
Then the Lady Vivien called to her that youth who had afore spoken to Sir Ewaine, and she bade him set Sir Ewaine upon the path that should lead him to that adventure he sought. And after that Sir Ewaine left the Lady Vivien without any further word and he took horse and departed thence. And that fair youth with the golden hair went before Sir Ewaine to the skirts of the forest that lay upon the other side of the valley from that side upon which Sir Ewaine had entered it. Then the youth showed Sir Ewaine a certain path that led into the forest and he said: "Take that path, fair lord, and it will bring you to your adventure."

So Sir Ewaine took the path as the youth directed and he travelled upon it for an hour or two and by and by he came to an open place in the woodland. And in the midst of that open place there was a high mound of earth covered with fair green grass and many sheep browsed upon the slopes of the mound and coadjacent thereunto. And on the mound there sat the being of whom Sir Sagramore had spoken, and Sir Ewaine was amazed at his hideous aspect. For he was of giant stature and swarthy black, and his hair was red as brick. His mouth gaped wide like a cavern and the teeth within were sharp like the teeth of a wild beast.

To this creature Sir Ewaine spake, saying, "Sirrah, whither shall I go to find that Adventure of the Fountain?"

Upon this that giant being laughed like the pealing of thunder and he said: "Ho! little man, have you come also to that adventure? The day before yesterday one came hither and sped but ill, and so also, I doubt not, it will fare with you. Take you yonder path, and I believe you will come to that adventure all too soon for your own good."

Sir Ewaine cometh to the valley of the fountain
So Sir Ewaine took the path that that being directed, and so entering the woodlands again he rode for a long while through the thick forests. Then after a while he came to a hill and he ascended the hill, and when he had reached the top thereof he found that the forest ceased and that the open country lay spread out before him and he

beheld a fair and level valley lying beneath the hill. And he beheld that the valley was very fertile with many fields and plantations of fair trees. And Sir Ewaine beheld in that valley a lake and a fountain that flowed into the lake and a tree that overshadowed the fountain, and he wist that this was the place where Sir Sagramore had met with that adventure aforetold of. So straightway he rode down into that valley and toward that place where was the enchanted fountain overshadowed by the tree. And when he reached that place he beheld the slab of stone and the silver bowl chained to the slab by a silver chain just as Sir Sagramore had beheld those things.

Then Sir Ewaine took the silver bowl into his hand and he dipped up water therein from the fountain, and he flung the water upon the marble slab as Sir Sagramore had done. *Sir Ewaine casteth water upon the slab*

Then straightway it befell as it had with Sir Sagramore, for first the earth began to tremble and to quake and then the sky began to thunder, and then there arose a great cloud that overspread the sky, so that it became all black like unto night time, although it was still the middle of the day. Then there came the great wind, the like of which Sir Ewaine had never before known in all his life, for it blew with such strength of fury that he was afraid it would blow him away from that place. Then there fell such a deluge of rain that he feared he would be drowned therewith. And whilst the rain fell in that wise he heard a multitude of voices in lamentation as though a great way off, just as Sir Sagramore had heard these voices.

Anon the rain ceased and the clouds passed away, and the sun came forth and shone with wonderful warmth and brightness, and thereupon a great flock of small birds came flying to that tree and perched in the branches thereof so that the tree was entirely filled with the multitude of feathered creatures gathered there. And that multitude of birds began to sing in such a wise, that when Sir Ewaine listened to that singing he wist not whether he were in paradise or upon earth, so sweet and piercing was the melody of their singing. And all these things befell with Sir Ewaine as they had befallen aforetime with Sir Sagramore.

Now, whilst Sir Ewaine stood listening in that wise, all bewitched by the singing of those birds, he was aware of one who came riding very rapidly toward him across the plain. And as that rider drew nigh unto Sir Ewaine, he beheld that he was a knight clad all in black armor and seated upon a great charger which was entirely black and which was hung with trappings as black as any raven. And the knight bore a shield which was altogether black and without any device whatsoever. And he was of a very terrible appearance, being huge of form and violent and fierce in his advance.

This black knight, when he had come close to that place where Sir Ewaine awaited him, cried out in a great voice: "Sir Knight, why didst thou come hither to meddle with my fountain? Know thou that thou hast brought a great deluge upon all this land so that thou hast wrought great damage to us who are the people thereof. But now thou shalt pay very dearly for the injury thou hast done. Prepare thyself straightway for battle!"

Unto this Sir Ewaine made reply: "Sir Knight, I wist not that in throwing water upon yonder slab I was doing injury to thee or to any one. Nevertheless, I am ready to meet thee in battle as thou dost make demand." Therewith Sir Ewaine dressed his shield and his spear and took his station in the meadow near the fountain and beside the lake, and put himself in such array for defence as he was able.

Sir Ewaine doeth battle with the Knight of the Fountain So when they both had prepared themselves in all ways they let go their horses the one against the other, in very violent assault, rushing together like a whirlwind. And so they met together in the midst of the course with an uproar as of thunder; the one smiting against the other with such violence that the spear of each was burst all into pieces unto the very truncheon thereof. And in that assault both knights would assuredly have been overthrown excepting for the wonderful address of each. For each drave spur into steed and shouted aloud so that each charger recovered his feet and fell not. Then each knight threw away the truncheon of his spear and each drew his sword and straightway fell to battle with might and main. And in that combat each knight gave the other many sore buffets and, for a long while, no one could have told how that encounter was like to go.

But at last Sir Ewaine waxed very furious with the opposition of that other knight, wherefore he arose in his stirrups and lashed at that black knight such a buffet that nor guard nor shield nor helm could withstand the stroke. For under that blow the black Knight of the Fountain reeled in his saddle as though he would fall from his horse. Then he drooped his shield and hung his head full low and catched at the horn of his saddle as though to stay himself from falling. Herewith Sir Ewaine lashed another buffet at him, and with that blow the sword of Sir Ewaine pierced through the helmet of the black knight and deep into his brain pan and with that stroke the black knight received his mortal hurt.

Then Sir Ewaine, perceiving that the black knight was so sorely hurt, repented him of what he had done in the heat of his battle and stayed his hand, though all too late. And he cried out: "Sir Knight, I fear me that I have given thee a very woeful hurt. I repent me of that, so yield thou thyself to me, and forthwith I will look to thy wound and will give thee such ease as I may."

But to this the black Knight of the Fountain made no reply. Otherwise he immediately wheeled his horse about, and set spurs to flank, and drove away with all speed from that place. And so rapidly did he race away from the field of battle that he appeared to fly, as it were, like to the shadow of a bird across the plain. *The Knight of the Fountain fleeth from Sir Ewaine*

At first Sir Ewaine was altogether amazed at the suddenness of the flight of the Black Knight, but presently he awoke and set spurs to his horse and sped away in pursuit as fast as he could race his horse forward. And ever Sir Ewaine pursued the Black Knight in that wise and called upon him to stay, and ever the Black Knight fled all the more rapidly away as though he heard not the voice of Sir Ewaine. And ever though he strove, Sir Ewaine could not reach the Black Knight in his flight. *Sir Ewaine pursueth the Black Knight*

Thus they sped as swift as the wind across the plain, the Black Knight fleeing and Sir Ewaine pursuing, and by and by Sir Ewaine was aware that they were approaching a walled town and a very tall and noble castle with many high towers, and steep roofs that overlooked the houses of the town. And Sir Ewaine perceived that many people were running hither and thither about the castle as though in great disturbance, and that many people were upon the walls of the town, watching the Black Knight and him as they drew nigh. And ever the knight rode toward the gate of the town and of the castle, speeding like the wind, and ever Sir Ewaine pursued him without being able to overtake him. So, in a little while, the Black Knight reached the drawbridge of the gate and he thundered across the drawbridge and Sir Ewaine thundered after him.

Now as the knight had approached the gateway of the town the portcullis had been lifted for to admit him, and so he rode through the gateway with all speed. But when Sir Ewaine would have followed, the portcullis was let fall for to keep him without.

Sir Ewaine is caught within the portcullis of the town Yet so great was the fury of Sir Ewaine's chase and so closely did he follow the Black Knight in pursuit that he was within the portcullis as it fell. And the portcullis fell upon the horse of Sir Ewaine and smote him just behind the saddle and cut him in twain, so that the half of the horse fell within the portcullis and the other half of the horse fell without the castle. And so violent was the blow of the falling of the portcullis, and so sudden the fall of the horse, that Sir Ewaine was flung down to the ground with so dreadful and terrible a shock that he lay in a swoon as though he had been killed.

So as Sir Ewaine lay there, there came a number of those who were in attendance at that part of the castle. These looked in through a wicket of iron and beheld Sir Ewaine where he lay in that swoon in the space between the portcullis and the inner gate. So when they beheld him lying thus with the half of his dead horse, they said: "Behold! yonder is the man who wounded our champion and who pursued him hither. Let him lie where he is until that our champion tells us what we shall do unto him. For lo! he is a prisoner here and cannot escape from our hands, and so we have it in our power to do with him whatsoever we please."

Thus they said, not knowing that even at that time their champion was lying very nigh to death because of the wound he had received at the hands of Sir Ewaine.

So these went away from that place, leaving Sir Ewaine lying as though dead in the swoon that his violent fall had caused him. But after a while life came back to him and he opened his eyes and gazed about him, and after that he made shift to arise, though with great pain. Then he beheld that he was a prisoner at that place, and that he lay with the half of his dead horse betwixt the portcullis and the inner gate of the castle so that he could neither get into the castle nor out but was there a prisoner like to a creature caught in a trap.

Then Sir Ewaine went to the wicket of the inner gate and he looked forth through the iron bars of the wicket for to see what sort of a place it was into which he had come. And he beheld that within the gate was the street of the town. And he perceived that the street was very steep and that it was cobbled with stones. And he beheld that the houses of the town that stood upon either side of the street were built either of brick or else of stone, and that they were fair and tall with overhanging gables and with shining windows of glass and roofs of bright red tiles. And he beheld that there were many booths and stores with fair fabrics and merchandise displayed for sale. And he saw that there were many people in the street but that all they were moving in one direction as though in great agitation. And as he stood, so gazing, he was aware of a great sound of lamentation that arose from all parts of the town, wherefore he thought that maybe the knight whom he had chased thither must now be lying nigh to death. At that he was much grieved, for not only was that a very noble and valorous knight, but his death would certes put Sir Ewaine himself into great jeopardy as soon as the people of the castle should come to deal with him in that place where he was now a prisoner.

And now followeth the history of the further adventures of Sir Ewaine as it is told in the books of chivalry that relate to these happenings, so I pray you to read that which followeth if that other which hath gone before hath been pleasing to you.

Chapter Third

How a damsel, hight Elose, who was in service with the Lady Lesolie of the Fountain, brought succor to Sir Ewaine in his captivity.

SO SIR EWAINE stood gazing out of the wicket of the gate as aforetold; and he wist not what to do to save his life; for he knew he could do naught but wait there until those who had to deal with him might come to slay him.

Now, as he stood thuswise in great trouble of spirit, he was aware of a damsel who came thitherward. And as that damsel approached, Sir Ewaine perceived that she was very comely of appearance, and that she had yellow curling hair and it seemed to Sir Ewaine that he had hardly ever beheld a damsel more fair than she who approached his place of captivity.

This damsel came close to the wicket where Sir Ewaine stood, and she gazed upon his face and her own face was pitiful and kind, and neither angry nor scornful. Then Sir Ewaine, beholding that her face was kind, said to her: "Damsel, why do you come to gaze thus upon a poor captive who is waiting for his death?"

To this the damsel made reply: "Alas, Sir Knight, I come hither because I take great pity that a noble champion such as you appear to be should be in so sad a case as this. For certes the people of this castle will come to slay you in a very little while." *The Damsel of the Fountain pitieth Sir Ewaine*

"Damsel," said Sir Ewaine, "thy pity is a great comfort to me, but it would be a still greater comfort if thou couldst help me to escape from this place."

To this the damsel made no reply. But presently she said: "Tell me, Sir Knight, why did you do so grievous a hurt to our knight-champion who was the defender of this land against those who would meddle with the fountain to bring a deluge upon our land. Wit you that because of the woeful buffets you gave him he lieth so near to death that he is like to die in a few hours."

"Damsel," said Sir Ewaine, "to tell you the very truth, I meant not to bring an injury upon this land, neither did I mean to visit so grievous a hurt as I did upon that good worthy knight your champion. But first I entered upon this adventure because a fellow of mine failed in it and because I deemed that it behooved me to redeem with mine own hand the honor he had lost to your champion. As for the hurts which he suffered at my hand—wit you that when a knight fights in battle with another knight, as I fought of late with your champion, that one knoweth not how hard he smites until the mischief is done. So it was with me, and when I smote I smote in the heat and the passion of battle. Then, when I perceived that I had hurt him so sorely I pursued your knight with intent to help him whom I had so sadly hurt. But ever your knight-champion fled away from me, so that at last I pursued him in anger; wherefore I rushed into this place without thinking, and so am caught here a helpless prisoner."

Then the damsel said, "Sir Knight, I pray you tell me what is your name and your degree?" To the which Sir Ewaine made reply: "My name is Sir Ewaine and I am King Uriens' son of Gore, and my mother is Queen Morgana, surnamed Le Fay."

Now when the damsel heard this announcement of the name and the degree of Sir Ewaine, she made great admiration, crying out: "Is it then possible that so famous a knight as thou art, and one so renowned in all the world both of chivalry and of common history, shouldst be caught a prisoner in this wise?" And she regarded Sir Ewaine through the aperture of the gate with very great wonder, and by and by she regarded him with still greater pity. Then after a little, she said: "Sir Knight Ewaine, I take great sorrow that so worthy a knight as thou art shouldst suffer harm. Now I am of a great mind for to help thee if thou wilt do my bidding in all things that I shall ordain for thee to do. For if I release thee from thy captivity, there are several things I would have thee do upon my commandment."

"Lady," said Sir Ewaine, "I believe that you mean me well, and I believe that you would not lay any command upon me that would be contrary to my knightly honor or my integrity as a right knight of royal blood to fulfill." And the damsel said: "Take no thought that I intend ill faith against thee, Sir Ewaine, for instead I am of a mind to be thy friend in this affair if so be thou wilt put thy trust in me."

Then Sir Ewaine said: "Lady, I yield myself to your will, and if you will set me free from this captivity I will do whatsoever you ordain for me to perform. But tell me, how mean ye for to bring me forth from this peril unless you may get the keys of this gate from the porter thereof?"

"Sir," said the damsel, "I cannot get those keys but I have another *The damsel* way than that to set you free. For wit you that though locks and *giveth succor* bars be strong, yet the power of enchantment is still stronger than *to Sir Ewaine* they." With this the damsel drew from her bosom a locket that hung there by a chain of gold, and she opened the locket and she brought forth therefrom a ring set with a clear red stone like to a pure ruby—bright—shining and very brilliant. And she said, "See you this ring?" and Sir Ewaine said, "Yea." "Well, Messire," said she, "this is a very wonderful ring, for it hath had many potent spells set upon it by the magician Merlin, who gave it in days gone by to my father, King Magnus of Leograns. So my father gave it to me and it is the most precious thing of all my possessions. For the property of this ring is of such a sort that if you turn the stone inward upon your hand so as to hide it within your palm, then you shall become invisible; and if you turn the stone out upon your hand again, then you shall become visible as you were before. Take this ring, Sir Ewaine, and when you have made yourself invisible by means of it, then you shall escape from your enemies. After you have so escaped, come you to the garden of this castle and I will be there. Do you come and lay your hand upon my shoulder, and then I will know you are there. After that I will then conduct you to a certain apartment where you shall be privily lodged until this present danger hath passed."

Therewith speaking, the damsel gave the ring to Sir Ewaine and he took it, giving her thanks beyond measure for her kindness to him. And immediately he set the ring upon his finger and turned the stone inward so as to hide it in his palm. Then lo! as soon as he had done that he became immediately invisible to the eyes.

Then the damsel Elose fled away from that place, lest those who would come to slay Sir Ewaine should find her there talking to him.

So, shortly after she had gone, there came a great party of armed men with intent to slay Sir Ewaine, and some of these were armed and all bore swords and guisarms. These came to the gate and flung it open, and rushed into the space between it and the portcullis with a great tumult, for they expected to find Sir Ewaine there and to slay him. But lo! he was gone and they beheld nothing there but the half of his dead horse and the saddle and the bridle and the trappings thereof. For there was neither sight nor sign of him anywhere to be seen.

At that they were all amazed beyond measure to find their prisoner gone, for they wist not how he could have escaped from that place. So they raised a great tumult and some cried out to hurry hither and others to hurry thither, and in the tumult and confusion Sir Ewaine passed out from their midst and none of them were aware of his going.

Sir Ewaine escapeth from the gateway After that Sir Ewaine went away from that place and into the town within the walls. And he came to the castle of the town and no one saw him in his going. And he entered the castle and the people of the castle saw him not.

How Sir Ewaine entereth the garden of the castle So, invisible to all, Sir Ewaine went to the privy garden of the castle, and he perceived that that was a very pleasant place, with many shady trees and with plats of flowers and with fountains and long straight walks where the lady of the castle might take her pleasure when she chose to be out of doors. And Sir Ewaine entered that garden and he perceived that there were several damsels therein and that all they were very sorrowful and downcast because that the knight-champion of that place had been slain, and several of them wept. But amongst these damsels was the damsel Elose, and she alone of all who were there was cheerful and bore a smiling countenance.

Then Sir Ewaine went to her and laid his hand upon her shoulder as she had bidden him to do, and thereupon she knew that he was there though she could not see him. So straightway she arose and went forth from out of the garden and Sir Ewaine followed her.

After that the damsel led Sir Ewaine to a certain part of the castle and up a long flight of steps and so brought him to an apartment that was immediately beneath the eaves of a certain part of the tower of the castle.

And Sir Ewaine beheld that here was a large and noble apartment hung with woven hangings representing pictures of battle and of court, and he beheld that the floor was spread with finely woven fabrics of divers sorts. And he saw that there were several large windows that overlooked the streets of the town and a fair prospect beyond. And the breeze blew into those windows very softly and pleasantly, and great flocks of pigeons flew about in the air with noisy and clapping flight, and numbers of other pigeons strutted on the tiles of the roof and bridled and cooed to each other in the red sunlight of the waning day. So this was a very pleasant place in which to dwell. And the damsel said to Sir Ewaine, "Here shall you abide until my further purpose is ripe."

Then the damsel Elose brought an ewer full of tepid water and *The damsel serveth Sir Ewaine* she poured the water into a basin, and the ewer and the basin were both of them of silver. And the damsel held the basin and Sir Ewaine bathed his hands and his face, and after that she gave him a large napkin of fine white linen and he dried his hands and his face thereon. So, when he was thus refreshed she brought him food and drink, and Sir Ewaine ate and drank with much appetite and was greatly uplifted in spirit. And by that time the evening was come.

Now all this while Sir Ewaine was greatly astonished that the damsel should be so kind to him, wherefore he said, "Damsel, why art thou so kind to me?" To this she made reply: "Messire, I have a purpose in all this, that by and by and in good season I will unfold to thee."

Then Sir Ewaine said to her: "I pray you, fair damsel, tell me now the mystery of that fountain and of the knight who guarded it? For I am very curious to know why there came that quaking of the earth and that thundering and rain when I cast water upon the slab beside the fountain."

"Sir," said Elose, "I will tell you that mystery." And so she did, as followeth:

"You are to know," quoth she, "that somewhile ago there was *The damsel telleth Sir Ewaine of the enchantment of the fountain* appointed a joust at a place not very distant from this. And to that joust there went the lady of this castle who is hight the Lady Lesolie. Thither also went the Lady Vivien, of whom thou either knowest or hast heard tell, for she is one of the greatest and most mischievous enchantresses in all of the world.

"At that jousting there was one knight who distinguished himself above all others, and he was Sir Sagron surnamed Coeur de Fer.

For that noble knight won the battle of the joust, overthrowing all who came against him without once suffering defeat himself. So to him was awarded the prize of battle, which prize was a fillet of gold. This fillet the victor had the right to bestow upon the lady whom he deemed the fairest of all who were there.

"Now the Lady Vivien thought that she would be chosen by whomsoever won that prize, for that day she had put on all the enchantments of beauty that she possessed. Nevertheless, and in spite of these charms, Sir Sagron bestowed the prize of beauty, not upon the Lady Vivien, but upon the Lady Lesolie, who is the countess of this castle where we are.

"Now when the Lady Vivien saw that she was passed over by Sir Sagron, she took great affront with Lady Lesolie who had been chosen, and vowed vengeance upon her.

"So afterward by her enchantments she had that slab of stone laid by the fountain and she ordained that whensoever any one should cast the water of the fountain upon the slab then there would come a great deluge to this land. Thereafter she established herself not very far distant from this valley of the fountain, and whenever a knight cometh by her castle, that knight she sets upon the adventure of the fountain.

Of Sir Sagron of the Fountain "Meantime Sir Sagron had offered himself as champion of the fountain, undertaking to defend it if the Lady Lesolie would upon her part consent to wed him and make him lord of this domain. To this the lady was constrained to say yea. So it was ordained that if Sir Sagron would defend the fountain without fail or default for the space of a year and a day, after that time she would give herself and all her domain to him as the lord thereof. So Sir Sagron hath ever since defended the fountain with great honor until to-day, when you overcame him in battle, and pursued him hither wounded unto death. Had he defended a fortnight longer, he had won his suit with the Lady Lesolie and would have been lord of this land. But now he will to-morrow awake in Paradise.

"This, Sir Ewaine, is the story of the mystery of the fountain, and now I tell thee I know not who will defend it unless haply it is thou who wilt do so."

"Fair damsel," quoth Sir Ewaine, "how may I look to defend the fountain who will immediately be slain if it be known that I am here?"

To this the damsel laughed and said: "Sir Ewaine, all that may come about if fortune be with me in these matters I am about to undertake."

Now by this time the darkness being come, the damsel lit two tapers of perfumed wax, and thereafter she conducted Sir Ewaine into another apartment. There he beheld a couch, very soft and comfortable and spread with a coverlet of crimson satin. And the damsel Elose said: "Sir Ewaine, doubtless thou art aweary. If that be so, here thou mayst rest thyself and be at ease." And therewith she set down the candles of wax upon a table and quitted the room and Sir Ewaine was left alone.

And Sir Ewaine was very weary, wherefore he laid aside his armor and disrobed himself and laid himself down upon that fair soft bed with great joy of comfort. And straightway thereafter he fell asleep as though he were a little weary child.

Now about the twelfth hour of the night and whilst Sir Ewaine lay thus asleep, he became aware of a great disturbance—the sound of weeping and a great outcry of lamentation that filled the entire silence of the night.

Anon came the damsel Elose, and she said: "Sir Ewaine, the knight Sir Sagron is dead whom thou wounded yesterday, and now they are bearing him to the church. Come and see!" So Sir Ewaine arose quickly and covered himself with a cloak, and he went with the damsel to a certain window that overlooked a street of the town. From that window and beneath him he beheld a great concourse of people that filled the entire street. Many of those were clad in armor of proof and others bare torches so that the entire night was aflame with the light thereof. And there were many women who rode upon horseback beside the armed knights. And all of this great assembly of people were crying out in lamentation so that it was as though all the hollow beneath the space of heaven were full of the voice of their sorrow. With this lamentation of many voices were mingled the sound of trumpets and the chaunting of priests and acolytes who recited the services for the dead. In the midst of all the press there

Sir Ewaine beholdeth the funeral at night

was a bier, and over the bier there had been spread a veil of white linen and upon the bier there lay stretched the knight-champion of that place with his hands crossed upon his sword. All about the bier were many people carrying long candles of wax, and these also added their lamentation to the voices of those others who lamented.

Then when Sir Ewaine beheld this spectacle he said: "Woe is me, Elose, this is surely a very sorry sight to behold! Now I grieve me greatly that I am the cause of this, for I meant not to slay that knight. Yet in the heat of battle who may stay the hand for to measure the stroke that one giveth to his enemy?"

Sir Ewaine beholdeth the Lady Lesolie of the Fountain Then anon as Sir Ewaine still gazed upon that scene, he beheld that a lady followed after the bier, and he saw that her hair was hanging loose and that she was in great disarray. But maugre that, it appeared to him that she was the most beautiful lady his eyes had ever looked upon. Then Sir Ewaine said to Elose, who was looking out of the window beside him, "What fair lady is that who followeth the bier of the dead knight?" To the which she made answer: "That is the lady of this castle, and she is making sorrow for the knight her champion who is slain."

Then Sir Ewaine gazed and gazed at that lady for as long as he could see her, and when she had gone by, he said: "Elose, certes that lady is the most beautiful dame that ever mine eyes looked upon. Now I tell thee truly that I do not wonder that your knight-champion was willing for to serve her for a whole year with faithfulness; for I would willingly serve for even a longer time than that to win her good regard."

At this Elose laughed with great good will. "Is it so with you, Sir Knight?" quoth she, "and do you then find that your heart is inclined toward this lady?" And Sir Ewaine said, "Yea, it is even so with me." Elose said: "And wouldst thou be pleased, Sir Ewaine, if I could devise it in such wise that the lady of this castle should look kindly upon thee?" And again Sir Ewaine said, "Yea."

Then Elose smiled very cheerfully upon Sir Ewaine and she said: "Well, Messire, let be till to-morrow and then we shall see what that *The damsel Elose serveth Sir Ewaine in the morning* day shall bring forth."

So when the next morning had come, Sir Ewaine arose greatly refreshed, and by and by Elose came to him with food with which to break his fast. And after he had broken his fast she brought a bowl of ivory with tepid water, and she brought a razor with a heft of ivory studded with gold, and she hung a fine linen towel upon her shoulder and she shaved Sir Ewaine so that his face was both fresh and clean. After that she brought him fine raiment—an undervest of soft cambric linen and a surcoat and hose of azure silk embroidered with silver, and a cloak with a clasp of gold, and with pears of silver hanging from the corners thereof. And she brought a circlet of gold for his head, such as became the son of a king. Then she looked upon Sir Ewaine and he was very comely.

After all this had been done in that wise, Elose left Sir Ewaine and went to where was the Lady Lesolie, and the lady sat alone in her bower in great sorrow that her knight-champion was dead. But Elose entered that place with a very cheerful countenance, and she said, "Lady, what cheer?"

Then the Lady Lesolie looked upon Elose with great indignation *The Lady* because of her cheerful aspect, and she said: "Damsel, I am much *Lesolie rebuketh the* displeased that thou shouldst appear so cheerful and gay of spirit *damsel* when thou beholdest me in such sorrow. And I think very ill of thee that thou who art the best beloved of all my damsels hast not come nigh me in all this time for to offer me cheer or comfort in mine affliction."

Now Elose was greatly in favor with the Lady Lesolie so that she feared her not, wherefore she still bore a very cheerful aspect. And she said: "Lady, I know not wherefore I should take such sorrow as I see the sorrow to be that you assume for Sir Sagron. I did not love him so much that I should take more than reasonable grief when he suffered such misfortune of battle as may befall any knight."

Then the Lady Lesolie's eyes sparkled very brightly with anger, and she said: "Ha! Damsel! Thou goest beyond all measure of the liberty of speech which I allow to thee. Mayhap I loved not Sir Sagron as he would have had me, yet I honored him a very great deal, and now that he is gone I know not who may defend the fountain in his stead. So, because thou dost smile and take cheer in this time of trouble, thy presence is displeasing to me, wherefore I would have thee gone from hence."

Then Elose said: "Very well, Lady, I will go as thou hast bidden me, but I think thou wilt be sorry that thou didst not talk more with me and that thou dost not inquire of me why I appear so cheerful as I do."

Therewith Elose turned as though to go forth from that place. But after she had gone a little distance, the Lady Lesolie arose and followed her to the door of the chamber and began coughing very softly. Then when Elose turned, the lady beckoned to her and said, "Come hither!" and Elose laughed and came. Then the lady said: "Thou art very saucy of disposition, but nevertheless I love thee more than thou deservest. Now tell me what it is that thou hast upon thy mind."

Then Elose said, "I will tell thee, but it must be where none may hear."

The lady said, "Come hither, then," and therewith she led Elose into a place where they were altogether by themselves, and when they were come there the Lady Lesolie said, "What is it, Elose?"

The damsel bespeaketh the Lady Lesolie Then Elose said: "Lady, there is in this castle a knight who loveth thee a very great deal, and this knight is exceedingly noble and of very great skill at arms, and he is a king's son, and he is a knight of King Arthur's court, and he is a knight of the Round Table. So great is the love of this knight for thee that thou mightest demand anything of him. Now it appeareth to me that since thou hast lost the knight who was our champion, thou wouldst do well to call upon this knight to defend thee. And if in good time thou shouldest choose him for thy lord, then it would be much to thy pride and greatly to the joy of this land."

Now all this while the lady had been regarding Elose very steadfastly, and when the maiden ended she said: "Who is this knight, and what is his name and his degree?" Elose said: "Lady, thou hast heard of him a great many times, for he is Sir Ewaine, the son of King Uriens of Gore and of Queen Morgana le Fay." Then the lady said in a very strange voice: "Elose, it is wonderful that a knight so famous as this should have been in our castle and yet we knew nothing thereof. Now tell me, when was it he came hither?" Then Elose was confused and said: "Lady, he hath only been here a little while, for he did but come this morning."

Then the Lady Lesolie smiled very curiously, and she said: "Bring that knight hither, that I may see him and speak with him." Then straightway Elose went to where Sir Ewaine was. And Elose said: "Sir Ewaine, arise and come with me, for my lady would have speech with thee."

So Sir Ewaine arose and went forth with Elose, and Elose brought him to where the Lady Lesolie was. And Elose introduced Sir Ewaine to the Lady Lesolie, and Sir Ewaine paid great homage to her for he beheld that she was very wonderfully beautiful. The lady looked at Sir Ewaine very steadily, and by and by she said, "Elose, this knight hath not the appearance of one who is a traveller new arrived from a journey; rather he appeareth like one who is fresh and well-bedight."

Then at first Elose was confused and wist not where to look. Then presently the lady said: "Elose, I believe this was the knight who slew Sir Sagron."

Then Elose looked very steadily into the lady's face, and anon she spake boldly and without fear, and she said: "Well, lady, what then? So much the better for thee if this knight overcame Sir Sagron, who was the best knight in all this land. For if this knight overcame Sir Sagron, then is he better than Sir Sagron, and so he is better to be the defender of the Fountain."

Then the lady said: "Say no more, but go ye both away until I meditate upon this for a while." And thereupon Elose and Sir Ewaine quitted the apartment of the lady and went away to another part of the castle.

After that they waited for word to come to them from the lady of the castle, yet no word came for a long while. But when the evening had come, the chatelaine sent a very courteous message to Sir Ewaine that it would pleasure her to have him sup with her. So Sir Ewaine went upon that command, and the lady received him very graciously and made place for him beside her at the table, and they sat and ate and drank together and talked of many things of court and field. And ever as they talked together the Lady Lesolie regarded Sir Ewaine very closely, and she perceived that he was very noble and haughty of appearance, and she wist that he was greater champion than she had ever beheld before.

The damsel bringeth Sir Ewaine to the Lady of the Fountain

Then, by and by, she said of a sudden to Sir Ewaine: "Messire, dost thou not think thou didst very ill to come hitherward to the destruction of our peace?"

Sir Ewaine promiseth to defend the Fountain

Then Sir Ewaine spake very boldly, saying: "Lady, I am very sorry to have caused thee grief, but I did only as any knight-adventurer would do, taking my chance of battle and of death with him as he took his chance with me. Yet now that the chance of war hath brought me hither, I cannot repent me of anything that hath befallen me. For that chance hath brought me into thy presence and hath made me acquainted with thee." Then the lady said: "Well, Messire, what am I to do now that thou hast slain the knight-champion of this place?" To the which Sir Ewaine made reply: "Lady, if thou wilt take me for thy champion, I will serve thee very faithfully and will ask no guerdon from thee. For I know of no greater joy that could befall me than to be thy chosen champion." Then the Lady Lesolie smiled and said: "Sir Ewaine, thou speakest very well, and I believe that thy deeds are every whit as trustworthy as thy words. So I will accept thee as my champion to do combat in my behalf and to protect my fountain and myself for a year and a day. If by the end of that time thou hast proved thyself to be entirely faithful, then I will consider anything else that thou mayst have to say to me."

So Sir Ewaine abided at that place and he defended the Fountain so well that no one came thither to assail it who was not overthrown, and from all whom he thus overthrew, Sir Ewaine took horse and shield and sent them away from that place afoot.

And Sir Ewaine dwelt in the Valley of the Fountain for nigh a year, and in that time he and the Lady Lesolie of the Fountain were betrothed to one another with intent to be wedded when the year was ended. And ever Sir Ewaine loved the Lady of the Fountain more and more, and ever she loved him more and more.

Yet oftentimes Sir Ewaine bethought him of the King's court and of his friends thereat and at those times he would long for them with a very great passion of desire. So it befell upon a day that Sir Ewaine and the Lady Lesolie were in the garden of the castle and Sir Ewaine sat sunk in deep and silent thought concerning those friends

and that court. And meanwhile the lady watched him askance. Then
by and by she said: "What is it that lieth upon thy mind, Messire,
that causeth thee to take so much thought to thyself?"

Then Sir Ewaine aroused himself and said: "Lady, it is that I think *Sir Ewaine*
much of my friends and companions of the court of King Arthur. *longeth for*
For now nigh to a year hath passed and in all of that time I have *the court of*
heard no single word of any of them." *the King*

Then the Lady Lesolie said, "Ewaine, art thou discontent with
us at this place?" He said: "Nay, lady, thou knowest I am very well
content and more than well content to be thus forever with thee.
Yet ne'ertheless I would that I might have word of my companions,
for I know not how it fareth with them. And furthermore, I would
fain know whether they who went in quest of Sir Launcelot with me
have yet heard anything of that noble and worthy champion."

Then the Lady Lesolie said: "Ah, Ewaine, I fear me that thou
thinkest so much of thy friends that thou wilt, in a little while, be
discontent to remain with us any longer." To which Sir Ewaine said:
"Lady, thou knowest very well that that could never be." And she
said, "Art thou sure of that?" "Yea," quoth Sir Ewaine, "I am well
assured of it."

Then the Lady of the Fountain said: "Ewaine, I have it in my
mind that thou shalt go and visit thy friends at the court of the great
king. For after thou hast seen them and hast satisfied thyself, I believe that thou wilt be better content to be here. So I lay it as my
command upon thee that thou shalt go to Camelot, and have con-
verse once again with thy friends and companions. Yet I would not
have thee remain too long away from us, wherefore I lay it as a further injunction upon thee that thou shalt return hither as soon as
possible, for we can ill spare our champion who is so dear to us."

he Lady of the Fountain:

Chapter Fourth

How Sir Ewaine returned to the court of King Arthur, and how
he forgot the Lady Lesolie and his duty to the Fountain.

O IT CAME about that the day after that day, Sir Ewaine took
horse and departed from the Valley of the Fountain as the
Lady Lesolie had commanded him to do; and he travelled
alone, going from that place in the same manner that he had come
thither.

Now as he went upon his way in return to Camelot he must
needs travel upon that same road by which he came thitherward. So
by and by he again beheld that huge herdsman oaf who sat upon the
mound as aforetold of, guarding his cattle. When this being beheld
Sir Ewaine he shouted to him aloud in a great voice, "Hello, little
man! Whither goest thou?" But to him Sir Ewaine made no reply,
but rode steadfastly upon his way.

Anon, and about the hour of noon, he came to within sight of
that wonderful valley wherein stood the enchanted castle of the Lady
Vivien. And Sir Ewaine rode down into the valley and toward the
castle, and as he drew nigh they of the castle were aware of his coming from afar.

So it was that as Sir Ewaine came nigh to the castle there issued
forth a multitude of people, who approached him singing and making joy and giving him great voice of welcome. For ever they cried
aloud: "Welcome, O noble champion! Welcome! And welcome still
again!"

So they met him and brought him as it were in triumph to the *Sir Ewaine*
castle, and when he had come nigh thereunto the Lady Vivien her- *cometh to the*
self came forth to add her welcome to his coming. And she wore *castle of*
a very smiling and cheerful countenance, and she also cried, as did *Vivien*
the others, "Welcome, Sir Ewaine! Welcome! Thrice welcome!" and
she said: "Messire, I well know that thou didst come forth victorious
from that adventure which thou didst undertake against the Knight

of the Fountain, wherefore it is that I am rejoiced to see thee. For, as thou already must know, I bore no very high regard for that knight whom thou didst overthrow."

Now Sir Ewaine was very well pleased with the welcome he found at that place, for he did not suspect that the Lady Vivien, who smiled so kindly upon him, nourished any thought of mischief against him. Wherefore he suffered them all to bear him into the castle in triumph and to relieve him of his armor and to bring him to a bath and to fit him with fine soft raiment wherewith he might with a good appearance come before the Lady Vivien in her bower.

After that Sir Ewaine went to where that lady was, and he sat with her and talked in great amity with her. Yet he knew not that all that while he talked with her she was planning mischief against him. So by and by, still in great amity, they went to a place where a noble feast was prepared, and there Sir Ewaine sat beside the Lady Vivien with great pleasure in being thus near to her. Then, after a while, having in mind those several mischiefs she had planned against the knights of King Arthur and of the Round Table, he said to her: "Lady, you who are so kind and fair to me, I know not why you do mischief against those others, my companions, who are of King Arthur's court; and I know not why you do mischief against the Lady Lesolie of the Fountain so as to bring trouble upon that land. She hath done you no ill that you should so practise evil against her."

Then the Lady Vivien assumed an appearance of great meekness and contrition, and she said: "Messire, what you say is true, and I repent me of all those evil things which I have done." And she said: "Would it pleasure you if all enchantment should be removed from that fountain, and if the land of the fountain should be left at peace?" Sir Ewaine said, "Lady, it would pleasure me beyond measure." Then the Lady Vivien said: "So it shall be, and I promise you very faithfully that that enchantment shall be entirely removed from that land this very day forward unto all time." Then she looked upon Sir Ewaine and smiled upon him in such wise that he was bewitched with her smiling, and she said, "Sir Ewaine, let there be peace betwixt us from this time forth for aye!" and he said, "Lady, God knows I bear you no ill will and so there is peace betwixt us."

Then the Lady Vivien said, "Sir, I would that thou wouldst accept a pledge of peace from me." And he said, "What is that pledge?" Quoth she, "I will show thee."

Thereupon saying, she smote her hands together, and in answer *The Lady* there came a fair young page clad in cloth of gold and with long, *Vivien giveth* curling ringlets of golden hair hanging down upon his shoulders. To *the ring of* this youth the lady gave sundry commands, and he departed, return- *forgetfulness* ing anon bearing in his hands a patten of gold and upon the patten was a fair white napkin of fine linen, and upon the napkin a ring of gold very cunningly wrought, and inset with a bright shining yellow stone. These the fair young page brought to the Lady Vivien, kneel- ing upon one knee, and she took the ring from the patten and gave it to Sir Ewaine, saying: "Sir, behold this ring! This I give to thee to wear as a pledge of the amity that lieth betwixt us." Therewith Sir Ewaine took the ring and set it upon his finger.

Now that ring was enchanted with very potent spells. For it was a ring of forgetfulness, so that whosoever wore it, that person would forget whatever the Lady Vivien would have him disremember.

So when Sir Ewaine set the ring upon his finger, that moment *Sir Ewaine* he forgot all about the Lady of the Fountain. And he forgot all the *forgetteth the* pledges that had passed betwixt himself and that lady, and he forgot *Lady Lesolie* all the other things that belonged to that part of his life. But all else he remembered: to wit, how he had undertaken that Adventure of the Fountain, and how he had overthrown the knight-champion of the Fountain and all other parts of his life.

Then Sir Ewaine looked at the Lady Vivien very strangely, like to one who is newly awakened from a sleep, and he said, "What is it we were speaking of anon?" And at that the Lady Vivien laughed and said, "Sir, it matters not." Sir Ewaine said, "Meseems I have had a dream, but I cannot remember what it was"; and then the Lady Vivien laughed again and said, "Neither does it matter what was thy dream." And she said: "It only matters that we are friends, and that thou wearest my pledge of amity upon thy hand. Now I prithee never remove that ring from thy finger, for from that moment the friendship that now exists shall cease betwixt us." Sir Ewaine said: "This ring shall remain upon my finger for aye, and I shall never take it from my finger even for a single moment."

So Sir Ewaine rested with great pleasure for that night at the castle of the Lady Vivien, and, when the next morning was come, he departed from the castle, betaking his way to the court of King Arthur.

For he said to himself: "Haply by this time they have some news of Sir Launcelot. So I will straightway return to the court of the King and learn if that be so."

Sir Ewaine returneth to the court of the King
Now Sir Ewaine, because he had forgotten all about his life at the Valley of the Fountain, had no thought that he had been gone from that court for a longer time than a fortnight, wherefore when he was come amongst his friends again and when he found that wellnigh a year had passed, he knew not what to think. "How is this," he said, "and what hath befallen me? Surely there was something that was like to a dream that I cannot remember. What is it that hath happened to me? I know not what it is." So Sir Ewaine was ashamed that he should not be able to remember what had happened to him for the year that had passed, wherefore he held his peace and said nothing concerning the matter. But ever Sir Ewaine feared lest he should betray to his friends that he had forgotten a whole year of his life. So it was he said to himself: "After that I have rested a little here at the court of the King I will set forth again in quest of news of Sir Launcelot. For maybe by and by I may be able to remember what I have forgotten of this year that hath passed."

King Arthur rideth afield
But Sir Ewaine did not immediately depart from the court, and so it chanced upon a certain day, the weather being very pleasant, King Arthur went afield with certain of his court and Sir Ewaine was one of those. That time it was early summer weather, and the breezes were soft and balmy, and full of the odor of growing things. So when the heat of the day was come the King ordained that a pavilion should be erected at a certain spot that pleased him very well, and he and the Queen and their courts sat in that pavilion at a fair feast which the attendants of the court had prepared for them.

There cometh a damsel to the King's pavilion
Now whilst they so sat, there came of a sudden a bustle and a sound of several voices talking without, and anon there came into the pavilion a damsel very fair of face and with curling yellow hair. And the damsel was clad in garments of yellow silk and she wore a frontlet of gold upon her head, and she wore shoes of variegated leather with

latchets of gold upon her feet. And she was further adorned with necklaces of gold and with armlets of gold, wherefore they who sat there were astonished at the beauty of the damsel and at the suddenness of her coming.

(Now you are to know that maiden was the damsel Elose, and yet Sir Ewaine knew her not because of the ring of forgetfulness which he wore.)

Then King Arthur arose where he sat, and he said: "Fair demoiselle, whence come you and what would you here? Tell us, I pray, who are you who cometh hither like to a fair vision from a dream."

Yet ever the damsel stood within the door of the pavilion, and because of the dazzling brightness of the sunlight whence she had come she could not at first see very well within the shadow of the tent. So she said, "I pray you tell me, is Sir Ewaine at this place?"

To that King Arthur, much wondering, said, "Yea, lady, yonder he sits," and thereupon the damsel Elose beheld Sir Ewaine where he was.

Then Elose entered farther into the pavilion and came to where Sir Ewaine sat. Her eyes shone very bright with anger, and she said: "Sir Ewaine, I denounce thee as a false knight and a traitor!" *The damsel Elose accuseth Sir Ewaine of treason*

Then Sir Ewaine looked upon the damsel with great astonishment, and said, "Who art thou, lady, who dost accuse me of being false?"

Upon that the damsel cried out in a very shrill voice, "Thou knowest very well who I am!"

But ever Sir Ewaine looked very steadily at her and almost he remembered her, but he could not quite remember her because of that ring which he wore. Wherefore he said, "Nay, I know thee not."

Then Elose smiled upon Sir Ewaine very bitterly, and she said: "Thou didst not forget me when thou didst lay in peril of thy life in the Castle of the Fountain; but now that thou art enjoying thyself with thy fellows, it pleases thee to forget so poor an one as I, who preserved thy life for thee. But that I could forgive thee if the need were to forgive it; yet I cannot forgive thee that thou hast also forgotten that dear lady, my mistress, unto whom thou didst pledge thy faith, and unto whom thou art bound in fealty. Messire, thou hast a very short memory."

Then Sir Ewaine cried out in an exceedingly bitter voice like one in great pain: "Lady, why say ye these things to me? I know you not."

Then Elose came very close to Sir Ewaine and she took his hand, and she said, "Do you not know me now?" He said, "Nay, I know thee not." Upon that the damsel raised her right hand with her glove in it, and she smote Sir Ewaine upon the face with the glove so that the mark of her glove lay upon his cheek. And Sir Ewaine made no defence against her assault, but ever he gazed very steadfastly at her, and he said very bitterly: "Lady, if thou wert a knight, thou wouldst not dare to do that to me, for either thou wouldst pay for that blow with thy life, or else I would wipe out the disgrace thereof with mine own blood."

But Elose laughed, and she went out from that pavilion and mounted her horse and rode away, leaving Sir Ewaine with his head bowed full low upon his breast as though he had been struck a mortal blow.

Then after the damsel had gone, King Arthur said, "Ewaine, who was that lady?" And at that Sir Ewaine lifted his head and cried out with great vehemence: "Sire, I know her not; nor can I remember that I have ever seen her before."

At that King Arthur was silent and all those who were there looked askance at Sir Ewaine and whispered together concerning those things that had happened. And Sir Ewaine was aware of how they regarded him and how they whispered together, yet he heeded them not, but ever sat with his head bowed low with shame and humiliation. And ever he strove to remember who that damsel was, but could not remember.

The King's court is adoubt concerning Sir Ewaine So after that time there was much talk amongst those at the court concerning that which had befallen in the King's pavilion. And many of them said to one another: "How is it possible for a knight of honor and of repute thus to forget one who had saved his life? And if he did indeed remember her, what of honor hath he who would deny her before those who know him?"

So those of the court spake together, and Sir Ewaine was aware that they regarded him with disfavor and he was hurt to the quick by that knowledge. So one day he came to King Arthur where he was, and he said: "Lord, I am aware that I am held in disrepute in this court. Now I crave thy leave to depart from hence at least for a season." And King Arthur said: "Messire, I will not deny that many things displeasing to me are said concerning thee. So if it be that thou art of a mind to quit us for a while until thou art able to approve thy truth and thy honor, and until thou hast disproved these things which thy calumniators say against thee, thou hast my fair leave to depart according to thy request."

So Sir Ewaine took his departure from court, and his heart was filled with bitterness and anger toward those who were one time his friends. For he ever said to himself: "Why is it that they should contemn me because I cannot remember that which I have forgot? For I cannot remember me of that damsel." *Sir Ewaine departeth from the court*

Thus he rode upon his way in great bitterness of spirit and with anger toward all the world, because that all the world appeared to be set against him.

Now Sir Ewaine journeyed for a long time he knew not whither, for he travelled somewhiles like to one in a dream.

So it befell one day that he came to a thick woodland of great extent, and there night overtook him and he wist not where he was nor how he should be able to come out of that wilderness. And whilst he was travelling thus in darkness and perplexity, he was suddenly aware of a light shining at a distance, and he followed that light until he came to a rude hut of the forest, which same stood in an open glade of no very great extent. To this forest habitation came Sir Ewaine, and he smote upon the door thereof with the butt of his spear and anon came one and opened the door, and that one was an ancient and grisly beldame of a most repulsive and forbidding appearance. When she beheld Sir Ewaine before her at the door of the hut she would have shut the door again, but he would not let her do so, but thrust his spear into the opening of the door so that she could not close it. *Sir Ewaine cometh to a lonely hut*

Then that beldame, finding that he would not be denied, spake to him very harshly, saying, "What would you here, Sir Knight?" Sir Ewaine said, "I would have lodging for the night."

Then the hag laughed very loud and shrill, and she said: "Well, since thou wilt not be denied, thou shalt have thy desire. Enter, and may thy lodging be for long."

So Sir Ewaine dismounted from his horse, and turned it loose to graze upon the grass by night. Meantime he himself entered the hut.

Here he beheld a great fire burning, with loud roaring in the chimney, and over the fire he beheld a great cauldron, in which was seething a stew of venison, the flavor of which filled the hut with a very savory odor. And Sir Ewaine beheld a great table, whereon were many platters of wood, and beholding these things spread as for a feast, he said, "Good dame, I pray thee tell me who dwells here in this hut with thee?" The beldame said, "My husband and my sons dwell here with me." Sir Ewaine said, "Certes, thou hast a great family." And at that the beldame laughed very violently and said, "Yea, that is true."

After that the hag ladled forth a mess of the stew into a wooden bowl, and she poured forth a great flagon of strong ale and she set these things upon the board with a hunch of black bread, and Sir Ewaine sat him down and ate and drank with great appetite. Then, after he had thus satisfied his hunger and his thirst he was very drowsy, wherefore he laid aside his armor and stretched himself upon a wooden bench that stood to one side and placed his helmet beneath his head and presently was enwrapped in a sound sleep.

The thieves return to the hut Now that hut was a den of thieves and that old hag was their housekeeper and there were twenty and seven in all of those thieves. So about the middle watch of the night that band of robbers returned with a considerable booty which they had seized from a party of townsfolk who were traversing a part of the forest that was not very far distant from that place. These beholding Sir Ewaine where he was sleeping, withdrew a little to one side and whispered together. And they whispered to the old beldame, saying, "Who is yonder man, and what doth he here?" She said: "He is an errant knight, who demanded housing awhile since. So here he lieth now asleep and at your mercy to dispose of as you see fit."

Then the captain of the thieves came softly to where Sir Ewaine lay, and he looked closely at him and he beheld the rich chain of gold about his neck and he beheld the ring upon his finger that the Lady

Vivien had given him. After that he withdrew a little and whispered to his fellow: "Here is a rich booty upon this sleeping knight. Now fetch hither cords and let us bind him. After that we may rob him at our ease, and after that again we may either slay him or else keep him here for a great ransom."

So some of the thieves brought a strong cord and they made a noose thereof, and first they privily took away all Sir Ewaine's weapons from him, and then they slipped the noose over his arms and in a trice and ere he was fully awake they had bound him several times about the body so that as to his hands and arms he was altogether helpless. *The thieves bind Sir Ewaine*

Thus Sir Ewaine was rudely awakened to find himself a captive in that place.

But when he saw who it was had made him captive, he assumed all the majesty of his high estate and he said: "Know ye what ye do? Wit ye that he whom you have thus bound is a king's son and a knight of the Round Table so that you have through me committed a very grievous offence."

Then several of those thieves were abashed at his words and at the great nobility of his bearing, but the captain of the band who was a hardened wretch, spake very boldly, saying: "It matters not who you are, only if you be truly a king's son and a knight of such worship, then will your ransom be all the greater." And he said: "First of all we will take this rich golden bawble from about your neck, and then we will take the fair golden ring from off your finger."

So the chief robber first took the chain from about Sir Ewaine's neck, as he said, and then he drew the ring from his finger, and because Sir Ewaine was bound he could in no wise prevent the robber chief from taking those jewels from him in that way. *The thieves rob Sir Ewaine of the ring of forgetfulness*

But lo! when the robber had plucked the ring from the finger of Sir Ewaine, then in an instant the magic of forgetfulness departed from him, and he remembered upon that instant all that had befallen him in the Valley of the Fountain. And he remembered the Lady Lesolie of the Fountain, and he remembered him of all the vows of faith he had plighted to her. And he knew now of why Elose had come to him at the King's court and had struck him in the face before them all; for he wist that the damsel had come because she *Sir Ewaine remembereth all* thought he had proved himself unfaithful and false to her lady. So it was as though a sword of remembrance had been struck through the heart of Sir Ewaine, wherefore he cried out in a loud and piercing voice, "Betrayed! Betrayed! Betrayed!" saying that word three times over. And the thieves wist not what he meant by those words, but thought that he meant that he had been betrayed by the beldame, not knowing that he meant that he had been betrayed by the Lady Vivien.

Then of a sudden in the fury of that remembrance of his own dishonor, it was as though the strength of ten descended upon Sir Ewaine. Wherefore, putting forth all his strength, he strained at his bonds so that they cut into his flesh. And he strained even more and more violently at his bonds until, of a sudden, they were burst and immediately he was free.

Sir Ewaine doeth battle with the thieves After that Sir Ewaine looked about him, but could find no weapon to his hand, wherefore he catched up the solid wooden bench whereon he had been lying awhile since. And he whirled that bench about his head and he smote with it upon the right hand and the left and he smote the thieves down upon the one side and the other. And so great was his fury that they bore back from before him in terror of his madness.

Sir Ewaine is wounded So Sir Ewaine might have slain all those thieves (though there were a score and seven of them in all) only for the captain of the band. He, beholding the fury of Sir Ewaine, ran to where there was a javelin that stood in a corner of that place. And he catched up the javelin and threw it at Sir Ewaine; and the javelin pierced through the shoulder of Sir Ewaine and pinned him fast to the wall of the hut.

Then Sir Ewaine wist that he was very sorely wounded, wherefore he roared aloud. And he strove with the javelin and anon he wrenched himself loose from the wall to which he had been pinned. Then he rushed at the thieves with the javelin still pinned through his shoulder and they made way before the terror of his onset.

Now as the robbers parted from before his onset, Sir Ewaine perceived that there was a way for him to the door. Thereupon he cast himself upon the door and he burst it open and fled away into *Sir Ewaine* the forest with the javelin still transfixed in his shoulder.

escapeth Therewith, perceiving that their captive was escaping from them, the thieves rushed after Sir Ewaine and pursued him with great out-cry. But ever they were afraid of the violence of his anger (for he had slain or broken the bones of eleven of them) wherefore they followed him not with as good a will as they would else have done. Hence it befell that Sir Ewaine made his escape from them and so got safe away into the cover of the night and of the forest, though sorely and woefully wounded.

After he had thus escaped from that danger, Sir Ewaine knew not what to do. For he was faint and bedizzied because of his wound and the agony thereof. But he wist that he must free himself from that javelin, wherefore he catched the haft of the weapon and he broke it in twain. After that he plucked out the javelin by the point which had transfixed his shoulder and with that a great issue of blood burst forth from the wound so that Sir Ewaine was nigh to swooning there-with.

But he did not swoon, but bare up under the passion of pain that lay upon him and from the issue of blood that followed what he had done. Wherefore, after he had rested him for a while, he went forward through the forest, tottering like a drunken man, now and then falling, and ever anon arising again and betaking his way he knew not whither.

A Damsel bringeth aid unto Sir Ewaine:

Chapter Fifth

How Sir Ewaine was succored and brought back to life by a certain noble lady, how he brought aid to that lady in a time of great trouble, and how he returned once again to the Lady Lesolie of the Fountain.

THUS SIR EWAINE wandered for all that night he knew not whither, and sometimes he fell and anon he would arise and go onward again. So against the dawn of day, he began to approach the outskirts of the forest and there, as he wandered painfully onward, he met a fagot-maker who had a cart and who was coming, all early in the morning, into the forest to chop fagots.

This fellow, beholding that figure of misery with a face like to wax and a body all covered with blood, wist not whether it was ghost or mortal man whom he beheld, wherefore he fell to crossing himself and pattering prayers for fear. But Sir Ewaine spake, though in a very weak and plaintive voice, saying: "Alas, good fellow! I pray you, for the sake of God's mercy to take pity upon me and to bear me hence in your cart to where I may secure aid and succor, else I must assuredly die all alone in the forest."

Then the woodchopper was aware that Sir Ewaine was no ghost or spirit left behind by the night, but that he was mortal man, and when he looked upon that sad woeful figure, he was moved to great pity, and said: "Alas, poor mortal, thou art in a sad plight indeed and so I will be glad to aid thee as thou desirest."

So after that the fagot-maker spread a soft thick bed of leaves *The* in his cart and laid the wounded knight thereon. And so he bore *woodchopper* Sir Ewaine out of the forest, with intent to take him to some place *Sir Ewaine* where he might be cherished with care and attention.

Thus it was that a poor woodchopper of the forest lent aid and assistance to one of the most noble knights of the Round Table and nephew to King Arthur. As for that fellow, he wist not who it was to whom he was giving aid, but only thought that it was some poor wretch who had fallen amongst thieves, for Sir Ewaine had neither armor nor weapons of any sort that might indicate how exalted was his estate, and even his golden chain of knighthood had been stolen from him by those thieves of the forest. Wherefore it was not possible for any one to know that he was other than a poor wayfarer of the forest. So the fagot-maker, unknowing who he was, bare that good knight out of the forest, and Sir Ewaine lay fainting, and all covered with blood and nigh to death, upon a bed of leaves in a poor woodchopper's cart.

Now when the fagot-maker had brought the wounded knight out of the woodlands and into the open country, he turned to find how it fared with him, for it seemed to the honest fellow that his burden was lying wonderful still and quiet. So the fagot-maker called out, "Friend, what cheer have you?" To this Sir Ewaine answered him not, for in the meantime as they travelled onward he had fallen into a swoon and now he lay like one who was dying or was dead.

Then the woodchopper came and looked upon the face of Sir Ewaine, and he beheld that it was white like to death. And he could not see that Sir Ewaine breathed, wherefore he thought that the wounded man was dead.

Thereat the poor knave was filled with great fear, for he said to himself: "Of a surety if they find me thus with a dead man lying in my cart, they will believe that I have committed a murder and they will hale me before the judge and they will hang me." Wherefore, reasoning in that wise, he began to cast about him how he might rid himself of that which was within his cart so that he should not thus be found in company with a dead man.

The woodchopper layeth Sir Ewaine beside a lake   Now at that time the cart chanced to be passing through a park coadjacent to a castle, the towers and the roofs and the chimneys of which might be seen through the leaves of the intervening trees. And at that place there was a little lake of water with many flags and sweet rushes growing around about the margin thereof, and this was a very secret, quiet place, for no one was nigh at that still early hour of day.

So here perceiving that no one could see what he would do, the fagot-maker stopped his cart and lifted Sir Ewaine out thereof and still he thought that the wounded man was dead. After that the woodchopper laid Sir Ewaine down very gently upon a soft bed of moss under the shadow of an oak tree and beside the margin of the lake. Having thus got rid of his burden in that wise he then went away and left the wounded knight lying alone in that place.

Now that part of the park where Sir Ewaine lay was a very fa- *The lady of* vorite spot of the lady of the castle, who was wont to take the air and *the castle* to walk with her court of damsels beside the lake. So it befell that *perceiveth Sir* morning, it being a very pleasant and cheerful day, that she walked *Ewaine* thither with those maidens in attendance upon her. So coming to that place, she perceived from afar where Sir Ewaine lay beneath the oak tree in the centre of the park. And when she saw him she said, "Who is yonder man and what does he do here?"

Then one of the damsels went more near to where Sir Ewaine lay, and she looked closely upon him and anon she said: "Lady, I believe this man is dead, for he is all covered with blood, and I do not see him move or breathe."

The lady said, "See if that be so," and therewith the damsel went closer to Sir Ewaine and reached forth and she laid her hand upon his bosom. Then she was aware that his heart beat, but only a little, and she knew that there was life in him. So she said: "Nay, he is not dead, but in a swoon that is like to death."

Then the lady came and also looked upon Sir Ewaine, and she was moved with pity to behold that great and noble frame of a man lying there in that way. Wherefore she said, "I am of a mind to save this man."

So after that she and her court retired to her castle, and when she was come there she took a very precious casket of ointment from a cabinet and gave it to that damsel who had touched Sir Ewaine. To her she said: "Take this ointment, damsel, to where that man lieth in a swoon. For wit you, this is a very potent oil to heal all manner of sickness and weakness even if one be upon the edge of death. Pour a little of this ointment upon the bosom of that man above his heart. Then rub it well with thy hand, and by and by he will revive. Take thou also yonder horse and some decent raiment fit for such a well-appearing man to wear, and let the horse be nigh to him when he *A damsel of* awakens. Then do thou observe him from secret place, and bring me *the castle* word of what he doeth." *bringeth* *succor to Sir* So the damsel did all as the lady had commanded her to do; she *Ewaine* took the horse, and the raiment and the precious balm and went to where Sir Ewaine lay in that deathly swoon. But when she came to anoint him with the ointment, she poured not a little upon him, nor did she rub with her hand the bosom of him who lay there; otherwise she poured the whole of the balm upon Sir Ewaine's bosom, and then she went away to a little distance and hid herself to observe what he would do.

So in a little she saw that the wounded man began to bestir himself and move his arms this way and that. Anon he uplifted himself from where he lay and gazed all about him, and so, being revived, remembered all that he had aforetime forgotten. Then he groaned with great travail of soul, for the memory of his dishonor came upon him and he still suffered a grievous pain from that sore wound in his shoulder. Then anon he beheld the horse near by and the garments that were beside the horse, and he thought that maybe those things had been placed there for his use, though who had been so kind to him he knew not. So he arose with great pain and he took the clothes from the horse and he went to the lake and bathed himself. After that he put on the clothes and mounted upon the horse with intent to depart from that place.

Then the maiden, who had beheld all that he did, came forth from the thicket where she had been hidden and whence she had observed him, and when Sir Ewaine saw her he said, "Maiden, was it thou who purveyed me with this horse and with these garments?" She said, "Nay, it was the lady to whom this place belongs." Sir Ewaine said, "Who is that lady?" And the maiden replied: "She is the widow of a very powerful lord, and she hath saved thy life this day. For she sent me with an ointment with which I bathed thee, and which gave thee strength to arise again. And she sent thee that horse and those clothes which thou hast put on." Sir Ewaine said: "Certes, she is most kind and charitable in her heart. Perhaps some time I may do her a service that will be equal to this service which she hath rendered to me."

Now the maiden did not suspect who it was with whom she spake, for his face was white like milk, and very haggard and wild with pain and weakness, so that his countenance showed none of that nobility that belonged to him. And, as aforesaid, he had no armor, for the thieves had taken away his armor and he had left it behind him in the hut whence he had escaped. So the maiden had no cause to think that he was one of great worship whom she beheld, so she said: "Good fellow, my lady hath need enough of aid, but I do not believe that thou art one who may help her in her trouble."

"Why dost thou think that?" quoth Sir Ewaine. "Thou shouldst not judge of my ability from what thou seest, for I may be other than what I appear to be."

Then the damsel was greatly astonished at the dignity of manner with which he spoke, for he spoke as one having authority and very calmly and haughtily. So she began to misdoubt that this was some one else than she had first thought him to be, wherefore she said, "I pray you, Sir, tell me who you are?" To the which he replied: "I am Sir Ewaine of King Arthur's court and of his Round Table, son to King Uriens of Gore and of the Lady Queen Morgana surnamed le Fay." *Sir Ewaine declareth himself to the maiden*

At this proclamation the damsel was greatly astonished, wherefore she cried out aloud: "Is it indeed possible that this is so, and that so famous and so remarkable a knight should have come to such a pass as that in which you were found?" and the damsel said: "Now the lady of this castle will be very highly honored when she comes to know that she hath lent succor to so noble and haughty a champion as you proclaim yourself to be. Let us go to her so that you may tell her the story of your misfortunes." And Sir Ewaine said: "So be it, and let us go."

So they both departed from that place and as they wended their way thence Sir Ewaine said: "Now tell me, damsel, what is the need of help that thy lady hath and concerning which thou didst speak to me anon?"

The damsel said: "I will tell thee. The lady of this castle is a widow, and at the death of her husband she had two very noble castles and two great estates belonging to those castles. Those castles and that land her lord bequeathed to her to have and to hold for her own. Now after she was thus left a widow, it befell that a certain very proud and haughty lord who was her neighbor, desired to make her his wife; but she would not listen to his suit, having great love for that worthy knight her husband who was dead. So she refused the *The damsel telleth Sir Ewaine concerning the lady of the castle* knight who desired to wed her and at that he was very angry. After that he came with a great array of armed men, and he despoiled her of one of her estates by force. And now, unless she should yield to him, he threatens to take away this other estate whereon she dwelleth and which is all that she hath in the world.

"So my lady is in a great pass and knoweth not what to do, having no knight for to defend her; for all those who should defend her, fall away from her in this time of trouble for fear of the anger of that lord who seeks her hand."

"Certes, this is a sad story which thou tellest me," said Sir Ewaine, "and indeed I will do what I may to help thy lady, who hath been so kind to me."

Thus talking together, they two approached the castle, and the lady of the castle, beholding them coming from a distance, was greatly surprised to see the damsel conversing in that wise with the wounded man whom she had been sent to succor.

Then when they were come to her the lady said to the damsel, "Didst thou use that balm as I told thee to do?" And the damsel said, "Yea." The lady said, "How much didst thou use thereof?" And the damsel said, "I used it all."

The lady of the castle is affronted at the maiden Then the lady when she heard how that the damsel had poured all of that balm at one time upon Sir Ewaine, was much affronted and very angry with her, and she said: "What is this that thou hast done? I cannot easily forgive thee this, for thou hast wasted several score pounds worth of the precious ointment upon a stranger whom we know not and who hath no appearance of worship."

Unto her the maiden made reply: "Lady, be not offended at this, for wit you that this stranger is of far greater worth than all the balm you could pour upon him."

At these words the lady was much surprised, wherefore she said, "Who is he that is of such great worth as thou sayst?" and the damsel replied: "Lady, this is none other than Sir Ewaine, Knight of the Round Table and nephew of King Arthur."

The lady giveth welcome to Sir Ewaine Then the lady of the castle cried out with astonishment and said, "Is this true that I hear?" And Sir Ewaine said, "Yea, Lady." Then the lady of the castle came to Sir Ewaine and took him by the hand, and said: "Welcome, welcome, Sir Ewaine! Now this is a great honor that hath befallen us at this place to have given aid and succor to a knight so famous in chivalry as thou art."

"Lady," quoth Sir Ewaine, "you do me honor beyond my worth, and so you put me under still greater obligations than I rested under afore this. Now I am most desirous of repaying you in some measure for all the kindness that you have visited upon me, wherefore, if it be sooth as I have been informed by this maiden that you have need of such a knight-champion at this place, then do I offer myself as such a champion, trusting that I may be of aid to you and so repay to you in some measure those favors which you have bestowed upon me."

At this the lady was rejoiced beyond all measure, and she said: "Messire, I accept thy offer of championship with all gratitude and with much pride, for indeed I believe it would not be possible to find in all of the world a champion as haughty and as puissant as thou art."

So it came about that Sir Ewaine abided at the castle of that widowed chatelaine for a long time, and until he was altogether healed of his wound. And every day he grew more strong and sturdy of body and more noble of appearance, so that all they of the castle took great pride in having him there as their champion.

Now it befell upon a day that there came to this castle that evil-minded lord of whom the damsel had spoken to Sir Ewaine, and this lord brought with him six other knights, and all these seven knights pitched their pavilions before the castle gates. And they mocked at those in the castle and dared any one to come forth therefrom, for they knew not, as you may believe, that Sir Ewaine was there as the champion of the castle.

So when Sir Ewaine heard how that knight mocked at the people of the castle, he was very wroth, wherefore he quickly made him ready, and donned a suit of rich armor that the lady had provided for him. And he mounted upon his horse, and so being in all wise prepared, he gave command to uplift the portcullis and to let fall the drawbridge. Then he rode forth from the castle, his horse's hoofs smiting the planks of the drawbridge with a noise like to thunder as he rode. And all of the people of the castle crowded out upon the walls, and when they beheld him ride past in that wise, they shouted with a loud voice because that such a champion was to defend the rights of their lady chatelaine.

Sir Ewaine doeth battle for the lady of the castle But when the knight and his companions who had come against the lady of the castle beheld that one champion ride forth in defence thereof, he was greatly surprised, and wist not what to think. So presently he rode forward to meet Sir Ewaine, and he said to him, "Sir, what knight art thou?" Sir Ewaine said: "I am the champion of the lady of this castle, and I come forth with intent to do battle in her behalf." Then that lord said, "What is thy estate?" To the which, Sir Ewaine, speaking with great pride and haughtiness, made reply: "It matters not that I tell thee at this present, but I may assure thee of this, that mine is a higher estate and a greater credit than thine own." Then the knight said, "Wouldst thou fight against us who are seven?" And Sir Ewaine said, "Yea, verily." And the knight said, "Thou art very foolish, but be it so."

So Sir Ewaine withdrew himself a little, and made himself ready in all wise for battle. Meantime that knight who had bespoken him withdrew to his party and he said to a knight who was the champion of his party, "Go thou forth against yon fellow." And the champion of that party did so.

Now that knight was the greatest and most powerful knight in all the country in which he dwelt. And he was very huge of girth and thick of limb, and so great had been his success at arms that he made sure that he could easily be able to overthrow his opponent. Wherefore he made him ready very proudly and took his station with great confidence. And when he was in all wise prepared, he shouted aloud and launched his horse against the horse of Sir Ewaine with full expectation that he would overthrow his enemy.

So they two rushed together like thunder and so met in the very middle of the course with such a crash of encounter that those who heard it stood appalled at the sound. But in that encounter the spear of the champion of that wicked lord's party broke all into splinters, but the spear of Sir Ewaine held so that the other was cast to earth with such force that he lay stunned and altogether devoid of life and motion.

How Sir Ewaine overthrew the enemies of the lady Then when the other knights of that party beheld how their champion had been overthrown so violently to earth, all they were greatly amazed at the result of that encounter; for as was said, there was no knight in all of that region who was so strong as that champion. Then they were filled with rage, and dropping their lances in rest, they all rushed upon Sir Ewaine together, with intent to overthrow him by force of numbers and might of metal, and afterward to slay him when he was unhorsed. But Sir Ewaine did not give them their will, but wheeled his horse with great address and dexterity and in such a wise as to separate those who thus came upon him in a body. Then suddenly he wheeled about again, and ere they were prepared for attack, he smote down one knight and then another and another, so that only three of those who assailed him were left. With that the others were filled with a great terror of the woeful buffets that Sir Ewaine struck, wherefore, without further combat, they all three turned and fled. But ever Sir Ewaine pursued them with great fury and he came nigh to one who was fleeing and smote him down from his horse. And he came nigh to another and smote him down also. Then last of all he overtook that lord who was the enemy of that lady, and he smote him so sorely with his sword that he would have fallen from his horse had not Sir Ewaine catched him ere he fell. Then Sir Ewaine plucked that knight out of his saddle and he laid him across the bow of his own saddle. So after having overthrown all those seven knights in that wise, he rode back again into the castle bearing that wicked lord lying across his saddle bow.

Now when those who stood upon the castle walls beheld what wonderful battle their champion did, they were amazed beyond measure at his prowess and they shouted aloud for joy at the victory of their champion over their enemies. So Sir Ewaine rode into the castle, in the midst of all that shouting and loud acclaim. And he came to where the lady was standing in a balcony that overlooked the courtyard of the castle, and he looked up to where she stood and he said: "Lady, lo! I have brought you back your enemy in payment for that blessed balm with which you brought me back to life."

Then the lady of the castle knew not what to do for joy. Wherefore she came down from where she was and catched Sir Ewaine by the hand and kissed it repeatedly. And she called upon Sir Ewaine as her savior, but Sir Ewaine withdrew his hand in great confusion, and said: "Lady, do not do so, for wit you I am a man who hath done a

The lady of the castle giveth praise to Sir Ewaine

dishonorable thing. And though I did that ill thing unwittingly, yet I am attainted because of that which I did."

Then the lady said: "Sir, I will not believe that you were ever dishonorable, and I would that you would remain always in this castle."

Then Sir Ewaine smiled and said: "I thank you for that wish. But it may not be, for now that I have done my service in your behalf and have brought your enemy to you to deal with at your pleasure, to-morrow I must depart upon my way once more."

Then Sir Ewaine delivered the captive knight from the pommel of his saddle into the hands of the lady, and afterward that wicked knight was bound with many securities and hostages to good behavior, and so he tormented that lady no more from that time forth unto the end of her life.

Sir Ewaine departeth from the castle as a pilgrim Now when the next day was come Sir Ewaine appeared before the lady of the castle and besought her that she would take back the armor she had given him and that in place of that armor she would purvey him the dress of a pilgrim. So that lady did as she was asked, and when she had done so Sir Ewaine clad himself as a pilgrim and departed from the castle of that chatelaine.

And Sir Ewaine wandered hither and thither as a pilgrim for several weeks; and after much journeying he came at last to that valley where dwelt the Lady of the Fountain. For ever his will led him thitherward, and so it came about that at last he beheld that town and castle once more. And when he beheld that place and when he brought to mind all that had befallen him of good and of ill thereat the tears arose into his eyes so that all things that he beheld swam as in a flood of water.

Sir Ewaine returneth to the Castle of the Fountain Then by and by he went toward that Castle of the Fountain and when he had come thereunto, he knocked upon the postern door and besought those who opened to him that he might have speech with the lady of the castle. So anon he was shown into the apartment where the lady was, and Elose was with her, and several others of the damsels of her court.

Now the hood of the cloak that Sir Ewaine wore, and the pilgrim's hat, so concealed his face that no one who was there knew who he was. Wherefore the Lady Lesolie, speaking as to a stranger, said, "Sir, what wouldst thou have of me?" And Sir Ewaine answered saying: "Lady, I come hither to bear to you a message from one who has unwittingly done you a great injury."

Upon this the lady cried out very vehemently: "Sir, if you come from that recreant knight, Sir Ewaine, then you may return unto him again who hath sent you hither." To which Sir Ewaine said, "Lady, I cannot return unto him, for it would be impossible."

At these words the Lady Lesolie's countenance fell, and for a while she spake not. Then after a while she said, "Dost thou bring ill news of him?" And Sir Ewaine said: "I know not whether the news be ill unto thee or not, but some while ago I beheld that unfortunate knight where he lay dying in a park beside a lake of water."

Then the Lady of the Fountain pressed her handkerchief to her lips as though to check an outcry, and after a little while she said, "Good Sir, tell me what you know." Sir Ewaine said, "I will do so." And he said: "You are to know that when Sir Ewaine left this court to return to the court of King Arthur, he fell in with the Enchantress Vivien, who gave him a ring of forgetfulness so that he disremembered all that had happened to him at your court. Afterward there came a young damsel from this place who put him to shame before all those who were his companions at the court of King Arthur. This that damsel did because she thought that Sir Ewaine was unfaithful to you. But he was not unfaithful and so he was shamed for no good reason. Now after being thus shamed before all the court of King Arthur in that wise, this woeful knight departed from his friends because he could not bear to dwell in his humiliation before them. So he left all those his friends and journeyed afar, and in his journeyings he fell among thieves, and these finding him unarmed, bound him whilst he slept, and robbed him and wounded him to death. So it was that I beheld him lying by the wayside, pierced through with a javelin and dying of that wound, and so have I come thither to tell you of this story."

Now when the Lady of the Fountain heard what that pilgrim had to say, she shrieked with great violence and immediately swooned away and fell upon the ground.

Then several of her maidens ran to her and these served her until by and by she revived from her swoon. Yet when she was thus recovered she straightway fell to smiting her hands together and crying aloud in a very bitter agony of spirit: "Woe is me that I should have disbelieved in the honor of that noble and worthy knight, for now because of my disbelief in him I perceive that I have lost him forever. For so hath died the best and truest knight that ever lived in all of the world." Saying this, she fell to weeping in great measure, and Elose strove to comfort her, also weeping, but the lady would not be comforted. Then Sir Ewaine said, "Lady, hast thou yet such a kind regard for the knight as this?" And the Lady Lesolie said with great passion: "Yea, truly, and so I always shall have, for methinks that never such another knight as he lived in this world."

Sir Ewaine declareth himself to the Lady of the Fountain Then Sir Ewaine said: "Lady, you understood not my words. Sir Ewaine is not dead, and if you will you may easily have him here again." She said, "How know you that?" Then Sir Ewaine cast off his hood and laid aside his hat and said: "Lady, I am that man; and if I have deceived thee in this, it is that I may again behold thy face that is so dear to me—yea, that is dearer than all the world besides." So saying, Sir Ewaine kneeled before the lady and embraced her about the knees, and she stooped and embraced his head and both of them wept with a great passion of love and joy. And so they were reconciled to one another.

And in that reconciliation there was much rejoicing, for all the town was bedraped with silken scarves and banners by day and illuminated by night because of joy for the return of the champion-defender of the Fountain. And there was feasting and drinking at the castle of the Fountain, and there was jousting from day to day for seven days, and in those joustings the knights of the court of the Fountain under the lead of Sir Ewaine defended their chivalry with such skill and valor that none of those that came against them were able to withstand them, but all those companies of knights-contestant were defeated, to the great glory of the Lady Lesolie of the Fountain.

Then after seven days of this rejoicing, Sir Ewaine was wedded with great pomp of circumstance to the Lady of the Fountain. And of that wedding it is to be recorded in the history of these things that Sir Ewaine and the Lady Lesolie rode to the minster upon milk-white horses, and that they were all clad in white samite embroidered with silver and inset with so many precious stones of all sorts and kinds that they glistened in the sunlight as though they were two figures of living fire. And it is recorded that tenscore damsels of wonderful beauty, clad all in white, preceded them upon the way, and spread the way with flowers, chaunting the while in voices of great rejoicing.

Thus Sir Ewaine was wedded at the castle of the Fountain, and after that he dwelt in the land of the Fountain with great peace and good content.

And Sir Ewaine ever defended the Fountain as he had aforetime, so that the fame of the Knight of the Fountain was known throughout the length and breadth of the land and in every court of chivalry. And many knights undertook the Adventure of the Fountain but in every case such errant knights were overthrown by the valor and the skill of the Knight of the Fountain. And in every case where that knight adventurer was thus overthrown, the Knight of the Fountain would take from him his horse and his shield and would send him away upon foot, disarmed and ashamed.

So, because of the valor of the Knight of the Fountain, it came about in course of time that a very noble and worthy court of chivalry became established at the castle of the city of the Fountain, insomuch that the renown of that court of the Fountain hath been handed down in the histories of chivalry even to this day, when knighthood no longer dwelleth upon the earth.

Such is the history of Sir Ewaine when he undertook the Adventure of the Fountain whilst upon the quest of Sir Launcelot. And now if you choose to read further you shall hear how Sir Percival and Sir Sagramore found Sir Launcelot in the Island of Joy and of how Sir Launcelot returned to his friends once more.

The Return of Sir Launcelot

ERE FOLLOWETH *the further history of Sir Launcelot of the Lake; of how Sir Percival and Sir Ector de Maris found Sir Launcelot where he was dwelling very peacefully and happily (albeit not with perfect content) in the Island of Joy, of which you have heard mention in that which hath gone before; of the notable affair-at-arms betwixt Sir Launcelot and Sir Percival, and of how Sir Launcelot, with Elaine the Fair, returned with Sir Percival and Sir Ector de Maris to the court of King Arthur. Likewise you shall there read of what befell that noble company in the Valley of the Fountain aforetold of.*

All this history is of such a sort that it hath given me great pleasure to write it; wherefore if so be it may give you a like sort of pleasure to read it, then shall I be very well content with that which I have done in my endeavor to set forth these several events aforesaid.

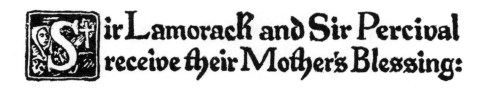

Sir Lamorack and Sir Percival receive their Mother's Blessing:

Chapter First

How Sir Percival met his brother, and how they two journeyed to the priory where their mother dwelt and what befell them thereafter.

OW RETURN we to Sir Percival and Sir Sagramore whom Sir Ewaine left (as aforetold of) still sleeping in that castle whence we departed so early in the morning—even before the break of day—to undertake the Adventure of the Fountain.

When those two good knights awoke and founds that Sir Ewaine had departed, they communed together in the bedchamber of Sir Percival. And they agreed that thereafter they two should join company and that in their further search for Sir Launcelot they should travel together as companions. So when they had broken their fast, they bade farewell to the lord of the castle, and departed upon their way, travelling very cheerfully together, side by side, and taking great joy in the gay and jocund weather, and in all the sweet freshness and the warmth of the springtide that embalmed them around about. *Sir Percival and Sir Sagramore depart together*

So they travelled as companions in arms for more than a year, and in that time they met with several bel-adventures, some of which are told of in books of chivalry and some of which are not told of. And I would that I could recount those adventures that befell them, but I cannot, for it would take another book as great as this to tell all of the things that happened to them in their journeyings. Yet it shall here be said that in those adventurings they fell in with a great many sorts of folk of different condition, both gentle and simple, and that several times they met certain knights-companion of the Round Table. And it shall here be said that they met in that wise with Sir Gawaine and Sir Bors de Ganis, concerning which meeting there shall be more said anon.

Of the manner in which they journey And if you would ask how they lodged them during their travels I would say that they lodged them in divers sorts and ways. For if it happened that at one time they would lodge them in such a noble castle as that where Sir Gawaine and Sir Percival met Sir Sagramore, then it would happen at another time that they would find shelter in the hut of some lonely shepherd upon the moorlands, and then it would happen at still another time that they would even have no shelter at all, but would maybe wrap themselves each in his cloak with nothing beneath him for a bed but the cold honest earth, and nothing above him for a coverlet but the silent company of God's own sky, all sprinkled over with a countless multitude of brightly shining stars. For so those good knights of old travelled errant in those days, taking whatever befell them in good part, and accepting all that came to them with a cheerful spirit.

If you would ask me in what sort of weather they travelled, I would tell you that they were content with whatsoever weather God sent to them; for if the weather were pleasant, as upon that first day of their journey, then they would travel very cheerfully up hill and down dale, in sunshine or shadow as the case might be; and if the weather were foul, then they would abide wheresoever heaven sent them shelter wherein to stay until the storm would pass by and be gone.

For this is true, that even wintry weather cannot chill a cheerful heart; wherefore, when the north wind would bluster loud and boisterously, and when the falling snow would be covering all the earth with frozen white, then those two worthy champions would be well content to lodge them at some wayside inn. For there they might warm them beside the roaring fire, whereof the blaze would shine in red sparks of light at several places upon the polished plates of their armor, and whilst they took cheer in the heat of the fire, and whilst they listened to the storm, how it beat and drummed upon the windows, and whilst they harkened at the wind, how it roared and thundered about the gables of the house, that while they would take great pleasure in the company of the good folk of the neighborhood, who would be gathered around a merry bowl of hot mulled ale, with roasted crab-apples bobbing afloat in it, singing merry songs the while and telling jolly contes, and laughing and making rude and homely sport in several ways that afforded good entertainment to those two belted knights who listened thereunto.

Thus you may know how in several ways it was that those two good worthy knights travelled during that considerable time when they were journeying together as companions in arms, for in this wise I have taken great pleasure in telling you thereof.

Now after those two had thus been companions in amity together for the space of a year or a little more than a year, it chanced upon a certain day that they found themselves at a place where a woodland ceased and where there began a very fair valley with a smooth shining river winding like a ribbon down the length thereof. And they sat at the head of that valley and they gazed down for some while thereinto, and they beheld that valley with great joy because it was so fair and fruitful. For in it were several meadow-lands, all smiling with verdure, and there were many fields of growing corn, and these fields and meadows rose ever upward until they cut against the sky, as smooth with fertility as though carved out with the edge of a sharp keen knife. And beside the river were banks of reeds and rushes and pollard willows and thickets of alder and aspen. And the broad highroad followed the course of the stream and there were several mills in the valley and broad ponds of water with bosky trees and with houses clustered upon the banks thereof. And ever the breeze blew mild and steady, and very balmy and warm, and great round white clouds moved slowly across the high arch of the bright blue sky. *Sir Percival and Sir Sagramore come to a fair valley*

All this Sir Percival and Sir Sagramore beheld and they took such joy in it that so I cannot forbear to tell you of it as I have done because of the joy that I also take in what they beheld. Wherefore I pray you to forgive me if I have recounted more of those things than need be, who am writing a history of chivalry and of knightly daring.

So those two worthies sat there where were the highlands at the edge of the forest, and gazed their fill down upon that valley, all spread out, as it were, upon a table beneath them, and when they had thus gazed their fill they aroused themselves from their pleasant contemplations and descended down into that valley, riding along beside the shining river.

So they followed the highway, and by and by came to where the road crossed the river by a high-arched bridge of stone. At that place were several houses of stone with white walls that stood sheltered with great, umbrageous trees and the walls of the houses touched the edge of the smooth and gently flowing river. Coadjacent to this place was a mill and a sheet of wide-spreading bright water where were so many swifts, flitting hither and thither above the smooth surface, that they resembled bees flying about a hive upon a warm day in June.

Sir Percival and Sir Sagramore meet a knight at the bridge Now as Sir Sagramore and Sir Percival approached that bridge aforesaid with intent to cross it, they were presently aware of another knight who came toward them from the other end thereof. And as they went forward he also came forward so that it was likely that they three would meet in the midst of the bridge. And they beheld that the knight rode upon a great Flemish charger as black as a coal, and that he was of a very noble, haughty appearance, showing no fear at their advance, though they were two and he was but one. For ever he rode forward very boldly, and with great spirit, even though it would bring him to meet them in the middle of the way.

There was no device of any sort upon the shield or the armor of that knight, for it appeared that he was minded to travel unknown; so they wist not who he was, but in his appearance they beheld that he was strong and big and very lusty.

Sir Sagramore exchanges words with the knight on the bridge Then as they approached one another Sir Sagramore bespake that knight, saying: "Sir, what mean you, coming so boldly thus against us? Would you who are one against two dispute the passage of this bridge with us?"

To this the other said: "Messire, I have no mind to assume any dispute with you; yet you must be aware that it would ill beseem any one of true knightly courage to draw aside and to give you way. For, as you say, you are two and I am but one; wherefore, if I should withdraw me from this meeting it might be that you would impute a lack of courage to me. So, meseems, it would be better for you to give way for me, for you could do so without any impeachment of fear, whilst I would do an injury to the pure nobility of my knighthood if I should give way to you."

Then Sir Sagramore said: "Sir Knight, it need not be that there should be two of us against one. Let my companion withdraw to the farther side of the bridge and let us two try a fall together. So it shall be decided which of us shall of a verity have the right first to cross this bridge."

"Well," said the stranger knight, "that falleth in with my will in the matter; therefore let it be as you say."

So, it being thus decided, Sir Percival drew away from the bridge upon his side, and those two knights-contestant made each himself ready for combat. Each chose his station, and when they were in all wise prepared, each set spur to horse and shouted to the assault and so dashed together across the space of bridge, each in a cloud of dust and with a noise like to thunder of horses' hoof beats upon the roadway of the bridge.

So they met in the very centre of the bridge with a crash one *The strange* might have heard a furlong or more away. In that encounter the spear *knight* of Sir Sagramore broke into many pieces but the spear of the other *overthrows* knight held so that Sir Sagramore was hurtled with great violence *Sir Sagramore* over the crupper of his horse, and, striking the ground with a roar of falling armor, he lay there like one who had been struck dead.

Now Sir Percival was greatly astonished to see so potent a knight as Sir Sagramore thus overthrown, wherefore he hurried forward with all speed to where his companion lay upon the ground. And Sir Percival leaped from his horse and went to his friend and found that he was not dead but only stunned by the violence of the fall he had suffered. For anon Sir Sagramore began to move and to bestir himself and so, after another while, Sir Percival was able to raise him up and set him upon his feet again, albeit Sir Sagramore's head was as light as a feather and swam like to running water.

Now all this while that other knight had been sitting very steadfastly observing Sir Percival what he was about. So when he beheld that no great harm had befallen that knight whom he had overthrown, he spake to Sir Percival, saying: "Sir Knight, are you satisfied upon your part, or will you also have to do with me in disputing the pass of this bridge?"

"Sir," quoth Sir Percival, "I would fain have had you go in peace, but since you have thus offered me the chance of battle or no battle, lo! I have no such choice, but must needs take this knight's quarrel upon myself. So make you ready that I may avenge his fall upon you."

Therewith Sir Percival gat Sir Sagramore to horse and cleared the bridge of him. Then he mounted upon his own horse and made him ready for that assault which he had undertaken.

So when he was in all wise prepared and perceiving that his enemy was also ready, he shouted to the charge and therewith drave forward in the assault.

Sir Percival and the strange knight do battle together Then again those two knights-contestant met in the centre of the bridge with such a violence of meeting that the spear of each was broken into splinters to the very truncheon thereof. And each would have fallen before the assault of the other except that, with spur and bridle-rein, each uplifted his charger to foot again. Thereupon, having no spear wherewith to do further battle, each knight voided his saddle and each drew his sword and made him ready for further battle. So they came together to assault afoot, and presently each fell to lashing at the other such violent buffets that the sound thereof could be heard in echo both far and near.

So they fought for a long time and in that while neither gained any advantage whatsoever over the other. But ever Sir Percival was more and more astonished at the valor and the prowess of his enemy, for, unless it were Sir Launcelot of the Lake, he knew not of any one in that land who might withstand his assault unless it were his own brother, Sir Lamorack.

So by and by Sir Percival stinted his battle, and he cried out, "Hold, Sir Knight!" and therewith upon that demand the other also stayed his assault, and stood leaning upon his sword, panting from the violence of the battle he had done.

Then Sir Percival said: "Sir, you assuredly fight a very wonderful battle, for I knew not there was any knight in this realm could withstand my assault, unless it were Sir Launcelot of the Lake or mine own brother who is Sir Lamorack of Gales. Wherefore I much marvel who you can be. Now I pray you tell me, are you Sir Launcelot, or are you my brother, Sir Lamorack?"

So spake Sir Percival, and at those words that other knight cried out in a loud voice: "What say you! What say you! Who are you who layeth claim to be brother to Sir Lamorack of Gales? Know I myself am Sir Lamorack of Gales, so that if you are my brother, then you can be none other than that good worthy knight Sir Percival." *Sir Lamorack and Sir Percival declare themselves*

Then Sir Percival cried out in a loud voice, "I am indeed Sir Percival!" and with that he uplifted the umbril of his helmet and showed his face. So also Sir Lamorack (for that other knight was indeed he) uplifted the umbril of his helmet and showed his face.

Then when Sir Percival beheld his brother's face and wist that it was indeed he against whom he had been doing battle, he cried out aloud: "My brother! My brother! Is it indeed thou with whom I have fought!" And Sir Lamorack also cried out, "My brother! My brother!" and thereupon each ran to the other and embraced him in his arms. And each kissed the other upon his cheek in great affection of spirit.

Then Sir Lamorack said: "My brother, I prithee tell me who was that knight whom I chanced to overthrow but now?" and Sir Percival said, "That was Sir Sagramore." Sir Lamorack said: "That is a great pity that I should have assaulted him and done him a hurt. Let us now go see how he doeth."

So they two went together to where Sir Sagramore was, and they found that he was now altogether recovered from his fall. And when Sir Sagramore heard that it was Sir Lamorack against whom he had run atilt, he made great exclamation of astonishment and he said: "Hah! I am not at all surprised that I should have met with such a mishap as that fall which I suffered, seeing that it was thou, Sir Lamorack, against whom I ran atilt." *Sir Lamorack knoweth Sir Sagramore*

After that there was much amicable talk betwixt the three. And after they had so talked for a considerable while, Sir Percival said to Sir Lamorack, "My brother, whither goest thou?" To this Sir Lamorack said: "I go to visit our mother at the Priory of Saint Bridget's. For wit you it hath now been three years since either of us hath seen her." Quoth Sir Percival: "Brother, what thou sayst is true, and I am greatly ashamed that it should be so long a time since I have beheld our mother. Now I am of a mind to go with thee upon this errand, and I will do so if my companion, Sir Sagramore, is willing to part company with me." And Sir Lamorack said, "I pray you do so."

Then Sir Sagramore said to Sir Percival: "Sir, I would not stay you from your duty. Go you with your brother in God's name and think naught of me." And Sir Percival said, "I will do so."

Sir Percival and Sir Lamorack depart together
So after a little while longer of friendly talk, Sir Percival and Sir Lamorack bade adieu to Sir Sagramore, and after that the two brothers betook their way toward the Priory of St. Bridget's as aforesaid and Sir Sagramore went his way alone.

Sir Percival and Sir Lamorack behold their mother
So Sir Percival and Sir Lamorack travelled upon their way for all that day, and upon the afternoon of the second day they came to that place where was the Priory of St. Bridget. Then you may suppose what joy that noble lady prioress, their mother, had in beholding her two knightly sons side by side before her once more. For it is recorded that when she beheld those two noble lords kneeling upon the ground so that she might bestow her blessing upon them, she wept very tenderly and said: "Ah, my dear sons! When your father was slain he left me four sons, of whom twain were slain by treachery so that now but you two are alive." And she said: "I pray God He may take you into His keeping and cherish you in all ways that be for your good, so that you may be spared your lives and not perish by violence as did your father and your two brothers."

After that they three sat together talking very tenderly to one another; and they sat together far into the night, so that it was past midnight when they parted company to seek their repose. And as they said good night to their mother, Sir Percival said: "Before the dawn of day cometh, dear mother, I must depart upon my journey once more." And Sir Lamorack said: "Is it so? Then I must depart with thee, my brother, for to keep thee company." At that the lady prioress fell to weeping, and still weeping she kissed them both and prayed that God might shield them both from sin and sorrow; and so they parted for the night.

So it befell that upon the first breaking of the morn, they two took horse and departed from that place. And when the lady prioress awoke, they were far upon their way. Then when the lady, their mother, found them gone, she cried out, "Alas! who would be a mother to suffer such partings as these!"

Now after Sir Lamorack and Sir Percival had left the Priory of St. Bridget's in that wise, they rode side by side through the dawning of the day, what time a thin, cool mist like to a veil of silver lay all about the meadow-lands; what time everywhere the birds were singing their pretty matins with great joy; what time the leaves of the trees rustled with the first breath of the coming day. Anon the sky grew bright like to shining silver, very clear and remote, and then anon uprose the glorious sun and sent his beams across the meadow-land and wold. *Sir Percival and Sir Lamorack depart from the Priory*

Then Sir Percival and Sir Lamorack drew rein and dismounted each from his steed. Each turned his horse to grass and then each opened his wallet and broke his fast, quenching his thirst at a forest fountain that burst out of a cleft rock near by, as clear as crystal and as cold as ice.

After that they had thus refreshed themselves they took horse again and once more travelled onward as before.

Now about the middle of the day, they being then journeying in a leafy woodland, they became aware of a sound of lamentation in a part of the forest and they wist that there was in that place some one who was in distress. So with one accord they followed that sound of lamentation a little to one side, and away from the path, and so, by and by, they came to a certain open glade of the woodlands where they perceived the figure of a knight stretched out upon the ground. And that knight was covered with blood and his armor was cleft and broken as with battle. Beside the knight there knelt an esquire clad all in garments pied of red and white. And as the esquire thus kneeled beside the knight he wiped the face of the knight continually with a napkin, and ever made that outcry of sorrow which they two had heard from a distance. *Sir Percival and Sir Lamorack hear a voice lamenting*

Then Sir Percival and Sir Lamorack rode forward into that glade and when the esquire perceived those two strange knights coming toward him, he arose and stood as though not rightly knowing whether to flee away or to remain where he was. This Sir Lamorack perceived and so called out: "Fair youth, be not afraid, but stay and tell us what is this sad sight which we behold, for we are knights errant and we mean ye well and not ill."

So the esquire, perceiving their intention to be friendly, remained where he was, and thereupon they two rode up to him and to where that figure of misfortune lay stretched in his blood upon the ground. Then Sir Lamorack said: "Is this noble knight living, or is he dead?" And the esquire said, "Alas, Messire! He is not dead, but mefeareth he is dying."

Sir Percival and Sir Lamorack succor a wounded knight Then Sir Lamorack and Sir Percival dismounted from their horses and they went to where lay the unfortunate knight aforesaid. And they examined him to see whether he were alive; and for a while they thought that he was dead, but after a while they perceived that he was not dead, but that he was grievously wounded and very nigh to death. Then Sir Lamorack lifted up his face and looked at that esquire, and he said, "Who is this knight, and how came he here?" "Messire," quoth the esquire, "I will tell you all. This is a very worthy knight hight Sir Tarn. He and his lady with only myself in attendance were riding this morning through this part of the forest with intent to go to the castle of a brother of Sir Tarn's. Right as we rode thus, there met us a very cruel and savage knight of these marches hight Sir Godwin. This Sir Godwin had with him several armed men and these fell upon my lord and his lady, and him they struck down with many dolorous blows and left for dead and her they have led captive away with them. As for me, I escaped from their hands into the thick woodlands and after they had gone I returned hither to lend such aid as I might to my sad, unfortunate lord."

"Ha!" said Sir Lamorack, "this is a very sorry story and that is indeed a wicked and unkindly knight who treated thy lord in this wise. Well do I know this Sir Godwin, for I slew his brother, Sir Gaudelin, for such another piece of mischief as this of which thou complainest." And Sir Lamorack said to Sir Percival: "Brother, let us put this good knight to such ease and comfort as we may, and then let us go to the castle of Sir Godwin and succor that lady of Sir Tarn whom he hath taken away captive." And Sir Percival also said, "Let us do so."

So they two dismounted from their horses and, with the help of that esquire they eased Sir Tarn of his armor. After that they searched his wounds and bathed them from the waters of a near-by fountain of the forest. And they bound up those wounds with such bandages as they had at hand and so brought all the ease and comfort they were able to the wounded man. So anon Sir Tarn opened his eyes and sighed, and anon he moved and upraised himself upon his elbow.

Then Sir Lamorack said: "Lie still, Sir Tarn, and move not for this while and until thou art better than thou now art. And take comfort to thyself, for I am Sir Lamorack of Gales and this is my brother, Sir Percival of Gales, and presently we go to the castle of Sir Godwin for to succor thy lady and to bring her to thee again. For indeed I have great faith that God will be with us in that undertaking, and that we shall bring you peace of soul as we have brought you comfort of body."

So Sir Lamorack comforted Sir Tarn, and after that they bade the wounded man adieu for the time and so left him and departed thence, betaking their way to the castle of Sir Godwin.

So after a while they perceived the castle of Sir Godwin where it was in the midst of the woodland. And they came close to the castle and when they were very near they dismounted from their horses and tied the bridles each to a sapling. After that they two went up to the gate of the castle and demanded admission. *Sir Percival and Sir Lamorack come to the castle of Sir Godwin*

Then presently the porter came to the gate and looked forth at them through the wicket, and he said: "Who are ye that demand admission, and what is your business?" Sir Lamorack said: "We be two knights who come to demand of Sir Godwin full satisfaction for the wounding of Sir Tarn and to demand that the lady of Sir Tarn be set free from durance."

So spake Sir Lamorack, and thereat the porter laughed and said: "Certes, ye be mad, or else ye be two fearless men to come thus upon such an errand." Therewith he shut the wicket and went away. And he went to where Sir Godwin was and told him how those two knights had come thither and what was their business.

When Sir Godwin heard that message he also laughed and he said to the porter: "Go thou and admit these two knights, and when they have entered the courtyard do thou shut to the gate after them. So we will have them catched as in a trap. After that we may deal with them as we please."

Sir Percival and Sir Lamorack enter the castle of Sir Godwin So the porter did as Sir Godwin commanded; he went and opened the gates to Sir Lamorack and Sir Percival and he said, "Come in!" and when they were within the castle he shut to the gate again so that they might not go forth until they of the castle chose to let them out again. And at that time Sir Percival and Sir Lamorack were in a courtyard of the castle and there was no way whereby they might escape from that place upon any side, for all the doors and passes were closed against them.

Anon came Sir Godwin, the lord of the castle, clad all in full armor. And he appeared at a balcony that overlooked the courtyard beneath, and he said: "Who are ye who come hither, meddling with that which concerns you not?"

Him answered Sir Lamorack very boldly: "Thou wicked and unworthy knight! Know thou that I am Sir Lamorack of Gales, and that I am he who slew thy brother, Sir Gaudelin, for such an offence as this that thou hast this morning committed. I and my brother, Sir Percival, are come hither with intent to punish thee for the evil thing which thou hast done this morning, for we will not suffer that such things shall be done as thou doest. For those were like the deeds that thy brother did and for them he died. So repent thee or his fate shall presently be thy fate also unless thou dost presently repent and make amends for the injury thou hast done."

So spake Sir Lamorack, and at that speech Sir Godwin was so filled with rage that it was as though all the light of heaven turned red before his eyes. For a while he could not speak because of that rage, and then by and by he cried out: "Hah! Hah! Art thou indeed Sir Lamorack who slew my brother? Now I am right glad of that. Make thine orisons, for this night thou shalt assuredly sup in Paradise with thy brother for company."

Sir Godwin attacks Sir Percival and Sir Lamorack in force Therewith he departed and was gone, and Sir Percival and Sir Lamorack knew not what was to happen next. Then, after a while, a door of the castle was suddenly opened upon the courtyard and a score or more of full-armed men rushed very violently into the space where Sir Lamorack and Sir Percival were. At that same time another door was opened upon the other side of the courtyard and thereupon there rushed in Sir Godwin and other armed men. All of these ran forward and flung themselves upon Sir Lamorack and Sir Percival with intent to overthrow them by dint of numbers.

But when Sir Percival and Sir Lamorack were aware of their coming, they straightway set themselves back to back and each whirled his bright shining sword about his head so that it flashed like lightning. Then there befell a great battle in that narrow courtyard, many against two. Yet ever those two bare themselves very valiantly so that in a little space of time there were six or ten men lying groaning upon the ground, and the pavement of the courtyard was become all slippery with blood. Yea; so great was the terror that those two spread about them that in a little while they who assaulted them drew away from the death that was measured out to those who were nearest to the two.

So, for a while, there came a pause in that battle, and in that pause Sir Lamorack perceived where Sir Godwin stood in the midst *Sir Lamorack slayeth Sir Godwin* of the castle folk, urging them to the attack. Thereat of a sudden the madness of battle fell upon Sir Lamorack, so that he waited not for another assault, but, shouting aloud, he ran at his enemy, whirling his sword about his head. At that fierce attack the castle folk scattered from before him like to chaff before the wind, and so Sir Lamorack and Sir Godwin stood face to face with no one to stay Sir Lamorack in his assault. Then Sir Lamorack whirled his sword and smote such a buffet that though Sir Godwin took that buffet upon his shield, yet his wits melted away from him because of the blow he had received. Then his defences fell low before him, his head hung upon his breast, he staggered, and his thighs trembled with weakness. Then he cried out, "Mercy! Mercy!" saying those words twice over. But Sir Lamorack would not hear him, but lifting up his sword he smote Sir Godwin again, and with that second stroke Sir Godwin fell down upon his knees to the ground. Then Sir Lamorack rushed off the helmet of Sir Godwin and he catched Sir Godwin's head by the hair and drew his neck forward. And he whirled up his sword and he smote Sir Godwin's head from his body so that it rolled down upon the stones of the courtyard.

Now when the followers of Sir Godwin beheld how their master was slain they were seized with a great terror of death insomuch that they crowded away to the extremities of the courtyard like to rats caught in a pit. And they held up their hands and cried aloud, "Mercy! Mercy!"

Then Sir Lamorack, panting for breath from his fight and leaning upon his sword, said, "Take your mercy." And he said, "Where is the major of this castle?" They say, "We will get him for you, lord," and therewith several ran upon that errand. Anon they came bringing a fat old man all trembling and quaking with fear. This fat old man kneeled down before Sir Lamorack, and Sir Lamorack said, "Art thou the major of this place?" And he said, "Yea, Messire." Sir Lamorack said, "What captives have ye here?" to the which the major replied, "There be seven captives, and four of those seven are ladies." Sir Lamorack said, "Take us to them."

So upon the command of Sir Lamorack the major arose from his knees, trembling with fear. And he conducted Sir Lamorack and Sir Percival to the keep of the castle and to the secret dungeons that were within the keep. There they found and liberated those seven poor and miserable creatures who were held prisoners in that place.

Sir Lamorack liberates the castle captives Amongst those ladies who were captive was the lady of Sir Tarn, and amongst the knights who were captive was Sir Percevant of Hind. All these seven captives Sir Lamorack and Sir Percival liberated and they gave great praise and loud acclaim to those two most worthy champions who had set them free from their piteous and miserable durance.

Then Sir Lamorack said, "Where is the treasure of this castle?" and in obedience to that command, the major conducted Sir Lamorack and Sir Percival to the treasure-house. There they found twelve great chests full of treasure, which same Sir Godwin had gathered by murder and robbery and rapine.

Then Sir Lamorack said: "Let this treasure be divided equally amongst these captives so that they may be recompensed for all the misery they have suffered."

So it was done as he commanded and thus it was that those who had been so sad in captivity were made glad in their liberation. Nor would Sir Lamorack take any of that treasure for himself; otherwise he gave it all to those who had suffered so much at the hands of Sir Godwin.

Then after all this was accomplished, it being then come eventide, Sir Lamorack said: "Let every living soul quit this place, for it is a den of thieves, and shall no longer be permitted to stand stone upon stone."

So all they of the castle came and stood without the walls, both young and old, strong and weak, man and woman, the sick and the well. And when all had thus come forth, Sir Lamorack gave command that torches should be set here and there to the castle. So it was done according to that command, and in a little while all that castle was in a flame of fire, so that the falling night was made bright with the illumination thereof. *Sir Lamorack setteth fire to the castle*

In the light of that illumination Sir Lamorack and Sir Percival rode away with the lady of Sir Tarn. And they brought the lady to where the wounded man lay—and he had then recovered his strength in a great measure and was in a way of regaining his life and his health once more.

So a pavilion was set up over Sir Tarn and after he was in all wise made comfortable, Sir Percival and Sir Lamorack departed from that place and went upon their way, riding through the night and all enwrapped around about by the darkness of the night and of the woodlands.

Thus it was that Sir Lamorack and Sir Percival met at that bridge in the valley; thus they visited together their mother, the prioress of St. Bridget's Priory; thus they destroyed that nest of thieves, and thus they departed once more upon their way.

And now followeth the story of how Sir Percival met Sir Ector de Maris; of how Sir Percival joined company with Sir Ector; of how they discovered a certain very wonderful isle in a lake of clear water, and of how Sir Ector had to do with a certain knight who was the champion of that island aforesaid.

Sir Percival and Sir Ector look
upon the Isle of Joy:

Chapter Second

How Sir Percival and Sir Ector de Maris came to a very wonderful place where was a castle in the midst of a lake.

HAT NIGHT Sir Lamorack and Sir Percival lay in the woodlands, each wrapped in his cloak, and each sleeping very soundly after all the travails of the day. And when the next morning had come Sir Percival awoke a little before the dawning of the day and Sir Lamorack still slept.

Then Sir Percival bethought him that he must again depart in quest of Sir Launcelot and that his brother, Sir Lamorack, was not upon that quest. So he rose very softly and he went aside and donned his armor so quietly that he did not disturb his brother's slumbers. After he had thus donned his armor, he took horse and rode alone into the forest, leaving Sir Lamorack still asleep where he lay. *Sir Percival leaveth Sir Lamorack asleep*

And Sir Percival traversed that woodland for a long while, not knowing whither he went, but trusting ever to God to bring him out thence all in good time. So as he journeyed he came about the prime of day to a certain open place where there was a crossroad and a wayside shrine and a little chapel. And as Sir Percival drew nigh to this place, he beheld that a knight in shining armor was kneeling at that wayside shrine, reciting his orisons.

Beside the kneeling knight there stood a noble dapple-gray warhorse, and the spear of the knight leaned against the bole of a near-by oak tree, and the shield of the knight hung suspended to the spear. And the knight wore neither helm nor bascinet, wherefore Sir Percival could see his face and so could know who he was. And Sir Percival knew that the knight who kneeled there was Sir Ector de Maris, the brother of Sir Launcelot of the Lake. *Sir Percival meets with Sir Ector de Maris*

Now though Sir Ector heard the sound of the footsteps of the horse as Sir Percival drew nigh, yet he neither ceased his orisons nor turned his head, but ever continued very steadfastly to recite his prayers. And so Sir Percival drew rein at a little distance and waited until Sir Ector was done his prayers, nor did he disturb the kneeling knight in any wise until he had crossed himself and arisen to his feet.

Then Sir Percival said, "This is well met, Sir Ector," and because the umbril of Sir Percival's helmet was uplifted, Sir Ector knew him and so he said, giving him greeting, "Well met indeed, Sir Percival."

Therewith Sir Percival dismounted from his horse, and he came to Sir Ector and clasped Sir Ector in his arms, and each kissed the other upon the cheek as though they had been brothers.

After that they went a little to one side and sat them down in the soft long grass of the wayside and beneath the shadow of a wide-spreading tree.

Then Sir Percival said to Sir Ector: "Sir, hast thou any news of thy brother, Sir Launcelot?" And Sir Ector said: "Nay, I have no news of him, but I had hoped that you might have news."

Sir Percival said, "I have no news," and he said, "Do you still go in quest of that noble and gentle knight your brother?" And Sir Ector said, "Yea." Sir Percival said: "So do I go upon that quest, and I would fain that we might travel somewhile together for the sake of companionship." And Sir Ector said: "So also would I wish it to be."

Now as they thus talked there came the hermit of that chapel to them where they sat, and he said to them: "Messires, will ye not break bread with me ere ye depart from this place?" Whereunto they said: "Yea; gladly will we do so."

So they all went together to the hermit's cell, and therewith he prepared for them such food as he had at his dwelling-place; to wit, sweet brown bread, with honey of the forest and berries freshly gathered from the thickets. So those two noble knights ate with great appetite and were fully refreshed and their hunger stayed.

Sir Percival and Sir Ector ride together Then, after they had thus eaten their fill, they gave many thanks to the good man for their refreshment and so departed from that pleasant place, riding side by side together, talking in pleasant discourse, and now and then chanting a bit of song, either one alone or both together. Meantime the warm sun shone very brightly, flickering ever and anon through the leaves and blazing of a sudden with a *Sir Percival and Sir Ector behold a fair valley* quick and wonderful glory as it catched upon the polished plates of their armor.

In this wise Sir Percival and Sir Ector travelled and by and by they came out of that forest. And they travelled for several days, until at last they one day came to a certain place whence they overlooked a valley. Here they drew rein upon the heights and looked down into that valley, and they beheld that it was a very fair place. And in the midst thereof they beheld that there was a lake of water, wonderfully clear and very blue and tranquil, as it were a part of the bright shining sky that lay within the cup of that valley. And they beheld that in the midst of the lake there was an island, and that upon the island there stood a castle, very tall and stately, and with many tall roofs of tile that shone all red like to several separate flames of fire against the mild blue sky behind. And they beheld that there was a little town of houses of stone and brick not far away from that castle, and they beheld that the rest of the island was very fertile and green, like to a pure emerald of bright fertility. And they beheld that there were several groves and plantations of trees and of fruit-trees at several places upon the island, so that, what with this and what with that, it was like a fragment of paradise planted in that place.

All these they beheld, as it were, upon the palm of the hand. And after they had gazed for a while, Sir Ector said: "Methinks that yonder is as fair a place as ever I saw in all of my life. Now let us descend thitherward and let us seek to discover to what noble lord yonder island castle belongeth." To the which Sir Percival said, "That meeteth altogether my wishes."

So thereupon those two rode down into that valley and so came to the margin of the lake. And they beheld that the waters of the lake were as clear as crystal and that all around the lake was a strand of yellow pebbles that appeared like pebbles of gold in the sunlight, wherefore it was as though that lake was altogether surrounded with the ring of gold. And beyond this strand of pebbles were meadows of long grass and of flowers, and chiefly these flowers were daffodils.

So those two knights proceeded along that golden strand, all in the shining sunlight, until, by and by, they came to a certain part of the lake that was nighest to the castle. And the island at that point sloped very gently down to the water, and as these two knights gazed across the waters they saw how that a wide, smooth meadow lay betwixt the castle and the waters of the lake, and that the meadow was besprinkled with an incredible number of bright daffodil flowers

Sir Percival and Sir Ector ride beside the lake

like to the meadows upon the other side of that strand of pebbles. And they perceived that there was a lady standing deep in the long grass of the meadow and in the midst of the flowers, and they saw that she wore many ornaments of gold set with jewels and that she carried a sparrow-hawk upon her wrist.

Then Sir Percival called to that lady across the water, saying, "Lady, what is this castle and who is the lord thereof?" To this the lady also called out in reply (speaking in a voice that was wonderfully high and clear), saying: "This is hight the Joyous Isle and yonder is the castle of Joyous Isle, and the lord of the castle is a very noble knight hight, le Chevalier Malfait. We of this castle are exceedingly proud of that knight, holding him to be the most noble champion in all of the world. For there have been several tournaments and jousts held in these marches, and in none of them hath any one been able to stand against our knight. And many knights have come hither at different times to try an adventure against our knight, but all these hath he overthrown with wonderful skill and strength."

Thus spake that lady; and to her Sir Percival said: "Certes, lady, this must be a very noble knight according to your accounting. Now I pray you tell me how came so puissant a knight as that into this remote place?"

Quoth she: "I cannot rightly tell you that, only I know that he came hither as a madman and that he was healed of his madness, and that he was wedded to the daughter of the king of this country, who is one of the most beautiful ladies in the world, and that since then he hath been living here at Joyous Isle."

Then Sir Percival said: "Lady, we came not hither upon any such adventure as that of trying the skill of your champion, but what you inform us concerning him giveth me a great appetite to try of what mettle he is. Now I pray you tell me, how may I come at this knight so as to adventure myself against him."

At this the lady laughed, and she said: "Messire, if such be your wish, you will find yourself very welcome at this place. If you would come at this adventure, you must travel by the margin of the lake a little farther upon the way you are going and until you have come to that part of the lake that is back of the castle. There you will find a ferryman and his two sons. Make your want known to this ferryman and he will take you into his boat and will ferry both you and your two horses across the water of the lake so that you may come to the other side."

So spake the lady; and after that Sir Percival gave her gramercy and therewith he and Sir Ector took their departure. And so they travelled some little while by the margin of the lake as the lady with the sparrow-hawk had directed, and by and by they came to that part of the lake that was back of the castle. Here they beheld a vessel such as the lady had described, and they beheld a hut beside the margin of the lake; and when they called there came forth out of the hut the ferryman and two others who were his sons. Of these Sir Percival made demand that they should transport him across the lake to the island and thereupon the ferryman immediately prepared to do so.

Then Sir Percival said to Sir Ector: "Sir, I pray you of your courtesy for one thing," and Sir Ector said, "What is that?" Sir Percival said: "I pray you that you will abide here and let me undertake this adventure alone. For I would not have it that two of us together should go forth against this one knight. And indeed I have great hope that I may be successful in this, even though I go thus alone, wherefore it is that I pray you of your courtesy that you will abide here, and patiently await my return."

So spake Sir Percival, and Sir Ector said: "Messire, let it be as you say and I will even abide here at this place and await your return. And if you should fail in that which you undertake, then will I also essay this adventure to discover if I may meet with better success."

So therewith Sir Percival entered the boat, and the ferryman and *Sir Percival* his two sons also entered it, and they bent to their oars and in a little *passeth to* while they had rowed Sir Percival across the water to the island that *Joyous Isle* lay upon the farther side.

Then when Sir Percival had safely come to the island in that wise, he rode up toward the castle through that very pleasant meadow aforetold of, and so came to the castle gateway. Here he beheld a bugle horn hanging by a chain. Then he took that bugle horn into his hands and blew upon it until the walls of the castle rang with the sound thereof. Anon, in answer to that blast, there came the porter of that castle and looked at Sir Percival through the wicket of the gate. And the porter said: "Messire, what would you have of us of this castle?"

Quoth Sir Percival: "Good man, I have heard news of the great prowess of the knight-champion of this castle, and so I have come hither to make a better acquaintance of that prowess. Now I, pray you to go to him and to tell him that there hath come an errant knight who would fain do battle with him in a friendly tilt if so be he will come forth hither without the castle and meet me in the meadow that lieth beneath the walls. For that meadow is a pleasant place, smooth and level, where two knights may have great joy in running atilt in friendly contest."

"Messire," quoth the porter, "it needs not that the knight of this castle should come forth out of the castle to meet you. For inside of this castle is a very pleasant tilt yard, and there is a gallery around about the tilt yard whence the lords and ladies of this place may view the contest between you and our knight. Wherefore, I pray you enter and take no fear, for you will be very well received at this place."

"I give you gramercy," said Sir Percival, "and I find that this is indeed a very gentle and kindly place whereunto I have come. So I pray you give me way and I will enter as you desire me to do."

Sir Percival entereth the castle of Joyous Isle So anon the portcullis of the castle was raised and the drawbridge was let fall and thereupon Sir Percival rode forward across the drawbridge and entered the castle and the courtyard thereof, the iron hoofs of his horse sounding very loud and noisy upon the stones of the pavement.

Then immediately there came several esquires running to him and asked of him what was his will and why he had come to that place. Sir Percival told them what he would have, and that he would have a friendly contest of arms with the knight of that place; whereunto the esquires said, "It shall be as you desire."

So two of those esquires ran to find the knight of the castle to tell him how that a challenger was come to run atilt against him, and meantime several other esquires led Sir Percival's horse to the tilt yard of the castle and others still again brought him a cup of fair spiced wine for his refreshment. Anon the folk of the castle began to gather in the balcony that overlooked the tilt yard, and Sir Percival, casting upward his eyes toward those who gathered there, beheld that

that was as fair a court of chivalry as ever had looked down upon any battle that he had fought in all of his life.

After that, and by and by, there came the knight-champion of the castle, riding into the farther extremity of the tilt yard, and when Sir Percival looked upon him it seemed to him that he had hardly ever seen so noble and haughty a figure as that castle champion presented.

Then straightway those two knights prepared each himself for the encounter, and when they were in all ways made ready the marshal of the lists came forward and proclaimed the conditions of battle—that it was to be ahorseback or afoot as the knights-contestant chose. After that proclamation the marshal withdrew a little to one side. Then he called upon those knights to make them ready. Then in another little while, and beholding that they were both ready in all wise, he blew a loud blast upon his trumpet, whereupon in an instant they quitted each his post and launched the one against the other like to two bulls rushing together in a charge. So they two met in the midst of the course with such an uproar of encounter that the ears of those who stood near by were stunned with the noise thereof. *Sir Percival doeth battle with the champion of Joyous Isle*

In that encounter each knight splintered his lance to the very butt thereof, and at the violence of the blow that each gave the other, the horse of each tottered back upon his haunches and would have fallen but for the address of the knight rider, who quickly recovered him with spur and voice and rein.

Then each knight voided his saddle and leaped to the ground, and each drew his sword from its sheath for an encounter afoot. Then flashed their swords like lightning in the sunlight, and blow followed blow with such great spirit and good will that the sound thereof deafened the ears of those who looked down upon that encounter from the balcony. And ever these two champions lashed at the other such buffets that it was a wonder that any skill and address at arms could have turned aside such strokes as fell in that friendly battle.

So they two fought for so long a time that those who onlooked were astonished at the strength and the courage and the endurance of those two champions, and in all that while neither knight had suffered aught of harm and neither had had aught of advantage over the other. *Sir Percival and the champion stint their battle*

Then at last the champion of the castle cried out, "Sir Knight, hold thy hand!" and thereupon Sir Percival ceased his battle and stood leaning upon the pommel of his sword, panting because of the great endeavor which he had put forth during that conflict. Then the knight-champion of the castle said: "Messire, I have met many knights in my day and amongst them I have encountered those who were regarded to be the best knights in the world, yet I make my vow that never until this time have ever I met any knight who hath proved himself to be so strong and so powerful as you have shown yourself to be in this battle. Now I pray you, Messire, that you of your courtesy will declare your name and degree, for I doubt me not that you are one whom we shall find to have conferred great honor upon us by coming to this place."

Sir Percival declareth himself
To this Sir Percival said: "Messire, your civility of words is equal to your address at arms. Gladly will I declare my name and degree, and happy will I be if it hath aught of significance to you, for I do not think that even Sir Launcelot of the Lake himself was ever a better knight than you have shown yourself to be. Know you that I am Sir Percival of Gales and that I am son to King Pellinore and brother unto Sir Lamorack of Gales. And now I beseech you upon your part to declare your name and title to me."

But to this speech the champion of the castle made no reply. Otherwise, when he heard what Sir Percival said, and when he heard the name and degree of Sir Percival, he gave forth a great cry, either of joy or of something different from joy. Therewith, and thus crying out, he flung away his sword and he flung away his shield, and he ran to Sir Percival and threw himself down upon his knees before Sir Percival and embraced him about the thighs. And he cried out: "What have I done! What have I done to do battle with thee in this wise!"

At this Sir Percival was very greatly astonished and he said: "Sir, what is this thou doest to kneel to me? Who art thou who sayst such words as these I hear? Now I pray thee that thou wilt immediately declare thyself to me who thou art!"

Sir Launcelot declareth himself
Then that knight, still kneeling, said: "Sir Percival, I am he whom men one time called Sir Launcelot of the Lake." Therewith saying, that knight of the castle lifted up the umbril of his helmet and Sir Percival beheld that it was indeed Sir Launcelot.

Then Sir Percival cried out even as Sir Launcelot had done, and thus crying out he said: "At last, at last I have found thee!" Therewith he lifted up Sir Launcelot into his arms, and he embraced Sir Launcelot and kissed him upon the cheek and they wept over one another with a great joy of meeting, and all those in the balcony who beheld that sight wondered what was its occasion.

Then Sir Launcelot said to Sir Percival: "Sir, let me bring you to my lady." And therewith he took Sir Percival by the hand and led him up into the gallery and to where the Lady Elaine sat in the midst of her court. And Sir Percival looked with a very earnest regard upon that lady, and it appeared to him that he had never before beheld so sweet and gentle and beautiful a countenance as that which he then looked upon. And Sir Percival said: "Lady, now that I see thee I wonder not that Sir Launcelot hath remained thus hidden away from the sight of all of us for these two years past. For if this island wherein ye dwell is a fair paradise then certes art thou a very fitting queen to that dwelling-place." *Sir Percival beholdeth Elaine the Fair*

So spake Sir Percival, and after he had spoken the Lady Elaine smiled very kindly upon him and she said: "Messire, your words are very fair and they flatter me far beyond my deserving. Great is your renown amongst us and I declare that you are very welcome to this place. Now I pray you put aside your armor and bathe and refresh yourself, and after that we shall all take gentle sport together."

Sir Percival said: "Lady, gladly would I stay with you at this present. But there is awaiting me at another place not far distant from this one whom Sir Launcelot will be even more glad to behold than he was glad to behold me. Now I pray you, suffer me first to go and bring that one hither and then will we both remain with you in greater joy of your company."

Quoth Sir Launcelot, "Who is it that could give me more pleasure to see than you, Sir Percival?"

"Sir," said Sir Percival, "it is your own brother, Sir Ector. For I left him upon the other side of the water of this lake whilst I came hither alone to try my fortune with you. Now I pray you let me go to him and bring him hitherward so that we may all rejoice together."

Then Sir Launcelot cried out: "This is indeed joy upon joy. Now I pray you, Sir Percival, go and bring him!" Therewith Sir Percival departed to fetch Sir Ector thither in accordance with that saying.

So Sir Percival rode down through the meadow of the island to the margin of the lake, and when he had come there the ferryman ferried him across the water as they had brought him across before. And Sir Percival found Sir Ector waiting for him, who, when he beheld Sir Percival coming, said: "Sir, what fortune had you in your adventure?" Quoth Sir Percival: "Oh, friend! that fortune which I had was greater than you or I could have deemed to be possible."

At these words Sir Ector was greatly astonished, and he said: "What great fortune is this of which thou speakest?" and Sir Percival said: "I will tell thee. Whom thinkest thou I have found upon this adventure? None other than thine own brother, Sir Launcelot, for he it is who is the lord of this castle."

Then Sir Ector cried out with astonishment, and he said: "Can this be so indeed?" And then he said: "Let us make haste and go to him upon the wings of the wind."

Sir Percival bringeth Sir Ector to Joyous Isle So again they entered the ferry and were ferried across the water. And after they were upon the farther side they rode together through that meadow of flowers and up to the castle.

Now as they drew nigh to the castle in that wise they beheld a great concourse of the castle folk coming forth to meet them and giving great sound of jubilation and rejoicing. At the head of these who approached to meet them came Sir Launcelot and the Lady Elaine, they two riding side by side, Sir Launcelot upon a great black horse, and she upon a white palfrey. And she was clad all in garments of white sarsanet embellished with pearls and embroidered with threads of silver, and she was adorned with ornaments of shining gold and she wore a golden crown upon her head such as was befitting the daughter of a king to wear. Her fair hair was enmeshed in a network of golden threads so that what with this and that her beauty shone from afar with exceeding lustre. And though Sir Ector had beheld her aforetime yet it was as though he had never beheld her until that day, for her joy and her pride of Sir Launcelot and in his meeting Sir Ector and Sir Percival again so illuminated her countenance that it was as though her beauty shone with a singular brightness from within; yea, it was as though her soul itself had illuminated her body of flesh with a pure and shining beauty that was other than of this world.

So as they met, Sir Launcelot and Sir Ector each leaped from his horse and they ran together and embraced and kissed each other and wept one upon another in such a wise that all of those who looked on wept also for joy of their joy. And then Sir Ector came to the lady and took her by the hand and kissed her hand and kissed it again and yet again. *Sir Ector and Sir Launcelot meet one another*

After that they all went up to the castle of the Joyous Isle together, and they entered into the castle with sounds of rejoicing and loud acclaim so that the very walls of the castle seemed, as it were, to cry out with joy. So after they had thus entered the castle, a number of attendants took Sir Percival and Sir Ector and made them comfortable in all wise. And they were given rich robes of royal make for to wear and after that there was feasting and rejoicing beyond measure.

Thereafter day followed day in great cheer and mirth and there were many joustings and tournaments held in honor of these two royal knights who had come thither.

Now one day Sir Launcelot and Sir Ector were walking together in the garden of that fair castle and they were alone, no attendants being with them at that time. Anon Sir Ector said to Sir Launcelot, "My brother, I pray ye read me a riddle." Quoth Sir Launcelot, "What is your riddle?" "It is this," said Sir Ector: "What should one do if a messenger came to him with command from a queen to whom he had sworn duty—that command being that he should show himself at court? Should that one neglect the command that his queen had transmitted to him, or should he obey that command." *Sir Ector bespeaketh Sir Launcelot*

Then Sir Launcelot turned his face aside so that Sir Ector might not read his eyes, and after a little he said, "I will not return to court."

"Why will ye not do so?" said Sir Ector, and Sir Launcelot made reply: "Because a duty that is greater than any queen's command keeps me here with this lady unto whom I have pledged all my truth and all my faith."

After that Sir Ector was silent for a little, and then after a little while he said: "Sir, you know very well that I would do naught to advise you against that which I believe to be your duty and your honor. But are you so doubtful of yourself that you fear to perform one duty lest you should fail in another duty? Now we are commanded by that queen whom you swore to serve to search you out and to find you and to tell you that it is her command unto you that you return to the court of the Great King and make your peace with her. Are you then so doubtful of your truth to the Lady Elaine that you fear to obey the command of the Queen?"

Then Sir Launcelot cried out, "Say no more to me of this!" and so Sir Ector said no more. So, shortly afterward they parted company.

After that they had so parted Sir Launcelot went to a certain chamber of the castle where he was alone and there he communed with his spirit, and these communings were very bitter and sad. Anon came the Lady Elaine to that place and knocked upon the door and demanded entrance, but for a while Sir Launcelot denied her. But ever she knocked, and so after a while he opened the door a little and admitted her into that place where he was.

Then the Lady Elaine came close to Sir Launcelot and looked very deeply into his eyes, and by and by she said, "Launcelot, what ails thee?" He said, "My brother hath been talking to me concerning certain matters." She said, "What was it he said to thee?" And Sir Launcelot replied, "I will not tell thee."

The Lady Elaine bespeaketh Sir Launcelot Then the Lady Elaine smiled into Sir Launcelot's face and she said: "It needs not that thou shouldst tell me what thy brother said, for I can guess very well what it was." Then she took Sir Launcelot's head into her embrace and she said, "Launcelot! Launcelot!" and he said, "Elaine! Elaine!" And the Lady Elaine said: "Alas, love, thou must return with these good knights unto the court of the King, for it is thy duty to do so. After that thou mayst return hither, and I pray God that thy staying away from this place may not be for very long."

Then Sir Launcelot said: "Elaine, I will not go away from this place unless it be that thou also goest with me. Wherefore, if thou wilt have me go to King Arthur's court, then go thou along with me. Otherwise, if thou wilt not do that, then I will disobey the Queen's commands and will stay forever here with thee."

Then the Lady Elaine smiled again though somewhat sadly and she said: "Ah, Launcelot, I am sorry for thee and for thy doubts. But as thou wilt have it so, so let it be and I will go with thee to the court of the King." Therewith she kissed Sir Launcelot upon the face and he kissed her as with a great passion.

So three days after that time all they departed from Joyous Isle— *They all* to wit, Sir Launcelot and Sir Percival and Sir Ector and the Lady *depart from* Elaine—and in the court who went along with them there also trav- *Joyous Isle* elled Sir Lavaine, the Lady Elaine's brother, who had aforetime been Sir Launcelot's companion at arms in that tournament at Astolat as aforetold of. These with their courts of esquires and ladies and demoiselles wended their way from that place with great state of departure and with all the pomp and circumstance that befitted the high estate of those who travelled.

So it was that Sir Launcelot was found, and now if you will read this history further you shall hear of a very pleasant adventure that befell them upon their way to the castle of King Arthur and of how Sir Ewaine and the Lady of the Fountain joined them and went with them to the court of the King.

ir Lavaine the Son of Pelles:

Chapter Third

*How Sir Launcelot and Sir Percival and Sir Ector and the Lady
Elaine progressed to the court of King Arthur, and how a very
good adventure befell them upon their way.*

OW, AS WAS said, Sir Launcelot and the Lady Elaine departed
for Camelot, together with Sir Percival and Sir Ector and
Sir Lavaine, for their intent was to return to King Arthur's
court. With them went a very noble court of knights and ladies, and
of many attendants of all degrees in waiting upon them. So it was that
whensoever their cavalcade would make a halt, that place where they
would rest would suddenly bloom forth, as it were, with the glory
of their coming. For upon such a halt there would immediately be
spread a number of pavilions of all sorts and colors for the accom-
modation of those lords and ladies, wherefore the green fields and
meadow-lands would presently be covered all over with a great multitude of gay colors of all sorts, bedazzling the eye with their brightness and their variety. Then all the air would be aflutter with silken
pennants and banners, and all would be bright with the shining of armor and the movement of gaily clad figures, and all would be merry
with the chatter and music of many voices talking together, and all
would be alive with movement and bustle—some running hither and
some running thither—and everywhere pages and esquires would be
busy polishing pieces of armor, and damsels would be busy in gentle
attendance upon the lady.

So it was that they made progression in that wise, all gay and *How they rest*
debonnaire, and so one day they made halt toward the sloping of the *within the*
forest
afternoon in a certain very pleasant woodland where a fair fountain
of water, as clear as crystal and as cold as ice, came gushing forth from
a mossy rock of the woodland. Here was a very pleasant meadow of
lush green grass all besprinkled with pretty flowers and around about
stood the trees of the forest, ever rustling and murmuring their leaves
in the soft and balmy breezes that caused their ancient heads to move,

311

very slowly this way and that, as though they were whispering to one another concerning the doings of those gay travellers aforesaid.

Now as those knights and ladies who had been travelling all that day were anhungered with journeying, a repast had been spread in the open air, and all they sat at table with only the blue sky and the bright floating clouds above their heads for a canopy, and only the soft green grass and the pretty flowers beneath their feet for a carpet. And so as they sat, pages and attendants ran hither and thither with plates and dishes and pattens of silver and of gold full of meats of all kinds, and with beakers and pitchers and goblets of silver and of gold full of wines of various sorts; and with these foods the attendants served that noble company as they sat at table. And all the stillness of the forest was filled full of the noise of the chanting of many voices, and of laughter and of snatches of song. What time there stood near by several minstrels who played upon harps for the entertainment of those who ate at the table.

A strange damsel appeareth in the forest So, as they sat, all enjoying themselves with feasting and good cheer, there came forth of a sudden from the forest a very beautiful damsel riding upon a milk-white horse with two esquires in attendance upon her—the one walking upon the one side of her horse, and the other upon the other. This damsel and the esquires were all clad in flame-colored satin and all these were adorned with many ornaments of gold. And the damsel wore about her neck several shining necklaces of gold inset with jewels of divers sorts, and she wore armlets of gold also inset with jewels upon her arms, and her hair was gathered into a net of gold. So it was, what with that flaming raiment and the shining of those several ornaments of gold, that she who came thither was all one living flame of fire.

So she drew nigh to them who sat at table, and they beheld that the face of that damsel was of a very singularly beautiful appearance, being like to ivory for whiteness; and they beheld that her lips were like to coral for redness, and that her eyes were like two jewels, very bright and shining. And they beheld that her hands were long and slender, and were adorned with many rings of wrought gold, so that each finger shone, as it were, with pure brightness because of those several hoops of gold that encircled them.

Such was the appearance of that damsel and all they who sat there at feast were astonished with wonderment when they beheld her, for they all wist that without doubt she was fay.

Now when that damsel had come pretty close to where they sat at their feast, she drew rein and cried out: "God save you, gentles! Now I pray you tell me if there is any knight here who hath a mind for an adventure that would doubtless be very pleasant for him to undertake?" *The damsel bespeaketh them*

To this Sir Launcelot made reply: "I dare say, fair maiden, that there are several knights here who would take pleasure in assuming any adventure that one so beautiful as you are might call upon him to perform. Speaking for myself, I shall be very glad to assume such an adventure; wherefore, I pray thee, tell me what that adventure is."

"I will tell you," said the damsel. "The adventure which I would have you undertake is hight the Adventure of the Fountain, and if you would assume it, you have only to take yonder path that leads through the woodlands in that direction and you shall come to it anon. For if you go in that way you will come, by and by, to a high mound, where you will find a huge black man sitting, watching a herd of cattle. Tell him that you are come to assume the Adventure of the Fountain, and he will direct you farther upon your way."

Then Sir Launcelot said: "This is a very strange thing that thou hast set me to undertake. Now I prithee tell me further concerning this adventure, and what will befall after I have bespoken that black herdsman of whom thou tellest." But at this the maiden only laughed and said: "The black man who sits upon the mound, he will tell you all that is necessary for you to know." Thereupon she turned her horse about and immediately departed with those two esquires who attended her. And so presently she reached the edge of the wood-land and disappeared into the forest whence she had emerged not a very long while before. And all that court of knights and ladies were equally amazed at her coming and at her going.

Then after she had thus gone Sir Launcelot said: "I know not what it is that this damsel has set me to do, but let us abide here to-night as we had purposed, and when to-morrow comes then we will all depart together in quest of this adventure which she calleth the

'Adventure of the Fountain.' For I doubt not that it is some very excellent undertaking that will afford us extraordinary entertainment."

They depart upon the Adventure of the Fountain Accordingly, that night they abided where they were, and when the early breaking of the day had come they departed thence upon the way that the damsel had pointed out.

After they had thus departed, they travelled for a considerable distance through the forest in that direction and anon they came to that mound of which the damsel had spoken. And they beheld that the mound stood in a wide open space of the woodland. And they beheld that there were many cattle grazing around about this mound and upon the mound, and they beheld that upon the mound there sat a gigantic being of such a hideous aspect that they were astonished at his appearance. For his skin was wellnigh black, and his half naked body was covered all over with hairs like to the hairs upon the body of an ape.

Then, when this being beheld them where they came, he roared at them in a great voice, saying, "Where go ye, little people, and what is your business?"

To him Sir Launcelot made reply: "Fellow, I came hither to assay that Adventure of the Fountain and these are my companions who come with me. Now tell me what that adventure is and what I shall do to fulfill it."

Then that gigantic oaf bellowed with loud laughter and he cried out: "Seekest thou that adventure? Now I warrant thee, thou wilt be well satisfied when thou hast found it. For so all have been satisfied who have come this way. Take thou yonder path and by and by thou wilt come to a certain valley that is very fair and beautiful. In that valley is a lake and there is a fountain nigh to the lake, and thou mayst know the fountain because a great tree stands beside it and shelters the waters thereof. Beside the fountain is a slab of stone and upon the slab is a silver bowl attached to the slab by a chain of silver. Dip up some water from the fountain into the silver bowl and cast the water upon the slab of stone, and thou shalt straightway meet with an adventure that will, I doubt not, satisfy all thy desires for a long time to come."

So spake that gigantic being in a voice like to thunder, and after he had spoken they presently all departed upon further quest of that adventure.

So they travelled a very long distance until by and by they came *They behold* to that steep hill aforetold of in this history. Thereafter they climbed *the valley of* to the top of this hill and found themselves at a place where the *the Fountain* forest ceased and whence beneath them lay a very fair valley. And they perceived from a distance the lake and the fountain of which they had been told, and after that they all rode down in that valley and to the place of the fountain.

Here, finding a fair level meadow, they pitched their pavilions around about the place of the fountain and Sir Launcelot and Sir Percival and Sir Ector and their knights armed themselves in all wise so as to be ready for any sort of adventure that might befall.

Thus being in all ways prepared, Sir Launcelot approached the *Sir Launcelot* fountain, and when he had come to it he found the silver cup chained *poureth water* to the slab of stone as the gigantic herdsman had said that he would *upon the slab* find it. So he took the silver cup into his hand, and he dipped up the water of the fountain therein, and he cast that water upon the slab of stone.

Then it befell just as it had aforetime befallen with Sir Sagramore and Sir Ewaine. For the earth trembled and shook so that all those who were there were filled with a great terror at the earthquake. Then there arose a mighty wind, so violent that all the pavilions that had been erected were overthrown and blown away before the blast. Then the skies thundered and thick dark clouds gathered over the heavens so that the light was presently altogether obscured, although it was hardly yet come to the prime of the day. After that the rain fell in such a deluge that all they who were there feared for some while that they would be drowned in that rainfall. And ever, as it rained, they heard, as from a distance, the voices of many raised, as it were in lamentation. For all this was just as it had been when Sir Sagramore and Sir Ewaine had come to that place.

Then after a while it ceased raining and the clouds cleared away from the sky, and the sun shone forth once more with an extraordinary brilliancy. And anon there came that multitude of birds flying, as aforetold of in this history, and these, descending upon the tree by the fountain, straightway fell to singing with such a piercing rapture of melody that the hearts of those who listened were altogether ravished with the charm of their song.

Then, whilst those who were there stood listening to that singing of the birds, they perceived a great distance away the form of a knight who came riding toward that place with great speed. And that knight was clad altogether in black armor and he rode upon a great black horse, and all the trappings and the furniture of that horse were as black as all the other things that belonged to that knight. So that knight came violently riding to where they were, and perceiving that great court of knights and ladies who stood there all drenched and wet with the rain, he cried out in a proud and menacing voice, "Who are ye, and which of ye was it who meddled with this fountain?"

To this Sir Launcelot replied, "Sir, it was I."

Then the black knight, speaking very fiercely, said: "Know ye that ye have done a very woeful mischief, for, because you have meddled with this fountain, ye have brought a deluge upon this land that hath done great damage to all they that dwell therein. Now make you straightway ready for battle, for I have great hopes of punishing you for the mischief you have done to this land by thus meddling with the fountain."

Then Sir Launcelot answered, speaking both with great pride and with dignity of demeanor. "Messire," quoth he, "never yet have I refused any call to battle, nor shall I do so at this present. As for that mischief of which you speak, wit you that I knew not I was making any mischief in what I did. Ne'ertheless, now that that mischief is done, I am ready to defend mine act since you have called upon me to do so."

So saying, Sir Launcelot withdrew to one side in that meadow near to the fountain as aforetold of; and the Knight of the Fountain likewise withdrew himself to that same place, and when they had come there each chose such ground as seemed to him to be best fitted for the encounter. Meantime, all they who were there gathered in a good place whence they might onlook that encounter and behold the upshot of the adventure.

So when all was ready for the encounter, as aforesaid, each knight shouted aloud and drave spur to horse and each charged against the other with all the fury of two wild bulls.

So they met in the midst of the course with such a roar of encountering spears and armor that the ears of those who heard it were stunned with the noise thereof. In that encounter the spear of each knight was shattered to splinters up to the hand that held it, and the horse of each sunk back upon his haunches as though he had encountered a stone wall. But each knight recovered his horse with spur and voice and with wonderful skill and dexterity, so that neither horse nor man suffered a fall from that encounter. *Sir Launcelot doeth battle with the Knight of the Fountain*

Then each knight voided his horse and leaped to the earth and each straightway drew his shining sword, all flashing in the bright sunlight. And each rushed upon the other with a great rage for battle, smiting and slashing with their swords, and dealing such dreadful buffets that those who beheld that battle were affrighted at the vehemence with which those two champions fought. So they did combat for a great while and in all that time neither suffered any great harm from the buffets of the other. Then, at last, that knight who did battle against Sir Launcelot cried out, "Stay thy hand for a little, Sir Knight, while I hold speech with thee!"

So Sir Launcelot ceased his battle and each knight-champion stood panting, leaning the while upon his sword. Then the Knight of the Fountain said: "I pray thee, Sir Knight, if so be thou wilt do me that courtesy for to tell me thy name. For I declare unto thee that never before this day have I ever met so great a champion in battle."

Then said Sir Launcelot: "Sir, wit you that I am Sir Launcelot of the Lake. As for you, I know not who you are, only know I for a certainty that you must be some very puissant champion, for never did I encounter a more worthy battle than this that I have met with to-day." *Sir Launcelot declareth himself*

Now when the Knight of the Fountain heard the name that Sir Launcelot declared, and when he wist who it was against whom he had been doing battle, he cried out in a loud and piercing voice, "What say you?" And again he cried out, saying: "Art thou indeed Sir Launcelot of the Lake? Then have I been fighting against him whom I love very dearly and whom I have sought for both long and far." So crying out, he threw aside his sword and his shield and ran to Sir Launcelot where he was. And he cast his arms around the body of Sir Launcelot and embraced him as with a great passion of joy.

Then Sir Launcelot was greatly astonished to find himself embraced by that strange knight, wherefore he said: "Messire, who art thou, and why dost thou embrace me in this wise?"

Sir Ewaine declareth himself Upon this the Knight of the Fountain uplifted the umbril of his helmet and he said: "Behold me! I am thy one-time companion in arms. I am Ewaine, the son of King Uriens of Gore." Therewith Sir Launcelot beheld the face of Sir Ewaine and knew him, and thus knowing him, he cried out with astonishment even as Sir Ewaine had cried out, saying: "Ewaine, is it thou against whom I have contended? Alas, what have I been doing to fight against thee in this wise!" Therewith he also cast aside his sword and shield and took Sir Ewaine into his arms and embraced him before them all, even as Sir Ewaine had embraced him. Then either kissed the other upon the face, and after that all the others of those who were one-time companions of Sir Ewaine came forth and also gave him greeting, rejoicing beyond measure to see him again.

Then Sir Launcelot brought Sir Ewaine to where was the Lady Elaine and he made the one acquainted with the other, and Sir Ewaine took the Lady Elaine's hand into his and kissed it with a great ardor of love. After that they all sat down together in full amity of discourse.

Then Sir Launcelot said to Sir Ewaine: "Messire, I prithee tell me how it is that you have come hither and are now dwelling here as the champion of this fountain. For certes, it is a very strange thing to find you thus engaged."

Sir Ewaine telleth his story To this Sir Ewaine made reply, "I will tell thee." And thereupon he told them all that had befallen him since he had left Sir Percival to go upon that Adventure of the Fountain in the which Sir Sagramore had failed to achieve success as aforetold. Meantime all they listened to him with great attention and with close regard. And when he had ended, all said that that was as wonderful an adventure as ever they had heard tell of in all of their lives.

Then Sir Ewaine said: "Gentles all, I pray you of your courtesy that you will wend with me to the castle where dwelleth my fair beloved lady, for certes it would be a great honor to her and to me to *They come to the castle of the Fountain* have you become acquainted with her."

So said Sir Ewaine, and all agreed with great joy to what he said, so shortly afterward they departed from that place and betook their way down that Valley of the Fountain to the castle of the Fountain as Sir Ewaine asked them to do, and they arrived at that place somewhat past the noon of the day.

There they were received with great joy and rejoicing, and after that for several days there was feasting and merrymaking and pleasant sports of all sorts at the castle of the Fountain.

✦   ✦   ✦

Now after several days had passed thus joyously at the castle of the Fountain, it chanced that Sir Ewaine and his lady and Sir Launcelot and the Lady Elaine were together in the garden of the castle, and no one else was there but they. So as they sat in discourse Sir Launcelot said to Sir Ewaine: "Messire, as we are going to the court of the King, will you not join our company with your fair Lady of the Fountain to accompany us? Certes it is that there would be great joy at court if so be we would all return together in that wise."

To this Sir Ewaine said: "Sir, that would indeed be a very good thing for us to do, and we will be glad to go with you as you ask us."

So straightway they of that place of the Fountain began to prepare themselves for journey, and three days after all the court of Sir Launcelot and his lady and all the court of Sir Ewaine and his lady made their departure from the Valley of the Fountain and betook their way toward Camelot. *They all depart from the castle of the Fountain*

Now the way they took led them toward that mound whereon sat that gigantic black man herding his cattle. And when this being perceived all those people passing that way, he sat there and laughed like to the pealing of thunder, though why he laughed not one of them wist, for there was naught of mirth to be seen in their progression. Yet ever that great black creature laughed and laughed until they had passed by and gone, still leaving him laughing in that wise.

And as they went still farther along that way they came by and by to where was the valley of the Lady Vivien. And they looked for that castle of the Lady Vivien whereunto Sir Ewaine had twice come as aforetold and, lo! it had entirely disappeared. Yea, there was not to be seen nor stick nor stone nor sign of it anywhere, and at that *The Lady Vivien hath vanished* they all greatly marvelled, much wondering what had become of that enchanted place.

Nor was it ever known what had become of it, nor was it ever known whether the enchantress had wearied of her mischiefs, or whether she feared the anger of so many who had now been raised up against her. Only this was known to be true, that she had betaken herself and her court and her castle altogether away from that place, nor was she seen there any more again.

Moreover, it is to be said at this place that from that time forth the enchantment of the fountain was removed and the cup and the slab of stone disappeared from where they lay, and thenceforward they of the valley were at peace. So endeth that part of the story of the Fountain.

They behold Camelot again Now when that noble concourse of knights and ladies who were in attendance upon Sir Launcelot and Sir Ewaine and their ladies drew nigh to the neighborhood of Camelot (which same was upon the fourth day after they had left the valley of the Lady Vivien) Sir Launcelot sent an herald messenger before them to announce their coming. So it befell that when they came within sight of the town, they beheld a great concourse of knights and esquires of the court who had come forth to meet them. These gave loud acclaim to Sir Launcelot and his companions, crying, "Welcome, ye glorious champions who are returning to us again!"

This welcome they gave on behalf of King Arthur, by whom they had been sent, for the King was glad beyond measure to have those champions who were so dear to his heart return to him once more. So it was that those who came to meet them cried out, "Welcome, welcome, ye glorious champions," in that wise. So rejoicing and giving welcome all they progressed toward the King's town—Sir Launcelot and his lady and Sir Ewaine and his lady, and their companions and all their courts, surrounded with great pomp of circumstance by those knights and esquires of the court of King Arthur, who had been sent to meet them.

And all they who had thus come forth from the town looked with great curiosity upon the Lady Elaine and the Lady Lesolie and all were astonished at the beauty and the grace of these two high dames. But more especially were they astonished at the beauty of the

Lady Elaine, for her loveliness shone like to a star in the midst of her court, wherefore they who looked upon her said to one another: "Certes, even Queen Guinevere herself is not more beautiful than yonder lady."

So they came to the King's town and they entered the town and *They kneel* they entered the castle of the King, and there they found King Arthur *before the* and Queen Guinevere sitting in state to receive them. Both the King *Queen* and the Queen were crowned with golden crowns, and each sat upon a throne to receive those who came in fitting pomp and with suffi- cient ceremony. So Sir Launcelot and the Lady Elaine and all those who were with them came before the King and Queen and kneeled down before them as they sat high aloft in royal state. Then as they kneeled there the King arose and descended from his throne and came forward and gave great welcome to them all; for his heart was filled with gladness and joy to behold them kneeling before him in that wise.

And all that while the Queen's face was smiling like to a beautiful mask. And ever she gazed very steadily at the Lady Elaine, beholding how that the countenance of that lady was exceedingly beautiful and very noble and gentle. And as the Queen gazed thus upon the Lady Elaine she hated her with great bitterness, yet ever she hid that hatred beneath a smiling countenance.

That day there was great feasting and rejoicing at the court of the King because of the return of Sir Launcelot and Sir Ewaine and Sir Percival and Sir Ector. And ever the Lady Guinevere took part in that rejoicing, albeit her heart was full of great bitterness and of a sort of despair.

Now the next day after that day, the Lady Guinevere sent for the *The Queen* Lady Elaine to come to her, and when she was come the Queen said *withdraweth* to her: "Lady, I have it in mind to do thee a singular honor that I *the Lady* would bestow upon thee, and this is that thou shouldst be in per- *Elaine from* sonal attendance upon me. To this end I have purveyed thee a room *Sir Launcelot* next to mine own chamber in mine own part of this castle, and there thou and thy attendants may lodge so that ye shall ever be near to my person. And ever thou shalt be in close attendance upon me and never shalt thou be parted from me for all the time that thou remainest at this place."

Thus spake the Lady Guinevere, for so, under the mask of friendliness and pretence of doing honor to the Lady Elaine, she purposed to separate Sir Launcelot from his lady and after that to keep them separate from one another. This she did, though why she should do it she could not rightly tell even to her own heart.

✦ ✦ ✦

So it was that Sir Launcelot returned to the court of the King; so it was that they were received at Camelot, and so it was that the Lady Elaine the Fair was separated from Sir Launcelot as I have recounted above.

Conclusion

OW AT THIS time the Lady Elaine was in very tender health, wherefore, after a day or two or three, she began to repine at being thus separated from Sir Launcelot as aforesaid; wherefore it befell that she grew lonely in that strange place and wept a great deal and ate little and slept little.

Now there was at this time with the Lady Elaine that Lady hight Dame Brysen before spoken of—she who went with the Lady Elaine to Sir Launcelot when he lay so nigh to death in the castle of Corbin. This lady saw how it was with the Lady Elaine and how that she pined in that wise for Sir Launcelot, and she wist that the Lady Elaine was like to fall sick unless she had sight of her lord. So Dame Brysen went to Sir Launcelot one day and she said to him: "Sir, if you find not some opportunity to see your lady, she will fall ill and maybe wane away to death because of her longing for you." Sir Launcelot said: "How may I see her?" Dame Brysen said: "Come to me this night in a certain passage of the castle during the mid-watch of the night and I will bring you to her. So you may cherish and comfort her for that while and so she will take good cheer once more."

So that night Sir Launcelot came to the place where Dame Brysen *How Sir* had appointed and Dame Brysen took him to where was the Lady *Launcelot visiteth the* Elaine. And when the Lady Elaine beheld Sir Launcelot she could *Lady Elaine* scarce control the transports of her joy in having him with her once more, for she catched him in her arms and held to him like as one sinking in deep waters holds to another who comes to save him. And ever she cried in her transport, "Thou art here! Thou art here!" And ever Sir Launcelot soothed her and spake words of comfort to her. So at last she took good cheer and smiled and laughed as she was wont to do aforetime.

323

So Sir Launcelot remained with the Lady Elaine for a long while, and Dame Brysen was with them for all that while, and the damsels of the court of the Lady Elaine were with them, for Sir Launcelot did not quit that place until the early watches of the morning were come, what time the Lady Elaine had fallen asleep like to a child who slumbers.

Then ere it was come the dawning of the day, Sir Launcelot took his departure and Dame Brysen conducted him thence as she had brought him thither.

The Queen is angered   Now there was a fair young damsel of the court of the Queen who acted as a spy upon Sir Launcelot. So when the next morning had come this damsel went to the Queen and told her how Dame Brysen had brought Sir Launcelot to the apartments of the Lady Elaine the night before, and when the Queen heard that news she was wroth as though she were gone wode, yet what she did and what she said and how she behaved hath never been told, for no one beheld her in the madness of her wrath but that damsel who was the spy and one other. Only it is known that after a while the Queen cried out in a voice very harsh and loud: "Where is that false traitor knight, Sir Launcelot! Bring him hither!" And then she said: "Let no one else come in to me but him, and when he comes let us be alone together!"

Sir Launcelot standeth before the Queen   So anon came Sir Launcelot conducted to that place where the Queen was, and then all those who were there withdrew, and no one was left in that apartment but Sir Launcelot and the Queen herself. So Sir Launcelot stood before the Queen and he said, "Here am I."

Then the Lady Guinevere looked for a long time upon Sir Launcelot, and her eyes were very wide as she stared upon him and her face was white like to wax. Anon she said, speaking in a voice that was very harsh but not loud: "Is it true that thou camest to this part of the castle last night?" and Sir Launcelot said, "Yea, lady." Then the Queen ground her white teeth together, and she said, still speaking in that same voice that was not loud: "Traitor! Traitor! how didst thou dare to come hither without my permission?"

Then Sir Launcelot looked very long into the Queen's face, and at last he said, "I am betrayed, it seems." "Yea," said the Queen, "thou art betrayed indeed, but it is thou who hast betrayed thyself."

Sir Launcelot said: "In what way have I betrayed myself, and in what way am I a traitor to thee or to anyone? Is not my duty first of all toward that lady to whom I have sworn my duty? What treason did I then do in cherishing her who is sick and weak and sad and helpless in this place where thou keepest her prisoner?"

So said Sir Launcelot and after that those two, to wit, the Queen and the knight champion, stared very fiercely at one another for a while. Then by and by the Queen's eyes fell before his eyes, and anon she fell to trembling. Then, of a sudden, she cried out in a very bitter voice: "Ah, Launcelot, Launcelot! May God have pity upon me for I am most unhappy!" Therewith she lifted her handkerchief to her eyes and so covered her face with it. And that while her face was altogether hidden excepting her lips which were all writhed and twisted with her passion. And yet she wept not, but ever her bosom rose and fell very violently as with a convulsion.

Then Sir Launcelot wist not what to do, albeit his heart was rent *Sir Launcelot* with love and pity. Then by and by he came close to her and he said: *pitieth the Queen* "Lady, lady! What is this you do! May God have pity on us both, for you tear my heart strings with your grief." Therewith, they two being alone, he sank down upon his knees before her, and he took her hands into his and strove to draw them away from her face. And for a while she would not let him withdraw her hands and then after a while she did let him, and so he held them imprisoned very tight in his own. Yet ever she kept her face turned away from him so that he could see but little of it. So with her face turned away she said after a while, "Launcelot! Launcelot! Art thou not sorry for me?" He said: "Yea, lady, I am sorry for thee and I am sorry for myself, and for which of the two I am more sorry I cannot tell. For God knoweth I would abide by my duty and my faith, and mefeareth thou wouldst have me do otherwise." Then the Queen said: "Launcelot, what is duty and what is faith when we measure these things with the measurement of happiness and unhappiness?" And Sir Launcelot said, "Lady, for God's sake, forbear."

Now as Sir Launcelot said those words he became of a sudden *The Lady* aware that some one was in that room. So he looked up and behold! *Elaine appeareth at* not far away from them there stood the Lady Elaine, and she was *that place* regarding them both and her face was as white as death, for she had entered that place without their knowing and she had heard much of that which had passed.

Then Sir Launcelot was aware that she had overheard his words to the Queen and with that he was overwhelmed with confusion and with pity. So he arose from his knees, though not quickly, and stood there before the Lady Elaine with folded arms and with his gaze downcast upon the floor. Then the Queen also looked up and likewise beheld the Lady Elaine where she stood, and therewith her face flamed all red like to fire.

Then the Queen arose very haughtily and she said: "Lady, this is well met, for I was about to send for you. Now tell me, was it by your will that this knight came last night to this part of the castle?" and the Lady Elaine said: "Yea, lady, it was by my will he came, for I was sad, and no one but he could comfort me."

Then the Queen's eyes sparkled with anger and she said: "Then you have broken an ordinance of the King's court, for well you know that such a thing as that is not permitted. For this I might punish you even unto death an I chose to do so. Yet I will not so punish you, but will have mercy upon you and will spare you. Nevertheless I command you that you quit this place with all expedition that is possible."

The Lady Elaine chideth the Queen So spake the angry Queen. But ever the Lady Elaine looked very proudly upon her. And when the Queen had ended that speech she said: "Lady, it shall be as you ordain, and to-morrow I shall be glad to depart from this place, for it is a place of great unhappiness to me. But tell me this, lady, ere I go: What would you say of one who took from another who harmed her not, all the happiness and joy that that other had in her life? And what would you say if that one who would so rob the other had for herself a lord who was the most noble and the most worthy knight of any in all of the world?"

At this speech the eyes of the Queen shone very wild like to the eyes of a hawk. And first she strove to speak and could not, and then she did speak, yet it was as though the words strangled her. And she said, "Go! Leave me! You know not what you say!" and other than that she could not say, but only strove to speak without any sound issuing out from her throat.

Then the Lady Elaine turned with great dignity and went away leaving those two alone together, and she neither turned her head nor paused at any time in her going.

Then the Queen, turning to Sir Launcelot, said: "Messire, I lay this command upon you, that though your lady shall depart, yet that you shall remain here at this court until such time as I give you leave to depart hence." Then she also turned and went away, and for a while Sir Launcelot remained, standing alone like to a statue of stone.

So the next day the Lady Elaine quitted the court of the King but Sir Launcelot remained. And he said not to any one that the Queen had commanded him to stay, for he would not betray her, so it was that all who were of the King's court thought that he stayed of his own will. *The Lady Elaine quitteth the court*

But ere the court of the Lady Elaine departed from that place Sir Lavaine, the brother of the Lady Elaine, came to Sir Launcelot and no one was present but they two. And Sir Lavaine said to Sir Launcelot: "Messire, do you not go hence with your lady?" and Sir Launcelot said: "Nay, but maybe I shall follow her anon."

Then Sir Lavaine said: "Sir, see you not that your lady, my sister, is in exceeding tender health?" and Sir Launcelot said, "Yea, I see it." Then Sir Lavaine said, speaking very fiercely: "What honor hath a man who will leave his own lady for the smiles of another woman? If you do such a thing you are dishonored as a knight and are a traitor to your troth." *Sir Lavaine accuseth Sir Launcelot of treason*

Then Sir Launcelot looked very steadily at Sir Lavaine and his face was exceedingly white and his eyes were like to coals of fire. Anon he said: "Messire, you speak bitter words, but you are safe from mine anger." Then Sir Lavaine laughed, though not with mirth, and immediately he went away from Sir Launcelot and left him where he was.

That same hour the Lady Elaine quitted the court of King Arthur, riding thence in a closed litter so that few, saving those immediately in attendance upon her, could know aught of what she thought or said or did.

And yet the whole world might have seen her countenance, for it was very calm and steadfast and without any mark of passion.

And all the world might have heard her words for those words were also without passion of any sort. Yea, I believe that at that time her soul itself was altogether cheerful and well-content and without any shadow of sorrow upon it.

For once, when Sir Lavaine spoke with great anger and indignation, she chid him for his heat, saying: "My brother, let be. What matters it? Could you but see into the future as I gaze thereinto, you would know that it mattereth but very little indeed that such things as this befall a poor wayfarer in this brief valley of tears."

And at another time she said: "My poor lord, Sir Launcelot! Him do I pity indeed, for God is like to chasten him before long, and to bend him and to bruise him as though he were a reed that was bent and bruised so that it may never be able to stand fully erect again. Yet even this mattereth but little; for the span of life is but very short, and all is in the hands of God."

So spake the Lady Elaine, very calmly and without passion or sorrow of any sort! For, as aforesaid, I believe that even at that time her eyes penetrated into the future and that she beheld therein what was to befall all of them.

Thus they journeyed by easy stages for two days, what time they came out from the mazes of the forest and into an open plain where they beheld a fair priory of the forest set in the midst of fair and fertile fields of corn and of rye. And the walls of the priory gleamed as white as snow in the sunlight, and the red roofs thereof shone like flames of fire against the deep blue sky against which they stood. And the road whereon they travelled went down beside the banks of a smooth and placid river, very bright and shining like to polished silver; and there were willows and aspens upon the one hand and smooth fields of ripening grain upon the other.

Now at that time the Lady Elaine was suffering great pangs of sickness, wherefore she said to those in attendance upon her: "Dear friends, it is well that we have come hither to this place. For this is a house of peace, and I am very sick. Wherefore I pray you let me rest here till God shall have dealt with me in my travails in such a manner as He shall see fit."

So spake the Lady Elaine, and upon that command they bare her to the gates of the priory. And they bare her into the priory and laid her upon a soft couch and there she had such ease in her sickness as they could bring to her at that time.

Meantime Sir Launcelot abided at the court of the King, very heavy of heart and very sorrowful of spirit. For his soul was dragged this way and that way. And whether he had gone away from the court or whether he had stayed as he did, in either case he would have been most unhappy. Yet to his present unhappiness was added many pangs like to the pangs of remorse. For he could not tell whether he did altogether ill or somewhat well in remaining at the King's court as he did.

Yet ever his thoughts went out after the Lady Elaine and he said to himself: "So soon as I can escape from this place with courtesy to the Queen, I will follow after her." Wherefore had he wist that even then she was lying so sick at the priory in the forest, it may well be believed that he would not have tarried a single moment longer, but would have flown to her upon the wings of the wind.

But Sir Launcelot knew not how it was with his lady, and so God was even then preparing a great punishment for him for which he might never hope to escape for as long as he should live.

The Nativity of Galahad

ERE FOLLOWETH *the story of the nativity of Sir Galahad and of how Sir Gawaine heard a miraculous prophecy concerning the Achievement of the Holy Grail, and of how it was prophesied that Sir Galahad should achieve that holy chalice. Also it shall be told how the infant Galahad was confided to the care of Sir Bors de Ganis, who alone knew what then became of him, until in due time he was manifested to the world as the greatest and the most puissant knight who ever lived.*

erlin Prophesieth from a Cloud of Mist:

Chapter First

How Sir Bors de Ganis and Sir Gawaine went forth in search of Sir Launcelot. How they parted company, and what befell Sir Gawaine thereafter.

OW THE history hath been told of those things that happened to several of the knights who went forth in quest of Sir Launcelot after that he went mad as aforetold; to wit, the history hath been told of Sir Percival and of Sir Ewaine and of Sir Sagramore and of Sir Ector de Maris. Here followeth an account of that which befell Sir Gawaine, when he, together with Sir Bors de Ganis, also went forth in search of Sir Launcelot.

After they two had left the court of King Arthur they joined company for a while. Thus travelling together as companions in arms, they met with several adventures, some of which are told in histories of chivalry and some of which are not. In such companionship there passed the spring and the summer and by and by it was the fall of the year.

Now some there be who love the summer time the best and some there be that love the spring; yet others still there be who love the autumn the best of all. And certes each season hath its beauties, so that one cannot wonder that there are some who love the beauties of the fall above the beauties of all other seasons. For in that time of the year there comes the nutting season, when country folk take joy in

How Sir Gawaine and Sir Bors rode forth together

being abroad in the hazel thickets, gathering the bright brown fruits of the hazel bushes. Then are days so clear and frosty, all early in the morning, that it is as though the whole vault of heaven were made of clear crystal. Then, when you look into the cold blue shadows of the wayside bank, there you behold everywhere the sparkling of many myriads of bright points of light where the thin frosts catch the shining of the early and yet slanting sun. Then do the birds cry with a wilder note as though heralding the approach of dreary winter. Then do the squirrels gambol in the dry, dead foliage in search of their winter store of food. Then is all the world clad very gloriously in russet and gold, and when the bright and jolly sun shines down through the thin yellow leaves of the woodland, all the earth appears to be illuminated with a wonderful splendor of golden light, so that it may be that even the glory of Paradise is not more wonderful than that unusual radiance.

Such was the world of autumn in which in the latter part of their journeyings in company those two noble knights made progress together. For anon they would ride along the smooth and dusty highways, where were hedgerows, growing thin of leaves but all bright with red and purple berries; and anon they would be riding through some thin woodland where the dry and fallen leaves rustled under foot with a sound like to a faint thunder of multitudinous rustlings; and anon they would be journeying along the wolds where the wind blew strong and free and the great white clouds sailed very smoothly and solemnly across the sky above their heads.

They meet Sir Percival and Sir Sagramore So travelling ever in that wise—sometimes here, sometimes there—they came one day in the early morning to where there was a smooth and shining lake, the chill waters whereof were all asmoke in the gentle warmth of the newly risen sun. And here were sedge and reeds, all fading brown and yellow, and at many places, wild fowl, disturbed at their coming, would spring up with loud and noisy splashings from the entangled water. So as they went beside that lake they beheld two knights coming toward them, riding side by side in the sunlight. And when they four had met together and had saluted one another and had bespoken one another, they found that those two knights were Sir Percival and Sir Sagramore, and that they also were journeying as armed companions, as aforetold of in this history.

So they four went a little farther to where there was a pleasant thatched farmhouse not far distant from the roadside, and there they broke their fast with bread and milk and fresh laid eggs and honey, which the farmer's wife served to them.

Then Sir Gawaine and Sir Bors besought Sir Percival and Sir Sagramore for news, and therewith they two told Sir Gawaine and Sir Bors how they had parted with Sir Ewaine and how that he had gone upon that Adventure of the Fountain. Then Sir Sagramore told them how it had befallen with him upon that same adventure, and to all this Sir Gawaine and Sir Bors listened very intently. And after Sir Sagramore had ended his story, Sir Bors and Sir Gawaine asked him many questions concerning those happenings, and he answered all that they asked him. Then Sir Gawaine said: "Well, Messire, I wot that all this mischief of which thou tellest us was brewed by that sorceress the Lady Vivien. Well I know her, and often have I had reason to chide her in times gone by for the mischiefs she was continually plotting against innocent folk. Now I have a mind to turn aside from my present quest and to find that lady and to bring her to repentance. And if I may not bring her to repentance then I shall compel her to undo all these mischiefs she hath done in this matter of the Fountain." Then Sir Sagramore said: "Sir, hearken to me and let be, or else thou wilt entangle thyself in those mischiefs also." *Sir Sagramore telleth of the Adventure of the Fountain*

So spake Sir Sagramore very wisely, but Sir Gawaine would not listen to what he said; otherwise he declared and affirmed that he would go and find the Lady Vivien and have speech with her so that he would either persuade or else compel her to better conduct. So ere Sir Percival and Sir Sagramore had departed from that farmhouse, Sir Gawaine had diligently inquired the way in which he should go so as to be likely to find the Lady Vivien, and after that he bade Sir Sagramore and Sir Percival farewell, and he bade Sir Bors farewell, and so took horse and rode away in quest of the Lady Vivien. *Sir Gawaine seeketh the Lady Vivien*

Now after Sir Gawaine had thus parted company with those other knights, he travelled all alone upon his way for the entire day, and that night he lodged in the woodland, near to where there was a fountain of clear pure water. And as he had no other shelter he wrapped himself in his cloak and laid his head upon his helmet and so fell asleep with great comfort and peace of mind.

So also he awoke very cheerfully in the dawning of the day, and laying aside his armor he went to the fountain of water near to which he had reposed and bathed himself therein and so was refreshed.

Sir Gawaine findeth the Lady Vivien Now after that and while Sir Gawaine was still unarmed, he was suddenly aware that several people were coming thitherward toward him through the yellow woodlands, and when they had come pretty near he beheld that those who approached were a company in attendance upon a lady. And he beheld that the company and the lady who rode in the midst of that company were clad all in flame-colored satin, so that the entire woodland was illuminated, as it were, by a great shining, flaming fire. And when that lady had come pretty nigh to Sir Gawaine, he knew who she was and wist that she was the Lady Vivien.

Then Sir Gawaine went to meet that lady, and he laid his hand upon the bridle rein of her palfrey and he said: "Lady, if I mistake not, thou art the Lady Vivien."

Quoth she: "Yea, I am that one, and thou, I perceive, art Sir Gawaine." To the which Sir Gawaine said, "Yea, I am he," and he said, "I have come hither with the especial purpose of having speech with thee."

Upon this the Lady Vivien looked at Sir Gawaine very strangely, and by and by she said, "What is it thou wouldst have of me, Messire?"

Sir Gawaine rebuketh the Lady Vivien Sir Gawaine said: "Lady, I am informed that thou hast done much mischief to a certain valley called the Valley of the Fountain, and I know that through this mischief thou hast brought mischance upon many good worthy knights. Now what I would have to say to thee is this: I would beseech thee to remove all of those mischievous enchantments from that Valley of the Fountain and so set that valley free from the ills that happen to it. This I beseech thee of thy gentleness to do, but if thou wilt not do it because I so beseech thee, then I will compel thee here and now to remove those enchantments."

Then the Lady Vivien's brows drew together into a frown and her cheeks grew very red and her eyes shown like sparks of fire, and she said: "Hah, Messire, methinks thou art very saucy in thy speech. What is it to thee what mischiefs I may do to others? Lo! I do no mischiefs to thee, wherefore this is none of thy affairs. Now I bid thee straightway to take thy hand from off my bridle rein or else a greater ill than thou hast any thought of will speedily befall thee."

Sir Gawaine said: "I will not take away my hand until thou hast promised me to do that thing which I have demanded of thee and to remove the enchantments of the Valley of the Fountain."

The Lady Vivien said, "Take away thy hand, Messire!" Sir Gawaine said, "I will not."

Then the Lady Vivien cried out: "Thou fool! Then thank thyself for what thou shalt suffer."

Now the Lady Vivien had in her hand a long white wand and as she spake she lifted this wand and smote Sir Gawaine with it upon the shoulder. And as she smote him she cried out: "Quit the shape that thou now hast and take instead the shape of a misshapen dwarf."

Then as she cried in that shrill and piercing voice, there befell a *The Lady* very wonderful thing, for, upon the instant, it happened in that wise *Vivien* as she commanded. For Sir Gawaine immediately began to shrink *bewitcheth Sir* and to shrivel so that in the space one might count five he had ceased *Gawaine* to be what he was and became instead a misshapen and diminutive dwarf.

Then all they of the Lady Vivien's party laughed and laughed until all the woods echoed with their mirth. And thus laughing, they took their departure, and rode away from that place, leaving Sir Gawaine standing there all bewildered and astonished with terror at what had befallen him.

So he stood for a little, like one in a maze, but after those others had entirely gone, he suddenly awoke, as it were, to his woful case. Then straightway he began running hither and thither, as though he had gone mad. And he ran in this direction and in that direction, seeking for the Lady Vivien, but nowhere could he discover any sign of her or her court. And ever as he ran he cried aloud in a voice of exceeding agony, "Have mercy! Have mercy!" But, as aforesaid, the lady and those who were with her had disappeared, and only the lonely woodlands surrounded him. Yet it appeared to him that he heard the sound of mocking laughter echoing through the forest, though whether that was really so or whether he was cheated by his fancy he could not certainly tell.

So after a while Sir Gawaine flung himself down upon the earth and wept with despair. Then after another while he bestirred himself and prayed God for help and wiped his eyes. And after that he gathered together the pieces of his armor which he could not now wear upon his shrunken and misshapen body, and he carried these pieces of armor away and hid them in a cave which he had observed not far distant from that place. Then he mounted upon his horse and rode away, not knowing whither to turn or what to do in the direful trouble that had fallen upon him.

Now after he had ridden for a while in that way, perched high upon his horse like some diminutive and withered ape, being still in the woodlands, he was aware of the sound of voices and of horses' hoofs coming toward him and then he was further aware of a company approaching from a distance through the half-naked forest.

The Forest company behold Sir Gawaine as a dwarf Then Sir Gawaine was filled with a great panic of shame, and he thought of naught but how he might hide himself and his misshapen body from those who were coming. But ere he was able to hide himself, those others had catched sight of him. And they saw how singularly small and deformed and withered was his shape, wherefore they shouted aloud and gave chase to him as though he had been a wild creature. So they pursued him for a long distance and at last they came up with him and surrounded him.

Then, finding that he could not escape, Sir Gawaine leaped down from his horse's back, and flinging himself upon the ground he covered his face with his hands and sought to bury it, as it were, under the earth, so that they who had caught him might not behold the shame of his misshapen countenance. But they dragged him to his feet and they pulled his hands away from his face and beheld it what it was. Then, when they beheld that his face was like the face of an ape they all shouted aloud again and again with laughter.

Then he who was the chief of that party said: "Who are you and how is it that a misshapen dwarf such as you should be riding about here in the forest upon a noble and knightly war-horse?" To the which Sir Gawaine said: "Sir, a great misfortune hath befallen me, and I am not he whom I was a little while ago." So said Sir Gawaine, and when they heard his speech they thought he jested wherefore they laughed again and again with a great uproar of laughter.

Then he who had spoken to Sir Gawaine turned to those others *They mock at* and said, "This poor creature is mad," but Sir Gawaine cried out: *Sir Gawaine* "Nay, I am not mad, but very miserable and unfortunate. For this morning I was a noble knight of royal lineage and now I am what you behold me."

At this speech they who heard laughed more than ever, for they thought no otherwise than that this poor dwarf was mad and was making sport for them.

Then he who had before spoken to Sir Gawaine spake still again, saying: "Sirrah, you are to know that the pet dwarf of the lady of the castle at which we dwell hath died only a few days ago. Now I will that you shall go with us to her, and that you shall serve her instead of the other creature who is dead. For certes you are the smallest and the most misshapen elf that ever I beheld in all of my life. What think you of this? If you go with us you shall have meat and drink in plenty and you shall have good clothes and lodging and fifty bright silver pennies a year for your hire."

Then Sir Gawaine cried out in a voice of great anguish: "I will not go with you for such a service. For if you did but know who I am and what it is that hath befallen me, you would know that such as I are not they to take such service upon them, nor am I one to make sport for a lady by exhibiting the miserable condition into which I have fallen from an one time high estate."

Thus said Sir Gawaine in a great agony of spirit, but still those that heard him did but laugh. Then seeing that he was of no mind to go with them, they bound his hands and his feet together so that he could not escape and so they constrained him to go whether he would or not.

After that they departed out of that forest and away therefrom, and by and by Sir Gawaine beheld that they were approaching a castle and that the castle was a very noble, stately, and lordly dwelling place.

So they came to the castle and entered into the courtyard thereof, *They bring* and after they had so arrived, he who was the leader of that party *Sir Gawaine* took Sir Gawaine up to a certain place where the lady of the castle *to the castle of* was, and he said to her: "Lady, behold this dwarf; we have caught *a lady* him in the woodlands and have brought him to you to serve you instead of that creature who died a while since. Saw ye ever such a wonderful dwarf as this?"

Then the lady of the castle looked upon Sir Gawaine and beheld how exceedingly diminutive he was and how exceedingly misshapen. And she was astonished at his appearance, and she said to him, "Who art thou, and whence comest thou?" She spake with such kindness and gentleness that Sir Gawaine was emboldened to tell her of his misfortune wherefore he cried out: "Lady, if I would tell you you would not believe me, for I am not what I appear to be, but am something altogether different. This morning I was a noble knight, but I have been enchanted and now I am what you behold me."

The lady pitieth Sir Gawaine

At this the lady of the castle also thought that Sir Gawaine was certainly mad, wherefore she said: "This poor creature is not in his senses. Take him hence and treat him very kindly. Let him be fed and clothed and then chain him with a very light chain of silver so that he may not escape until he hath become used to this place, and yet so that he may not be burdened with these chains."

So spoke the lady very kindly and gently, but Sir Gawaine was filled full of an utter despair at her words. So he was taken away and fed like to some pet creature and he was chained as the lady had said and ever he wept for pure despair.

Now the lady of that castle was very tender of heart, wherefore she pitied Sir Gawaine because he appeared to be so misshapen and deformed. So ever she spoke kindly and gently to him and she would not suffer that any of the people of the castle should torment him. Thus it was that though at first Sir Gawaine was minded to escape from the castle, yet afterward he would not escape, for he said to himself: "Why should I leave this place; and where can I, poor wretch that I be, find a better and kinder shelter in my misfortunes than I have at this castle?" So he became gentle and tractable and would not have quitted that place even if he could have done so.

How Sir Gawaine dwelleth at the castle

And Sir Gawaine abode in that castle for more than a year, and ever the lady treated him with kindness and with gentle tenderness and ever he treated her with such courtliness as a knight royal might bestow upon a lady. So great was his courtliness of demeanor that the lady marvelled much thereat, yea, insomuch that she said to herself: "Certes this poor creature must have been reared in a noble court or else he must have dwelt a long time in such a place, for to have learned such courtliness of manner as he showeth."

And sometimes it befell that the lady would question Sir Gawaine as to what had happened to him in times gone by; but Sir Gawaine had taught himself wisdom upon that point and now he would tell her nothing; for he was aware that whenever he had been moved to speak about himself and what had befallen him, then they who heard him would think him to be mad, and would laugh at him and mock him, wherefore he would no longer give any one the chance to declare that he was mad. So ever he held his peace and ever the lady of the castle wondered how it was that he had come to have so much of gentleness and dignity of demeanor.

So that winter and another winter passed, and during all that time Sir Gawaine abode at the castle of the gentle lady as aforesaid. Then came the springtime and the summertime again, and the season when all the trees were green and bosky and when the days were warm and balmy once more.

Now it befell about the middle of that summer that the lord and the lady of the castle whereof Sir Gawaine was now the dwarf went forth ahawking, and a very gay court of the castle folk went with them. With these the lady took her dwarf, for it was now come that she could hardly ever bear to be parted from him. And it befell that when the heat of the day had come the lord of the castle gave orders that a pavilion should be pitched in a pleasant shady place, and there he and his lady took their midday meal and rested until the sun should shed a less fervid heat.

That time Sir Gawaine was wandering very sadly about the skirts of the forest, making great moan of that enchantment that lay upon him. So as he wandered he was suddenly aware of a bird with plumage of gold that sat upon the ground at a little distance, regarding him with eyes that were very bright and shining. Now when Sir Gawaine beheld that bird, his heart leaped very strangely in his breast, for he bethought him that this was that same golden bird of the Lady Nymue of the Lake which she had sent to him one time before to guide him to the valley where Sir Pellias was abiding. For it hath been aforetime told in that Book of King Arthur (which hath been written before this book) how that same golden bird had

Sir Gawaine beholdeth the golden bird

conducted Sir Gawaine and Sir Ewaine and Sir Marhaus of Ireland through the forest to where Sir Pellias was at that time in great trouble and anxiety of soul. So Sir Gawaine, beholding that bird there in the forest, wist that it was the Lady Nymue's bird, and he thought that if he should follow it now, maybe it might bring him to the Lady of the Lake, and that she would release him from his deformity.

So Sir Gawaine went back to that pavilion whence he had come, and he took a palfrey that he found there, and no one stayed him, for the dwarf was now permitted to go whithersoever he pleased. So Sir Gawaine mounted the palfrey and departed without saying a single word to any one, and no one stayed him in his going.

So Sir Gawaine came again to where he had seen the bird and the bird was still sitting upon the ground where he had first beheld it.

Sir Gawaine followeth the golden bird into the forest Then as Sir Gawaine approached the bird it took wing and flew with shrill chirping to a little distance and then settled again upon the ground. And when Sir Gawaine approached it again, again it took wing and flew chirping to a little distance. So ever it flew and so ever Sir Gawaine followed, and thus it conducted him into the forest and away from that place where was the pavilion of the lord and lady.

Thus ever the golden bird led the way and ever Sir Gawaine followed, until, at last, the bird brought Sir Gawaine out of the forest and to a strange place which he had never beheld before. For beyond the edge of the woodland he beheld a dreary valley, naked and bare, and covered all over with a great multitude of stones and rocks. And in that valley could be seen no sign of vegetation or of herbage of any sort, but only those naked and desolate rocks and stones all shining bright in the heat of the sun as though they were ribs of stones shining in a furnace of fire.

Sir Gawaine beholdeth the cloudy mist And Sir Gawaine beheld that in the centre of the valley there was a cloud of thick mist in the shape of a solid pillar of smoke. And he beheld that that cloud of mist moved not in any way but remained fixed in its place as it were a pillar of stone.

Then Sir Gawaine looked for that golden bird and he beheld it perched upon the high branches of a tree near by. And he saw that the bird had folded its wings as though to rest, wherefore he knew that there must be somewhat at this place for him to undertake, and that the bird must have conducted him to this place for that purpose.

So Sir Gawaine, in that enchanted appearance of a dwarf, went down into the valley and drew near to that pillar of mist. And he came close to the cloud and he stood and looked upon it. Then as he so stood, a voice issued of a sudden out of the midst of the cloud saying, "Gawaine! Gawaine! is it thou who art there?" And Sir Gawaine was astonished beyond all measure that a voice should thus address him from out of the midst of the pillar of cloud, for he had long since ceased to think that any creature, mortal or otherwise, would know him in the guise into which the Lady Vivien had bewitched him.

But though he was so astonished, yet he answered in the voice of the dwarf, saying, "Who art thou who callest upon the name of Gawaine, the son of Lot of Orkney?"

Then the voice replied: "I who speak to thee am Merlin. Here for *Sir Gawaine* twelve years have I been lying asleep, enclosed in a coffer of stone, *heareth the* yet once in every six years I awake for one hour of life and at the end *voice of* of that hour I relapse into sleep again. This is my time for waking, *Merlin* and so hast thou been brought hither that thou mightest hear that prophecy that I have to utter.

"And this is my prophecy:

"The Sacred Grail that has been lost to the earth for so long shall *Of the* be brought back to that earth again. Yea, the time draweth nigh and *prophecy of* now is when he who shall achieve the Quest of that Holy Chalice is *Merlin* about to be born into the world."

And the voice from out of the cloud continued, saying:

"When that babe is born into the world he shall be taken away by that knight who is most worthy to handle him, and after he hath been taken away he shall be hidden by that knight from the eyes of man until his time hath come.

"You, who are a sinful man, may not have that babe in your keeping, but there is one who hath but little of sin and he may do so. So do you according to the ordination of this command:

"Follow that golden-winged thing that hath conducted you hither and it will lead you to where you may become purified of your enchantment. After that you shall follow that golden bird still farther and it will lead you to where you shall find Sir Bors de Ganis. He it is who is most worthy in all of the world at this present for to handle that babe, and so he shall care for him and shall hide him in a place of safety until his time shall be come.

"Bid Sir Bors to follow that golden bird along with you and it shall bring you both to where you shall find that wonderful infant aforesaid.

"Thereafter, when that babe shall have been taken away by Sir Bors, go you forth and proclaim to all men that when eighteen years have passed, then shall the Knights of the Round Table depart in quest of the Holy Grail. And do you proclaim this prophecy: that when that Grail hath been recovered, then soon after shall come the end of the Round Table, and so shall end the days of all this chivalry that shall forever be remembered to all the world.

"And this is the prophecy of the Grail which you have been brought hither to hear, so go you forth and declare it abroad so that all good worthy knights may know that this prophecy hath been uttered."

So spake that voice, and then it ceased and Sir Gawaine listened for a while, but still it spake no more. Then Sir Gawaine cried out aloud: "Merlin, what may I do to free thee from the enchantment that lieth upon thee?" And he waited for a reply, but no reply was vouchsafed him. And he cried out again, "Merlin, what may I do to free thee from where thou liest?" but still no answer was given to him.

Sir Gawaine striveth to enter the cloud of mist Then Sir Gawaine went forward with intent to enter that cloud of mist, but lo! it was like to a wall of adamant and he could nowhere enter into it. And he strove at several places but still there was no place where he might penetrate it. For the enchantment that lay upon that pillar of mist was so potent that it was not possible for any one to enter it saving only the enchantress Vivien, who herself had created that cloud by her powerful enchantments.

And ever Sir Gawaine called repeatedly upon the name of Merlin, but at no time did Merlin answer him. Then by and by Sir Gawaine was aware that the golden bird that had brought him to that place was flitting hither and thither near by, as though it were very restless to depart. So Sir Gawaine was aware that it behooved him presently to quit that place whither he might never return again. So once more he called aloud upon Merlin, saying, "Farewell, Merlin," and it appeared to him that he heard a voice, very faint and distant as though sounding from a dream that is fading, and he seemed that voice said, "Farewell."

Thereafter Sir Gawaine mounted his palfrey and turned him about and departed from that place, still in the guise of a dwarf, and so that prophecy of Merlin was completed.

✛   ✛   ✛

And never more after that time was the voice of Merlin heard again, *Of the sleep of* for no one saving Sir Gawaine ever found that valley with its pillar of *Merlin* cloud. Yet it may be that Merlin did but sleep, for it was prophesied of him that at the ending of the age he should come forth again into the world, but whether he should come forth in the spirit or in the flesh, no one knew. Yea, there be many who opine that Merlin hath awakened again and is alive this very day, for such miracles are performed in these times that it is hardly possible to suppose otherwise than that the spirit of Merlin is in the world once more. Wherefore it is that many suppose that he is now again alive, though haply in the spirit.

✛   ✛   ✛

Now followeth the story of the birth of Galahad, who was the most famous knight who ever lived in the world and who achieved the Quest of the Grail as was foretold by Merlin in that prophecy herein recounted. So I pray you to read that story as it shall presently be told.

ir Bors de Ganis, the good:

Chapter Second

How Sir Bors and Sir Gawaine came to a priory in the forest, and how Galahad was born at that place.

O SIR GAWAINE followed the golden bird away from that valley of enchantment where Merlin lay bound in sleep in the stone coffer (and concerning that stone coffer and the enchantment of Merlin it was aforetold of at length in the Book of King Arthur). And ever he followed that winged golden creature both long and far, and ever the bird ceased not to flit before him, but led him onward in a certain direction. So thus it befell that toward the evening of that same day Sir Gawaine, still following the golden bird, came out of the forest again and to a wonderful place, lit by a strange golden light that was not like the light of the moon nor like the light of the sun nor like any other kind of light that was to be found in the world of mortal man. For though it was toward evening when Sir Gawaine came to that place, yet everywhere there was that golden radiance both upon earth and in the sky. And in this light Sir Gawaine beheld a wide and circular lake, very still and shining, and without any ripple upon the face thereof, so that it was rather like to a lake of crystal than to a lake of water. And all about the margin of the lake there bloomed an incredible number of tall flowers, both lily flowers and asphodels.

Then, as Sir Gawaine drave his horse forward through those flowers, he became aware that this was that magic lake where dwelt the Lady Nymue of the Lake and where dwelt Sir Pellias who was her lord and the knight-champion of the lake—for he had beheld that lake aforetime by moonlight when he had followed Sir Pellias to that place.

Now as Sir Gawaine thus advanced amidst the flowers, he was aware that a little distance away there stood a pavilion of green satin adorned with golden figures of cherubim and so he went forward toward that pavilion, for ever the golden bird led him thitherward.

347

So as he came toward that pavilion there issued forth therefrom a lady who came to meet him. And that lady was clad all in a garment of shining green; and she wore about her neck many bright and glistering ornaments of gold inset with stones about her wrists and arms. And her hair was perfectly black and her face was white like to ivory for whiteness and her eyes were black and shining like to two jewels set in ivory. And Sir Gawaine immediately knew that lady who she was and that she was the Lady of the Lake herself; for so she appeared to King Arthur and so she appeared to several others, as you may read of if it should please you in those volumes of this history that were written before this volume.

So the Lady of the Lake came forward to meet Sir Gawaine, and she beheld Sir Gawaine how that he was bewitched into the guise of a dwarf as aforetold. And the lady said: "Certes, Messire, this is a great misfortune that hath befallen thee. Now I prithee come with me until I make an end of thy enchantment."

So the Lady of the Lake took the horse of Sir Gawaine by the bridle, and she led the horse through those flowers for some little distance, and so brought him to the margin of the waters of the lake. And when they had come there the Lady of the Lake stooped and dipped up some of the water of the lake into her hand; and she flung the water upon Sir Gawaine, crying out in a high and piercing voice: "Cease from thy present shape, and assume that shape that is thine own!"

The Lady of the Lake healeth Sir Gawaine of his enchantment Therewith, upon an instant, the enchantment that had rested upon Sir Gawaine was released from him and he became himself again, resuming his own knightly appearance instead of that semblance of a misshapen dwarf into which the enchantment of the Lady Vivien had cast him.

Then Sir Gawaine leaped down from off the back of that poor palfrey upon which he had been riding, and he kneeled down before that fair and gentle Lady of the Lake, and he set the palms of his hands together and gave her words of pure gratitude beyond stint that she had removed that enchantment from him. And ever the Lady of the Lake looked down upon Sir Gawaine and smiled very kindly upon him. And she said: "Messire, abide this night in yonder pavilion, for it hath been prepared for thee to rest in. To-morrow, after thou hast thus rested and refreshed thyself, then thou shalt go forward upon thy way again."

Then the Lady of the Lake gave her hand to Sir Gawaine and *The Lady of* he took it and kissed it. And after that she turned and approached *the Lake* the lake, and at that time the sky was all golden both with the glory *departeth* of the fading day and with that other glory, the strange magic light that embalmed that wonderful lake as aforetold. And Sir Gawaine, still kneeling upon the strand of the lake, beheld that the Lady of the Lake reached the water, and stretched forth her foot and set it upon the surface of the lake as though the water had been a sheet of clear glass. And as soon as that lady thus touched the water of the lake, she immediately disappeared from sight, and thenceforth was seen no more at that time.

After that Sir Gawaine arose from where he kneeled, and he went toward the pavilion and as he approached it there came forth two esquires to meet him. And those esquires were people of the lake, for they also were clad in garments of green like the garments of the Lady of the Lake, and those garments also shone with a singular lustre as did her garments. And their hair was perfectly black and each wore a fillet of gold about his head.

These came to Sir Gawaine and conducted him to the pavilion *Sir Gawaine* and into the pavilion. In the pavilion was a couch and Sir Gawaine *is served by* seated himself thereon, and after he had done so the two esquires *the people of* brought a table of gold and placed it before him. Then they spread *the lake* a napkin of white linen upon the table and anon they set before Sir Gawaine a very bounteous feast of various meats, and of manchets of white bread and of divers wines both red and white. So Sir Gawaine ate and drank and refreshed himself, and meantime the two esquires of the lake served him in all ways.

After that Sir Gawaine laid him down to sleep, and he slept very peacefully and gently and without any anxiety whatsoever. And when the morning had come he bestirred himself and presently there came to him those two esquires and aided him to arise. And they brought new rich garments for him to wear, and they brought him food wherewith to refresh himself, and after that they brought him a suit of splendid armor, polished like a mirror and inlaid with various singular devices in gold.

Then those esquires of the lake armed Sir Gawaine and brought him forth from the pavilion, and Sir Gawaine beheld a noble and lordly war-horse caparisoned in all ways, and in all ways fitting for a Knight Royal to ride upon. And the esquire said to him: "Sir, this is your horse, and it hath been purveyed expressly for you."

So Sir Gawaine viewed the war-horse and saw how noble it was, and he mounted upon it with great joy of possession and he gave thanks without measure to those two esquires who had served him. After that he rode away from that place with such lightness of heart and with such peace and happiness of spirit as doth not often come to any man in this life.

Sir Gawaine followeth the golden bird once more

Then presently there came that golden bird once more and flitted before Sir Gawaine as it had aforetime done, chirping very shrilly the while. And Sir Gawaine followed the bird once more as aforetime, and it led him as it had before done ever in a certain direction. So it brought him onward in that wise until about the middle of the day, what time he came forth into an open place of the forest and there beheld before him the forest hermitage several times mentioned in these histories.

And Sir Gawaine saw that a noble black war-horse stood beside that forest sanctuary, and he saw that a great spear leaned against a tree beside the hermitage and that a shield hung from the spear. And when Sir Gawaine had come close enough he knew by the device upon that shield that it was Sir Bors de Ganis who was there at the hermitage.

Now as Sir Gawaine approached the cell of the hermit of the forest, the horse of Sir Bors neighed aloud, and the horse of Sir Gawaine neighed in answer. Therewith, as though that neighing had been a summons, the door of the hut opened and the hermit appeared in the doorway, shading his eyes with his hand from the glare of the sun. So when he perceived that it was Sir Gawaine who approached that lonely place he cried out aloud: "Welcome Sir Gawaine! Welcome to this place! Sir Bors is here and awaiting thee. For it hath been told him in a dream that thou wouldst meet him here at this time to-day, and so he is here awaiting thy coming in fulfillment of that dream."

Sir Gawaine meets Sir Bors again

So Sir Gawaine dismounted from his horse and he entered the

cell of the hermit and there he beheld Sir Bors kneeling at prayer at a little altar, and Sir Gawaine stood and waited until Sir Bors had finished his orisons. And when Sir Bors had crossed himself and had arisen to his feet, he turned with great joy and took Sir Gawaine into his arms; and either embraced the other and either kissed the other upon the cheek.

After that they sat down and the hermit brought them food and they ate of the simple fare of the hermit's cell, and meantime Sir Gawaine told Sir Bors all that had happened to him since they had parted company. To all that was said Sir Bors listened with deep attention, for he was much, astonished at that which had befallen Sir Gawaine and at the enchantment he had suffered at the hands of the Lady Vivien. And indeed it was, of a surety, a very wonderful adventure, such as any one might well have marvelled to hear tell of.

But when Sir Gawaine told Sir Bors concerning the prophecy of Merlin, then Sir Bors became all enwrapped as with a certain exaltation of spirit. Wherefore, when Sir Gawaine had finished that part of his story, Sir Bors cried out: "How wonderful is this miracle that thou tellest me! Know ye that certain things of this sort have been presented before me of late in several dreams, but lo! now they have been manifested to thee in reality." And he said: "Let us straightway arise and go forth hence, for methinks that even now we have tarried too long in performing the bidding of this prophecy." Accordingly they arose and they gave thanks in full measure to that good old hermit and they bade him farewell. Thereafter they went forth and mounted their horses and took shield and spear in hand and departed thence, and after they had so departed, straightway the golden bird appeared once more and flew chirping before them.

Then Sir Bors, beholding the bird, said: "Lo! is not yonder the bird that has been sent to lead us upon our way?" And Sir Gawaine said, "Yea; that is it." And then Sir Bors said, "Let us follow it apace."

So they followed the bird, and ever it flew before them, leading *Sir Gawaine* them upon the way. Thus they travelled for a long while, until at *and Sir Bors* last, toward the sloping of the afternoon, they became aware that the *golden bird* forest wherein they rode was becoming thinner. And anon they were *They come to* aware of the ringing of a bell somewhere not a great distance away. *the priory of* And the bird led them toward where that bell was ringing, and so in *the valley* a little pass they came forth out of the forest and into a very fertile valley. And there was a smooth river, not very broad, that flowed down through the valley, and beside the river there was a fair priory, not large in size but very comely, with white walls and red roofs and many shining windows, very bright in the sun. And all about the priory were fair fields and orchards and gardens, all illuminated very bright and warm, in the full light of the slanting sun that was now turning all the world to gold by its bright, yellow and very glorious shining.

So when Sir Bors and Sir Gawaine entered this pleasant plain, the golden bird that had led them thitherward suddenly chirped very loud and shrill, and straightway flew high aloft into the air and immediately disappeared over the tree tops. Thereupon those two champions knew with certainty that this must be the place whither they were to come, and they wist that here they should doubtless find that young child of which the prophecy of Merlin had spoken. So they went forward toward the priory with a certain awe, as not knowing what next of mystery was to happen to them.

They meet Sir Lavaine So as they approached that holy place, the gateway of the priory was suddenly opened, and there came forth a young knight of a very noble and haughty appearance, and both Sir Gawaine and Sir Bors knew that one, that he was Sir Lavaine, the brother of the Lady Elaine, and whilom the companion in arms of Sir Launcelot of the Lake. And as they drew more near they beheld that the face of Sir Lavaine was very sad and that he smiled not at all as he gave them greeting, saying: "Ye are welcome, Messires, and ye come none too soon, for we have been waiting for you since the morning." And he said, "Dismount and come with me."

So Sir Bors and Sir Gawaine dismounted from their horses and straightway there came several attendants and took the steeds and led them away to stable. Then Sir Lavaine turned, and he beckoned with his hand, and Sir Bors and Sir Gawaine followed after as he had commanded them to do. So Sir Lavaine brought them through several passageways and from place to place until at last he brought them to a small cell of the priory, very cold and bare and white as snow.

They behold the Lady Elaine In the centre of the cell there lay a couch and upon the couch there lay a figure as still as death and Sir Bors and Sir Gawaine beheld that it was the Lady Elaine who lay there. Her hair lay spread out all over the pillow of the couch, shining like to pure gold, and in the midst of the hair her face shone very white, like to pure clear wax for whiteness. Her eyes looked, as it were, from out of a faint shadow and gazed ever straight before her and she never stirred nor moved her gaze as Sir Bors and Sir Gawaine and Sir Lavaine entered her cell; for it was as though her looks were fixed upon something very strange that she beheld a great distance away.

Then Sir Lavaine, speaking in a whisper, said, "Come near and behold," and thereupon Sir Bors and Sir Gawaine came close to the couch upon which the Lady Elaine lay. So when they had come nigh, Sir Lavaine lifted the coverlet very softly and they beheld that a new-born babe lay beside the lady upon that couch. Then they wist that that babe was the child of Sir Launcelot of the Lake and the Lady Elaine; and they wist that this was the babe of whom Merlin had spoken in his prophecy. For the child was very wonderfully beautiful, and it was as though a certain clear radiance of light shone forth from its face; and it lay so perfectly still that it was like as though it did not live. So Sir Bors and Sir Gawaine knew because of these and several other things that this must indeed be that very child whom they had come to find. Yea, it was as though a voice from a distance said: "Behold! this is that one who shall achieve the Quest of the Holy Grail according to the prophecy of Merlin." *They behold the young child*

So Sir Bors and Sir Gawaine kneeled down beside the bed and set their palms together, and Sir Lavaine stood near them, and for a while all was very silent in that place. Then suddenly the Lady Elaine spake in that silence in a voice very faint and remote but very clear, and as she spake she turned not her eyes toward any one of them, but gazed ever straight before her. And she said, "Sir Bors, art thou there?" and Sir Bors said, "Yea, Lady."

Then she said: "Behold this child and look you upon him, for this is he who shall achieve the Quest of the Holy Grail and shall bring it back to the earth again. So he shall become the greatest knight that ever the world beheld. But though he shall be the greatest champion at arms that ever lived, yet also he shall be gentle and meek and without sin, innocent like to a little child. And because he is to be so *The Lady Elaine bespeaketh Sir Bors* high in chivalry and so pure of life, therefore his name shall be called Galahad." And she said again, "Sir Bors, art thou there?" and he said, "Yea, Lady."

She said: "My time draweth near, for even now I behold the shining gates of Paradise, though it yet is that I behold them faintly, as through a vapor of mist. Yet anon that mist shall pass, and I shall behold those gates very near by and shining in glory; for soon I shall quit this troubled world for that bright and beautiful country. Nevertheless, I shall leave behind me this child who lieth beside me, and his life shall enlighten that world from which I am withdrawing." Then she said for the third time, "Sir Bors, art thou there?" And Sir Bors wept, and he said, "Yea, Lady, I am here."

Then the Lady Elaine said: "Take thou this child and bear him hence unto a certain place that thou shalt find. Thou shalt know that place because there shall go before thee a bird with golden plumage, and it shall show thee where thou art to take this child. Leave the child at that place whither the bird shall lead thee, and tell no man where that place is. For this child must hide in secret until the time shall come when he shall be manifested to the world." And she said, "Hearest thou me, Sir Bors?" And Sir Bors, still weeping, said, "Yea, Lady."

Then she said: "Go and tarry not in thy going, for the ending is very near. Wait not until that end cometh, but go immediately and do as I have asked thee to do."

Sir Bors departeth with the young child Then, still weeping, Sir Bors arose from where he kneeled, and he took the young child and he wrapped it in his cloak and he went out thence and was gone, taking the babe with him.

And this while Sir Gawaine and Sir Lavaine also wept, and ever Sir Gawaine still kneeled and Sir Lavaine stood beside him.

Such is the story of the nativity of Sir Galahad, who afterward achieved the Quest of the Holy Grail as was prophesied in the prophecy of Merlin.

✦ ✦ ✦

The passing of Elaine the Fair That same day the Lady Elaine died about the middle watch of the night, departing from this world in great peace and good content, and Sir Gawaine and Sir Lavaine were with her at the time of her passing.

Then Sir Gawaine said, weeping, "Let me go and fetch Sir Launcelot of the Lake hither." But Sir Lavaine, speaking very sternly, said: "Let be and bring him not, for he is not worthy to be brought hither. But as for you, do you depart, for I have yet that to do I would do alone. So go you immediately and return unto the court of the King. But when you have come to the King's court, I charge you to say nothing unto any one concerning the birth of the child Galahad, nor of how this sweet, fair lady is no more, for I have a certain thing to do that I would fain perform before those things are declared. So when you have come to court say nothing of these matters of which I have spoken." To the which Sir Gawaine said, "Messire, it shall be as you desire in all things."

So immediately Sir Gawaine went forth and called for his horse, and they brought his horse to him and he mounted and departed from that place, leaving Sir Lavaine alone with his dead.

Sir Gawaine departeth from the priory

And it remaineth here to be said that Sir Gawaine went directly from that place to the court of the King, and when he had come there he told only of those adventures that had happened to him when the Lady Vivien had bewitched him. But of those other matters: to wit, of the nativity of Galahad and of the death of the Lady Elaine, he said naught to any one but concealed those things for the time being in his own heart.

Yet ever he pondered those things and meditated upon them in the silent watches of the night. For the thought of those things filled him at once with joy and with a sort of terror; with hope and with a manner of despair; wherefore his spirit was troubled because of those things which he had beheld, for he knew not what their portent might be.

he Barge of the Dead 🙟🙟

Conclusion

OW AFTER Sir Bors had departed and after Sir Gawaine had departed as aforesaid—the one at the one time and the other at the other—there came several of those of the priory to that cell of death. And they lifted up that still and peaceful figure and bare it away to the chapel of the priory. And they laid it upon a bier in the chapel and lit candles around about the bier, and they chanted all night in the chapel a requiem to the repose of the gentle soul that was gone. And when the morning light had dawned Sir Lavaine came to that chapel when the candles were still alight in the dull gray of the early day and he kneeled for a long time in prayer beside the bier.

Thereafter and when he had ended his prayers, he arose and departed from that place, and he went to the people of the priory, and he said to them, "Whither is it that this river floweth?" They say: "It floweth down from this place past the King's town of Camelot, and thence it floweth onward until it floweth into the sea to the southward."

Sir Lavaine said, "Is there ere a boat at this place that may float upon the river?" And they say to him: "Yea, Messire, there is a barge *Sir Lavaine* and there is a man that saileth that barge and that man is deaf and *findeth a boat* dumb from birth." At that Sir Lavaine said: "I pray you to bring me to where that deaf and dumb bargeman is."

So one of those to whom he spake took him to a certain place where was that barge, and the deaf and dumb bargeman. And the bargeman was a very old man with a long beard as white as snow and he gazed very steadfastly upon Sir Lavaine as he drew near thitherward. So Sir Lavaine came close to the bargeman and he made signs to him, asking him if he would ferry him down the stream to the King's

357

town, and the dumb bargeman understood what Sir Lavaine would have and he made signs in answer that it should be as Sir Lavaine desired.

Sir Lavaine with the dead lady departeth in the barge

After that Sir Lavaine gave command that the barge should be hung and draped all with white samite embroidered with silver and he gave command that a couch of white samite should be established upon the barge, and the covering of the couch was also embroidered with silver. So when all was in readiness there came forth a procession from the chapel, bearing that still and silent figure, and they brought it to the barge and laid it upon the couch of white samite that had been prepared for it. Thereafter Sir Lavaine entered the barge and took his station in the bow of the boat and the deaf and dumb man took his station in the stern thereof.

Then the bargeman trimmed the sail and so the barge drew slowly away from that place, many standing upon the landing-stage and watching its departure.

So they descend the flood

And after that the barge floated gently down the smooth stream of the river, and ever the deaf and dumb man guided it upon its way. And anon they floated down betwixt banks of rushes, with here and there a row of pollard willow-trees and thickets of alder. And all about them was the pleasant weather of the summertime, with everything abloom with grace and beauty.

Then anon, departing from those marshy stretches with their rushes and their willows and their alders, they drifted past some open meadow-lands, with fields and uplands all trembling in the still hot sunlight. And after that they came to a more populous country where were several small towns and villages with here and there a stone bridge crossing the river. And at those places of habitation many came and stood upon a bridge beneath which they passed, and others stood upon the smooth and grassy banks of the stream and gazed in awe at that wonderful barge as it drifted by adown the flood. And they who thus gazed would whisper and marvel at what they beheld and would cross themselves for awe and terror.

So ever they floated onward until at last they came to within sight of the town of Camelot.

After that, in a little they came to the town and as they passed by the town walls, lo! a great multitude of people came and stood upon the walls and gazed down upon that white bedraped barge and those who were within. And all the people whispered to one another in awe, saying: "What is this and what doth it portend? Is this real or is it a vision that we behold?"

But ever that barge drifted onward past the walls and past those *So they come* who stood thereon, and so, at last, it came to a landing-place of stone *to Camelot* steps not far distant from the castle of the King. There the dumb bargeman made fast the barge to the iron rings of the landing-stage, and so that strange voyage was ended.

Now at that time King Arthur and many of the lords and some of the ladies of his court sat at feast in the royal hall of the castle, and amongst those was Sir Launcelot and Queen Guinevere. So as they sat thus, there came one of a sudden running into the hall as in affright, and thereat all looked upon him and wondered wherefore he came into the hall in that way. Then King Arthur said, "What ails thee that thou comest hither to us thus?"

Then he who came kneeled before King Arthur, and he said: *King Arthur* "Lord, here is a wonderful thing. For down by the river there hath *heareth news* come a barge to the landing-stairs of the castle, and that barge is hung *of the barge* all with white samite embroidered with silver. And in the barge and upon a couch of white samite there lieth a dead lady so beautiful that I do not think her like is to be found in all of the earth. And a dumb man sits in the stern of the boat, and a noble young knight sits in the bow of the boat with his face shrouded in his mantle as though for grief. And that knight sits there as silent and as motionless as the dead lady, and the dumb man sits there also, like to an image of a man rather than a man of flesh and blood. Wherefore it is that I have come hither to bring you word of this wonderful thing."

Then King Arthur said: "This is indeed a most singular story that thou tellest us. Now let us all straightway go and see what this portendeth."

So the King arose from where he sat, and he descended therefrom, and he went forth out of the hall, and all who were there went with him.

Now first of all there went King Arthur, and among those who *King Arthur* were last there went Sir Launcelot of the Lake. For when he had *and his court* heard of that dead lady he bethought him of the Lady Elaine and *go to where is* *the barge* of how she was even then in tender health, wherefore he repented him with great bitterness of heart that he was not with her at that time instead of lingering at court as he did. And he said to himself: "Suppose that she should die like to this dead lady in the barge— what would I do if that should have happened unto me?" So it was that his feet lagged because of his heavy thoughts, and so it was that he was near the last who came to the riverside where was that barge as aforesaid.

Now, there were many of the towns folk standing there, but upon King Arthur's coming all those made way for him, and so he came and stood upon the upper step of the landing-stairs and looked down into the boat. And he beheld that figure that was lying there and knew it that it was the Lady Elaine who lay there dead.

Then the King looked for a little upon that dead figure as it were in a sort of terror, and then he said, "Where is Sir Launcelot?"

Sir Launcelot beholdeth the dead
Now when the King so spake, they who stood there made way, and Sir Launcelot came through the press and stood also at the head of the stairs and looked down into the barge. Then of a sudden— as it were in an instant of time—he beheld with his very eyes that thing which he had been thinking of anon; for there before him and beneath him lay in very truth the dead image of that dear lady of whom he had been thinking only a moment before.

Then it was as though Sir Launcelot had suddenly been struck with a shaft of death, for he neither moved nor stirred. Nay, it was not to be perceived that he even so much as breathed. But ever he stood there gazing down into that boat as though he had forgotten for that while that there was anybody else in all of the world saving only himself and that dead lady. And many of those who were there looked upon the face of Sir Launcelot, and they beheld that his coun- tenance was altogether as white as the face of that dead figure who lay in the barge beneath them.

Sir Lavaine accuseth Sir Launcelot
Then a great hush of silence fell over all and every voice was stilled, and at that hush of silence Sir Lavaine lifted the hood from his face and looked up from where he sat in the boat at the feet of the dead lady, and so beheld Sir Launcelot where he stood. Then upon the instant Sir Lavaine stood up in the barge and he cried out in a great loud harsh voice: "Hah! art thou there, thou traitor knight?

Behold the work that thou hast done; for this that thou beholdest is thy handiwork. Thou hast betrayed this lady's love for the love of another, and so thou hast brought her to her death!"

So said Sir Lavaine before all those who were there, but it was as though Sir Launcelot heard him not, for ever he stood as though he were a dead man and not a living man of flesh and blood. Then of a sudden he awoke, as it were, to life, and he clasped the back of his hands across his eyes, and cried out in a voice as though that voice tore his heart asunder, "Remorse! Remorse! Remorse!" saying those words three times over in that wise.

Then he shut his lips tight as though to say no more, and thereupon turned and went away from that place.

And he turned neither to this side nor to that, but went straight *Sir Launcelot* to the castle of the King, and there ordered that his horse should *departeth* be brought forth to him upon the instant. So when his horse was brought he mounted it and rode away; and he bade farewell to no one, and no one was there when he thus departed.

So for a long while Sir Launcelot rode he knew not whither, but after a while he found himself in the forest not far away from the cell of the hermit of the forest. And he beheld the hermit of the forest, that he stood in an open plat of grass in front of his cell and that he was feeding the wild birds of the woodland; for the little feathered creatures were gathered in great multitudes about him, some resting upon his head and some upon his shoulders and some upon his hands. And a wild doe and a fawn of the forest browsed near by and all was full of peace and good content.

But at the coming of Sir Launcelot, all those wild creatures took alarm; the birds they flew chirping away, and the doe and the fawn they fled away into the thickets of the forest. For they wist, by some instinct, that a man of sin and sorrow was coming thitherward; wherefore they were afeared and fled away in that wise.

But Sir Launcelot thought nothing of this, but leaped from his horse, and ran to the hermit and flung himself down upon the ground before him and embraced him about the feet. And the hermit was greatly astonished and said, "What ails thee, Sir Launcelot?" Whereunto Sir Launcelot cried out: "Woe is me! Woe is me! I have sinned very grievously and have been grievously punished and now my heart is broken!"

Then the hermit perceived that some great misfortune had befallen Sir Launcelot, wherefore he lifted Sir Launcelot to his feet and after that he brought him into his cell. And after they were in the cell together, he said: "Now tell me what ails thee, Sir Launcelot. For I believe that in telling me thou shalt find a great deal of ease."

So Sir Launcelot confessed everything to the hermit—yea, everything to the very bottom of his soul, and the good, holy man hearkened to him.

Then after Sir Launcelot had said all that lay upon his heart, the hermit sat for a while in silence, communing with his spirit. And after a while he said: "Messire, God telleth me that if thy sin hath been grievous, so also hath thy punishment been full sore. Wherefore meseemeth I speak what God would have me say when I tell thee that though neither thou nor any man may undo that which is done, nor recommit that which is committed, yet there is this which thou or any man mayest do. Thou mayst bathe thy soul in repentance as in a bath of clear water (for repentance is not remorse but something very different from remorse), and that having so bathed thyself thou mayst clothe thyself as in a fresh raiment of new resolve. So bathed and so clad, thou mayst stand once more upon thy feet and mayst look up to God and say: 'Lo, God! I am Thy handiwork. I have sinned and have done great evil, yet I am still Thy handiwork, who hath made me what I am. So, though I may not undo that which I have done, yet I may, with Thy aid, do better hereafter than I have done heretofore.'

"For every man may sin, and yet again may sin; yet still is he God's handiwork, and still God is near by His handiwork to aid him ever to a fresh endeavor to righteousness.

"So, though thou hast sinned, thou art still the creation of God and may yet do His will in the world who hath sent thee hither."

Then Sir Launcelot wept, and he said, "There is much comfort in thy words."

After that he abode for three days in the cell of the hermit and at the end of that time he went forth again into the world, a broken yet a contrite man, and one full of a strong resolve to make good the life that God thenceforth intended him to live.

So by and by you shall hear of further adventures that befell him; yet not at this place.

So it was with Sir Launcelot, and now it only remaineth to be said that, after his departure from the King's court as aforesaid, they brought the dead figure of the Lady Elaine to the minster at Camelot and there high mass was said for the peace of her pure and gentle soul. So for two days (what time Sir Launcelot was bathing himself in the waters of repentance as aforetold) that figure lay in state in the minster and with many candles burning about it, and then it was buried in the minster and a monument of marble was erected to the memory of that kind and loving spirit that had gone.

So endeth the history of the Nativity of Galahad and so therewith this book also cometh to an end.

Yet after a while, if God giveth me life to finish that work which I have undertaken in writing these histories (and I pray He may give me to finish that and several other things), then I shall tell you many things more than these. For I shall tell you how Sir Launcelot came back again into the world, and I shall tell you of the history of the Quest of the Grail, and I shall tell you of other knights who came in later days to make the court of King Arthur even more glorious than it was before.

Already two histories have been written concerning these things and this makes the third, and another, I believe, will complete that work which I have assigned myself to do; wherefore, as was said, I pray that God may grant that I shall be able to finish that fourth book and so end my work that I have here undertaken. Amen.

THE END